Homeplaces

Homeplaces

*Stories of the South
by Women Writers*

edited by Mary Ellis Gibson

University of South Carolina Press

Copyright © 1991 University of South Carolina

Published in Columbia, South Carolina, by the University of
South Carolina Press

"224" watercolor by Kip Gerard
Portfolio Gallery
Columbia, South Carolina

jacket and text by Rebecca Blakeney

Manufactured in the United States of America

Library of Congress Cataloging-in-Publication Data

Homeplaces : stories of the South by women writers / edited by Mary
  Ellis Gibson.
    p. cm.
  Includes bibliographical references.
  ISBN 0–87249–784–4 (hard-cover : acid-free). — ISBN 0–87249–785–2
(paper : acid-free)
  1. Short stories, American—Southern States. 2. Short stories,
American—Women authors. 3. Women—Southern States—Fiction.
4. Southern States—Fiction. 5. Home—Fiction. I. Gibson, Mary
Ellis, 1952– . II. Title: Homeplaces.
PS551.H65 1991
813′.01089287—dc20   91–4678

Contents

Acknowledgments

"First Dark," copyright © 1959 by Elizabeth Spencer. From *The Stories of Elizabeth Spencer* by Elizabeth Spencer. Used by permission of Doubleday, a division of Bantam Doubleday Dell Publishing Group, Inc.

"The Business Venture", Copyright © 1987 by Elizabeth Spencer, from *Jack of Diamonds* by Elizabeth Spencer. Reprinted by permission of the publisher, Dutton, an imprint of New American Library, a division of Penguin Books USA Inc.

"The Long Afternoon" from *The Wind Shifting West* by Shirley Ann Grau. First published by Alfred A. Knopf, Inc. Copyright © 1973 by Shirley Ann Grau. Reprinted by permission of Brandt and Brandt Literary Agents, Inc.

"One Summer" from *The Black Prince and Other Stories* by Shirley Ann Grau. First published by Alfred A. Knopf, Inc. Copyright, 1955 by Shirley Ann Grau. Copyright © renewed 1983 by Shirley Ann Grau. Reprinted by permission of Brandt and Brandt Literary Agents, Inc.

"Flight" from *Nine Women* by Shirley Ann Grau. Copyright © 1985 by Shirley Ann Grau. Reprinted by permission of Alfred A. Knopf, Inc.

"A Tender Man" from *The Sea Birds Are Still Alive* by Toni Cade Bambara. Copyright © 1974, 1976, 1977 by Toni Cade Bambara. Reprinted by permission of Random House Inc.

"Madame Bai and the Taking of Stone Mountain" (pp. 59–69) from *Confirmation: An Anthology of African American Women* by Amiri Baraka Ed. and author Toni Bambara. Copyright © 1983. By permission of William Morrow and Co., Inc.

"The Welcome Table" from *In Love & Trouble: Stories of Black Women*, copyright © 1970, 1967 by Alice Walker, reprinted by permission of Harcourt Brace Jovanovich, Inc.

"A Sudden Trip Home in the Spring" from *You Can't Keep a Good Woman Down*, copyright © 1971 by Alice Walker, reprinted by permission of Harcourt Brace Jovanovich, Inc.

"Mother Tongue" first published in *The Greensboro Review* number 45 (Winter 1988–89). Reprinted by permission of Molly Best Tinsley.

"Zoe" first published in *Shenandoah*. Reprinted by permission of Molly Best Tinsley.

Copyright © 1982 by Ntozake Shange. From the book *Sassafrass, Cypress & Indigo* and reprinted with permission from St. Martin's Press, Inc., New York.

Copyright © 1987 by Ntozake Shange. From the book *Ridin' the Moon in Texas* and reprinted with permission from St. Martin's Press, Inc., New York.

"A Pilgrim Notebook, Part I: The Odyssey" first published in a different form in *Obsidian*. Published by permission of Opal J. Moore.

"A Happy Story" first published in *Callaloo*, vol. 12, no. 2. Reprinted by permission of The Johns Hopkins University Press.

"A Man Among Men" from *How Far She Went*. Copyright © by Mary Hood. Used by permission of the University of Georgia Press.

"Manly Conclusions" from *How Far She Went*. Copyright © by Mary Hood. Used by permission of the University of Georgia Press.

"Finding the Chain" from *And Venus Is Blue* by Mary Hood. Copyright © 1986 by Mary Hood. Reprinted by permission of Houghton Mifflin Co.

Introduction

At the end of Elizabeth Spencer's early story "First Dark," a woman and a man walk away from an old house and a small southern town. The narrative voice has warned us already that the woman is escaping a trap. The problem with towns and houses like this, the narrator tells us, is that they make people into "bemused custodians" of the grave. In the end the woman gets her coat, walks out the door, puts the key under the mat, and doesn't look back. "First Dark," standing at the beginning of this collection, can be read as a farewell and a greeting in southern fiction. In the more than thirty years since it was first published in 1959 both southern writers and the characters they have created have walked away from homeplaces or have found their homes changed almost beyond recognition.

This collection focuses on homeplaces in all their many meanings, and it represents a variety of ways women writers have thought about home, estrangement from home, and the relationships between individuals and family traditions in the last twenty years. As the south has been redefined by urbanization, suburbanization, changes in women's roles, integration and the continuing struggle against racism, southern writers have taken the measure of these changes.

Women writers in particular, though by no means exclusively, have often approached these changes by exploring the illusory boundary between the public and the private. These stories show how redefinitions of home are caught in the larger web of relations between genders, races, classes, or regions. Many protagonists in these stories are women who have found their own places in home and culture shifting. The central characters in Opal Moore's "A Happy Story" and in Shirley Ann Grau's "Flight" live in a world where the anticipated life is not the one they actually experience. The patterns of the artist's storytelling and the stories people tell themselves to live by are always in flight.

The changing nature of home is reflected in these stories not only in the lives of women who are surprised by the new designs of their culture but also, and still more, in the lives of girls and young women who must try to find ways to grow up when the definitions of home are changing all around them. In Molly Best Tinsley's story "Zoe" a teenage girl attempts to find some stable point in the rootless world of the upscale condominium complex where her mother entertains a series of lovers. In the selection from Ntozake Shange's *Sassafrass, Cypress & Indigo* family solidarity is not in question, but the dangers of growing up black and female create fear that forges a bond between Indigo and her mother.

Of course the redefinitions of home and transformations of place in the South affect men as well as women. We can measure these changes as they affect men by contrasting Shirley Ann Grau's early story "One Summer" with Mary Hood's recent treatments of fathers and sons in her stories "Manly Conclusions" and "A Man Among Men." Grau's protagonist MacDonald Addams comes to terms with his grandfather's death and in the process creates for himself a picture of his own life taking the same course his father's has: he too will become a small-town doctor, marry, settle down into a life that he both mildly resents and ultimately accepts. In Hood's "Manly Conclusions" the definition of manhood is similarly passed from father to son, but now the very place called home is changing. Dennis Petty's house is encroached upon by the summer and weekend houses of rich people from Atlanta. All rural land is posted. Territorial disputes become violent. And the whole change—the suburbanization even of the country—is caught up in the larger legacy of war over territory. Dennis's father, a Vietnam vet, in spite of himself passes on to his son a legacy of violence, anger, and the struggle to control it.

What makes these stories so complex a representation of home is that they show home as the scene of mutual affection and protection against violence and as the place where the violence of racism or sexism is most intimately and immediately felt. This treatment of violence carries on the traditions of William Faulkner, Flannery O'Connor, and Margaret Walker; like O'Connor in particular, several of these writers show us how even global events play out in local communities. As in O'Connor's "The Displaced Person," an intense study of fascism, oppression, and moral responsibility, in Toni Cade Bambara's "Madame Bai and the Taking of Stone Mountain" and in Hood's stories the effects of distant conflict are brought immediately home and mirrored in local turmoil. Bambara's story, set during the time of the serial murders of black children in Atlanta, shows us the overtly violent side of a culture which, in the shadows of a Confederate monument carved in granite and its own racist ideology, is rapidly becoming cosmopolitan thanks to foreign trade and foreign war.

At the same time that they carry on this investigation of southern violence, community, and morality, these stories allow us to see the distance between current writers and previous generations of writers of southern fiction. No character in these stories, and virtually none in the many stories I read in putting this anthology together, acts from motives I would characterize as nostalgic: no one invokes memories of the Old South to justify their actions or to explain themselves to themselves. Motives for cruelty come from feelings of rage, or displacement, or the cultural reflexes of an unexamined and often unacknowledged racism. The knitting together of community comes from the recognition that community cannot now be made from geographic stability but must be made from the human capacity to remember and to regenerate significant ties of affection. Thus Sarah in Alice Walker's "A Sudden Trip Home in the Spring" and Cliffie in Hood's "Finding the Chain" return home, briefly, and leave, probably for good. Both have no continuing home to which they can return. Each takes with her the memories she values, and each is enabled to let go of the rest.

In the concern with home, with displacement and death, with the necessity of creating community, these stories have significant thematic connections. Many of them also examine the new dimensions of American race relations in the years following the Civil Rights movement.

As I chose these stories I felt that the changing sense of place in the American South could best be represented by including an equal number of African-American and white writers. I agree with Reynolds Price's observation that if any single characteristic distinguishes southern literature from the literature of other regions, it is the importance of race, in the fabric of southern culture and in its literary history. The suggestions for further reading and classroom use at the end of this anthology point out that African-American women writers outside the South are increasingly drawn to novels with southern settings or to novels exploring the history of slavery. Writers such as Toni Morrison, Gloria Naylor, Sherley Ann Williams, and Paule Marshall have in their recent novels written powerfully about slavery and southern culture in ways that will, I believe, have a lasting impact on the literary self-understanding of southerners. The stories I have collected here, though contemporary in their settings, have similarly the effect of redefining the meanings of "southern" and of home.

Most of the stories here that directly examine racism are by African-American writers; of the white writers in this anthology only Elizabeth Spencer is concerned directly with questions of race, though racial issues form important threads in the background of the stories by Shirely Ann Grau (much of Grau's other work is more explicitly about race). The settings of Molly Best Tinsley's stories and of those by Mary Hood involve, instead of a focus on racism, an examination of nationalism and of regional change.

In Spencer's "The Business Venture" we see the only direct examination by a white writer in this anthology of race in southern middle-class life since the Civil Rights movement. Spencer's "The Business Venture" presents us with a very uncomfortable picture of small-town southern life among relatively privileged young whites. She sees acutely the pressures of group solidarity among teenagers and young adults and subtly captures that mixture of enmity and attachment among people united by race, class, and old ties in a small town. These are the people who choose to stay home, though even they move to the new housing developments. They operate on the racist principles they have inherited, the principles assumed in segregated academies and less than elegant—but socially significant—small-town private clubs. When one of their number begins a business and perhaps a love affair with a black man, the outcome is not pretty. The business venture turns out to have dangerous consequences.

Several of the stories here by Opal Moore, Ntozake Shange, Alice Walker, and Toni Cade Bambara treat the consequences of racism still more fully than Spencer's powerful story does, though, as I have suggested, all of these writers are also concerned with other issues and themes. Alice Walker's "The Welcome Table" and Opal Moore's "A Pilgrim Notebook" make an especially interesting pair. The protagonist in Moore's story is dogged by the possibility of violence, by white society's expectation that as a black man he is himself violent. Ben's success in the corporate world makes possible both an affluent life and new sorts of discrimination to accompany older forms of fear. On a highway in the Middle West he feels suddenly surrounded by hostility, and it is an experience which makes geography irrelevant. Moore implies that the geography of racism is at once universal and has its own particular history: "Even safe inside his car, safe inside his era, he'd felt as if he were running—only steps ahead of some ancestor African—disoriented, afraid, rough feet clouded in red dust, running in circles. . . . He'd sworn that he would never return to Mississippi. But in the end, it didn't matter. The world was Mississippi."

Like Spencer's "The Business Venture," Alice Walker's "The Welcome Table" is a powerful presentation of the delusions and hypocrisy of racism; in this story the very South that haunts Moore's story comes to life and the defense of the group occurs at the expense of the excluded. In "The Welcome Table," as in "The Business Venture," the surface of white social convention would appear to be unruffled. Spencer's story leaves us at this point wondering about the futures of the business partners and their supposed friends, but Walker allows a triumph in death for the victim of racism. The old woman in Walker's story unconsciously tests white Christianity and finds it wanting, and it is she, not those who reject her, who goes on to her own spiritual reward.

Whether or not they are writing explicitly about relations between African-Americans and American whites, all the writers represented in this anthology find themselves attracted to stories of cultural clash, stories of the way otherness is constructed and confronted. Molly Best Tinsley's "Mother Tongue" is just such a story of familial and cultural estrangement which becomes, finally, self-estrangement.

Despite the changes and dislocations of home in the stories collected here, these stories also testify to the great variety that now characterizes southern culture and to the delight of exploring that variety. From Shange's Texas women's rodeo to the conclusion of Hood's "Finding the Chain," these stories do present their protagonists' joy in living. And the writers exhibit their own senses of the absurd and the ironic, their various delight in language and in art. Grau's "Flight," Shange's "Ridin' the Moon in Texas," and Moore's "A Pilgrim Notebook" achieve power in their daring forms and styles. Moore and Grau take us deeply inside the consciousness of characters in extreme situations. Shange's language itself, the particular texture and the energy of the speaking voice, is her principal source of power. At the very beginning of "Ridin' the Moon in Texas," which is excerpted from a series of writings to accompany images, Shange creates an individual language: "Houston Rodeo & Livestock Show ain't never seen the same since we come riding in from Arcola. All colored and correct. . . . and I'll say one thing. That flock of niggahs on them gorgeous horses and them wagons, now that was something to look at! Must be why ain't none of us forget it. The trailride and all. And the rodeos. The black ones, of course, white folks don't quite have the hang of it. I mean, how you sposed to look, your image, on your horse. It takes a colored point of view." Elizabeth Spencer achieves a different power, capturing the speech and thoughts of a very different character in "The Business Venture," while Mary Hood relies on a central carefully crafted symbol to bring home the point of her story.

The stories included in this volume, then, were chosen for this power of language and of craft and for their astuteness about place and cultural change in the contemporary South. In order to emphasize the historical coherence of this group of stories, I have arranged the writers chronologically in the order of their birth. I include early stories by Shirley Ann Grau and Elizabeth Spencer to reflect the range of their writings and the scope of the changes in Southern place, family, and culture that their works measure. Although no collection of only eight writers can fully represent the variety of fine writing now being produced by southern women writers and by women writers outside the South who treat southern history and culture, this collection does provide an introduction to the work of these writers; by selecting two or three stories by each, I have tried to represent something of the depth and variety of their work and to indicate the changing concerns of recent southern fiction.

While this anthology does focus on the writing of southern women and on writing about the South, gathering stories into such a collection necessarily raises the unanswerable question of what is southern. At this point, anthologists customarily insert their disclaimers, defining "southern" tautologically to encompass whatever they wish to include. Any definition of southernness, my own included, is in some respects arbitrary. Of the writers here, Elizabeth Spencer could be considered both an important force in southern fiction and one of the most widely respected of southern writers, yet she lived in Europe and in Canada for many years and many of her fine stories are set in Canada. Toni Cade Bambara, who lived in Georgia for eighteen years, was born and reared in the northeast and recently moved to Philadelphia. Opal Moore has lived in Virginia for a number of years, but most of her published work is set in the Middle West, and she is now working on a group of stories about displacement and dislocation which is set in Las Vegas. Molly Best Tinsley has lived most of her adult life in the area around Washington, D.C., and she teaches at the Naval Academy; whether this qualifies as "southern" is an interesting question. Yet Tinsley's stories are particularly appropriate for this volume because they so carefully examine cultural displacement and the relatively homogeneous anonymity of contemporary suburban life. In sum, these writers and their stories can tell us about our own lives in the South an in regions beyond, for each writer is attuned to the ways place and community and cultural change are connected.

When I began thinking about this anthology and a title to encompass these themes, I was drawn to the southern expression "homeplace." Echoing in my memory was the voice of my mother during most of my childhood speaking of going "down home." And those trips themselves provoked many stories about so-and-so's "homeplace"—always stories in the past tense, reflecting on the distance the speaker had come from home or the destruction of the world as she or he had known it. As anyone who rides through the rural South can see, homeplace is now, often enough, a bare chimney in a field or, more likely, a weathered farmhouse with a house trailer or a brick ranch on the highway side of the yard. Outside many southern cities and towns homeplaces grand enough to be saved may be seen surrounded by subdivisions, their old trees reminding us by their age of the farm that once was there. Less grand homeplaces have disappeared so completely that the landscape itself, reshaped by graders, pavement, or landscaping, may be unrecognizable; the former inhabitants are elsewhere—driving cars and eating foods with names unheard of in 1960. These transformations of home and its meanings are a new source for southern fiction, and the eight writers I have included here have explored old and new ways of imagining what a homeplace might be. Their writing can tell us much about the ways work, places, and families create one another in the contemporary South.

Mary Ellis Gibson
University of North Carolina at Greensboro

Homeplaces

Elizabeth Spencer

First Dark

When Tom Beavers started coming back to Richton, Mississippi, on weekends, after the war was over, everybody in town was surprised and pleased. They had never noticed him much before he paid them this compliment; now they could not say enough nice things. There was not much left in Richton for him to call family—just his aunt who had raised him, Miss Rita Beavers, old as God, ugly as sin, deaf as a post. So he must be fond of the town, they reasoned; certainly it was a pretty old place. Far too many young men had left it and never come back at all.

He would drive in every Friday night from Jackson, where he worked. All weekend, his Ford, dusty of flank, like a hard-ridden horse, would sit parked down the hill near Miss Rita's old wire front gate, which sagged from the top hinge and had worn a span in the ground. On Saturday morning, he would head for the drugstore, then the post office; then he would be observed walking here and there around the streets under the shade trees. It was as though he were looking for something.

He wore steel taps on his heels, and in the still the click of them on the sidewalks would sound across the big front lawns and all the way up to the porches of the houses, where two ladies might be sitting behind a row of ferns. They would identify him to one another, murmuring in their fine little voices, and say it was just too bad there was nothing here for young people. It was just a shame they didn't have one or two more old houses, here, for a Pilgrimage—look how Natchez had waked up.

One Saturday morning in early October, Tom Beavers sat at the counter in the drugstore and reminded Totsie Poteet, the drugstore clerk, of a ghost story. Did he remember the strange old man who used to appear to people who were coming into Richton along the Jackson road at twilight—what they called "first dark"?

"Sure I remember," said Totsie. "Old Cud'n Jimmy Wiltshire used to tell us about him every time we went 'possum hunting. I could see him plain as I can see you, the way he used to tell it. Tall, with a top hat on, yeah, and waiting in the weeds alongside the road ditch, so'n you couldn't tell if he was standing down in the ditch or not. It would look like he just grew up out of the weeds. Then he'd signal to you."

"Them that stopped never saw anybody," said Tom Beavers, stirring his coffee. "There were lots of folks besides Mr. Jimmy that saw him."

"There was, let me see . . ." Totsie enumerated others—some men, some women, some known to drink, others who never touched a drop. There was no way to explain it. "There was that story the road gang told. Do you remember, or were you off at school? It was while they were straightening the road out to the highway—taking the curves out and building a new bridge. Anyway, they said that one night at quitting time, along in the winter and just about dark, this old guy signaled to some of 'em. They said they went over and he asked them to move a bulldozer they had left across the road, because he had a wagon back behind on a little dirt road, with a sick nigger girl in it. Had to get to the doctor and this was the only way. They claimed they knew didn't nobody live back there on that little old road, but niggers can come from anywhere. So they moved the bulldozer and cleared back a whole lot of other stuff, and waited and waited. Not only didn't no wagon ever come, but the man that had stopped them, he was gone, too. They was right shook up over it. You never heard that one?"

"No, I never did." Tom Beavers said this with his eyes looking up over his coffee cup, as though he sat behind a hand of cards. His lashes and brows were heavier than was ordinary, and worked as a veil might, to keep you away from knowing exactly what he was thinking.

"They said he was tall and had a hat on." The screen door flapped to announce a customer, but Totsie kept on talking. "But whether he was a white man or a real light-colored nigger they couldn't say. Some said one and some said another. I figured they'd been pulling on the jug a little earlier than usual. You know why? I never heard of *our* ghost *saying* nothing. Did you, Tom?"

He moved away on the last words, the way a clerk will, talking back over his shoulder and ahead of him to his new customer at the same time, as though he had two voices and two heads. "And what'll it be today, Miss Frances?"

The young woman standing at the counter had a prescription already out of her bag. She stood with it poised between her fingers, but her attention was drawn toward Tom Beavers, his coffee cup, and the conversation she had interrupted. She was a girl whom no ordinary description would fit. One would have to know first of all who she was: Frances Harvey. After that, it was all right for her to be a little odd-looking, with her reddish hair that curled back from her brow, her light eyes, and her high, pale temples. This is not the material for being pretty, but in Frances Harvey it was what could sometimes be beauty. Her family home was laden with history that nobody but the Harveys could remember. It would have been on a Pilgrimage if Richton had had one. Frances still lived in it, looking after an invalid mother.

"What were you-all talking about?" she wanted to know.

"About that ghost they used to tell about," said Totsie, holding out his hand for the prescription. "The one people used to see just outside of town, on the Jackson road."

"But why?" she demanded. "Why were you talking about him?"

"Tom, here—" the clerk began, but Tom Beavers interrupted him.

"I was asking because I was curious," he said. He had been studying her from the corner of his eye. Her face was beginning to show the wear of her mother's long illness, but that couldn't be called change. Changing was something she didn't seem to have done, her own style being the only one natural to her.

"I was asking," he went on, "because I saw him." He turned away from her somewhat too direct gaze and said to Totsie Poteet, whose mouth had fallen open, "It was where the new road runs close to the old road, and as far as I could tell he was right on the part of the old road where people always used to see him."

"But when?" Frances Harvey demanded. "Last night," he told her. "Just around first dark. Driving home."

A wealth of quick feeling came up in her face. "So did I! Driving home from Jackson! I saw him, too!"

For some people, a liking for the same phonograph record or for Mayan archaeology is enough of an excuse to get together. Possibly, seeing the same ghost was no more than that. Anyway, a week later, on Saturday at first dark, Frances Harvey and Tom Beavers were sitting together in a car parked just off the highway, near the spot where they agreed the ghost had appeared. The season was that long, peculiar one between summer and fall, and there were so many crickets and tree frogs going full tilt in their periphery that their voices could hardly be distinguished from the background noises, though they both would have heard a single footfall in the grass. An edge of autumn was in the air at night, and Frances had put on a tweed jacket at the last minute, so the smell of moth balls was in the car, brisk and most unghostlike.

But Tom Beavers was not going to forget the value of the ghost, whether it put in an appearance or not. His questions led Frances into reminiscence.

"No, I never saw him before the other night," she admitted. "The Negroes used to talk in the kitchen, and Regina and I—you know my sister Regina—would sit there listening, scared to go and scared to stay. Then finally going to bed upstairs was no relief, either, because sometimes Aunt Henrietta was visiting us, and *she'd* seen it. Or if she wasn't visiting us, the front room next to us, where she stayed, would be empty, which was worse. There was no way to lock ourselves in, and besides, what was there to lock out? We'd lie all night like two sticks in bed, and shiver. Papa finally had to take a hand. He called us in and sat us down and said that the whole thing was easy to explain—it was all automobiles. What their headlights did with the dust and shadows out on the Jackson road. 'Oh, but Sammie and Jerry!' we said, with great big eyes, sitting side by side on the sofa, with our tennis shoes flat on the floor."

"Who were Sammie and Jerry?" asked Tom Beavers.

"Sammie was our cook. Jerry was her son, or husband, or something. Anyway, they certainly didn't have cars. Papa called them in. They were standing side by side by the bookcase, and Regina and I were on the sofa—four pairs of big eyes, and Papa pointing his finger. Papa said, 'Now you made up these stories about ghosts, didn't you?' 'Yes, sir,' said Sammie. 'We made them up.' 'Yes, sir,' said Jerry. 'We sho did.' 'Well, then, you can just stop it,' Papa said. 'See how peaked these children look?' Sammie and Jerry were terribly polite to us for a week, and we got in the car and rode up and down the Jackson road at first dark to see if the headlights really did it. But we never saw anything. We didn't tell Papa, but headlights had nothing whatever to do with it."

"You had your own *car* then?" He couldn't believe it.

"Oh no!" She was emphatic. "We were too young for that. Too young to drive, really, but we did anyway." She leaned over to let him give her cigarette a light, and saw his hand tremble. Was he afraid of the ghost or of her? She would have to stay away from talking family.

Frances remembered Tommy Beavers from her childhood—a small boy going home from school down a muddy side road alone, walking right down the middle of the road. His old aunt's house was at the bottom of a hill. It was damp there, and the yard was always muddy, with big fat chicken tracks all over it, like Egyptian writing. How did Frances know? She could not remember going there, ever. Miss Rita Beavers was said to order cold ham, mustard, bread, and condensed milk from the grocery store. "I doubt if that child ever has anything hot," Frances's mother had said once. He was always neatly dressed in the same knee pants, high socks, and checked shirt, and sat several rows ahead of Frances in study hall, right in the middle of his seat. He was three grades behind her; in those days, that much younger seemed very young indeed. What had happened to his parents? There was some story, but it was not terribly interesting, and, his people being of no importance, she had forgotten.

"I think it's past time for our ghost," she said. "He's never out so late at night."

"He gets hungry, like me," said Tom Beavers. "Are you hungry, Frances?"

They agreed on a highway restaurant where an orchestra played on weekends. Everyone went there now.

From the moment they drew up on the graveled entrance, cheerful lights and a blare of music chased the spooks from their heads. Tom Beavers ordered well and danced well, as it turned out. Wasn't there something she had heard about his being "smart"? By "smart," Southerners mean intellectual, and they say it in an almost condescending way, smart being what you are when you can't be anything else, but it is better, at least, than being nothing. Frances Harvey had been away enough not to look at things from a completely Southern point of view, and she was encouraged to discover that she and Tom had other things in common besides a ghost, though all stemming, perhaps, from the imagination it took to see one.

They agreed about books and favorite movies and longing to see more plays. She sighed that life in Richton was so confining, but he assured her that Jackson could be just as bad; *it* was getting to be like any Middle Western city, he said, while Richton at least had a sense of the past. This was the main reason, he went on, gaining confidence in the jumble of commonplace noises—dishes, music, and a couple of drinkers chattering behind them—that he had started coming back to Richton so often. He wanted to keep a connection with the past. He lived in a modern apartment, worked in a soundproof office—he could be in any city. But Richton was where he had been born and raised, and nothing could be more old-fashioned. Too many people seemed to have their lives cut in two. He was earnest in desiring that this should not happen to him.

"You'd better be careful," Frances said lightly. Her mood did not incline her to profound conversation. "There's more than one ghost in Richton. You may turn into one yourself, like the rest of us."

"It's the last thing I'd think of you," he was quick to assure her.

Had Tommy Beavers really said such a thing, in such a natural, charming way? Was Frances Harvey really so pleased? Not only was she pleased but, feeling warmly alive amid the music and small lights, she agreed with him. She could not have agreed with him more.

"I hear that Thomas Beavers has gotten to be a very attractive man," Frances Harvey's mother said unexpectedly one afternoon.

Frances had been reading aloud—Jane Austen this time. Theirs was one house where the leather-bound sets were actually read. In Jane Austen, men and women seesawed back and forth for two or three hundred pages until they struck a point of balance; then they got married. She had just put aside the book, at the end of a chapter, and risen to lower the shade against the slant of the afternoon sun. "Or so Cud'n Jennie and Mrs. Giles Antley and Miss Fannie Stapleton have been coming and telling you," she said.

"People talk, of course, but the consensus is favorable," Mrs. Harvey said. "Wonders never cease; his mother ran away with a brush salesman. But nobody can make out what he's up to, coming back to Richton."

"Does he have to be 'up to' anything?" Frances asked.

"Men are always up to something," said the old lady at once. She added, more slowly, "In Thomas's case, maybe it isn't anything it oughtn't to be. They say he reads a lot. He may just have taken up with some sort of idea."

Frances stole a long glance at her mother's face on the pillow. Age and illness had reduced the image of Mrs. Harvey to a kind of caricature, centered on a mouth that Frances could not help comparing to that of a fish. There was a tension around its rim, as though it were outlined in bone, and the underlip even stuck out a little. The mouth ate, it took medicine, it asked for things, it gasped when breath was short, it commented. But when it commented, it ceased to be just a mouth and became part of Mrs. Harvey, that witty tyrant with the infallible memory for the right detail, who was at her terrible best about men.

"And what could he be thinking of?" she was wont to inquire when some man had acted foolishly. No one could ever defend accurately the man in question, and the only conclusion was Mrs. Harvey's; namely, that he wasn't thinking, if, indeed, he could. Although she had never been a belle, never a flirt, her popularity with men was always formidable. She would be observed talking marathons with one in a corner, and could you ever be sure, when they both burst into laughter, that they had not just exchanged the most shocking stories? "Of course, he—" she would begin later, back with the family, and the masculinity that had just been encouraged to strut and preen a little was quickly shown up as idiotic. Perhaps Mrs. Harvey hoped by this method to train her daughters away from a lot of sentimental nonsense that was their birthright as pretty Southern girls in a house with a lawn that moonlight fell on and that was often lit also by Japanese lanterns hung for parties. "Oh, he's not like that, Mama!" the little girls would cry. They were already alert for heroes who would ride up and cart them off. "Well, then, you watch," she would say. Sure enough, if you watched, she would be right.

Mrs. Harvey's younger daughter, Regina, was a credit to her mother's long campaign; she married well. The old lady, however, never tired of pointing out behind her son-in-law's back that his fondness for money was ill-concealed, that he had the longest feet she'd ever seen, and that he sometimes made grammatical errors.

Her elder daughter, Frances, on a trip to Europe, fell in love, alas! The gentleman was of French extraction but Swiss citizenship, and Frances did not marry him, because he was already married—that much filtered back to Richton. In response to a cable, she had returned home one hot July in time to witness her father's wasted face and last weeks of life. That same September, the war began. When peace came, Richton wanted to know if Frances Harvey would go back to Europe. Certain subtly complicated European matters, little understood in Richton, seemed to be obstructing Romance; one of them was probably named Money. Meanwhile, Frances's mother took to bed, in what was generally known to be her last illness.

So no one crossed the ocean, but eventually Tom Beavers came up to Mrs. Harvey's room one afternoon, to tea.

Though almost all her other faculties were seriously impaired, in ear and tongue Mrs. Harvey was as sound as a young beagle, and she could still weave a more interesting conversation than most people who go about every day and look at the world. She was of the old school of Southern lady talkers; she vexed you with no ideas, she tried to protect you from even a moment of silence. In the old days, when a bright company filled the downstairs rooms, she could keep the ball rolling amongst a crowd. Everyone—all the men especially—got their word in, but the flow of things came back to her. If one of those twenty-minutes-to-or-after silences fell—and even with her they did occur—people would turn and look at her daughter Frances. "And what do you think?" some kind-eyed gentleman would ask. Frances did not credit that she had the sort of face people would turn to, and so did not know how to take advantage of it. What did she think? Well, to answer that honestly took a moment of reflection—a fatal moment, it always turned out. Her mother would be up instructing the maid, offering someone an ashtray or another goody, or remarking outright, "Frances is so timid. She never says a word."

Tom Beavers stayed not only past teatime that day but for a drink as well. Mrs. Harvey was induced to take a glass of sherry, and now her bed became her enormous throne. Her keenest suffering as an invalid was occasioned by the absence of men. "What is a house without a man in it?" she would often cry. From her eagerness to be charming to Frances's guest that afternoon, it seemed that she would have married Tom Beavers herself if he had asked her. The amber liquid set in her small four-sided glass glowed like a jewel, and her diamond flashed; she had put on her best ring for the company. What a pity no longer to show her ankle, that delicious bone, so remarkably slender for so ample a frame.

Since the time had flown so, they all agreed enthusiastically that Tom should wait downstairs while Frances got ready to go out to dinner with him. He was hardly past the stair landing before the old lady was seized by such a fit of coughing that she could hardly speak. "It's been— it's been too much—too *much* for me!" she gasped out.

But after Frances had found the proper sedative for her, she was calmed, and insisted on having her say.

"Thomas Beavers has a good job with an insurance company in Jackson," she informed her daughter, as though Frances were incapable of finding out anything for herself. "He makes a good appearance. He is the kind of man"—she paused—"who would value a wife of good family." She stopped, panting for breath. It was this complimenting a man behind his back that was too much for her—as much out of character, and hence as much of a strain, as if she had got out of bed and tried to tap-dance.

"Heavens, Mama," Frances said, and almost giggled.

At this, the old lady, thinking the girl had made light of her suitor, half screamed at her, "Don't be so critical, Frances! You can't be so critical of men!" and fell into an even more terrible spasm of coughing. Frances had to lift her from the pillow and hold her straight until the fit passed and her breath returned. Then Mrs. Harvey's old, dry, crooked, ineradicably feminine hand was laid on her daughter's arm, and when she spoke again she shook the arm to emphasize her words.

"When your father knew he didn't have long to live," she whispered, "we discussed whether to send for you or not. You know you were his favorite, Frances. 'Suppose our girl is happy over there,' he said. 'I wouldn't want to bring her back on my account.' I said you had to have the right to choose whether to come back or not. You'd never forgive us, I said, if you didn't have the right to choose."

Frances could visualize this very conversation taking place between her parents; she could see them, decorous and serious, talking over the fact of his approaching death as though it were a piece of property for agreeable disposition in the family. She could never remember him without thinking, with a smile, how he used to come home on Sunday from church (he being the only one of them who went) and how, immediately after hanging his hat and cane in the hall, he would say, "Let all things proceed in orderly progression to their final confusion. How long before dinner?" No, she had had to come home. Some humor had always existed between them—her father and her—and humor, of all things, cannot be betrayed.

"I meant to go back," said Frances now. "But there was the war. At first I kept waiting for it to be over. I still wake up at night sometimes thinking, I wonder how much longer before the war will be over. And then—" She stopped short. For the fact was that her lover had been married to somebody else, and her mother was the very person capable of pointing that out to her. Even in the old lady's present silence she heard the unspoken thought, and got up nervously from the bed, loosing herself from the hand on her arm, smoothing her reddish hair where it was inclined to straggle. "And then he wrote me that he had gone back to his wife. Her family and his had always been close, and the war brought them back together. This was in Switzerland—naturally, he couldn't stay on in Paris during the war. There were the children, too—all of them were Catholic. Oh, I do understand how it happened."

Mrs. Harvey turned her head impatiently on the pillow. She dabbed at her moist upper lip with a crumpled linen handkerchief; her diamond flashed once in motion. "War, religion, wife, children—yes. But men do what they want to."

Could anyone make Frances as angry as her mother could? "Believe what you like then! You always know so much better than I do. *You* would have managed things somehow. Oh, you would have had your way!"

"Frances," said Mrs. Harvey, "I'm an old woman." The hand holding the handkerchief fell wearily, and her eyelids dropped shut. "If you should want to marry Thomas Beavers and bring him here, I will accept it. There will be no distinctions. Next, I suppose, we will be having his old deaf aunt for tea. I hope she has a hearing aid. I haven't got the strength to holler at her."

"I don't think any of these plans are necessary, Mama."

The eyelids slowly lifted. "None?"

"None."

Mrs. Harvey's breathing was as audible as a voice. She spoke, at last, without scorn, honestly. "I cannot bear the thought of leaving you alone. You, nor the house, nor your place in it—alone. I foresaw Tom Beavers here! What has he got that's better than you and this place? I knew he would come!"

Terrible as her mother's meanness was, it was not half so terrible as her love. Answering nothing, explaining nothing, Frances stood without giving in. She trembled, and tears ran down her cheeks. The two women looked at each other helplessly across the darkening room.

In the car, later that night, Tom Beavers asked, "Is your mother trying to get rid of me?" They had passed an unsatisfactory evening, and he was not going away without knowing why.

"No, it's just the other way around," said Frances, in her candid way. "She wants you so much she'd like to eat you up. She wants you in the house. Couldn't you tell?"

"She once chased me out of the yard," he recalled.

"Not really!"

They turned into Harvey Street (that was actually the name of it), and when he had drawn the car up before the dark front steps, he related the incident. He told her that Mrs. Harvey had been standing just there in the yard, talking to some visitor who was leaving by inches, the way ladies used to—ten minutes' more talk for every forward step. He, a boy not more than nine, had been crossing a corner of the lawn where a faint path had already been worn; he had had nothing to do with wearing the path and had taken it quite innocently and openly. "You, boy!" Mrs. Harvey's fan was an enormous painted thing. She had furled it with a clack so loud he could still hear it. "You don't cut through my yard again! Now, you stop where you are and you go all the way back around by the walk, and don't you ever do that again." He went back and all the way around. She was fanning comfortably as he passed. "Old Miss Rita Beavers' nephew," he heard her say, and though he did not speak of it now to Frances, Mrs. Harvey's rich tone had been as stuffed with wickedness as a fruitcake with goodies. In it you could have found so many things: that, of course, he didn't know any better, that he was poor, that she knew his first name but would not deign to mention it, that she meant him to understand all this and more. Her fan was probably still somewhere in the house, he reflected. If he ever opened the wrong door, it might fall from above and brain him. It seemed impossible that nowadays he could even have the chance to open the wrong door in the Harvey house. With its graceful rooms and big lawn, its camellias and magnolia trees, the house had been one of the enchanted castles of his childhood, and Frances and Regina Harvey had been two princesses running about the lawn one Saturday morning drying their hair with big white towels and not noticing when he passed.

There was a strong wind that evening. On the way home, Frances and Tom had noticed how the night was streaming, but whether with mist or dust or the smoke from some far-off fire in the dry winter woods they could not tell. As they stood on the sidewalk, the clouds raced over them, and moonlight now and again came through. A limb rubbed against a high cornice. Frances's coat blew about her, and her hair blew. She felt herself to be no different from anything there that the wind was blowing on, her happiness of no relevance in the dark torrent of nature.

"I can't leave her, Tom. But I can't ask you to live with her, either. Of all the horrible ideas! She'd make demands, take all my time, laugh at you behind your back—she has to run everything. You'd hate me in a week."

He did not try to pretty up the picture, because he had a feeling that it was all too accurate. Now, obviously, was the time she should go on to say there was no good his waiting around through the years for her. But hearts are not noted for practicality, and Frances stood with her hair blowing, her hands stuck in her coat pockets, and did not go on to say anything. Tom pulled her close to him—in, as it were, out of the wind.

"I'll be coming by next weekend, just like I've been doing. And the next one, too," he said. "We'll just leave it that way, if it's O.K. with you."

"Oh yes, it is, Tom!" Never so satisfied to be weak, she kissed him and ran inside.

He stood watching on the walk until her light flashed on. Well, he had got what he was looking for; a connection with the past, he had said. It was right upstairs, a splendid old mass of dictatorial female flesh, thinking about him. Well, they could go on, he and Frances, sitting on either side of a sickbed, drinking tea and sipping sherry with streaks of gray broadening on their brows, while the familiar seasons

came and went. So he thought. Like Frances, he believed that the old
lady had a stranglehold on life.

Suddenly, in March, Mrs. Harvey died.

A heavy spring funeral, with lots of roses and other scented flowers
in the house, is the worst kind of all. There is something so recklessly
fecund about a south Mississippi spring that death becomes just another
word in the dictionary, along with swarms of others, and even so pure
and white a thing as a gardenia has too heavy a scent and may suggest
decay. Mrs. Harvey, amid such odors, sank to rest with a determined
pomp, surrounded by admiring eyes.

While Tom Beavers did not "sit with the family" at this time, he
was often observed with the Harveys, and there was whispered specula-
tion among those who were at the church and the cemetery that the
Harvey house might soon come into new hands, "after a decent interval." No one would undertake to judge for a Harvey how long an
interval was decent.

Frances suffered from insomnia in the weeks that followed, and at
night she wandered about the spring-swollen air of the old house,
smelling now spring and now death. "Let all things proceed in orderly
progression to their final confusion." She had always thought that the
final confusion referred to death, but now she began to think that it
could happen any time; that final confusion, having found the door ajar,
could come into a house and show no inclination to leave. The worrisome thing, the thing it all came back to, was her mother's clothes.
They were numerous, expensive, and famous, and Mrs. Harvey had
never discarded any of them. If you opened a closet door, hatboxes as
big as crates towered above your head. The shiny black trim of a great
shawl stuck out of a wardrobe door just below the lock. Beneath the lid
of a cedar chest, the bright eyes of a tippet were ready to twinkle at you.
And the jewels! Frances's sister had restrained her from burying them
all on their mother, and had even gone off with a wad of them tangled
up like fishing tackle in an envelope, on the ground of promises made
now and again in the course of the years.

("Regina," said Frances, "what else were you two talking about
besides jewelry?" "I don't remember," said Regina, getting mad.

"Frances makes me so mad," said Regina to her husband as they were driving home. "I guess I can love Mama and jewelry, too. Mama certainly loved *us* and jewelry, too.")

One afternoon, Frances went out to the cemetery to take two wreaths sent by somebody who had "just heard." She drove out along the winding cemetery road, stopping the car a good distance before she reached the gate, in order to walk through the woods. The dogwood was beautiful that year. She saw a field where a house used to stand but had burned down; its cedar trees remained, and two bushes of bridal wreath marked where the front gate had swung. She stopped to admire the clusters of white bloom massing up through the young, feathery leaf and stronger now than the leaf itself. In the woods, the redbud was a smoke along shadowy ridges, and the dogwood drifted in layers, like snow suspended to give you all the time you needed to wonder at it. But why, she wondered, do they call it bridal *wreath*? It's not a wreath but a little bouquet. Wreaths are for funerals, anyway. As if to prove it, she looked down at the two she held, one in each hand. She walked on, and such complete desolation came over her that it was more of a wonder than anything in the woods—more, even, than death.

As she returned to the car from the two parallel graves, she met a thin, elderly, very light-skinned Negro man in the road. He inquired if she would mind moving her car so that he could pass. He said that there was a sick colored girl in his wagon, whom he was driving in to the doctor. He pointed out politely that she had left her car right in the middle of the road. "Oh, I'm terribly sorry," said Frances, and hurried off toward the car.

That night, reading late in bed, she thought, I could have given her a ride into town. No wonder they talk about us up North. A mile into town in a wagon! She might have been having a baby. She became conscience-stricken about it—foolishly so, she realized, but if you start worrying about something in a house like the one Frances Harvey lived in, in the dead of night, alone, you will go on worrying about it until dawn. She was out of sleeping pills.

She remembered having bought a fresh box of sedatives for her mother the day before she died. She got up and went into her mother's closed room, where the bed had been dismantled for airing, its wooden parts propped along the walls. On tne closet shelf she found the shoe box into which she had packed away the familiar articles of the bedside table. Inside she found the small enameled-cardboard box, with the date and prescription inked on the cover in Totsie Poteet's somewhat prissy handwriting, but the box was empty. She was surprised, for she realized that her mother could have used only one or two of the pills. Frances was so determined to get some sleep that she searched the entire little store of things in the shoe box quite heartlessly, but there were no pills. She returned to her room and tried to read, but could not, and so smoked instead and stared out at the dawn-blackening sky. The house sighed. She could not take her mind off the Negro girl. If she died . . . When it was light, she dressed and got into the car.

In town, the postman was unlocking the post office to sort the early mail. "I declare," he said to the rural mail carrier who arrived a few minutes later, "Miss Frances Harvey is driving herself crazy. Going back out yonder to the cemetery, and it not seven o'clock in the morning."

"Aw," said the rural deliveryman skeptically, looking at the empty road.

"That's right. I was here and seen her. You wait there, you'll see her come back. She'll drive herself nuts. Them old maids like that, left in them old houses—crazy and sweet, or crazy and mean, or just plain crazy. They just ain't locked up like them that's down in the asylum. That's the only difference."

"Miss Frances Harvey ain't no more than thirty-two, -three years old."

"Then she's just got more time to get crazier in. You'll see."

That day was Friday, and Tom Beavers, back from Jackson, came up Frances Harvey's sidewalk, as usual, at exactly a quarter past seven in the evening. Frances was not "going out" yet, and Regina had telephoned her long distance to say that "in all probability" she should not be receiving gentlemen "in." "What would Mama say?" Regina asked. Frances said she didn't know, which was not true, and went right on cooking dinners for Tom every weekend.

In the dining room that night, she sat across one corner of the long table from Tom. The useless length of polished cherry stretched away from them into the shadows as sadly as a road. Her plate pushed back, her chin resting on one palm, Frances stirred her coffee and said, "I don't know what on earth to do with all of Mama's clothes. I can't give them away, I can't sell them, I can't burn them, and the attic is full already. What can I do?"

"You look better tonight," said Tom.

"I slept," said Frances. "I slept and slept. From early this morning until just 'while ago. I never slept so well."

Then she told him about the Negro near the cemetery the previous afternoon, and how she had driven back out there as soon as dawn came, and found him again. He had been walking across the open field near the remains of the house that had burned down. There was no path to him from her, and she had hurried across ground uneven from old plowing and covered with the kind of small, tender grass it takes a very skillful mule to crop. "Wait!" she had cried. "Please wait!" The Negro had stopped and waited for her to reach him. "Your daughter?" she asked, out of breath.

"Daughter?" he repeated.

"The colored girl that was in the wagon yesterday. She was sick, you said, so I wondered. I could have taken her to town in the car, but I just didn't think. I wanted to know, how is she? Is she very sick?"

He had removed his old felt nigger hat as she approached him. "She a whole lot better, Miss Frances. She going to be all right now." Then he smiled at her. He did not say thank you, or anything more. Frances turned and walked back to the road and the car. And exactly as though the recovery of the Negro girl in the wagon had been her own recovery, she felt the return of a quiet breath and a steady pulse, and sensed the blessed stirring of a morning breeze. Up in her room, she had barely time to draw an old quilt over her before she fell asleep.

"When I woke, I knew about Mama," she said now to Tom. By the deepened intensity of her voice and eyes, it was plain that this was the important part. "It isn't right to say I *knew*," she went on, "because I had known all the time—ever since last night. I just realized it, that's all. I realized she had killed herself. It had to be that."

He listened soberly through the story about the box of sedatives. "But why?" he asked her. "It maybe looks that way, but what would be her reason for doing it?"

"Well, you see—" Frances said, and stopped.

Tom Beavers talked quietly on. "She didn't suffer. With what she had, she could have lived five, ten, who knows how many years. She was well cared for. Not hard up, I wouldn't say. Why?"

The pressure of his questioning could be insistent, and her trust in him, even if he was nobody but old Miss Rita Beavers' nephew, was well-nigh complete. "Because of you and me," she said, finally. "I'm certain of it, Tom. She didn't want to stand in our way. She never knew how to express love, you see." Frances controlled herself with an effort.

He did not reply, but sat industriously balancing a match folder on the tines of an unused serving fork. Anyone who has passed a lonely childhood in the company of an old deaf aunt is not inclined to doubt things hastily, and Tom Beavers would not have said he disbelieved anything Frances had told him. In fact, it seemed only too real to him. Almost before his eyes, that imperial, practical old hand went fumbling for the pills in the dark. But there had been much more to it than just love, he reflected. Bitterness, too, and pride, and control. And humor, perhaps, and the memory of a frightened little boy chased out of the yard by a twitch of her fan. Being invited to tea was one thing; suicide was quite another. Times had certainly changed, he thought.

But, of course, he could not say that he believed it, either. There was only Frances to go by. The match folder came to balance and rested on the tines. He glanced up at her, and a chill walked up his spine, for she was too serene. Cheek on palm, a lock of reddish hair fallen forward, she was staring at nothing with the absorbed silence of a child, or of a sweet, silver-haired old lady engaged in memory. Soon he might find that more and more of her was vanishing beneath this placid surface.

He himself did not know what he had seen that Friday evening so many months ago—what the figure had been that stood forward from the roadside at the tilt of the curve and urgently waved an arm to him. By the time he had braked and backed, the man had disappeared. Maybe it had been somebody drunk (for Richton had plenty of those to offer), walking it off in the cool of the woods at first dark. No such doubts had occurred to Frances. And what if he told her now the story Totsie had related of the road gang and the sick Negro girl in the wagon? Another labyrinth would open before her; she would never get out.

In Richton, the door to the past was always wide open, and what came in through it and went out of it had made people "different." But it scarcely ever happens, even in Richton, that one is able to see the precise moment when fact becomes faith, when life turns into legend, and people start to bend their finest loyalties to make themselves bemused custodians of the grave. Tom Beavers saw that moment now, in the profile of this dreaming girl, and he knew there was no time to lose.

He dropped the match folder into his coat pocket. "I think we should be leaving, Frances."

"Oh well, I don't know about going out yet," she said. "People criticize you so. Regina even had the nerve to telephone. Word had got all the way to her that you came here to have supper with me and we were alone in the house. When I tell the maid I want biscuits made up for two people, she looks like 'What would yo' mama say?' "

"I mean," he said, "I think it's time we left for good."

"And never came back?" It was exactly like Frances to balk at going to a movie but seriously consider an elopement.

"Well, never is a long time. I like to see about Aunt Rita every once in a great while. She can't remember from one time to the next whether it's two days or two years since I last came."

She glanced about the walls and at the furniture, the pictures, and the silver. "But I thought you would want to live here, Tom. It never occurred to me. I know it never occurred to Mama . . . This house . . . It can't be just left."

"It's a fine old house," he agreed. "But what would you do with all your mother's clothes?"

Her freckled hand remained beside the porcelain cup for what seemed a long time. He waited and made no move toward her; he felt her uncertainty keenly, but he believed that some people should not be startled out of a spell.

"It's just as you said," he went on, finally. "You can't give them away, you can't sell them, you can't burn them, and you can't put them in the attic, because the attic is full already. So what are you going to do?"

Between them, the single candle flame achieved a silent altitude. Then, politely, as on any other night, though shaking back her hair in a decided way, she said, "Just let me get my coat, Tom."

She locked the door when they left, and put the key under the mat—a last obsequy to the house. Their hearts were bounding ahead faster than they could walk down the sidewalk or drive off in the car, and, mindful, perhaps, of what happened to people who did, they did not look back.

Had they done so, they would have seen that the Harvey house was more beautiful than ever. All unconscious of its rejection by so mere a person as Tom Beavers, it seemed, instead, to have got rid of what did not suit it, to be free, at last, to enter with abandon the land of mourning and shadows and memory.

The Business Venture

We were down at the river that night. Pete Owens was there with his young wife, Hope (his name for her was Jezzie, after Jezebel in the Bible), and Charlie and me, and both the Houston boys, one with his wife and the other with the latest in a string of new girlfriends. But Nelle Townshend, his steady girl, wasn't there.

We talked and watched the river flow. It was different from those nights we used to go up to the club and dance, because we were older and hadn't bothered to dress, just wore slacks and shorts. It was a clear night but no moon.

Even five years married to him, I was in love with Charlie more than ever, and took his hand to rub the reddish hairs around his wrist. I held his hand under water and watched the flow around it, and later when the others went up to the highway for more whiskey, we kissed like two high school kids and then waded out laughing and splashed water on each other.

The next day Pete Owens looked me up at the office when my boss, Mr. McGinnis, was gone to lunch. "Charlie's never quit, you know, Eileen. He's still passing favors out."

My heart dropped. I could guess it, but wasn't letting myself know I really knew it. I put my hard mask on. "What's the matter? Isn't Hope getting enough from you?"

"Oh, I'm the one for Jezzie. You're the main one for Charlie. I just mean, don't kid yourself he's ever stopped."

"When did any of us ever stop?"

"You have. You like him that much. But don't think you're home free. The funny thing is, nobody's ever took a shotgun to Charlie. So far's I know, nobody's ever even punched him in the jaw."

"It is odd," I said, sarcastic, but he didn't notice.

"It's downright peculiar," said Pete. "But then I guess we're a special sort of bunch, Eileen."

I went back to typing and wished he'd go. He'd be asking me next. We'd dated and done a few things, but that was so long ago, it didn't count now. It never really mattered. I never thought much about it.

"What I wonder is, Eileen. Is everybody else like us, or so different from us they don't know what we're like at all?"

"The world's changing," I said. "They're all getting like us."

"You mean it?"

I nodded. "The word got out," I said. "You told somebody, and they told somebody else, and now everybody is like us."

"Or soon will be," he said.

"That's right," I said.

I kept on typing letters, reeling them on and off the platen and working on my electric machine the whole time he was talking, turning his hat over and picking at a straw or two off the synthetic weave. I had a headache that got worse after he was gone.

Also at the picnic that night was Grey Houston, one of the Houston brothers, who was always with a different girl. His former steady girlfriend, Nelle Townshend, kept a cleaning and pressing shop on her own premises. Her mother had been a stay-at-home lady for years. They had one of those beautiful old Victorian-type houses—it just missed being a photographer's and tourist attraction, being about twenty years too late and having the wooden trim too ornate for the connoisseurs to call it the real classical style. Nelle had been enterprising enough to turn one wing of the house where nobody went anymore into a cleaning shop, because she needed to make some money and felt she had to be near her mother. She had working for them off and on a Negro back from the Vietnam war who had used his veterans' educational benefits to train as a dry cleaner. She picked up the idea when her mother happened to remark one night after she had paid him for some carpenter work, "Ain't that a dumb nigger, learning dry cleaning with nothing to dry-clean."

Now, when Mrs. Townshend said "nigger," it wasn't as if one of us had said it. She went back through the centuries for her words, back to when "ain't" was good grammar. "Nigger" for her just meant "black." But it was assuming Robin had done something dumb that was the mistake. Because he wasn't dumb, and Nelle knew it. He told her he'd applied for jobs all around, but they didn't offer much and he might have to go to Biloxi or Hattiesburg or Gulfport to get one. The trouble was, he owned a house here. Nelle said, "Maybe you could work for me."

He told her about a whole dry cleaning plant up in Magee that had folded up recently due to the old man who ran it dying on his feet one day. They drove up there together and she bought it. Her mother didn't like it much when she moved the equipment in, but Nelle did it anyway. "I never get the smell out of my hair," she would say, "but if it can just make money I'll get used to it." She was dating Grey at the time, and I thought that's what gave her that much nerve.

Grey was a darling man. He was divorced from a New Orleans woman, somebody with a lot of class and money. She'd been crazy about Grey, as who wouldn't be, but he didn't "fit in," was her complaint. "Why do I have to fit in with her?" he kept asking. "Why shouldn't she fit in with us?" "She was O.K. with us," I said. "Not quite," he said. "Y'all never did relax. You never felt easy. That's why Charlie kept working at her, flirting and all. Then she'd have been one of us. But she acted serious about it. I said, 'Whatever you decide about Charlie, just don't tell me.' She was too serious."

"Anybody takes it seriously ought to be me," I said.

"Oh-oh," said Grey, breaking out with fun, the way he could do—in the depths one minute, up and laughing the next. "You can't afford that, Eileen."

That time I raised a storm at Charlie. "What did you want to get married for? You're nothing but a goddamn stud!"

"What's news about it?" Charlie wanted to know. "You're just getting worked up over nothing."

"Nothing! Is what we do just nothing?"

"That's right. When it's done with, it's nothing. What I think of you—now, that's something." He had had some problem with a new car at the garage—he had the GM agency then—and he smelled of clean lubricating products and new upholstery and the rough soap where the mechanics cleaned up. He was big and gleaming, the all-over male. Oh, hell, I thought, what can I do? Then, suddenly curious, I asked: "*Did you make out with Grey's wife?*"

He laughed out loud and gave me a sidelong kiss. "Now that's more like it."

Because he'd never tell me. He'd never tell me who he made out with. "Honey," he'd say, late at night in the dark, lying straight out beside me, occasionally tangling his toes in mine or reaching for his cigarettes, "if I'd say I never had another woman outside you, would you believe it?"

I couldn't say No from sheer astonishment.

"Because it just might be true," he went on in the dark, serious as a judge. Then I would start laughing, couldn't help it. Because there are few things in the world which you know are true. You don't know (not anymore: our mamas knew) if there's a God or not, much less if He so loved the world. You don't know what your own native land is up to, or the true meaning of freedom, or the real cost of gasoline and cigarettes, or whether your insurance company will pay up. But one thing I personally know that is *not* true is that Charlie Waybridge has had only one woman. Looked at that way, it can be a comfort, one thing to be sure of.

It was soon after the picnic on the river that Grey Houston came by to see me at the office. You'd think I had nothing to do but stop and talk. What he came about was Nelle.

"She won't date me anymore," he complained. "I thought we were doing fine, but she quit me just like that. Hell, I can't tell what's the trouble with her. I want to call up and say, 'Just tell me, Nelle. What's going on?'"

"Why don't you?" I asked.

Grey is always a little worried about things to do with people, especially since his divorce. We were glad when he started dating Nelle. She was hovering around thirty and didn't have anybody, and Grey was only a year or two younger.

"If I come right out and ask her, then she might just say, 'Let's decide to be good friends,' or something like that. Hell, I got enough friends."

"It's to be thought of," I agreed.

"What would you do?" he persisted.

"I'd rather know where I stand," I said, "but in this case I think I'd wait awhile. Nelle's worrying over that business. Maybe she doesn't know herself."

"I might push her too soon. I thought that, too."

"I ought to go around and see old Mrs. Townshend," I said. "She hardly gets out at all anymore. I mean to stop in and say hello."

"You're not going to repeat anything?"

See how he is? Skittery. "Of course not," I said. "But there's such a thing as keeping my eyes and ears open."

I went over to call on old Mrs. Townshend one Thursday afternoon when Mr. McGinnis's law office was closed anyway. The Townshend house is on a big lawn, a brick walk running up from the street to the front step and a large round plot of elephant ears in the front yard. When away and thinking of home, I see right off the Townshend yard and the elephant ears.

I wasn't even to the steps before I smelled clothes just dry-cleaned. I don't guess it's so bad, though hardly what you'd think of living with. Nor would you particularly like to see the sign outside the porte-cochere, though way to the left of the walk and not visible from the front porch. Still, it was out there clearly, saying "Townshend Dry Cleaning: Rapid Service." Better than a funeral parlor, but not much.

The Townshend house is stuffed with things. All these little Victorian tables on tall legs bowed outward, a small lower shelf, and the top covered katy-corner with a clean starched linen doily, tatting around the edge. All these chairs of various shapes, especially one that rocked squeaking on a walnut stand, and for every chair a doily at the head. Mrs. Townshend kept two birdcages, but no birds were in them. There never had been any so far as I knew. It wasn't a dark house, though. Nelle had taken out the stained glass way back when she graduated from college. That was soon after her older sister married, and her mama needed her. "If I'm going to live here," she had said, "that's got to go." So it went.

Mrs. Townshend never raised much of a fuss at Nelle. She was low to the ground because of a humpback, a rather placid old lady. The

Townshends were the sort to keep everything just the way it was. Mrs. Townshend was a LeMoyne from over toward Natchez. She was an Episcopalian and had brought her daughters up in that church.

"I'm sorry about this smell," she said in her forthright way, coming in and offering me a Coke on a little tray with a folded linen napkin beside it. "Nelle told me I'd get used to it and she was right: I have. But at first I had headaches all the time. If you get one I'll get some aspirin for you."

"How's the business going?" I asked.

"Nelle will be in in a minute. She knows you're here. You can ask her." She never raised her voice. She had a soft little face and gray eyes back of her little gold-rimmed glasses. She hadn't got to the hearing-aid stage yet, but you had to speak up. We went through the whole rigmarole of mine and Charlie's families. I had a feeling she was never much interested in all that, but around home you have to do it. Then I asked her what she was reading and she woke up. We got off the ground right away, and went strong about the President and foreign affairs, the picture not being so bright but of great interest, and about her books from the library always running out, and all the things she had against book clubs—then Nelle walked in.

Nelle Townshend doesn't look like anybody else but herself. her face is like something done on purpose to use up all the fine skin, drawing it evenly over the bones beneath, so that no matter at what age, she always would look the same. But that day she had this pinched look I'd never seen before, and her arms were splotched with what must have been a reaction to the cleaning fluids. She rolled down the sleeves of her blouse and sat in an old wicker rocker.

"I saw Grey the other day, Nelle," I said. "I think he misses you."

She didn't say anything outside of remarking she hadn't much time to go out. Then she mentioned some sort of decorating at the church she wanted to borrow some ferns for, from the florist. He's got some he rents, in washtubs. "You can't get all those ferns in our little church," Mrs. Townshend said, and Nelle said she thought two would do. She'd send Robin, she said. Then the bell rang to announce another customer. Nelle had to go because Robin was at the "plant"—actually the old cook's house in back of the property where they'd set the machinery up.

I hadn't said all I had to say to Nelle, so when I got up to go, I said to Mrs. Townshend that I'd go in the office a minute on the way out.

But Mrs. Townshend got to her feet, a surprise in itself. Her usual words were, You'll excuse me if I don't get up. Of course, you would excuse her and be too polite to ask why. Like a lot of old ladies, she might have arthritis. But this time she stood.

"I wish you'd let Nelle alone. Nelle is all right now. She's the way she wants to be. She's not the way you people are. She's just not a bit that way!"

It may have been sheer surprise that kept me from telling Charlie all this till the weekend. We were hurrying to get to Pete and Hope Owens's place for a dinner they were having for some people down from the Delta, visitors.

"What did you say to that?" Charlie asked me.

"I was too surprised to open my mouth. I wouldn't have thought Mrs. Townshend would express such a low opinion as that. And why does she have it in the first place? Nelle's always been part of our crowd. She grew up with us. I thought they liked us."

"Old ladies get notions. They talk on the phone too much."

To our surprise, Nelle was at the Owenses dinner, too. Hope told me in the kitchen that she'd asked her, and then asked Grey. But Grey had a date with the little Springer girl he'd brought to the picnic, Carole Springer. "If this keeps up," Hope said to me while I was helping her with a dip, "we're going to have a Springer in our crowd. I'm just not right ready for that." "Me either," I said. The Springers were from McComb, in lumber. They had money but they never were much fun.

"Did Nelle accept knowing you were going to ask Grey?" I asked.

"I couldn't tell that. She just said she'd love to and would come about seven."

It must have been seven, because Nelle walked in. "Can I help?"

"Your mama," I said, when Hope went out with the tray, "she sort of got upset with me the other day. I don't know why. If I said anything wrong, just tell her I'm sorry."

Nelle looked at her fresh nail polish. "Mama's a little peculiar now and then. Like everybody." So she wasn't about to open up.

"I've been feeling bad about Grey is all," I said. "You can think I'm meddling if you want to."

"Grey's all right," she said. "He's been going around with Carole Springer from McComb."

"All the more reason for feeling bad. Did you know they're coming tonight?" She smiled a little distantly, and we went out to join the party. Charlie was already sitting up too close to the wife of the guest couple. I'd met them before. They have an antique shop. He is tall and nice, and she is short (wears spike heels) and nice. They are the sort you can't ever remember what their names are. If you get the first names right you're doing well. Shirley and Bob.

"Honey, you're just a doll," Charlie was saying (if he couldn't think of Shirley, Honey would do), and Pete said, "Watch out, Shirley, the next thing you know you'll be sitting on his lap."

"I almost went in for antiques myself," Nelle was saying to Bob, the husband. "I would have liked that better, of course, than a cleaning business, but I thought the turnover here would be too small. I do need to feel like I'm making money if I'm going to work at it. For a while, though, it was fun to go wandering around New Orleans and pick up good things cheap."

"I'd say they'd all been combed over down there," Bob objected.

"It's true about the best things," Nelle said. "I could hardly afford those anyway. But sometimes you see some pieces with really good design and you can see you might realize something on them. Real appreciation goes a long way."

"Bob has a jobber up in St. Louis," Shirley said. "We had enough of all this going around shaking the bushes. A few lucky finds was what got us started."

Nelle said, "I started thinking about it because I went in the living room a year or so back and there were some ladies I never saw before. They'd found the door open and walked in. They wanted to know the price of Mama's furniture. I said it wasn't for sale, but Mama was just coming in from the kitchen and heard them. You wouldn't believe how mad she got. 'I'm going straight and get out my pistol,' she said."

"You ought to just see her mama," said Hope. "This tiny little old lady."

"So what happened?" Shirley asked when she got through laughing.

"Nothing real bad," said Nelle. "They just got out the door as quick as they could."

"Yo' mama got a pistol?" Charlie asked, after a silence. We started to laugh again, the implication being plain that a Charlie Waybridge *needs* to know if a woman's mother has a pistol in the house.

"She does have one," said Nelle.

"So watch out, Charlie," said Pete.

Bob remarked, "Y'all certainly don't change much over here."

"Crazy as ever," Hope said proudly. It crossed my mind that Hope was always protecting herself, one way or the other.

Shirley said she thought it was just grand to be back, she wouldn't take anything for it, and after that Grey and Carole arrived. He had another drink and then went in to dinner. Everybody acted like everything was okay. After dinner, I went back in the kitchen for some water, and there was Charlie, kissing Shirley. She was so strained up on tiptoe, Charlie being over six feet, that I thought, in addition to being embarrassed, mad, and backing out before they saw me, What they need is a stepladder to do it right.

On the way home, I told Charlie about catching them. "I didn't know she was within a country mile," he said, ready with excuses. "She just plain grabbed me."

"I've been disgusted once too often," I said. "Tell it to Bob."

"If she wanted to do it right," he said, "she ought to get a stepladder." So then I had to laugh. Even if our marriage wasn't ideal, we still had the same thoughts.

It sometimes seemed to me, in considering the crowd we were always part of, from even before we went to school, straight on through, that we were all like one person, walking around different ways, but in some permanent way breathing together, feeling the same reactions, thinking each other's thoughts. What do you call that if not love? If asked, we'd all cry Yes! with one voice, but then it's not our habit to ask anything serious. We're close to religious about keeping everything light and gay. Nelle Townshend knew that, all the above, but she was drawing back. A betrayer was what she was turning into. We felt weakened because of her. What did she think she was doing?

I had to drive Mr. McGinnis way back in the woods one day to serve a subpoena on a witness. He hadn't liked to drive since his heart attack, and his usual colored man was busy with Mrs. McGinnis's garden. In the course of that little trip, coming back into town, I saw Nelle Townshend's station wagon turn off onto a side road. I couldn't see who was with her, but somebody was, definitely.

I must add that this was spring and there were drifts of dogwood all mingled in the woods at different levels. Through those same woods, along the winding roads, the redbud, simultaneous, was spreading its wonderful pink haze. Mr. McGinnis sat beside me without saying much, his old knobby hands folded over a briefcase he held upright on his lap. "A trip like this just makes me think, Eileen, that everybody owes it to himself to get out in the woods this time of year. It's just God's own garden," he said. We had just crossed a wooden bridge over a pretty little creek about a mile back. That same creek, shallower, was crossed by a ford along the road that Nelle's car had taken. I know that little road, too, maybe the prettiest one of all.

Serpents have a taste for Eden, and in a small town, if they are busy elsewhere, lots of people are glad to fill in for them. It still upsets me to think of all the gossip that went on that year, and at the same time I have to blame Nelle Townshend for it, not so much for starting it, but for being so unconscious about it. She had stepped out of line and she didn't even bother to notice.

Once the business got going, the next thing she did was enroll in a class—a "seminar," she said—over at the university at Hattiesburg. It was something to do with art theory, she said, and she was thinking of going on from there to a degree, eventually, and get hold of a subject she could teach at the junior college right up the road. So settling in to be an old maid.

I said this last rather gloomily to Pete's wife, Hope, and Pete overheard and said, "There's all kinds of those." "You stop that," said Hope. "What's supposed to be going on?" I asked. (Some say don't ask, it's better not to, but I think you have to know if only to keep on guard.)

"Just that they're saying things about Nelle and that black Robin works for her."

"Well, they're in the same business," I said.

"Whatever it is, people don't like it. They say she goes out to his house after dark. That they spend too much time over the books."

"Somebody ought to warn her," I said. "If Robin gets into trouble she won't find anybody to do that kind of work. He's the only one."

"Nelle's gotten too independent is the thing," said Pete. "She thinks she can live her own life."

"Maybe she can," said Hope.

Charlie was away that week. He had gone over to the Delta on business, and Hope and Pete had dropped in to keep me company. Hope is ten years younger than Pete. (Pete used to date her sister, Mary Ruth, one of these beauty-queen types, who had gone up to the Miss America pageant to represent Mississippi and come back first runner-up. For the talent contest part of it, she had recited passages from the Bible, and Pete always said her trouble was she was too religious but he hoped to get her over it. She used to try in a nice way to get him into church work, and that embarrassed him. It's our common habit, as Mary Ruth well knew, to go to morning service, but anything outside that is out. Anyway, around Mary Ruth's he used to keep seeing the little sister Hope, and he'd say, "Mary Ruth, you better start on that girl about church, she's growing up dynamite." Mary Ruth got involved in a promotion trip, something about getting right with America, and met a man on a plane trip to Dallas, and before the seat-belt sign went off they were in love. For Mary Ruth that meant marriage. She was strict, a woman of faith, and I don't think Pete would have been happy with her. But he had got the habit of the house by then, and Mary Ruth's parents had got fond of him and didn't want him drinking too much: they made him welcome. So one day Hope turned seventeen and came out in a new flouncy dress with heels on, and Pete saw the light.)

We had a saying by now that Pete had always been younger than Hope, that she was older than any of us. Only twenty, she worked at making their house look good and won gardening prizes. She gave grand parties, with attention to details.

"I stuck my neck out," I told Hope, "to keep Nelle dating Grey. You remember her mama took a set at me like I never dreamed possible. Nelle's been doing us all funny, but she may have to come back someday. We can't stop caring for her."

Hope thought it over. "Robin knows what it's like here, even if Nelle may have temporarily forgotten. He's not going to tempt fate. Anyway, somebody already spoke to Nelle."

"Who?"

"Grey, of course. He'll use any excuse to speak to her. She got mad as a firecracker. She said, 'Don't you know this is nineteen seventy-*six*? I've got a business to run. I've got a living to make!' But she quit going out to his house at night. And Robin quit so much as answering the phone, up at her office."

"You mean he's keeping one of those low profiles?" said Pete.

Soon after, I ran into Robin uptown in the grocery, and he said, "How do you do, Mrs. Waybridge," like a schoolteacher or a foreigner, and I figured just from that, that he was on to everything and taking no chances. Nelle must have told him. I personally knew what not many people did, that he was a real partner with Nelle, not just her hired help. They had got Mr. McGinnis to draw up the papers. And they had plans for moving the plant uptown, to an empty store building, with some investment in more equipment. So maybe they'd get by till then. I felt a mellowness in my heart about Nelle's effort and all—a Townshend (LeMoyne on her mother's side) opening a dry cleaning business. I thought of Robin's effort, too—he had a sincere, intelligent look, reserved. What I hoped for them was something like a prayer.

Busying my thoughts about all this, I had been forgetting Charlie. That will never do.

For one thing, leaving aside women, Charlie's present way of life was very nearly wild. He'd got into oil leases two years before, and when something was going on, he'd drive like a demon over to East Texas by way of Shreveport and back through Pike and Amite counties. At one time he had to sit over Mr. McGinnis for a month getting him to study up on laws governing oil rights. In the end, Charlie got to know as much or more than Mr. McGinnis. He's in and out. The in-between times are when he gets restless. Drinks too much and starts simmering up about some new woman. Once tried, soon dropped. Or so I like to believe. Then, truth to tell, there is really part of me that not only wants to believe but at unstated times does believe that I've been the only one for Charlie Waybridge. Not that I'd begrudge him a few times of having it off down in the back of the gym with some girl who came in from the country, nor would I think anything about flings in New Orleans while he was in Tulane. But as for the outlandish reputation he's acquired now, sometimes I just want to say out loud to all and sundry, "There's not a word of truth in it. He's a big, attractive, friendly guy, O.K.! But he's not the town stud. He belongs to *me*."

All this before the evening along about first dark when Charlie was seen on the Townshend property by Nelle's mother, who went and got the pistol and shot at him.

"Christ, she could have killed me," Charlie said. He was too surprised about it even to shake. He was just dazed. Fixed a stiff drink and didn't want any supper. "She's gone off her rocker," he said. "That's all I could think."

I knew I had to ask it, sooner or later. "What were you doing up there, Charlie?"

"Nothing," he said. "I'd left the car at Wharton's garage to check why I'm burning too much oil. He's getting to it in the morning. It was a nice evening and I cut through the back alley and that led to a stroll through the Townshend pasture. That's all. I saw the little lady out on the back porch. I was too far off to holler at her. She scuttled off into the house and I was going past, when here she came out again with something black weighting her hand. You know what I thought? I thought she had a kitten by the neck. Next thing I knew there was a bullet smashing through the leaves not that far off." He put his hand out.

"Wonder if Nelle was home."

I was nervous as a monkey after I heard this, and nothing would do me but to call up Nelle.

She answered right away. "Nelle," I said, "is your little mama going in for target practice these days?"

She started laughing. "Did you hear that all the way to your place? She's mad 'cause the Johnson's old cow keeps breaking down our fence. She took a shot in the air because she's tired complaining."

"Since when was Charlie Waybridge a cow?" I asked.

"Mercy, Eileen. You don't mean Charlie was back there?"

"You better load that thing with blanks," I said, "or hide it."

"Blanks is all it's got in it," said Nelle. "Mama doesn't tell that because she feels more protected not to."

"You certainly better check it out," I said. "Charlie says it was a bullet."

There was a pause. "You're not mad or anything, are you, Eileen?"

"Oh, no," I warbled. "We've been friends too long for that."

"Come over and see us," said Nelle. "Real soon."

I don't know who told it, but knowing this town like the back of my hand, I know *how* they told it. Charlie Waybridge was up at Nelle Townshend's and old Mrs. Townshend shot at him. Enough said. At the Garden Club Auxiliary tea, I came in and heard them giggling, and how they got quiet when I passed a plate of sandwiches. I went straight to the subject, which is the way I do. "Y'all off on Mrs. Townshend?" I asked. There was a silence, and then some little cross-eyed bride, new in town, piped up that there was just always something funny going on here, and Maud Varner, an old friend, said she thought Nelle ought to watch out for Mrs. Townshend, she was showing her age. "It's not such a funny goings-on when it almost kills somebody," I said. "Charlie came straight home and told me. He was glad to be alive, but I went and called Nelle. So she does know." There was another silence during which I could tell what everybody thought. The thing is not to get too distant or above it all. If you do, your friends will pull back, too, and you won't know anything. Gradually, you'll just turn into, Poor Eileen, what does she think of all Charlie's carryings-on?

Next, the injunction. Who brought it and why? I got the answer to the first before I guessed the second.

It was against the Townshend Cleaners because the chemicals used were a hazard to health and the smell they exuded a public nuisance. But the real reason wasn't this at all.

In order to speed up the deliveries, Nelle had taken to driving the station wagon herself, so that Robin could run in with the cleaning. Some people had begun to remark on this. Would it have been different if Nelle was married or had a brother, a father, a steady boyfriend? I don't know. I used to hold my breath when they went by in the late afternoon together. Because sometimes when the back of the stationwagon was full, Robin would be up on the front seat with her, and she with her head stuck in the air, driving carefully, her mind on nothing at all to do with other people. Once the cleaning load got lighter, Robin would usually sit on the back seat, as expected to do. But sometimes, busy talking to her, he wouldn't. He'd be up beside her, discussing business.

Then, suddenly, the business closed.

Nelle was beside herself. She came running to Mr. McGinnis. Her hair was every which way around her head and she was wearing an old checked shirt and no makeup.

She could hardly make herself sit still and visit with me while Mr. McGinnis got through with a client. "Now, Miss Nelle," he said, steering her through the door.

"Just when we were making a go of it!" I heard her say; then he closed the door.

I heard by way of the grapevine that very night that the person who had done it was John Houston, Grey's brother, whose wife's family lived on a property just below the Townshends. They claimed they couldn't sleep for the dry-cleaning fumes and were getting violent attacks of nausea.

"Aren't they supposed to give warnings?" I asked.

We were all at John and Rose Houston's home, a real gathering of the bunch, only Nelle being absent, though she was the most present one of all. There was a silence after every statement, in itself unusual. Finally John Houston said, "Not in cases of extreme health hazard."

"That's a lot of you-know-what," I said. "Rose, your family's not dying."

Rose said: "They never claimed to be dying." And Pete said: "Eileen, can't you sit right quiet and try to use your head?"

"In preference to running off at the mouth," said Charlie, which made me mad. I was refusing, I well knew, to see the point they all had in mind. But it seemed to me that was my privilege.

The thing to know about our crowd is that we never did go in for talking about the "Negro question." We talked about Negroes the way we always had, like people, one at a time. They were all around us, had always been, living around us, waiting on us, sharing our lives, brought up with us, nursing us, cooking for us, mourning and rejoicing with us, making us laugh, stealing from us, digging our graves. But when all the troubles started coming in on us after the Freedom Riders and the Ole Miss riots, we decided not to talk about it. I don't know but what we weren't afraid of getting nervous. We couldn't jump out of our own skins, or those of our parents, grandparents, and those before them. "Nothing you can do about it" was Charlie's view. "Whatever you decide, you're going to act the same way tomorrow as you did today. Hoping you can get Alma to cook for you, and Peabody to clean the windows, and Bayman to cut the grass." "I'm not keeping anybody from voting—yellow, blue, or pink," said Hope, who had got her "ideas" straight from the first, she said. "I don't guess any of us is," said Pete, "them days is gone forever." "But wouldn't it just be wonderful," said Rose Houston, "to have a little colored gal to pick up your hand-kerchief and sew on your buttons and bring you cold lemonade and fan you when you're hot, and just love you to death?"

Rose was joking, of course, the way we all liked to do. But there are always one or two of them that we seriously insist we know—really *know*—that they love us. Would do anything for us, as we would for them. Otherwise, without that feeling, I guess we couldn't rest easy. You never can really know what they think, what they feel, so there's always the one chance it might be love.

So we—the we I'm always speaking of—decided not to talk about race relations because it spoiled things too much. We didn't like to consider anyone of us really involved in some part of it. Then, in my mind's eye, I saw Nelle's car, that dogwood-laden day in the woods, headed off the road with somebody inside. Or such was my impression. I'd never mentioned it to anybody, and Mr. McGinnis hadn't, I think, seen. Was it Robin? Or maybe, I suddenly asked myself, Charlie? Mysteries multiplied.

"Nelle's got to make a living is the whole thing," said Pete, getting practical. "We can't not let her do that."

"Why doesn't somebody find her a job she'd like?" asked Grey.

"Why the hell," Charlie burst out, "don't you marry her, Grey? Women ought to get married," he announced in general. "You see what happens when they don't."

"Hell, I can't get near her," said Grey. "We dated for six months. I guess I wasn't the one," he added.

"She ought to relocate the plant uptown, then she could run the office in her house, one remove from it, acting like a lady."

"What about Robin?" said Hope.

"He could run back and forth," I said. "They do want to do that," I added, "but can't afford it yet."

"You'd think old Mrs. Townshend would have stopped it all."

"That lady's a mystery."

"If Nelle just had a brother."

"Or even an uncle."

Then the talk dwindled down to silence.

"John," said Pete, after a time, turning around to face him, "we all know it was you—not Rose's folks. Did you have to?"

John Houston was sitting quietly in his chair. He was a little older than the rest of us, turning gray, a little more settled and methodical, more like our uncle than an equal and friend. (Or was it just that he and Rose were the only ones so far to have children—what all our parents said we all ought to do, but couldn't quit having our good times.) He was sipping bourbon. He nodded slowly. "I had to." We didn't ask any more.

"Let's just go quiet," John finally added. "Wait and see."

Now, all my life I'd been hearing first one person then another (and these, it would seem, appointed by silent consensus) say that things were to be taken care of in a certain way and no other. The person in this case who had this kind of appointment was evidently John Houston, from in our midst. But when did he get it? How did he get it? Where did it come from? There seemed to be no need to discuss it.

Rose Houston, who wore her long light hair in a sort of loose bun at the nape and who sat straight up in her chair, adjusted a fallen strand, and Grey went off to fix another drink for himself and Pete and Hope. He sang on the way out, more or less to himself, "For the times they are a-changing . . ." and that, too, found reference in all our minds. Except I couldn't help but wonder whether anything had changed at all.

The hearing on the dry cleaning injunction was due to be held in two weeks. Nelle went off to the coast. She couldn't stand the tension, she told me, having come over to Mr. McGinnis's office to see him alone. "Thinking how we've worked and all," she said, "and how just before this came up the auditor was in and told us what good shape we were in. We were just about to buy a new condenser."

"What's that?" I asked.

"Takes the smell out of the fumes," she said. "The very thing they're mad about. I could kill John Houston. Why couldn't he have come to me?"

I decided to be forthright. "Nelle, there's something you ought to evaluate . . . consider, I mean. Whatever word you want." I was shaking, surprising myself.

Nobody was around. Mr. McGinnis was in the next county.

Once when I was visiting a school friend up north, out from Philadelphia, a man at a party asked me if I would have sexual relations with a black. He wasn't black himself, so why was he curious? I said I'd never even thought about it. "It's a taboo, I think you call it," I said. "Girls like me get brainwashed early on. It's not that I'm against them," I added, feeling awkward. "Contrary to what you may think or may even believe," he told me, "you've probably thought a lot about it. You've suppressed your impulses, that's all." "Nobody can prove that," I said, "not even you," I added, thinking I was being amusing. But he only looked superior and walked away.

"It's you and Robin," I said. I could hear myself explaining to Charlie, Somebody had to, sooner or later. "You won't find anybody really believing anything, I don't guess, but it's making people speculate."

Nelle Townshend never reacted the way you'd think she would. She didn't even get annoyed, much less hit the ceiling. She just gave a little sigh. "You start a business, you'll see. I've got no time for anything but worrying about customers and money."

I was wondering whether to tell her the latest. A woman named McCorkle from out in the country, who resembled Nelle so much from the back you'd think they were the same, got pushed off the sidewalk last Saturday and fell in the concrete gutter up near the drugstore. The person who did it, somebody from outside town, must have said something nobody heard but Mrs. McCorkle, because she jumped up with her skirt muddy and stockings torn and yelled out, "I ain't no nigger lover!"

But I didn't tell her. If she was anybody but a Townshend, I might have. Odd to think that, when the only Townshends left there were Nelle and her mother. In cases such as this, the absent are present and the dead are, too. Mr. Townshend had died so long ago you had to ask your parents what he was like. The answer was always the same. "Sid Townshend was a mighty good man." Nelle had had two sisters: one died in her twenties, the victim of a rare disease, and the other got married and went to live on a place out from Helena, Arkansas. She had about six children and could be of no real help to the home branch.

"Come over to dinner," I coaxed. "You want me to ask Grey, I will. If you don't, I won't."

"Grey," she said, just blank, like that. He might have been somebody she met once a long time back. "She's a perpetual virgin," I heard Charlie say once. "Just because she won't cotton up to you," I said. But maybe he was right. Nelle and her mother lived up near the Episcopal church. Since our little town could not support a full-time rector, it was they who kept the church linens and the chalice and saw that the robes were always cleaned and hung in their proper place in the little room off the chancel. Come to think of it, keeping those robes and surplices in order may have been one thing that started Nelle into dry cleaning.

Nelle got up suddenly, her face catching the light from our old window with the wobbly glass in the panes, and I thought, She's a grand-looking woman, sort of girlish and womanish both.

"I'm going to the coast," she said. "I'm taking some books and a sketch pad. I may look into some art courses. You have to have training to teach anything, that's the trouble."

"Look, Nelle, if it's money— Well, you do have friends, you know."

"Friends," she said, just the way she had said "Grey." I wondered just what Nelle was really like. None of us seemed to know.

"Have a good time," I said. After she left, I thought I heard the echo of that blank, soft voice saying, "Good time."

It was a week after Nelle had gone that old Mrs. Townshend rang up Mr. McGinnis at the office. Mr. McGinnis came out to tell me what it was all about.

"Mrs. Townshend says that last night somebody tore down the dry cleaning sign Nelle had put up out at the side. Some colored woman is staying with her at night, but neither one of them saw anybody. Now she can't find Robin to put it back. She's called his house but he's not there."

"Do they say he'll be back soon?"

"They say he's out of town."

"I'd get Charlie to go up and fix it, but you know what happened."

"I heard about it. Maybe in daylight the old lady won't shoot. I'll go around with our yardman after dinner." What we still mean by dinner is lunch. So they put the sign up and I sat in the empty office wondering about this and that, but mainly, Where was Robin Byers?

It's time to say that Robin Byers was not any Harry Belafonte calypso-singing sex symbol of a "black." He was strong and thoughtful-looking, not very tall, definitely chocolate, but not ebony. He wore his hair cropped short in an almost military fashion so that, being thick, it stuck straight up more often than not. From one side he could look positively frightening, as he had a long white scar running down the side of his cheek. It was said that he got it in the army, in Vietnam, but the story of just how was not known. So maybe he had not gotten it in the war, but somewhere else. His folks had been in the county forever, his own house being not far out from town. He had a wife, two teenaged children, a telephone, and a TV set. The other side of Robin Byers's face was regular, smooth, and while not especially handsome it was good-humored and likable. All in all, he looked intelligent and conscientious, and that must have been how Nelle Townshend saw him, as he was.

I went to the hearing. I'd have had to, to keep Mr. McGinnis's notes straight, but I would have anyway, as all our crowd showed up, except Rose and John Houston. Rose's parents were there, having brought the complaint, and Rose's mama's doctor from over at Hattiesburg, to swear she'd had no end of allergies and migraines, and attacks of nausea, all brought on by the cleaning fumes. Sitting way in the back was Robin Byers, in a suit (a really nice suit) with a blue-and-white-striped "city" shirt and a knit tie. He looked like an assistant university dean, except for the white scar. He also had the look of a spectator, very calm, I thought, not wanting to keep turning around and staring at him, but keeping the image in my mind like an all-day sucker, letting it slowly melt out its meaning. He was holding a certain surface. But he was scared. Half across the courtroom you could see his temple throbbing, and the sweat beads. He was that tense. The whole effect was amazing.

The complaint was read out and Mrs. Hammond, Rose's mother, testified and the doctor testified, and Mr. Hammond said they were both right. The way the Hammonds talk—big Presbyterians—you would think they had the Bible on their side every minute, so naturally everybody else had to be mistaken. Friends and neighbors of the Townshends all these years, they now seemed to be speaking of people they knew only slightly. That is until Mrs. Hammond, a sort of dumpling-like woman with a practiced way of sounding accurate about whatever she said (she was a good gossip because she got all the details of everything), suddenly came down to a personal level and said, "Nelle, I just don't see why if you want to run that thing you don't move it into town," and Nelle said back right away just like they were in a living room instead of a courthouse, "Well, that's because of Mama, Miss Addie. This way I'm in and out with her." At that, everybody laughed, couldn't help it.

Then Mr. McGinnis got up and challenged that very much about Mrs. Hammond's headaches and allergies (he established her age, fifty-two, which she didn't want to tell) had to do with the cleaning plant. If they had, somebody else would have such complaints, but in case we needed to go further into it, he would ask Miss Nelle to explain what he meant.

Nelle got up front and went about as far as she could concerning the type of equipment she used and how it was guaranteed against the very thing now being complained of, that it let very few vapors escape, but then she said she would rather call on Robin Byers to come and explain because he had had special training in the chemical processes and knew all their possible negative effects.

And he came. He walked down the aisle and sat in the chair and nobody had ever seen such composure. I think he was petrified, but so might an actor be who was doing a role to high perfection. And when he started to talk you'd think that dry cleaning was a text and that his God-appointed task was to preach a sermon on it. But it wasn't quite like that, either. More modern. A professor giving a lecture to extremely ignorant students, with a good professor's accuracy, to the last degree. In the first place, he said, the cleaning fluid used was not varsol or carbon tetrachloride, which were known not only to give off harmful fumes but to damage fabrics, but something called "Perluxe" or perchlorethylene (he paused to give the chemical composition), which was approved for commercial cleaning purposes in such and such a solution by federal and state bylaws, of certain numbers and codes, which Mr. McGinnis had listed in his records and would be glad to read aloud upon request. If an operator worked closely with Perluxe for a certain number of hours a day, he might have headaches, it was true, but escaping vapor could scarcely be smelled at all more than a few feet from the exhaust pipes, and caused no harmful effects whatsoever, even to shrubs or "the leaves upon the trees." He said this last in such a lofty, rhythmic way that somebody giggled (I think it was Hope), and he stopped talking altogether.

"There might be smells down in those hollows back there," Nelle filled in from where she was sitting, "but it's not from my one little exhaust pipe."

"Then why," asked Mrs. Hammond right out, "do you keep on saying you need new equipment so you won't have any exhaust? Just answer me that."

"I'll let Robin explain," said Nelle.

"The fact is that Perluxe is an expensive product," Robin said. "At four dollars and twenty-five cents a gallon, using nearly thirty gallons each time the accumulation of the garments is put through the process, she can count on it that the overheads with two cleanings a week will run in the neighborhood of between two and three hundred dollars. So having the condenser machine would mean that the exhaust runs into it, and so converts the vapors back to the liquid, in order to use it once again."

"It's not for the neighbors," Nelle put in. "It's for us."

Everybody had spoken out of order by then, but what with the atmosphere having either declined or improved (depending on how you looked at it) to one of friendly inquiry among neighbors rather than a squabble in a court of law, the silence that finally descended was more meditative than not, having as its most impressive features, like high points in a landscape, Nelle, at some little distance down a front bench, but turned around so as to take everything in, her back straight and her Townshend head both superior and interested; and Robin Byers, who still had the chair by Judge Purvis's desk, collected and severe (he had forgotten the giggle), with testimony faultlessly delivered and nothing more he needed to say. (Would things have been different if Charlie had been there? He was out of town.)

The judge cleared his throat and said he guessed the smells in the gullies around Tyler might be a nuisance, sure enough, but couldn't be said to be caused by dry cleaning, and he thought Miss Townshend could go on with her business. For a while, the white face and the black one seemed just the same, to be rising up quiet and superior above us all.

The judge asked, just out of curiosity, when Nelle planned to buy the condenser that was mentioned. She said whenever she could find one secondhand in good condition—they cost nearly two thousand dollars new—and Robin Byers put in that he had just been looking into one down in Biloxi, so it might not be too long. Biloxi is on the coast.

Judge Purvis said we'd adjourn now, and everybody stood up of one accord, except Mr. McGinnis, who had dozed off and was almost snoring.

Nelle, who was feeling friendly to the world, or seeming to (we all had clothes that got dirty, after all), said to all and sundry not to worry, "we plan to move the plant uptown one of these days before too long," and it was the "we" that came through again, a slip: she usually referred to the business as hers. It was just a reminder of what everybody wanted not to have to think about, and she probably hadn't intended to speak of it that way.

As if to smooth it well into the past, Judge Purvis remarked that these little towns ought to have zoning laws, but I sat there thinking there wouldn't be much support for that, not with the Gulf Oil station and garage right up on South Street between the Whitmans' and the Binghams', and the small-appliance shop on the vacant lot where the old Marshall mansion had stood, and the Tackett house, still elegant as you please, doing steady business as a funeral home. You can separate black from white but not business from nonbusiness. Not in our town.

Nelle came down and shook hands with Mr. McGinnis. "I don't know when I can afford to pay you." "Court costs go to them," he said. "Don't worry about the rest."

Back at the office, Mr. McGinnis closed the street door and said to me, "The fumes in this case have got nothing to do with dry cleaning. Has anybody talked to Miss Nelle?"

"They have," I said, "but she doesn't seem to pay any attention."

He said I could go home for the day and much obliged for my help at the courthouse. I powdered my nose and went out into the street. It wasn't but eleven-thirty.

Everything was still, and nobody around. The blue jays were having a good time on the courthouse yard, squalling and swooping from the lowest oak limbs, close to the ground, then mounting back up. There were some sparrows out near the old horse trough, which still ran water. They were splashing around. But except for somebody driving up for the mail at the post office, there wasn't a soul around. I started walking, and just automatically I went by for the mail because as a rule Charlie didn't stop in for it till noon, even when in town. On the way I was mulling over the hearing and how Mrs. Hammond had said at the door of the courtroom to Nelle, "Aw right, Miss Nellie, you just wait." It wasn't said in any unpleasant way; in fact, it sounded right friendly. Except that she wasn't looking at Nelle, but past her, and except that being older, it wasn't the ordinary thing to call her "Miss," and except that Nelle is a pretty name but Nellie isn't. But Nelle in reply had suddenly laughed in that unexpected but delightful way she has, because something has struck her as really funny. "What am I supposed to wait *for*, Miss Addie?" Whatever else, Nelle wasn't scared. I looked for Robin Byers, but he had got sensible and gone off in that old little blue German car he drives. I saw Nelle drive home alone.

Then, because the lay of my home direction was a shortcut from the post office, and because the spring had been dry and the back lanes nice to walk in, I went through the same way Charlie had that time Mrs. Townshend had about killed him, and enjoyed, the way I had from childhood on, the soft fragrances of springtime, the forsythia turned from yellow to green fronds, but the spirea still white as a bride's veil worked in blossoms, and the climbing roses, mainly wild, just opening a delicate, simple pink bloom all along the back fences. I was crossing down that way when what I saw was a blue car.

It was stopped way back down the Townshend property on a little connecting road that made an entrance through to a lower town road, one that nobody used anymore. I stopped in the clump of bowdarc trees on the next property from the Townshends'. Then I saw Nelle, running down the hill. She still had that same laugh, honest and joyous, that she had shown the first of to Mrs. Hammond. And there coming to meet her was Robin, his teeth white as his scar. They grabbed each other's hands, black on white and white on black. They started whirling each other around, like two schoolchildren in a game, and I saw Nelle's mouth forming the words I could scarcely hear: "We won! We won!" And his, the same, a baritone underneath. It was pure joy. Washing the color out, saying that the dye didn't, this time, hold, they could have been brother and sister, happy at some good family news, or old lovers (Charlie and I sometimes meet like that, too happy at some piece of luck to really stop to talk about it, just dancing out our joy). But, my God, I thought, don't they know they're black and white and this is Tyler, Mississippi? Well, of course they do, I thought next—that's more than half the joy—getting away with it! Dare and double-dare! Dumbfounded, I just stood, hidden, never seen by them at all, and let the image of black on white and white on black—those pale, aristocratic Townshend hands and his strong, square-cut black ones—linked perpetually now in my mind's eye—soak in. It's going to stay with me forever, I thought, but what does it mean? I never told. I didn't think they were lovers. But they were into a triumph of the sort that lovers feel. They had acted as they pleased. They were above everything. They lived in another world because of a dry cleaning business. They had proved it when they had to. They knew it.

But nobody could be counted on to see it the way I did. It was too complicated for any two people to know about it.

Soon after this we got a call from Hope, Pete's wife. "I've got tired of all this foolishness," she said. "How did we ever get hung up on dry cleaning, of all things? Can you feature it? I'm going to give a party. Mary Foote Williams is coming home to see her folks and bringing Keith, so that's good enough for me. And don't kid yourself. I'm personally going to get Nelle Townshend to come, and Grey Houston is going to bring her. I'm getting good and ready for everybody to start acting normal again. I don't know what's been the matter with everybody, and furthermore I don't want to know."

Well, this is a kettle of fish, I thought: Hope, the youngest, taking us over. Of course, she did have the perspective to see everything whole.

I no sooner put down the phone than Pete called up from his office. "Jezzie's on the warpath," he said. (He calls her Jezzie because she used to tell all kinds of lies to some little high school boy she had crazy about her—her own age—just so she could go out with Pete and the older crowd. It was easy to see through that. She thought she might just be getting a short run with us and would have to fall back on her own bunch when we shoved her out, so she was keeping a foothold. Pete caught her at it, but all it did was make him like her better. Hope was pert. She had a sharp little chin she liked to stick up in the air, and a turned-up nose. "Both signs of meanness," said Mr. Owens, Pete's father, "especially the nose," and buried his own in the newspaper.)

"Well," I said doubtfully, "if you think it's a good idea . . ."

"No stopping her," said Pete, with the voice of a spectator at the game. "If anybody can swing it, she can."

So we finally said yes.

The morning of Hope's party there was some ugly weather, one nasty little black cloud after another and a host of restless crosswinds. There was a tornado watch out for our county and two others, making you know it was a widespread weather system. I had promised to bring a platter of shrimp for the buffet table, and that meant a whole morning shucking them after driving out to pick up the order at the Fish Shack. At times the lightning was popping so close I had to get out of the kitchen. I would go sit in the living room with the thunder blamming so hard I couldn't even read the paper. Looking out at my backyard through the picture window, the colors of the marigolds and pansies seemed to be electric bright, blazing, then shuddering in the wind.

I was bound to connect all this with the anxiety that had got into things about that party. Charlie's being over in Louisiana didn't help. Maybe all was calm and bright over there, but I doubted it.

However, along about two the sky did clear, and the sun came out. When I drove out to Hope and Pete's place with the shrimp—it's a little way north of town, reached by its own side road, on a hill—everything was wonderful. There was a warm buoyancy in the air that made you feel young and remember what it was like to skip home from school.

"It's cleared off," said Hope, as though in personal triumph over Nature.

Pete was behind her at the door, enveloped in a huge apron. "I feel like playing softball," he said.

"Me, too," I agreed. "If I could just hear from Charlie."

"Oh, he'll be back," said Pete. "Charlie miss a party? Never!"

Well, it was quite an affair. The effort was to get us all launched in a new and happy period and the method was the tried and true one of drinking and feasting, dancing, pranking, laughing, flirting, and having fun. I had a new knife-pleated silk skirt, ankle length, dark blue shot with green and cyclamen, and a new off-the-shoulder blouse, and Mary Foote Williams, the visitor, wore a slit skirt, but Hope took the cake in her hoop skirts from her senior-high-school days, and her hair in a coarse gold net.

"The shrimp are gorgeous," she said. "Come look. I called Mama and requested prayer for good weather. It never fails."

"Charlie called," I said. "He said he'd be maybe thirty minutes late and would come on his own."

A car pulled up in the drive and there was Grey circling around and holding the door for Nelle herself. She had on a simple silk dress with her fine hair brushed loose and a pari of sexy new high-heeled sandals. It looked natural to see them together and I breathed easier without knowing I hadn't been doing it for quite a while. Hope was right, we'd had enough of this foolishness.

"That just leaves John and Rose," said Hope, "and I have my own ideas about them."

"What?" I asked.

"Well, I shouldn't say. It's y'alls' crowd." She was quick in her kitchen, clicking around with her skirts swaying. She had got a nice little colored girl, Perline, dressed up in black with a white ruffled apron. "I just think John's halfway to a stuffed shirt and Rose is going to get him all the way there."

So, our crowd or not, she was going right ahead.

"I think this has to do with you-know-what," I said.

"We aren't going to mention you-know-what," said Hope. "From now on, honey, my only four-letter words are 'dry' and 'cleaning.'"

John and Rose didn't show up, but two new couples did, a pair from Hattiesburg and the Kellmans, new in town but promising. Hope had let them in. Pete exercised himself at the bar and there was a strong punch as well. We strolled out to the pool and sat on white-painted iron chairs with cushions in green flowered plastic. Nelle sat with her pretty legs crossed, talking to Mary Foote. Grey was at her elbow. The little maid passed out canapés and shrimp. Light was still lingering in a clear sky barely pink at the edges. Pete skimmed leaves from the pool surface with a long-handled net. Lightning bugs winked and drifted, and the new little wife from Hattiesburg caught one or two in her palm and watched them crawl away, then take wing. "I used to do that," said Nelle. Then she shivered and Grey went for a shawl. It grew suddenly darker and one or two pale stars could be seen, then dozens. Pete, vanished inside, had started some records. Some people began to trail back in. And with another drink (the third, maybe?), it wasn't clear how much time had passed, when there came the harsh roar of a motor from the private road, growing stronger the nearer it got, a slashing of gravel in the drive out front, and a door slamming. And the first thing you knew there was Charlie Waybridge, filling the whole doorframe before Pete or Hope could even go to open it. He put his arms out to everybody. "Well, whaddaya know!" he said.

His tie was loose two buttons down and his light seersucker dress coat was crumpled and open but at least he had it on. I went right to him. He'd been drinking, of course, I'd known it from the first sound of the car—but who wasn't drinking? "Hi ya, baby!" he said, and grabbed me.

Then Pete and Hope were getting their greetings and were leading him up to meet the new people, till he got to the bar, where he dropped off to help himself.

It was that minute that Perline, the little maid, came in with a plate in her hand. Charlie swaggered up to her and said, "Well, if it ain't Mayola's daughter." He caught her chin in his hand. "Ain't that so?" "Yes, sir," said Perline. "I am." "Used to know yo' mama," said Charlie. Perline looked confused for a minute; then she lowered her eyes and giggled like she knew she was supposed to. "Gosh sakes, Charlie," I said, "quit horsing around and let's dance." It was hard to get him out of these moods. But I'd managed it more than once, dancing.

Charlie was a good strong leader and the way he danced, one hand firm to my waist, he would take my free hand in his and knuckle it tight against his chest. I could follow him better than I could anybody. Sometimes everybody would stop just to watch us, but the prize that night was going to Pete and Hope, they were shining around with some new steps that made the hoop skirts jounce. Charlie was half drunk, too, and bad on the turns.

"Try to remember what's important about this evening," I said. "You know what Hope and Pete are trying for, don't you?"

"I know I'm always coming home to a lecture," said Charlie and swung me out, spinning. "What a woman for sounding like a wife." He got me back and I couldn't tell if he was mad or not, I guess it was half and half; but right then he almost knocked over one of Hope's floral arrangements, so I said, "Why don't you go upstairs and catch your forty winks? Then you can come down fresh and start over." The music stopped. He blinked, looked tired all of a sudden, and, for a miracle, like a dog that never once chose to hear you, he minded.

I breathed a sigh when I saw him going up the stairs. But now I know I never once mentioned Nelle to him or reminded him right out, him with his head full of oil leases, bourbon, and the road, that she was the real cause of the party. Nelle was somewhere else, off in the back sitting room on a couch, to be exact, swapping family news with Mary Foote, who was her cousin.

Dancing with Charlie like that had put me in a romantic mood, and I fell to remembering the time we had first got serious, down on the coast where one summer we had all rented a fishing schooner. We had come into port at Mobile for more provisions and I had showered and dressed and was standing on deck in some leather sandals that tied around the ankle, a fresh white T-shirt, and some clean navy shorts. I had washed my hair, which was short then, and clustered in dark damp curls at the forehead. I say this about myself because when Charlie was coming on board with a six-pack in either hand, he stopped dead still. It was like the first time he'd ever seen me. He actually said that very thing later on after we'd finished with the boat and stayed on an extra day or so with all the crowd, to eat shrimp and gumbo and dance every night. We'd had our flare-ups before, but nothing had ever caught like that one. "I can't forget seeing you on the boat that day," he would say. "Don't be crazy, you'd seen me on that boat every day for a week." "Not like that," he'd rave, "like something fresh from the sea." "A catfish," I said. "Stop it, Eileen," he'd say, and dance me off the floor to the dark outside, and kiss me. "I can't get enough of you," he'd say, and take me in so close I'd get dizzy.

I kept thinking through all this in a warm frame of mind while making the rounds and talking to everybody, and maybe an hour, more or less, passed that way, when I heard a voice from the stairwell (Charlie) say: "God Almighty, if it isn't Nelle," and I turned around and saw all there was to see.

Charlie was fresh from his nap, the red faded from his face and his tie in place (he'd even buzzed off his five-o'clock shadow with Pete's electric razor). He was about five steps up from the bottom of the stairs. And Nelle, just coming back into the living room to join everybody, had on a Chinese-red silk shawl with a fringe. Her hair, so simple and shining, wasn't dark or blond either, just the color of hair, and she had on the plain dove-gray silk dress and the elegant sandals. She was framed in the door. Then I saw Charlie's face, how he was drinking her in, and I remembered the day on the boat.

"God damn, Nelle," said Charlie. He came down the steps and straight to her. "Where you been?"

"Oh, hello, Charlie," said Nelle in her friendly way. "Where have *you* been?"

"Honey, that's not even a question," said Charlie. "The point is, I'm *here*."

Then he fixed them both a drink and led her over to a couch in the far corner of the room. There was a side porch at the Owenses', spacious, with a tile floor—that's where we'd all been dancing. The living room was a little off center to the party. I kept on with my partying, but I had eyes in the back of my head where Charlie was concerned. I knew they were there on the couch and that he was crowding her toward one end. I hoped he was talking to her about Grey. I danced with Grey.

"Why don't you go and break that up?" I said.

"Why don't you?" said Grey.

"Marriage is different," I said.

"She can break it up herself if she wants to," he said.

I'd made a blunder and knew it was too late. Charlie was holding both Nelle's hands, talking over something. I fixed myself a stiff drink. It had begun to rain, quietly, with no advance warning. The couple from Hattiesburg had started doing some kind of talking blues number on the piano. Then we were singing. The couch was empty. Nelle and Charlie weren't there. . . .

It was Grey who came to see me the next afternoon. I was hung over but working anyway. Mr. McGinnis didn't recognize hangovers.

"I'm not asking her anywhere again," said Grey. "I'm through and she's through. I've had it. She kept saying in the car, 'Sure, I did like Charlie Waybridge, we all liked Charlie Waybridge. Maybe I was in love with Charlie Waybridge. But why start it up all over again? Why?' 'Why did you?' I said. 'That's more the question.' 'I never meant to, just there he was, making me feel that way.' 'You won't let me make you feel any way,' I said. 'My foot hurts,' she said, like a little girl. She looked a mess. Mud all over her dress and her hair gone to pieces. She had sprained her ankle. It had swelled up. That big."

"Oh, Lord," I said. "All Pete and Hope wanted was for you all— Look, can't you see Nelle was just drunk? Maybe somebody slugged her drink."

"She didn't have to drink it."

I was hearing Charlie: "All she did was get too much. Hadn't partied anywhere in months. Said she wanted some fresh air. First thing I knew she goes tearing out in the rain and whoops! in those high-heeled shoes—sprawling."

"Charlie and her," Grey went on. Okay, so he was hurt. Was that any reason to hurt me? But on he went. "Her and Charlie, that summer you went away up north, they were dating every night. Then her sister got sick, the one that died? She couldn't go on the coast trip with us."

"You think I don't know all that?" Then I said: "Oh, Grey!" and he left.

Yes, I sat thinking, unable to type anything: it was the summer her sister died and she'd had to stay home. I was facing up to Charlie Waybridge. I didn't want to, but there it was. If Nelle had been standing that day where I had stood, if Nelle had been wearing those sandals, that shirt, those shorts— Why pretend not to know Charlie Waybridge, through and through? What was he really doing on the Townshend property that night?

Pete, led by Hope, refused to believe anything but that the party had been a big success. "Like old times," said Pete. "What's wrong with new times?" said Hope. In our weakness and disarray, she was moving on in. (Damn Nelle Townshend.) Hope loved the new people; she was working everybody in together. "The thing for you to do about *that* . . ." she was now fond of saying on the phone, taking on problems of every sort.

When Hope heard that Nelle had sprained her ankle and hadn't been seen out in a day or so, she even got Pete one afternoon and went to call. She had telephoned but nobody answered. They walked up the long front walk between the elephant ears and up the front porch steps and rang the old turning bell half a dozen times. Hope had a plate of cake and Pete was carrying a bunch of flowers.

Finally Mrs. Townshend came shuffling to the door. Humpbacked, she had to look way up to see them, at a mole's angle. "Oh, it's you," she said.

"We just came to see Nelle," Hope chirped. "I understand she hurt her ankle at our party. We'd just like to commiserate."

"She's in bed," said Mrs. Townshend; and made no further move, either to open the door or take the flowers. Then she said, "I just wish you all would leave Nelle alone. You're no good for her. You're no good I know of for anybody. She went through all those years with you. She doesn't want you anymore. I'm of the same opinion." Then she leaned over and from an old-fashioned umbrella stand she drew up and out what could only be called a shotgun. "I keep myself prepared," she said. She cautiously lowered the gun into the umbrella stand. Then she looked up once again at them, touching the rims of her little oval glasses. "When I say you all, I mean all of you. You're drinking and you're doing all sorts of things that waste time, and you call that having fun. It's not my business unless you come here and make me say so, but Nelle's too nice to say so. Nelle never would—" She paused a long time, considering in the mildest sort of way. "Nelle can't shoot," she concluded, like this fact had for the first time occurred to her. She closed the door, softly and firmly.

I heard all this from Hope a few days later. Charlie was off again and I was feeling lower than low. This time we hadn't even quarreled. It seemed more serious than that. A total reevaluation. All I could come to was a question: Why doesn't he reassure me? All I could answer was that he must be in love with Nelle. He tried to call her when I wasn't near. He sneaked off to do it, time and again.

Alone, I tried getting drunk to drown out my thoughts, but couldn't, and alone for a day too long, I called up Grey. Grey and I used to date, pretty heavy. "Hell," said Grey, "I'm fed up to here and so are you. Let's blow it." I was tight enough to say yes and we met out at the intersection. I left my car at the shopping-center parking lot. I remember the sway of his Buick Century, turning onto the Interstate. We went up to Jackson.

The world is spinning now and I am spinning along with it. It doesn't stand still anymore to the stillness inside that murmurs to me, I know my love and I belong to my love when all is said and done, down through foreverness and into eternity. No, when I got back I was just part of it all, ordinary, a twenty-eight-year-old attractive married woman with family and friends and a nice house in Tyler, Mississippi. But with nothing absolute.

When I had a drink too many now, I would drive out to the woods and stop the car and walk around among places always known. One day, not even thinking about them, I saw Nelle drive by and this time there was no doubt who was with her—Robin Byers. They were talking. Well, Robin's wife mended the clothes when they were ripped or torn, and she sewed buttons on. Maybe they were going there. I went home.

At some point the phone rang. I had seen to it that it was "out of order" when I went up to Jackson with Grey, but now it was "repaired," so I answered it. It was Nelle.

"Eileen, I guess you heard Mama turned Pete and Hope out the other day. She was in the mood for telling everybody off." Nelle laughed her clear, pure laugh. You can't have a laugh like that unless you've got a right to it, I thought.

"How's your ankle?" I asked.

"I'm still hobbling around. What I called for, Mama wanted me to tell you something. She said, 'I didn't mean quite everybody. Eileen can still come. You tell her that.'"

Singled out. If she only knew, I thought. I shook when I put down the phone.

But I did go. I climbed up to Nelle's bedroom with Mrs. Townshend toiling behind me, and sat in one of those old rocking chairs near a bay window with oak paneling and cane plant, green and purple, in a window box. I stayed quite a while. Nelle kept her ankle propped up and Mrs. Townshend sat in a tiny chair about the size of a twelve-year-old's, which was about the size she was. They told stories and laughed with that innocence that seemed like all clear things—a spring in the woods, a dogwood bloom, a carpet of pine needles along a sun-dappled road. Like Nelle's ankle, I felt myself getting well. It was a new kind of wellness, hard to describe. It didn't have much to do with Charlie and me.

"Niggers used to come to our church," Mrs. Townshend recalled. "They had benches in the back. I don't know why they quit. Maybe they all died out—the ones we had, I mean."

"Maybe they didn't like the back," said Nelle.

"It was better than nothing at all. The other churches didn't even have that. There was one girl going to have a baby. I was scared she would have it right in the church. Your father said, 'What's wrong with that? Dr. Erskine could deliver it, and we could baptize it on the spot.'"

I saw a picture on one of those little tables they had by the dozen, with the starched linen doilies and the bowed-out legs. It was of two gentlemen, one taller than the other, standing side by side in shirt-sleeves and bow ties and each with elastic bands around their upper arms, the kind that used to hold the sleeves to a correct length of cuff. They were smiling in a fine natural way, out of friendship. One must have been Nelle's father, dead so long ago. I asked about the other. "Child," said Mrs. Townshend, "don't you know your own grandfather? He and Sid thought the world of one another." I had a better feeling when I left. Would it last? Could I get it past the elephant ears?

I didn't tell Charlie about going there. Charlie got it from some horse's mouth that Grey and I were up in Jackson that time, and he pushed me off the back steps. An accident, he said; he didn't see me when he came whamming out the door. For a minute I thought I, too, had sprained or broken something, but a skinned knee was all it was. He watched me clean the knee, watched the bandage go on. He wouldn't go out—not to Pete and Hope's, not to Rose and John's, not to anywhere—and the whiskey went down in the bottle.

I dreamed one night of Robin Byers, that I ran into him uptown but didn't see a scar on his face. I followed him, asking, Where is it? What happened? Where's it gone? But he walked straight on, not seeming to hear. But it was no dream that his house caught fire, soon after the cleaning shop opened again. Both Robin and Nelle said it was only lightning struck the back wing and burned out a shed room before Robin could stop the blaze. Robin's daughter got jumped on at school by some other black children who yelled about her daddy being a "Tom." They kept her at home for a while to do her schoolwork there. What's next?

Next for me was going to an old lady's apartment for Mr. McGinnis, so she could sign her will, and on the long steps to her door, running into Robin Byers, fresh from one of his deliveries.

"Robin," I said, at once, out of nowhere, surprising myself, "you got to leave here, Robin. You're tempting fate, every day."

And he, just as quick, replied: "I got to stay here. I got to help Miss Nelle."

Where had it come from, what we said? Mine wasn't a bit like me; I might have been my mother or grandmother talking. Certainly not the fun girl who danced on piers in whirling miniskirts and dove off a fishing boat to reach a beach, swimming, they said, between the fishhooks and the sharks. And Robin's? From a thousand years back, maybe, superior and firm, speaking out of sworn duty, his honored trust. He was standing above me on the steps. It was just at dark, and in the first streetlight I could see the white scar, running riverlike down the flesh, like the mark lightning leaves on a smooth tree. When we passed each other, it was like erasing what we'd said and that we'd ever met.

But one day I am walking in the house and picking up the telephone, only to find Charlie talking on the extension. "Nelle . . ." I hear. "Listen, Nelle. If you really are foolin' around with that black bastard, he's answering to *me*." And *blam!* goes the phone from her end, loud as any gun of her mother's.

I think we are all hanging on a golden thread, but who has got the other end? Dreaming or awake, I'm praying it will hold us all suspended.

Yes, praying—for the first time in years.

Shirley Ann Grau

The Long Afternoon

Like the weeks that had preceded it, the day was hot. There wasn't a speck of dust or a breath of air moving. Under the burning white light of the sun, things seemed closer than they were really. Hilda Marie Merrick, who was called Patsy, sat on the edge of the front porch and dangled her bare legs. She had been home from the hospital a week, and there was nothing to do. She lifted her right leg to stare attentively at the red polish on her toenails. She'd been up since eight, when the morning got too hot for sleeping. She'd washed her hair and set it too tightly; her head was beginning to ache. "When I woke up this morning, I wanted to die," she called over her shoulder.

In the living room, by the open window, her mother sealed the letter she had just finished and began writing the address. "Did you, dear?"

"Yes, I did." Patsy reached one finger to loosen the tightest of the curls. "Mother, do you know that there is not a single person left in this town that I would care to talk to. They have gone to camp, every single one of them."

Mrs. Merrick's voice took on a faint warning color. "The doctor told you no."

"I don't care what he said. I just don't care."

"Now you're being silly."

"I wouldn't hurt myself. I could be so careful."

"No."

There was the soft rubbing sound of pen on paper, and over by the hedge the ragged sound of a cricket.

"Do you know something?" Patsy said. "You would think that with the way they all came down to the hospital and stood around, looking all worried and wanting to do every little thing for me—a person would think that they wouldn't go off to camp and leave me where I haven't got a single person I know in town."

"Oh, Patsy."

"It is not often that eleven-year-old people have their appendix out, and as serious as mine."

"It wasn't serious."

"It was. I could feel it. You just don't know what it was like."

"Baby, how spoiled you got."

"You don't know." Patsy's hand felt lightly for the scar. "It's still sore."

Across the street a power mower started noisily, and from farther away still came the empty sound of a horse's hoofs and the singsong chant of a fruit vendor.

The street was paved on one side only. The city council had started to surface it months before, only to discover that they had overestimated the available funds. They had then announced that unless the people who lived on the street paid for it themselves, it would stay that way. It had stayed that way.

A small girl, not more than eight or so, came up the center of the half-paved road and in through the Merricks' gate, walking with the measured, scuffing tread of her age. Her hair was pulled back freshly into two pigtails, which stuck out from the nape of her neck; from each one dropped a ribbon. The starchiness of her dress was already beginning to wilt in the heat. One hand was stuck into the skirt pocket. The other hand held a brown roll—an old-fashioned leather music case. She climbed the steps, smiled shyly at Patsy and Mrs. Merrick, and, with a sidling glide, slipped in the front door. Between her thin, nubby shoulders her dress was already stained by perspiration.

"I didn't look like that," Patsy said, "at her age."

"Yes, you did," her mother said.

"No."

Mrs. Merrick began putting the note paper back in the box. "Why are you so trying, dear?"

"I was born that way." Patsy pointed her nose at the white, hot sky. "Mother, I itch all over."

"The heat powder is in the downstairs bathroom."

"It's not that kind of thing. I feel just like I could shake myself once or twice and my skin would fall right off. Like I'm not attached to it at all."

"The heat is bad," Mrs. Merrick said. Her gray eyes had a misty look as they stared out at the lawn. And her pencil was busy making little doodling marks.

From inside the house came the first hesitant chords of the scale.

"Here we go." Patsy gave a long, whistling sigh. "Why does Claude have to take pupils here?"

"Because there isn't any other place."

"Oh, hells bells!"

Inside, fumbling fingers began striking G-major chords. Patsy closed her eyes and tried seeing how long she could hold her breath. Her eyes popped open when a truck stopped, but she was so intent on holding her breath that she didn't wonder about the large crate two men unloaded. She went on counting.

The men balanced the crate on the edge of the steps and wiped the perspiration from their chins. "Where you reckon you want this?" one asked. He had bright china-blue eyes behind the tight folds of lids squinched up against the glare.

Patsy shrugged and went on with her silent counting. Fifty-one, fifty-two, fifty-three . . . She heard the door bell and then her mother's surprised murmur. She always manages to sound surprised, Patsy thought. And at that exact moment, without thinking, without deciding, she took a long breath of air. Fifty-eight.

"Patsy, honey," her mother called. "Come see—the new television's here."

She got up and ambled into the hall. Her mother was signing the receipt, on the top of the packing case. In the little room on the left that they called the music room she could see the bent small back of the pigtailed girl and the bent long back of her brother Claude. His finger moved directingly up and down, keeping time.

Patsy sat down in the hall, in one of the round-backed chairs that had belonged to her grandmother, and waited until the men had just passed her and were at the front door. "Mama," she said, "I'm growing again. I got to get a bigger bra."

The men coughed with laughter, and her mother closed the front door sharply after them. To Patsy, she said, "Just what are you trying to do?"

"Nothing." Patsy stared after the men, puzzled. She had not expected the laugh—a look maybe, or a wink. "I hate people."

"Young lady, you'd better find something to do," her mother said, and left her.

The little pigtailed musician departed, grinning broadly this time. Her dress was soaked with perspiration, her glasses were blurred and smeary, too, but she did not seem to notice. She had put her music away so hastily that the white edges showed ragged at the ends of the rolled case. Only one of the leather straps was fastened; the other dragged in the dirt. She skipped out the front gate and began to run back the way she had come, following the exact center of the street, so that one foot ran on concrete, the other on mud. It gave her a kind of lopsided, jack-rabbit pace.

"If there was any traffic, she'd get killed," Patsy said with satisfaction. She had returned to the porch.

"But there isn't," Claude said. He swung his long leg over a chair and sat astride it. The Coke bottle in his hand dripped bits of ice to the porch floor.

"You didn't bring me one," Patsy said.

"This is the last."

"Now, that's not true. I saw a whole case."

"They're all warm." He held out the bottle. "You want the rest of this?"

"No." She threw back her head and stared at the bright blue ceiling. Wasps were building their round mud nests up against one corner. "You've got all sorts of germs I don't want to catch."

"Okay."

"You drink noisier than anybody I ever knew."

"More noisily," he corrected.

"Why do you have to wear those silly-looking shorts?"

He tipped his head back and finished the Coke with a gurgle.

"And those long socks are the silliest things I ever did see."

"Quit it."

"You're too thin to wear things like that—that's what Mama told you."

"One day," Claude said, "I'm going to strangle you."

"Mama did tell you you were too thin for shorts. I heard her."

He yawned.

"You got the biggest teeth I ever saw," she said. "Like a horse."

"Do you want to fight?" He pulled out his handkerchief and dried his hands. "I haven't got time now. Later this evening, huh?"

Patsy turned away. "I don't want to be here this evening. I won't be here this evening at all."

Mrs. Merrick appeared. She was one of those women who never step outside without a hat—in winter because it is cold and in summer because it is sunny. Now she wore a light-green straw with a wide, flopping brim.

"You're always wearing green," Patsy said accusingly.

"Idiot child, shut up." Claude balanced the bottle on one finger.

"Really, Claude," Mrs. Merrick said. "Don't be nasty to her."

"You heard her," Patsy said. "You heard what she told you."

Claude shrugged, and blew through loose lips: "Ruuuuup."

"I wish I had eyes pretty as yours, Mama," Patsy said.

"Honey, you have lovely eyes."

"Brown." Patsy crinkled up the corners of her mouth in disgust. "Everybody's got brown eyes. And anyhow it makes me look like Claude."

"God forbid," Claude said softly, and his mother threw him a warning glance.

"Patsy, honey, don't you want to come along with me?" she said.

"Where?"

"I'm going to pick up the laundry."

"Nuh-uh."

"It would give you something to do," Mrs. Merrick said. "We'll be right back."

A ride across the little town to the Negro section, which was called Bridge City. Then a talk with the laundress while her oldest son brought out the bundle and put it in the back seat of the car and her other kids swung from an old tire hung from the branches of the big chinaberry tree.

"No," she said.

"Did Mary Beth finish her lesson, Claude?" Mrs. Merrick asked.

"Yep. Lucille won't be along until three-thirty."

"Why do I have to have a brother who gives music lessons?" Patsy demanded.

"Now, dear," her mother said.

"Why can't it ever be quiet around here."

"Hilda Marie, you are being mean, plain and simple mean, to your only brother," her mother said.

"I want to be mean. I want to."

Mrs. Merrick only waved as she headed for the garage.

"You *are* crazy," Claude told Patsy pleasantly and went inside to put back the Coke bottle.

Patsy threw her head far back over her chair, pressing until the wood cut into the back of her neck and little lights danced in front of her eyes.

"Fool jackass!" she cried at the top of her voice. "Crazy fool jackass!"

At lunch, Mr. Merrick, a short, very heavy man, looked longingly at the other plates and then began his own low-calorie fare.

"I don't see how you eat that without salt," Patsy said. "And so dreadful to begin with."

"I don't either, kitten," her father said.

"You'd think Claude would put on some weight, instead of being a bean pole like he is," Patsy said.

"Like is not a conjunction," Claude said.

"Now don't begin that," her mother said.

"What grades did you get in English?" Claude asked.

"I got a B-plus, Mr. Jackass."

"That's enough," her father said.

Patsy moved her fork in circles around her plate, following the gold bands. "I reckon I am not hungry. I would like to be excused."

"You're not sick, dear?" her mother asked.

Patsy turned at the door, with one hand holding the frame. "I am dying," she said. "I am dying of loneliness with everyone away."

"What an act," Claude said.

Patsy retreated to a porch chair and propped her feet up on the railing. She was trying with all her might to see if she could pop the back hook of her bra by hunching her shoulders when her father came out and sat beside her.

"Dessert?" He offered her a plate.

She shook her head sadly. "Like I said, I am not hungry." She regretted the first word the minute it was out of her mouth, but he did not correct her.

He still held out the plate. "Chocolate cake."

She took it. "Mama said it wasn't polite to offer things with your left hand."

"She's absolutely right," Mr. Merrick said, "but I am not going to fight, kitten, so stop trying."

"I wish you would stop calling me that name. I hate that name more than anything."

"Hilda Marie?" he suggested.

She made a face.

"What, then?"

She did not answer.

"Don't forget to take the plate in with you, kitten, when you go," Mr. Merrick said, getting up.

"Daddy," she said. He turned.

"Can't I come to town with you?"

He put one foot on the step and leaned his elbow on his knee. "Kitten, you'd be in the office half an hour and you'd get tired and want to come home. And I'd have to stop and bring you."

"No," she said. "No, I wouldn't." But he shook his head and was gone.

In the shade of the big red honeysuckle, an orange-striped cat stretched lazily, and then it sauntered over to the deeper shade of the butterfly bush. The long, hot afternoon was beginning.

Claude came out and started down the steps.

"Everybody's leaving," Patsy said. He didn't answer or turn, so she followed him, scuffing her heels on the gravel of the walk. "Where are you going?" she asked.

His car was at the curb. "I'm going to see Joyce."

"Like that?" She pointed to his shorts. "I didn't think you'd want anybody outside the family to see you like that."

"Look, twerp . . . Why don't you find something to do? Anything."

"That's what everybody tells me. You going to play bridge?"

"Yes, I *am*."

"I could play with you."

"If you could play."

"You could teach me."

"No," Claude said.

"It wouldn't take long."

"Not on your life." He got in the car and pulled the door to.

She stuck her head in the window. "If I had a car, I could drive around and visit people way over in Jackson, if I had a car."

He switched on the ignition and started the motor. "Well, you haven't. Now move before you get hurt."

The car drove away. She stood and watched, swinging her right leg back and forth so that her sandal scuffed along the gutter edge. After the car disappeared, she stared down at her moving foot. Then, carefully, she bent her sandal back against the cement. Pressing with all her weight, she snapped the sole so that it flapped loosely as she walked.

In the side yard a mulberry tree was dropping its full purple berries into the grass. She heard them squish under her feet. From a branch just over her head she pulled one of the nubby berries, and put it in her mouth. It prickled for an instant and tasted of dust. Then the heavy, overripe juice flooded out on her tongue. She reached up for a cluster of berries this time. They crushed between her grasping fingers. She whistled softly between her teeth and wiped her hand across the front of her skirt.

Claude had left one of his hunting knives on the back porch. She picked it up and began tossing it idly into the ground, trying without success to spear a small fragment of wood. Tiring of this, she left the knife sticking in the ground and wandered over to the sunny end of the porch to inspect her geraniums—four little pots of earth, each with a couple of scraggly stems reaching up into the air. Only one had a leaf, a shriveled brown bit that wrapped itself around the dead stalk.

Patsy filled the watering can and poured a little water on each one. Then she went into the kitchen.

"Fanny."

The short, stocky black woman turned around. "Yeah?"

"We got any coffee grounds?" Even as she asked, Patsy was making for the coffeepot.

"What you want that for?"

"My geraniums." They had been on her bedside table at the hospital, and she had loved each single one. "Mama says coffee grounds are good for plants."

"Ain't nothing gonna help them plants. Watch out my floor!" Fanny said as Patsy carried a handful of dripping grounds. "They is dead."

Patsy sprinkled the grounds around the bare twigs, watered them again, and went back in the kitchen. She got herself a glass of water and leaned on the refrigerator, drinking and swinging her leg so that the broken sandal flapped slowly.

Fanny turned. She was perched on a high red stool at the sink, polishing demitasse spoons. "What I hearing?"

Patsy held up her foot.

"Might just as well throw them out. They ain't no more good than those plants of yours," Fanny said.

Patsy rubbed the back of her thighs against the cool enamel of the refrigerator. "This is the longest day."

"Iffen you want things to do, you could get that big silver pitcher from out the dining room and polish it up."

"Did Estes come yet?" He was Fanny's boy, a couple of years older than Patsy. He came sometimes to keep his mother company, if he didn't have anything else to do. "Did he?" Patsy demanded.

"No, he ain't, yet."

Patsy stood on one leg and curled the lifted foot around the other ankle. She watched Fanny's movements, narrowing her left eye with the effort of her perception. "Lord, but you sure are slow."

The hand stopped its motion. "You come all the way back here to pester me?"

"Nuh-uh. Fanny, why don't you give them to him?"

Fanny reached her rag into the jar of pink silver polish. "Give who to who?"

"You just don't listen to me. Give those spoons, the ones right there, to Estes."

"Now, why I want to do that?"

"He could sell them for a lot of money." Patsy squatted down on the floor.

"You mama say for you not to sit like that. She say it ain't becoming for a young lady."

Patsy pretended not to hear. "Don't you want to make a lot of money?"

Fanny turned around again. "And what you mama going to say to that?"

"She wouldn't know."

"And what the police gonna say when they see you mama's initials all over the tops of them spoons?"

"We could take the initials off," Patsy said, "or take them over to Atlanta, where nobody'd know."

"You been looking too much at that television. I told you mama that."

"That's got nothing to do with it."

"You looking at it all day in the hospital there, I told her it ain't good."

"You talk so much. Yack, yack, yack."

Fanny swung back to her work, so violently that she had to catch hold of the counter for balance. "I ain't even begun to talk."

Chewing her lip, Patsy gazed up at the crosspiece of the doorway. After a minute, she said, "I bet you anything I could chin myself on that."

Fanny whistled—"Euuuuuuu."

"Well, I could."

"And bust all that stitching the doctor put in your stomach. And pour your insides all out over the floor."

Patsy stood up, her arms moving nervously. That was a nightmare she had sometimes: the hole in her stomach opening up. Sometimes, when she woke up, she would reach inside her pajamas and run her fingers along the new scar, just to be sure that it still held together.

"Fanny, what would you do if I was sick right here?"

"Iffen you gonna get sick, you just plain better go out in the back yard, where it don't matter none," Fanny said calmly.

Patsy pounded her fist against the door. "You are just so mean that I am going to make my mama fire you, and then I'm gonna tell everybody about you, and you won't be able to get another job, and you'll starve to death. That's what I'll do."

"Man, man," Fanny said to the chrome-plated faucet of the sink. "She sure is changed. They must put something else in her when they took that appendix out."

Before she thought, Patsy said, "You reckon they did?"

"You reckon they did?" Fanny mimicked in a high-pitched voice. "You reckon they did?"

"Crazy fool jackass!" Patsy exploded as she banged out the door. "Crazy fool jackass!"

Fanny shouted after her, "They done fill you up with all sorts of garbage to make you act so ugly! That what they done!"

Tucking her hands in the back belt of her shorts, Patsy sauntered around the corner of the house, still whispering to herself, "Fool jackass, crazy fool jackass."

She spotted Jo Dillard's rumpled black head, almost hidden by one of the big old hydrangea bushes. The Dillards lived next door. "What are you doing by my house?" Patsy asked.

Jo turned her head slowly, and the clear, blue, five-year-old gaze focused first on Patsy's feet, then climbed her body, coming almost indifferently to her face.

"I asked you what you doing by my house."

The eyes climbed down the body again. "Digging," Jo said. She pointed with her left hand. "See?" Behind the hydrangea bush was a little hole she was making with an old wavy-bladed bread knife.

"What you doing that for?"

"Nothing. Digging."

"You're lying."

Jo did not answer.

"Tell me."

"Huh?"

"You tell me."

Jo turned back to her work. Two thin sinews stood out on the back of her neck, beneath the ragged fringe of her clipped hair.

"You are the ugliest-looking kid I have ever seen," Patsy told her. "You are positively the ugliest thing. And you get uglier every day. You do."

The eyes lifted, circled her face, and wandered off.

"And the way you do everything with your left hand—that's the silliest thing, too."

The child went on digging, her head bent.

"Tell me." Patsy's voice dropped, and she crouched down by the smaller figure.

The child watched the ground intently, fascinated by each small load of mud. A round white marble came to the surface. Two small, squarish fingers went down and picked it up; the hand closed over it.

"What you find?"

The knife continued to lift small pats of dirt.

"What did you find in my garden? Give it here."

The blade fell to the ground. Jo clenched both hands around the marble. Her fingers wove tightly together.

Patsy picked up the knife. She scraped it against the brick foundation and ran her finger over the wavy edge of the blade. "I am going to kill you," she said. "And a dozen policemen will come to take you away."

With a small whinny of fear, Jo scuttled home, her hands still clenched.

Patsy jumped up and, waving the knife over her head, shouted, "Don't come back! Don't ever come back!"

She tossed the knife up against the trunk of the hydrangea bush and walked away, wiping her dirty hands on her bare thighs. A window flew up, and Mrs. Dillard called, "Patsy, what are you doing! Patsy . . ." She pretended not to hear as she strolled to the back of the yard, rolling her hips under the tight white shorts.

In the quiet of the hot afternoon, she could hear the clicking of the dial phone. "Maybe she is calling the police," she told herself aloud. "And they will come and get me in one of the white cars with the chrome siren on top. And my scar will pop, and I'll bleed all over everything." She fingered her side; it was sore to the touch.

Inside her own house, the phone began to ring. She cocked her head, listening. She could almost hear Mrs. Dillard's angry words.

"She is old and ugly," Patsy said aloud. From a low branch a fat swallow beat a clumsy retreat. "She is old and fat and ugly and I hate her."

Dragging her feet so that the tips of her toes brushed the crispy edges of the grass, she went around the two chinaberry trees, grown close together and circled by an old wisteria vine with ragged shreds of flowers still among its leaves. She was hidden from the house.

Her mother appeared on the side porch and called, "Patsy!"

"She is old and ugly and I hate *her*, too," Patsy whispered.

"Patsy, come her this instant. This very instant."

Patsy reached out and took hold of the sharp rough bark of the tree. "No," she whispered.

Fanny popped out the kitchen door. Through the vines Patsy saw the sun glint on her black skin.

"What she did this time?"

Mrs. Merrick opened the screen and came down into the yard; her heels made a sharp clatter on each step. "This is just too much."

"What she did?"

"Patsy!" Her mother folded her hands and rested her chin on them. She was really angry; that was a sure sign.

"Ugly," Patsy whispered.

Right in front of her were crosspieces of wood nailed to the trunk of one of the chinaberry trees—the steps leading up to the tree house. She tilted back her head. Vaguely, through the dense foliage, she could see the brown, weathered boards. Slowly and carefully, so as not to hurt her scar, she began to climb.

"Patsy! . . . Look in the back yard, Fanny." Mrs. Merrick started across the grass.

Patsy reached the platform, railless and tiny: only four boards wide. She sat down cross-legged on the wood that had been warped by winter rains and stained almost black by the falling berries.

"I won't ever come down," she whispered. The sound startled her, so she went on talking to herself silently. I'll live up here. Until I get old and die. I'll stay until I get old and older and die.

Below, hidden by the feathery leaves, her mother demanded, "Patsy, come here immediately."

I won't ever come down. I won't.

She clenched her fists and closed her eyes in determination. But already, under the lids, the tears were beginning.

One Summer

You forget most things, don't you? It's even hard to remember in the hurry and bustle of spring what the slow unwinding of fall was like. And summer vacations all blur one into the other when you try to look back at them. At least, it's that way for me: a year is a long time.

But there's one summer I remember, clear as anything; the day, a Thursday in August.

It had been a terrific summer, the way it always is here. There was dust an inch thick on everything. The streams were mostly all dry. Down in the flaky red dust of the beds—where the flood in spring was so fast you couldn't cross it and where now there was just a foot or two of slimy smelling water—you could find the skeletons of fishes so brittle that they crumbled when your foot touched them. The wells were always dug extra deep just for summers like this: there's always water if you go down deep enough for it. There was plenty of water for drinking and washing and even maybe enough to keep the gardens watered, but nobody did; most of the plants withered and crumbled away. By August, cracks were beginning to show in the ground, too, crisscross lines maybe half an inch wide showing under the brown dead grass.

So that when this big pile of thunderheads came lifting out of the south everybody watched them, wondering and hoping.

I was sitting on Eunice Herbert's porch, over in the coolest part, behind the wooden jalousies. There was a swing there, and an electric fan on a little black iron table, and two or three black iron stands of ferns, all different kinds—her mother was crazy about them. Maybe it wasn't cooler there, but with the darkness from the closed jalousies and the smell of wet mud from the fern pots, it seemed comfortable.

Eunice was the prettiest girl in town, there wasn't any doubt of that. She had hair so blond that it looked almost silver white. All summer long she kept it piled up on top of her head with a flower stuck right on top; she got the idea from the cover of *Seventeen*, she said. Whenever she was at a party, there was nearly always a fight between some boys. It was just sure to happen, that's all; I was in enough to know. I almost had got thrown out of school because of one of them: at the spring party in the gym of the big yellow-brick high school. I don't remember how it started. I was just dancing with some girl when over at the table where Eunice was sitting two fellows started to fight. I remember dropping the girl's arm and walking over. Not wanting to fight, not really, but somehow I did; and somehow I got a Coke bottle in my hand and started swinging. It was the bottle that nearly got me expelled. My father had to do an awful lot of talking so I could go on and finish the year with the rest of my class.

One thing though—it set things up fine between Eunice and me. In those two months she hadn't had a date with another fellow.

That hot Thursday afternoon in August we were sitting on her porch swing, holding hands under the wide skirt of her dress, which she had spread out so that her mother wouldn't see anything but two people sitting and talking. Her mother was inside, doing something, I never found out what, but every ten minutes or so she'd stick her head out the door and ask: "You children want something?" And Eunice would say: "Oh, Mamma, no," with her voice going up a little on the last word.

We were just sitting there swinging back and forth, staring at the green little leaves of the ferns. I was feeling her soft thin fingers. There was a kind of shivering going up and down my back that wasn't just the electric fan blowing on my wet shirt.

Then her mother stuck her head out the front door to the porch for maybe the fifteenth time that afternoon—she was a little woman with a tiny face that reminded me of a squirrel somehow, with a nervous twitching nose. "Children," she said (and I could feel Eunice's fingers stiffen at the word), "just you look out there—" she pointed to the south; "here's a big pile of rain clouds, coming right this way."

"Yes, ma'am," I said. We'd noticed the clouds come up half an hour past.

And then because she kept staring at us we had to get up and walk over and peer out through the little open squares in the jalousies and look at the sky.

"It looks like rain," I said, because somebody had to say something.

Without turning around I heard Mrs. Herbert take a seat in one of the wicker chairs. I heard the cane creak and then the rockers begin to move softly back and forth on the wood flooring. Alongside me I could feel Eunice stiffen like a cat that's been hit by something. But there wasn't anything she could do: her mother was going to sit and talk to us for the rest of the afternoon. I might just as well go sit in one of the single chairs.

The afternoon was so quiet that from my house—just across the street and one house down—you could hear our cook, Mayline, singing at the top of her voice:

> *"Didn't it rain, little children,*
> *Didn't it rain, little children,*
> *Didn't it rain?"*

So she'd noticed that big mass of clouds too.

"Is that Mayline I hear?" Mrs. Herbert said. The words came out slowly, one for each creak of her rocker.

"Yes, ma'am," I said and sat down in the red-painted straight chair.

Eunice dropped down in the middle of the swing and folded her hands on her lap and didn't say anything.

"Well," her mother said with just an edge of annoyance, "if you children are doing anything you don't want me to see . . ."

"Oh, Mamma," Eunice said, staring down at her hands.

"Yes, ma'am," I said, and then changed it to "No, ma'am," and all the while I was thinking of a way to get us out of there.

From the corner of my eye I saw that Eunice's mother was getting that hurt bewildered look all mothers use.

And then—just at the right minute—we heard Morris Henry come running down the street. He was a poppy-eyed little black monkey

Negro, no taller than a twelve-year-old, but strong as a man and twice as quick. He had little hands, like a child's or a girl's maybe, with nails that he always chewed down to the quick. Even when there wasn't anything more to bite on, he'd keep chewing away at the fingers with his wide flaring yellow teeth.

He came running down the road—you could hear the sound of his bare feet on the dirt road quite a ways in front of him. He took a short cut through the empty lot at the corner and came bursting through the high dry grass that went up like a puff of smoke all around him.

With the dust in his nose he started sneezing, but he didn't stop. He tore down the middle of our street at top speed, both hands holding to his trousers so they wouldn't fall off. He took our fence with a one-hand jump, made a straight line through the yard to the kitchen door, and was up the steps two at a time. The door slammed after him.

It was quiet then with him inside my house. All you could see was the path he'd broken for himself through the dry stalks of the zinnias in the front yard.

"My goodness," Mrs. Herbert said. "Hadn't you better go see what's wrong?"

"Yes, ma'am," I said.

"I'll come with you," Eunice said quickly.

We yanked open the screen door and we were all the way down the steps and halfway to the front gate before we heard it slam, we were running that fast.

"The front way," I said. And we rushed up the front steps and in the front door.

We had to stop for a minute: the parlor was always kept with the blinds drawn, and coming out of the sun we couldn't see a thing. I could hear Eunice breathing heavily alongside me. She was so close it was the easiest thing in the world to put my arm around her. I kissed her hard, and for as long as I dared with people so close—the voices in the kitchen sounded excited.

"You hurt," she said.

And I just grinned at her; it was the sort of hurt she liked.

And then we went into the kitchen to see what had happened.

Little Morris Henry was sitting in a red-painted kitchen chair and my mother was holding his thin little shoulder, that was all bulged and lumpy with muscle. Over in a corner Mayline stood with her mouth open and a streak of flour on her black face.

Next to my shoulder I could hear Eunice let her breath out with a quick hissing whisper. No one seemed to have noticed that we had come in. Mayline was looking over in our direction and her eyes rested right on us, but there wasn't any recognition in them. They were just empty brown eyes; only they weren't brown any more, but bright live metal. They were eyes like flat pieces of silver.

Because we didn't know what to do, we stood very still and waited.

In a minute my mother looked around. She seemed to feel that we were there; she couldn't have seen us, we were behind her. But she looked over. Keeping her hand on Morris Henry's shoulder she twisted her head around and looked at us.

"He says there's something wrong with the old gentleman. . . ." Her voice wandered off. She had spoken in such a whisper and the words had slipped so gradually that you couldn't quite tell when she stopped. I wondered if I had really heard anything at all.

She seemed to realize this, because she repeated louder this time, in a way that you couldn't mistake: "He says there's something wrong with the old gentleman."

That would be my grandfather. Everybody called him that. They never did use his name. When they were talking about him it was "the old gentleman" and to his face they always said "sir."

"The old gentleman's gone fishing on the Scanos River," they'd say. And that would mean he'd taken his little power boat out into the middle of the muddy red yellow river and stopped the motor and thrown over his line and was sitting there waiting for the fish to bite; and they always did; he was a fine fisherman.

Or maybe Luce Rogers, who was Mayline's husband—of a sort and not a legal sort—would stick his head in the kitchen door and wipe his shiny face with his broad hand and look at Mayline and shake his head and say sadly: "Baby, I can't set with you this morning. I got to go to work." And Mayline would look at him from under her lids, not quite believing him because he didn't like to work and he sure had a wandering eye. So she would suck in one corner of her mouth and hold it between her teeth and stare at him, nodding her head just a little. And he would open his eyes very wide and shake his head and say: "You ain't got no cause to suspicion me, baby. I was just plain walking past the place when the old gentleman yells at me from the porch."

And Mayline would relax for a little while anyhow, because that would mean that my grandfather had found some work for him to do, like mowing the grass maybe or washing the windows, or doing some other work that the regular girl, whose name was Wilda Olive, couldn't do. It was just about the only time Luce Rogers worked—when my grandfather caught him.

That Thursday afternoon in the kitchen, it was Eunice who moved first. She slipped around me—she was standing almost half behind me in the doorway—and went up to my mother and put her arms around her.

"You better sit down, Mrs. Addams," she said. She had the chair all pulled out from the table and ready. "You look a little pale."

That wasn't true; my mother looked perfectly all right. But that was Eunice's way—she'd used that line in the high-school play a couple of months before and she didn't see any reason not to use it again. Or maybe it was because she didn't really know what to say either.

Anyhow, my mother did sit down. And she leaned one arm against the table and beat a little tattoo on it with her fingers.

The minute she sat down, Morris Henry bounced up and went over and stood by the window, chewing his little knuckles. Eunice stood next to my mother and looked over at me. And I looked down at the ground.

My mother began tapping the heel of her shoe against the floor. That was a sure sign she was thinking. Finally she said to me: "Mac-Donald—"

"Yes, ma'am," I said.

She was the only one who ever used my full name like that. To most people I was just Mac. But she liked that full name, maybe because it had belonged to her family. Or maybe she just liked the sound of it.

"Go see if there's a car in the neighborhood we can borrow. . . . Go outside and look.

"Eunice," she was giving orders now, "put in a call for Dr. Addams. . . . I've got to put on a regular dress." She only wore a kind of smock-like affair around the house, because of the heat.

I went out in the yard and looked up and down the block. There wasn't a single car in any driveway. It wasn't surprising, because most people either took the car down to the business section with them if they were going to work, or if they left them at home their wives took them to the market or the movies. I had known that I wasn't going to find anything when I went out.

I went back up the stairs into the hall. Eunice had finished calling and had put the phone back on the little black wood table that teetered if you touched it too hard. She was leaning against the wall, at an angle with it, and her legs were crossed. The way she had hunched her shoulders her peasant blouse was slipping way down on one side.

Eunice waved at me to come back. She had just called my father's office. He wasn't there. Nobody had expected that he would be. He was out making his calls. He had a big practice—he was probably the most popular doctor in the county or maybe even in this part of the state—and there was no telling exactly where he was.

Eunice put down the phone for a minute. "Isn't it just dreadful, Mac?" she said in a whisper; "about your grandfather, I mean."

"Yeah," I said. I was looking at the smooth stretch of her shoulder.

She saw my gaze and pulled up the cloth.

"You the prettiest girl in this town," I said, "bar none." I had told her that before, and she always answered the same way.

She gave a little giggle and said: "Men . . ."

My mother came out into the hall. She just looked at us and walked over and took the phone off the hook. There was somebody on the party line. She broke through that in a minute and had the operator. "Can you find Dr. Addams?" she said. "Tell him it's his father."

That was the way you located either of the two doctors in this town, if you needed them fast. You just called up Shirley Williams, who was the operator, and told her. And sooner or later my father would make a call and she'd recognize his voice and give him the message. It worked fast that way; much faster than you'd think. I was sure that in about half an hour my father would know about it wherever he was.

She hung up the phone and looked at us. "This is just no time for you to behave like children. . . . MacDonald, is there a car we can borrow?"

"No, ma'am," I said.

"I'll just have to walk then." She took a sunshade out of the closet and slammed the door. She was halfway down the walk before she turned to look at me.

"I reckon you better come along," she said slowly. "I might need you to take a message."

My grandfather wouldn't ever have a telephone in his house. There was always somebody passing by soon enough to take a message for him, he said.

She pointed me back into the house. "Go get a hat," she said. "It's killing out here."

On the way out I said to Eunice: "I'll see you tonight."

It was an agreement we had. During the last two months, almost every night I'd slip out of my room and throw one small piece of gravel against her window screen. And then when she'd looked out I'd blink my flashlight real quick, just once. And she would slip down. . . . If her folks ever found out, there'd really be a row. Though they didn't have to worry. Eunice wasn't that sort of a girl. We'd just stand out in the dark, not even talking, so no one would notice us. Until the mosquitoes got too bad; and then I'd kiss her good-night.

"I'll see you tonight," I told her as I grabbed my hat and rushed out after my mother.

The sun was so hot you could feel it tingling your skin right through the clothes. It was so hot you didn't sweat any more. My mother went right on walking very fast, so that we covered the five blocks to my grandfather's house in maybe two minutes. And all the while I had my eyes on the big pile of thunderheads, the ones that had just come up and were hanging there in the sky promising rain. The people we passed, sitting on their shaded porches, who nodded or waved to us, were watching them too and they called out to ask us if we had seen them.

My mother answered them, hardly politely sometimes, we were walking so fast.

As it turned out we needn't have been in such a hurry after all.

My grandfather had died that hot afternoon in August, while everybody for miles around was watching the big pile of thunderheads. And nobody was paying much attention to an old man.

He had tumbled out of his chair in the living-room and died there on the floor with his mouth full of summer dust from the green flowered carpet. Wilda Olive, the colored woman who kept house for him, found him there about an hour later. She'd been puttering around in the back yard, making like she was sweeping off the walk, but really, just like everybody else, keeping an eye on those clouds.

She came in to tell him about the rain that might be coming and found him where he'd done a jackknife dive into the carpet. For a while she just stood looking at him, with his seersucker coat rumpled up in back and his bald head buried under his arm, bald head that was getting just a little dusty on the floor. She took a couple of steps backwards (she didn't even go near or touch him) and she lifted up her apron and put it over her head and began to cry. It was one of those long aprons that wrap all around and it was big enough to cover up her head. She just stood there, bent over in the dark from the heavy linen folds, and wailing. Not high, the way a white woman would cry, but a kind of flat low tone that you could almost see curling its way up through the layers of heat in the day.

Morris Henry, who happened to be passing by in the street, had heard it and gone in to look. After one look his poppy eyes stuck out even more than usual; and he headed straight for our house, at a run. And my mother and I came rushing over in the full heat of the afternoon sun. . . .

Minute we stepped through the front gate we began to hear Wilda Olive's moaning. My mother nodded toward the pecan tree in the north corner of the yard. "You just sit down there and wait for me," she said.

Of course, I didn't do anything of the sort. I followed her right inside.

She pushed past Wilda Olive and bent over the old man and stretched out her hand but didn't quite touch him and pulled back her hand and straightened up and just stood there. Finally she reached over and pulled the apron from Wilda Olive's head. "Stop that," she said sharply.

Wilda Olive didn't seem to hear her. My mother held up her own hand, with fingers outspread, and looked at it carefully. Then slapped Wilda Olive hard as she could. That hushed her.

"We'll need some ice water," my mother told her. "It's perishing hot out, walking." Wilda Olive went to the kitchen. And my mother came and stood on the porch. "MacDonald," she said when she saw me, "I thought I told you to stay out in the yard under the tree."

She wasn't really paying any attention to me; I could tell that from her tone; so I didn't move. She took one of the cane rockers from where it was leaning backwards against the porch wall and turned it around and sat down, very slowly. Very slowly, with one hand she rubbed the left side of her face, the two skins rubbing together smoothly and squeaking just a little from the wet of the perspiration.

Wilda Olive brought the ice water and disappeared. "Let's hope she doesn't start that racket again," my mother said, and listened carefully. But everything was quiet. "We'll just wait for your father," she said.

I sat down on the edge of the porch, my feet stuck through the railing and hanging down. It was so hot it was hard to breathe.

There was a little bead of sweat collected very slowly on my neck, right over the little hump of bone there. I hunched my shoulders so that the shirt would not touch and break it. I felt it getting bigger and bigger until it had enough force to cross the bone and begin to wiggle slowly down my back. It was all the way down to within an inch of my belt when my father came driving up.

My mother jumped up and went out to meet him. Her feet in their white sandals went by me very fast and I noticed for the first time how small they were and how brown and smooth the turn of her ankle. I'd never thought of my mother as having nice legs before. . . .

My mother stood against the side of the car leaning in through the window, the sun full and hard on her white print dress. I saw the line of her thighs and her narrow hips. It was funny for me to be thinking of my mother that way now, with my grandfather lying all doubled up on the floor inside and dead. I saw something I'd never seen before: she had as good a figure as Eunice Herbert.

When my father went inside, she sat down, not saying anything to me, rocking herself slowly, her foot beating out the time. There was a fuzz of yellow hair all up her leg; I saw that out of the corner of my eye.

Then my father came out and sat on the arm of her chair. I looked up and saw how she sat there with her eyes tight closed. My father was writing out the death certificate, the way he had to; I recognized the form. I'd seen them lying around his office enough.

And I thought how he was writing his father's name: Cecil Percival

Addams. I could see his hand printing out the name, slow and steady. He was writing out his father's name on a death certificate.

Just the way it would be for me someday. What he was doing now, I would be doing for him someday. I would sit where he was now; and there would be my wife alongside me, crying a little bit and trying now to show it. I would be a doctor, too, writing just the way he was now. And he would be lying dead inside.

And then we'd all move up one step again. And it would be my son who'd be looking down at me, lying still and dusty. I'd never thought of that before.

The trickle of sweat reached to my belt, broke, and spread, cold on my hot skin. I shivered. The thunderheads were still piled up in the south, shining gray-bright in the sun. They struck me as being very lonesome.

My father signed the paper and laid it out on the railing. "Jeff'll need that," he said quietly. Jeff was the undertaker, a little man, quick and nervous and bald, who wore black suits in the winter and white linen ones in the summer. His wife had run off with a railroad engineer and disappeared. He had a married daughter over to the north in Birmingham and he visited her twice a year.

My mother bent her head over in her lap with a quick sharp movement. My father slipped his arm around her.

"Honey," he said, "don't. Let's go home."

He lifted her up and they walked to the car. I could tell from the way he braced himself that he was almost carrying her. And even a small woman like my mother is a heavy load in one arm. I hadn't thought my father was that strong.

My mother slipped in the front seat and made room for me alongside her.

"No," my father said. "Let him stay here."

My mother shook her head doubtfully.

"Somebody's got to," my father said as he got behind the wheel. "He's almost a man. And there isn't going to be anything for him to do."

My mother didn't look convinced.

"Look," my father said shortly, "he's staying."

"There's a phone next door in the Raymond place," my mother said faintly, "MacDonald, if you want to call."

"Yes, ma'am," I said.

"Stay on the porch, son, if you want to," my father said. "Just see that Jeff gets the certificate. And keep an eye on Wilda Olive."

"Yes, sir," I said.

As they drove off, my mother rubbed her face deep down in my father's shoulder, the way a girl does sometimes on a date coming home.

And just for a second I could really feel Eunice's cheek rubbing against my shoulder and hear the soft sound it made on the cloth. And there was the tickle of her hair on my chin. And the far faint odor that wasn't really perfume—though that was part of it—but was the smell of her hair and her skin.

Then all of a sudden I didn't have that picture any more. I was back on my grandfather's porch, watching my father drive off with my mother. She had her face buried deep down in his shoulder. My father's arm went up and around to pull her closer to him. Then I couldn't see any more, the dust on the road was so thick.

I looked around. In the whole afternoon there wasn't a thing moving, except me. Except my breathing, up and down. And that seemed sort of out of place.

For a while I sat on the porch. Then I thought that maybe I ought to have a look at Wilda Olive. I didn't want to go through the house, so I walked all the way around it, outside, around to the kitchen door. "Wilda Olive." I thought I called loud but my voice softened in the heat until it was just ordinary speaking tone.

She was in the kitchen, scouring out the sink, quietly, like nothing had happened. She looked up and saw me. "Yes, sir," she said.

She'd never said "sir" to me before. The old man's death had changed that. I had moved up one step. I was in my father's place. It was funny how quick it all happened.

"Yes, sir," she said.

"You all right?" That sounded silly. But I'd said it, so I stuck my hands down deep in my pockets and lifted up my jaw and waited for her to answer.

"Yes, sir." She dropped her eyes. Ordinarily she would have gone back to her work and let me stand there to do what I wanted. But that had changed, too. Now she stood waiting for me. Not going on with her work because of me.

"You were cutting up pretty bad when we came," I told her.

"Yes, sir," she said. There wasn't the slightest bit of expression in her face now.

"Well," I said, "I'll be out front if you want me—on the porch, because it's too hot inside." That wasn't the reason. I didn't want to stay inside with the old man. But she mustn't know that. I wanted to go around, the way I'd come—through the garden—but I knew she was expecting me to go straight through the house. And so I did, walking fast as I could without seeming to hurry.

I had hardly got out on the porch before I saw Eunice coming. She had a red ruffled parasol held high against the sun and she was carrying something wrapped in a checked kitchen towel in her other hand. I watched her open the gate and come up to the porch.

"I thought you'd be steaming hot," she said, "so I brought you over a Coke." She unwrapped the towel and there it was, the open bottle, still with ice all over the outside.

"Thanks," I said. I drank the Coke, but I couldn't think of anything else to say. Somehow she didn't belong here. Somehow I just didn't want her here.

She took the bottle from me when I had finished. "I got to get back," she said. "I promised Mamma to help with dinner."

"Thanks," I said again.

At the foot of the steps she turned. "I'm awful sorry."

The sun was shining on her just the way it had on my mother.

"It's okay," I said. "It's okay."

She was gone then. And there was only the Coke taste in my mouth to remind me that she had been there. And that was gone soon, and there was just the dust taste. And there wasn't a trace of her. I just couldn't believe that she had been there . . . it was funny, the way things were beginning not to seem real.

That evening they came, the little old people who had been my grandfather's friends . . . or maybe his enemies. Time sort of evened out all those things.

Jeff, the undertaker, had come and gone and the house was really and truly empty now; I found I could breathe better. (That was another strange thing: I had never feared my grandfather, living and moving; but dead, he made me afraid. . . .)

Matthew Conners was the first. I saw him way off down the road, coming slowly, picking his way carefully between the ruts, testing the deepest ones with his cane, lifting himself carefully over them.

The sun had gone down but the sky was still full of its light, hard and bright. The rain clouds hadn't moved.

Matthew came up the walk and stood at the foot of the steps. "He come back yet?"

"No, sir," I said. "Jeff'll have him along soon."

Matthew Conners nodded. His head bobbed quickly up and down on the sinewy cords of his neck. He'd been a handsome man once, they said; the bad boy of the southern counties. There was a picture of him in an album of my grandfather's; very tall, very thin, with hair carefully pompadoured in front. Even in the picture you could see how bright the stripes of his tie were. He'd never married. He'd gone on living in the two rooms behind his hardware store (which was on the busiest corner in town, next to the post office). Until one day he sold the business to a nephew. He kept the rooms, though, and lived there. He spent most of his days there, sitting on the doorstep, not saying much to people who were passing, just sitting there, as if he were waiting.

Matthew Conners climbed slowly up the porch steps and sat down on the chair where my mother had sat and put the cane down between his knees and crossed his hands on it and waited.

I saw those hands, blue spots and heavy-veined, crossed and folded together, and I thought how maybe at that very minute Jeff was pressing my grandfather's hands together. . . .

They came all evening, the old people. After Matthew Conners came Vance Bonfield and the short, very fat woman who was his wife, Dorothy, her double chins dripping with perspiration.

I said: "Good evening." They nodded but didn't answer.

And then Henry Carmichael, walking because he didn't live far at all. By this time the porch chairs were all filled—there were only three of them. I started to bring out another chair, but the old man just shook his bald shiny head in my direction and went in the house. Slowly and with great care he began bringing out a dining-room chair, his old hands trembling with its weight. He brought two chairs out, stopped and counted them carefully with one finger. Then he took a handkerchief out of his coat pocket, wiped his face carefully, and with a tired sigh sat down with the others.

They didn't seem to talk to each other at all, beyond the first hello, just sat there waiting, with their hands folded.

So I sat down on the steps and waited, too. Only thing is, I was careful not to fold my hands. I put them out flat, one on each knee.

The long summer twilight had just about worn out when Jeff and his four Negro helpers brought my grandfather back, in a shining wood coffin this time, and put him in the living-room. I heard Wilda Olive begin to cry, softer this time; so I didn't bother to stop her. I don't think I could have anyway. The old men didn't seem to notice; they didn't turn their heads or say anything. They just sat staring out at the front lawn.

I moved out into the side yard and sat down under the locust tree. The dry ground had cracked up, pulling apart the tangled grass roots. In one of the cracks there was a lily bulb, shriveled and dry. I tried to think what kind it must have been, but I couldn't ever remember seeing a flower in that spot.

My father came back. He parked his car, came in the gate, and walked straight up to me. He held out his hand. I wasn't sure whether he wanted to shake mine or give me a pull to my feet. I reckon he did both.

"Go ahead home, son," he said, still holding my hand.

I found myself saying very softly and slow and sure, as if I wasn't in a bit of a hurry: "Don't you reckon you going to need me here?"

"That's all right," my father said.

"You be all right?"

"Sure," my father said, and turned away, walking toward the house. "You just hurry. Your mother's waiting supper on you."

I couldn't help feeling that my father wanted me to stay, that he wanted company somehow, but couldn't have it. So I left, walking as fast as I could.

When I caught sight of our house, even if it was so hot, I began to run.

My mother was sitting very quietly in the parlor waiting for me. She had a copy of the *Ladies' Home Journal* in her hands, but she wasn't reading it. She was just using it for something to hold on to. She was wearing the same light print dress she had on before, but now the fresh starchness was gone. The lace on the organdy collar wasn't standing out stiff any more and there were perspiration spots on the shoulders.

She didn't look up from the book when I came in. "Just wash your hands down here, MacDonald. Mayline won't mind if you use the kitchen sink this once."

"Yes'm," I said.

"And we'll eat dinner right away—and then get dressed."

"Yes'm," I said.

"We can keep fresher that way—for the evening." She hesitated over the last words. It was one thing about my mother; wakes always scared her a lot; she'd said so once.

"You hungry, MacDonald?" she asked finally, standing up and putting the magazine back on the table under the lamp.

"No'm," I said. "Not much, just sort of."

After supper my mother and I walked back over to the house. She was wearing a black chiffon dress; and the dye gave off a peculiar smell in the heat: not sour like perspiration, nor sweet like some flowers, nor bitter like Indian grass, but a mixture of all three. I had got dressed too, because I had to: a white suit and a tie, a black tie that had been part of my father's navy uniform. Under the coat I could feel the cotton of the shirt get wet and stick to my body.

Mrs. Herbert was out in the front yard cutting zinnias with a big shiny pair of scissors. She was the only woman I ever knew who kept her house filled with zinnias, and the strong woody odor of them was in all the rooms. Standing there in the half dark she looked like one of those flowers, with her thin body and her frizzy ragged-looking red-brown hair. (Eunice said her mother never had her hair just cut, but singed; she thought it was good for it.)

Eunice was sitting on the top step of the porch. When my mother stopped to say a word to Mrs. Herbert, she came down and stood a little way farther down the fence, leaning on the top rail, her fingers crumbling the dry heads of cornflowers.

"You look nice, all dressed up like that," Eunice said to me softly.

"It's plenty hot," I said. "With a tie and all."

"It makes you look different."

"How?"

"I don't know," she said. "Just different."

My mother had turned around now and was standing waiting for me.

"I got to go," I said. "I got to be there. . . ."

Eunice nodded. It was funny how, being a blonde like she was, her eyelashes were almost black. And when she stood looking down the way she did now, they were just a black semicircle on her cheeks. Usually I would have spent the evening on her porch or at a movie with her. And now I couldn't because my grandfather had to have a wake.

"Look," I said. "I won't be all that late tonight. . . . I'll let you know when I get home."

She nodded, still looking down, the eyelashes still making that dark mark on her cheeks.

I turned around and walked off quick as I could after my mother. And all the way over—in the first dark, which was dusty and uncertain to the eye—I was angry. I kept asking myself why I had to be a part of the old man's dying.

My mother took my arm, formally, and I wondered suddenly if I did look different or something.

The windows of the house were all wide open, it was so hot, and there was a light in every room. Very dim light, from a single bulb that was either small or shaded over with brown paper. The rooms were crowded and full of talk, buzzing whispers that didn't seem to say anything, and vague nodding heads. There were people here who'd come from all parts of the county and some from Montgomery, even. All people I knew, but I had a hard time recognizing them, their faces were so different in the half light.

Out in the kitchen there were two new colored women, working under Wilda Olive's direction. They were cooking everything, emptying out the cupboards. There wasn't any reason to watch the larder any more; the stuff had to be used up. Wilda Olive had never had anyone to help her before; she'd never had anyone to boss about—the way she did now. And she was really fixing a supper, for all the people who'd come. Not even the white women stopped or interfered with her. The smell of cooking was all over the house, making the air so heavy I couldn't catch my breath. I had to go outside.

There was only one light globe burning with all its brightness, full away—the one out in the yard. The summer moths were flying around in big swooping circles, and two little kids—a boy and a girl—were standing in the circle of light, swatting them down with pieces of folded newspaper. Each time they hit one, it would disappear with a tiny popping sound and a puff of something like smoke.

The whole yard was full of kids, the youngest ones who were not allowed in the house. They were wandering around, making up games to play or fighting or just sitting, or calling for their mothers in hushed uncertain voices. Mamma Lou Davis, a big fat colored woman, had posted herself at the front gate, to make sure that they didn't wander away.

In the far corner of the garden, next to the row of leathery old live-forever bushes, a bunch of kids had begun to play funeral. They'd found a trowel somewhere and they dug a little hole. Then very carefully they filled it and heaped it so that the mud came to a mound on top. The sticks they'd tied together like a cross wouldn't stand up in the loose dry ground, so they pulled off the silvery leaves from bushes and stuck them all over the mound, like feathers. Then they stood in a circle, solemn all of them, with their hands folded behind their backs, and sang:

> "We will gather by the river,
> The beautiful, beautiful river,
> We will gather by the river . . ."

There were more verses, dozens of them, but they only seemed to know those three lines. So they sang them over and over again.

There was one—a girl with a fat round face—who was sitting on the ground a foot or two away from the group. Her fresh starched pinafore dress was getting all dusty and rumpled, and every time the group paused for breath, in that second or two of quiet, she'd ask: "Which river? Which river? Where?" Not paying any attention to her, they'd go on singing:

> "Gather by the beautiful river."

Their voices together were thin and high-pitched and ragged.

Eunice and her mother came (her father was the druggist and had to stay at the store until it closed at eleven); they didn't see me. I could tell from the polite and cautious way Eunice was looking around that she was searching for me as she followed her mother inside.

I just stood there in the far corner of the yard, not thinking much of anything, just sort of letting my mind float out on the heavy waves of jasmine odor. It couldn't have been long—not much more than a half-hour—when I saw Eunice come out on the porch again. She walked right straight over to the railing this time and stood there, with her right hand rubbing up and down her throat. You could see that she wasn't steady on her feet. Almost immediately her mother came rushing out of the door and put her arm around her and whispered in her ear, and then the two of them came down the steps and got in their car and drove away.

Mamma Lou Davis spoke to me from her stand near the gate: "That little girl sure got plenty sick, green sick. . . ."

"Yeah," I said.

"It plain affect some people that way, dying does." One of the kids, a little boy, made a dash for the gate and the street beyond. Mamma Lou's broad black hand caught him neatly on the top of the head and turned him back into the yard.

"She weren't in there long," Mamma Lou said. "But she got plenty sick."

"Yes," I said, "I could tell that."

I looked over on the porch and saw the extra chairs had been filled. Asa Stevenson had come, a short man, almost a midget. (They said he had killed three wives with his children. He had ten or eleven kids, all told, and every one of them was big and strapping; every one of them was exactly his image.) And Mrs. Martha Watkins Wood, a big woman with yellow wrinkled skin stretched tight across her heavy bones, and with the long sad face of a tired old horse, had come out from Montgomery.

Now in the circle on the porch, all the chairs were filled. Old Carmichael had known just who was coming, had expected them. With the arrival of Mrs. Wood the circle was complete. You could almost see it draw up on itself and close—a solid circle of wooden chairs. And at that precise moment I noticed that the silence was gone. They began talking, their voices light and rustling in the hot night air. Nobody went near them.

Over in the corner of the yard one of the kids was still singing:

"We will gather at the river,
Gather at the beautiful river. . . ."

By ten o'clock it had turned very quiet. The kids had fallen asleep—most of them—on the porch steps or out on the grass. A couple of them were using the little grave they had dug for a pillow. Mamma Lou was still at the gate, but she was sitting now, on a camp stool somebody had brought her from the house. I recognized the stool—it was the one my grandfather used when he went fishing.

Inside, the people seemed to have no more to say. They sat in the chairs that had been brought from all parts of the house for them, and looked at each other, and occasionally one of the women managed a smile, a kind of hesitant one, that seemed even littler in the half light.

From her position on the lowest step little Trudy Wilson shivered with a nightmare and began to cry. Her mother's heels made a kind of running clatter on the straw matting of the hall. They were the first to leave, the Wilsons, even though Trudy had waked up from her dream and was smiling again. The people with the children left first, and then the people who had a distance to drive. And then the people who had a business day coming with tomorrow. Until there were only my parents and me and the old people on the porch.

"Do you suppose they'll stay all night?" my mother asked.

"How could I know?" my father said. "They'll leave when they get ready and not before."

That was true enough. Hoyt Stevenson, who'd driven over with his wife and their three daughters and his father, had tried to get the old man to drive back with them. He tried for at least ten minutes, talking to the man in a low voice. And the old man just didn't answer, just kept shaking his head.

That's the way it was with all of them. So their families got together and figured out a way that they could get home to bed and not worry about the old people's getting home. Jim Butts, who owned the sawmill and who could afford a big car and a chauffeur, offered to ride home with somebody and leave his car and the colored driver. That's the way they did it. Finally there was just Butts's big light-yellow-colored Cadillac parked out front with the fuzzy-haired Negro asleep at the wheel, his arms wrapped all around it. And our car, which was parked up the drive, next to the house.

"Ruby, honey," my father said, "why don't you go to bed?"

My mother smiled at him limply. "I reckon I will. . . ."

Wilda Olive came in softly, carrying a round wicker tray with small cups of coffee.

My father took two. "I'll need them to stay awake."

"Thank you," my mother said. "I nearly forgot you were here, Wilda Olive."

"Yes'm," she said softly, gave me my cup of coffee, and went out on the porch to bring the rest to the old me.

I tasted the coffee. It had brandy in it.

"Say," my father said, "she sure made this a stiff dose."

"I'm so tired," my mother said. "It'll make me light-headed as anything."

"You can be in bed by that time," my father told her; "go ahead."

She stood up. "Come on, MacDonald," she said to me.

"I'm staying."

She appealed to my father. "I couldn't ever walk home alone at this time of night."

"MacDonald," my father said.

"Okay." I got up.

My father put his coffee cup down slowly. "What did you say?"

"Yes, sir."

My mother was tugging at my arm.

"Can I come back?"

My father shook his head.

"Don't you want company?"

"Go home," my father said.

My mother pulled my arm. "MacDonald, please—" And outside she gave a sigh of annoyance. "I'd think you'd have some sense. Can't you see your father's all upset without you pestering him?"

"Yes, ma'am," I said.

When we were almost home I asked her: "Why do you suppose he didn't want company?"

"Sometimes you want to be alone, MacDonald."

"I wouldn't," I said. I saw her staring at me with a funny kind of look. I rubbed my hand quick all over my face to wipe off whatever expression she was worried about.

On our porch I stopped and took off my coat and tie. I dropped them on a chair. Meanwhile she had opened the door.

"Come on in, son."

I shook my head. "I reckon I need a walk." I started down the steps.

"MacDonald," my mother said, "you aren't coming to bed?"

"No'm."

"Your father said—"

"I don't care—" and because I didn't want to hear her answer to that, I bolted around the corner of the house. I didn't quite know where I wanted to go, so I just stood for a minute, just looking around. There was a thin flat hard sliver of moon pasted up in the west. The sky was almost bright blue and there were piles of thunderheads all over it now, shining clear in the light. There wasn't a bit of air. The dust wasn't even blowing. Everything was still and moldy and hot in the moonlight.

It was the sort of night when you breathe as shallow as you can, hoping to keep the heat out of your body that way, because your body is hot enough already. And you feel like you have a fever and maybe you do—on a thermometer—but you know it's just summer, burning.

I began to walk, not going anywhere, just wading through the dark and the heat. There were mockingbirds singing, like it was day. In the houses all the windows were wide open, and even out in the streets you could hear the hum of electric fans.

I passed a couple of colored boys walking, in step down the sidewalk. They rolled big white eyes at me as they went past. They were wearing sneakers; you couldn't hear their steps at all even in the quiet.

I wasn't thinking of anything. I was just moving around feeling how good the little breeze that made was. I walked through the town, through the business section, the closed stores and the grocery and the movie house; and the railroad station, open, but empty; and the rails shining white in the light, but empty too. I kept on walking until I had swung back through town in a circle and started back toward home. And the first thing I knew I was passing my grandfather's house. I saw the big jasmine bush at the corner of the lot—dusty but full of yellow flowers.

I went around to the side yard out of the reach of the street light and climbed over the fence. It was just a wire and wood fence and I had to swing over quick before my weight brought it down.

I was right by the kitchen window, so I looked in. Wilda Olive was standing there, at the kitchen table. She was dressed in a black linen dress so starched that it stood out all around her like stiff paper. And her hair was just combed and pulled straight on top her head and shining with lacquer. She wasn't asleep; her eyes were open.

Out in the yard, so close that I could almost put my hand down and touch it, a mockingbird was singing. I looked around carefully trying to see him. I saw a spot of gray close by the back porch that could have been the bird, but I wasn't sure.

My father was in the dining-room—I slipped over and looked through that window. He was sitting in one of the armchairs, all hunched down in it so that his head rested against the back. He was facing toward the living-room doors. My grandfather was in the first room, the one with the curtains drawn and the light shining dull brown through them.

And the old people were still on the porch. I could hear their voices, light and rustling.

I walked around the house and stood on the front steps, listening to them.

"There was plenty of timber for a house," Vance Bonfield was saying. He was a little wrinkled man, with a full head of clear black hair, which he dyed carefully every week. "But Cecil Addams wouldn't have any of plain pine. He had to have that cypress brought out from Louisiana."

"Wasn't him," Matthew Conners said. "His wife wanted it. Wanted a house just like she used to have. That's what it was."

Vance looked at him, blinking his pale-blue eyes slowly.

"Her name's plain gone from my memory," he said. "Do you happen to recall it?"

"Linda," Mrs. Wood said.

"Louise." Mrs. Bonfield's double chin quivered with the word.

"It was Lizette," Matthew Conners said.

"Ask him," Vance said, and lifted his thin old hand to point to me.
(I jumped; I hadn't really thought they'd noticed me.)

"Ask him," Henry Carmichael said; "young people always remember better."

"Not so," Matthew Conners said, and banged with his cane on the
porch boards. "They just got less to remember."

And then I said as loud as I could, because some of them were deaf:
"Her name was Eulalie."

They looked at me and slowly shook their heads.

And I added quickly "Lalia for short."

They sighed together: "Aahh"; they looked relieved.

"That's a bright young boy," Matthew Conners said. "A bright
young fellow."

They looked at me. "He's a fine young fellow."

"Looks like his grandpa," Vance said. "A man's looks goes on in his
sons."

Wilda Olive brought out a round of whiskies.

Looking at her, Vance said: "I can remember when she was the
prettiest high-brown girl in this part of the state."

Matthew Conners cackled to himself, remembering. "And wasn't it
a hell of a to-do when he brought her home after his wife died."

"I remember," they said.

I stood looking at them, wondering what it was they remembered,
all of them together. Something I didn't know, something I couldn't
know. Nor my father. Something my grandfather had known, who was
dead.

Wilda Olive served them the drinks as if she never heard.

Vance held the glass in his hand, which shook so that the ice
tingled. "Yes, sir," he said. "She was the prettiest thing you ever laid
eyes on. Skin all yellow and burning."

Wilda Olive went inside. I looked after her and tried to see how she
had looked years ago, when she had been pretty, so pretty that she'd
caught my grandfather's eye. But all I saw was a colored woman,
middle-aged and getting sort of heavy, with grieving lines down her
cheeks.

"Prettiest thing," Vance said. "Sort of thing a young man can have,
if he wants it."

"Man can't have anything long," Matthew Conners said.

They were looking at me. I began backing away.

"He's got a girl already," Asa Stevenson said, and hunched his dwarfed shoulders. "He got in a fight over her and near got thrown out of school."

"Who?" Mrs. Bonfield's fat chin lifted up and stared at me.

And Vance put in: "The Herbert girl, what's her name?"

I was backing off. They called to me: "Wait."

I had to stop.

"What's her name?" Matthew Conners leaned forward and rested his thin wrinkled chin on his cane. "What's her name?"

"I don't know," I said. The words sounded stupid and I knew they heard that too, but the only thing I could do was repeat: "I don't know."

"Not know your girl's name," Carmichael said, shaking his head. "Not know your girl's name . . ." His voice trailed off. "How do you call her to come out to you?"

Matthew Conners cackled softly. "You plain got it twisted, man. He's the one that come out. . . ."

"She's a pretty girl," Mrs. Wood said, her voice high and shrill in her solemn long face.

"You're right to pick a pretty girl," Vance said. "While you can."

I saw the hate in their eyes and I began to be sick. I backed away, down the steps and around the corner of the porch. This time they didn't seem to notice and let me go.

"It isn't long a man has anything," Matthew Conners was saying, and the ice cubes in his glass rattled. "It isn't long."

I climbed back over the fence, and the wire squeaked with my weight. I walked along the other side, slowly, curling my toes in the hard dry grass at each step.

Finally I sat down under the big locust tree near the street; I knew they couldn't see me there.

There was a funny sort of quivering in my stomach. I leaned back against the rough bark of the tree and looked up through the leaves at the sky that was almost bright blue. Out of the corner of my eye I could catch the sheen of the moon on the car waiting in the street. And that same moon made little blobs of light all around me. It was hot; I just sat there with my arms wrapped around my knees, feeling the sweat run down my back. I noticed a movement over on the porch. I looked more carefully. One of the old men, my grandfather's friends, was wiping his face slowly on a white handkerchief.

I sat under the locust tree and stared up at the sky that was so bright the stars looked uncertain and dim. I don't know how long I sat there before I began to notice something different. The rustling of voices was changing. I shifted my eyes from the sky to the porch.

Their talk was drying up quickly. The words got fewer and farther apart. They began watching each other with a quick sidewise slanting of eyes. And mouths came to a stiff closed line. They began to fidget nervously in their chairs.

Then one by one, with an imperceptible murmur, they slipped away. Singly, each singly, they left. I watched them leave, quiet and alone, and I thought: that's how they came.

The road ended here. They had to walk one way. And soon there were five of them, scattered down the length of the road, poking their way along, feeling the way with their sticks, black on a bright road.

I got up and went over and woke Claude, the chauffeur. He pushed his cap back on his head and rubbed his face with one hand.

"Claude," I said, "there they go."

"Huh?" He held his hand pressed to his face so that his stub nose was all pushed to one side.

"There they go," I repeated. "You better catch them."

He opened his eyes and looked down the road. "Christ Almighty," he said, starting the engine, "they plain near got away."

He swung the car around and went after them. I stood leaning on the gatepost watching. He drove up to the last man, drove a little past him and stopped, got out, opened the door quick. The old man never stopped walking, just kept walking until he was right abreast of the car, and then Claude stepped up and took his arm and almost lifted him into the car. Then he closed the door, quietly (I couldn't hear a sound), and went on after the next one. He did that until they were all safely in the car.

I started home then, and all the way I kept thinking of the picture of the old people moving down the road.

And suddenly I remembered the last time I had seen my grandfather—two days ago. We had both gone to the same place fishing. In deep summer there was only one place around here that you could fish in, only one place where the water stood deep and cool. He'd showed it to me himself the summer past—in an old gravel pit, way back behind the worn-out holes and the sandy ridges. It was quite a trick getting into it; it's hard climbing in loose gravel. I got to the top of the ridge and stood looking down at the line of aspens and willows and red honeysuckle bushes that grew around the pool. Then I noticed that my grandfather was already there, sitting on his camp stool, his rod in his hand. And at first I grinned and thought how surprised he would be to see me; and how much better it was to fish with company, even though you never say a word.

I started to climb down to him, and some loose gravel rolled away under my feet. He looked up and saw me. And he got up and grabbed his stool and his bait box and hurried away up the other side of the ridge. And I noticed a funny thing: his line wasn't out. He'd been sitting there, holding his rod, and waiting, but he hadn't cast out his line. He'd just been sitting there, waiting. . . .

And I understood then. . . . Why Matthew Conners had sold his store and didn't seem to notice the people passing by who talked to him. Why Mrs. Martha Watkins Wood wouldn't keep a servant full time in the big old empty house of hers in Montgomery, just day help. Why Vance Bonfield and his wife suddenly took separate rooms after sleeping in the same bed for forty-six years. Why Henry Carmichael shouted at the noisy grandchildren who climbed the wisteria vines to peer into the windows of his room. Why old people wanted to be left alone. . . .

There was the fear in my grandfather's eyes the day at the gravel pool. Even from a distance I had seen it. The fear that had made the old man pick up his bait basket and scurry off as fast as his stiffening legs could go.

The fear of dying . . . the fear that grows until at last it separates you from the people you know: the dusty-eyed old people who want to be left alone, who go off alone and wait. Who fish without a line.

One day I'll be that afraid. . . . All of a sudden I knew that. Knew that for the first time, I'll be old and afraid.

I'll be old and restless in company and want to be alone. Because loneliness is more bearable than company, when you are waiting; because it's a kind of preparation for that coming final loneliness.

I could feel it starting, just the beginning of fear.

I'll be old and sit on porches and talk in dry rattling whispers and remember the past and the things that I had when I was able to have them. And in the shaded parlors, in the faces of dead friends, see the image of my fear. The fear that will live with me: will follow me through the day and lie down with me at night and join me again in the morning, until there isn't any more morning and I don't get up at all. . . .

I began to run, not knowing where I was going, not caring. And there was the fear running with me, just with me.

It was so hot, I was running through a blank solid wall. I had to breathe and I kept trying, but there wasn't any air, just heat.

From far away there was the pounding of my own feet on the ground. I looked down at them, moving. I could hear the strangling sound of my own breathing, but that was far away too.

Only, the mockingbird was singing louder and louder and there was a spot of gray flying alongside me. Like it was laughing at me, trying to run away from it.

I was getting tired, so tired; I tried but I couldn't keep up the pace. It was hard too to keep my balance; I kept falling forward. I stretched out my arms; they touched something and I held on to it tightly. I stood shaking my head until my eyes cleared. It was a fence, a picket fence. And just beyond was our house. I had come home. Not thinking about it, I had come home. All the hot noisy outside had come down to this: our green-painted clapboard house with the olive-colored shutters and the big black screen porch all around it. But somehow I couldn't go inside.

I lifted my eyes. And there were the thunderheads. They were right behind the house, right in line with it, but miles up in the sky. Just where they'd been all day. They'd turned red with the sunset and disappeared with the first dark and then reappeared silver-white with the moon. And there they were, hanging cool-looking and distant.

I looked away from them, down and across the street, to the light in the side window of the Herberts' house. That would be Eunice, waiting for me. For just a minute I saw her face and her eyes that crinkled at the corners and the way her hair was piled up on top of her head with a flower stuck in it.

I thought of all these things and I just turned away from the yellow square of light. And I took a couple of steps backward until I pressed up against the big thick barberry hedge. One of the crooked thorns scratched my hand; I looked at it, bleeding slightly; it didn't hurt. Somehow nothing much seemed real—not Eunice, nor my house, nor the hedge that had cut me. Nothing but the pile of thunderheads up in the sky and the fear that had caught up with me, was running circles around me.

Circles and circles around me. Like the mockingbird that was singing louder and louder. The brown-gray bird.

Very slowly I sat down, leaning my back against the sharp thorns of the hedge. And listened.

Flight

"There's nothing you can do?"

"We are fairly sure now that the primary site is the liver. That's somewhat unusual."

"But you can't help her?"

"I am sorry. There is nothing at all we can do."

"I'll go home now, Michael. It's time."

"Mother, why not wait a bit longer?"

"Tomorrow, I think. I'll go tomorrow."

"It's a long flight."

"It was just as long when I flew here to visit you, Michael."

"You were stronger then, Mother."

"There was more time then, too. Or I thought there was. Will you see to the tickets? I'll go back the way I came, that flight through Dallas."

"Mother, please wait until you are stronger."

"I will not get stronger. You have talked to the doctors. And I know they are right."

"You could stay here. We are all here."

"I will take the plane home tomorrow, Michael. . . . Now I am sleepy. . . . Is it raining outside? I hear rain very clearly." Water: whispering, giggling.

She, the small child, waited for rain, watched across Mr. Beauchardrais's pasture as the clouds gathered, black and silver. Heavy clouds with ball and chain lightning dancing between them, silently. The spiky clumps of pasture grass faded to pale yellow, glimmering, reflecting like water to the sky.

She sat in the porch corner, wedged comfortably against peeling boards which were corded like the veins in her mother's hands, her father's arms. Sometimes she even imagined that the house's blood flowed through those raised twisting networks in the wood.

Mouse, people called her for her habit of sitting silent and still in corners. And Doodle Bug for the hours she spent under the house, crawling between the low brick foundation pillars, creeping cautiously through broken glass and slate to settle comfortably, flat on her back, at the center of the house, where the damp air smelled of mildew and tomcats and a heavy sweet stickiness that was the breath of the ground itself. . . .

While her mother's feet thudded up and down across the boards overhead, she lay on her back and watched the spiders weaving the thick gray webs around the water pipes. Watching for the Black Widow, small with a single red dot on its stomach. . . . When it rained, neighborhood dogs and cats sheltered under the house, politely, deliberately ignoring each other. Huddled against the underside of the front steps, a calico fed her latest litter while two dogs slept, twitching and yelping in their dreams. . . .

She sat cross-legged on the porch where the sun-bleached wood was so hard her small pocketknife could barely scratch a mark. She had to be very careful; if her parents caught her testing the strength of the boards, she would get a paddling for sure. As if the boards were something to be guarded, as if they were worth anything at all. . . .

She watched the rain. It began with a yellowish kind of darkness in the air, then a shiver while leaves rushed into the neatly swept hard clay yard and spun in rising circles. Just like the cartoons she saw on Saturday afternoons, when her mother had extra money to send her to the movies. (On good days her father walked to work and saved his carfare in a jelly glass on the kitchen counter. For her.) When those cartoon characters ran, they left swirls of motion behind them like the wind and the dead leaves.

Rain meant her father rode the streetcar and no extra coins went into the kitchen glass.

She settled back—no movie this week, that was for sure—and waited for the rain.

On the tin roof, drops tapped, then knocked, then rattled like hailstones. A whispering, a hissing ran along the roof gutters to the cistern at the corner of the house.

Her mother called loudly, "Willie May, come quick. Come help me."

In the backyard her mother was putting chicks and ducklings into the poultry shed. Willie May hated to touch them—the small bony bodies felt skeletal and evil in her hands. She held her breath as she hurriedly put the small blobs safely under shelter. They were so stupid that they would stand in the rain, gawking in curious confusion, and drown.

Afterwards, back in the porch corner again, wet clothes plastered tight to shoulders, nostrils filled with the scent of her own dripping hair, she watched the air turn smoky gray. She sniffed the sweet moisture-laden dust and occasionally, after a close crash of thunder, she could smell the sharp, nose-tickling odor of ozone.

Another time her mother called her. That once in September during the hurricane season. "Willie May," her mother cried, voice shaking with fear and pain, "Willie May, help me." The child she was carrying was born too soon, a small hairy boy who gasped a couple of times and was perfectly still.

Willie May ran off into the rain, hiding in the heavy tangle of titi bushes and myrtle trees on the other side of the street. She shivered all over—not with cold, because it was September and very warm, and not with fear of the weather, because though the winds were high they were not nearly hurricane strength. She huddled against the trunk of a big wax myrtle, and rain and leaves and bark pelted down on her. Her arms and hands twitched, like a puppet, her body shook so hard that she could scarcely breathe. Perhaps she'd even stopped breathing for a while, because she found herself lying full length on the ground, one ear and eye pasted shut by soft oozing mud.

It was still raining hard and the sky was darker, not with the greenish dark of a hurricane, but the gray dark of night. Looking out carefully from her shelter, across the empty ground, she could see that all the lights in her house were on.

She went home then, because she had no other place to go. The deep gutters on each side of the dirt street were filled to the top (crawfish would like that, she thought), the water was ankle deep on the three loose boards that served as a bridge to her house. She inched her way across, carefully. The boards shivered and quaked, about to wash away. In the morning she would have to go hunting for them and put them back in their place. She'd most probably find them near the Duquesnay house where the ground rose just a bit. An Indian mound, people said, and children frightened each other with stories of walking ghosts.

Out of the darkness her father said, "Willie May."

She hadn't known he was there. His voice came from the dark corner of the porch by the living room window. She stared, dazzled by the bright square of light, saw nothing. Mosquitoes, attracted to the moisture of her eyes, swarmed on her, and she blinked rapidly.

"You ran off," her father said, "when your mama called you. You left her and the baby died."

She wanted to say: I didn't kill him.

But no sound came out.

"Your mama knew you were afraid when you saw the baby, but she thought you'd know enough to run to Rosie's house."

No, she hadn't thought of that. Never once thought of running the three blocks to her Aunt Rosie's house and telling her. She'd thought of nothing but digging under the weeds and bushes, hiding. Like a mouse gone back to earth.

I'm sorry, she wanted to say.

But again no words.

The water-washed boards suddenly shifted sideways and she fell into the muddy night-black rushing water, coming up coughing and choking, crying with fear, scrambling up the bank of the ditch to the firm hard-swept mud of the front yard.

Her father did not move. She would not have known he was there, except in the quiet night she could hear his breathing.

"Mother, please stay. You're comfortable here and the doctors are so good."

"I do not need doctors now."

"Mother, listen. We only want to take care of you. Don't you understand. We love you."

Oh, I understand. The trap. The trap that caught my father and my mother and even me. But that was years ago, not now. No more love.

She would run away again. Only, when she went to earth this time, it would be for good. And she would choose her own spot.

"The baby didn't die because of you," her mother said.

But Willie May knew better. She knew.

"He died because he was born too soon. If I hadn't strained and fought with that window because the rain was pouring in, and if the window hadn't been stuck . . . He wasn't your fault. But you shouldn't have run away."

She hung her head and the old guilt and disgust settled in her stomach while her chest ached so much that she thought she too would die.

"Your duty," her mother said, "you don't ever run away from your duty to your family. Not ever. Not until you die."

Willie May thought wearily, and with horror: You aren't ever free. Something always holds you, stops you, brings you back.

"Good evening, Mrs. Denham. Will you have your sleeping pill now?" The night nurse: round black face under a round white cap.

"You still wear your cap, Nurse. None of the others do."

"The hospital doesn't require it any more, Mrs. Denham." She had a habit of repeating the patient's name over and over again. Perhaps she had been taught to do that. "But I worked hard for this bit of organdy and I intend to keep on wearing it."

"I know what it is to work hard for something."

"Yes," the nurse said.

Then there were the usual little night sounds: rubber-shod feet thudding ever so softly, and the soft silky whispering of nylon-clad thighs moving up and down the halls.

I did not come for this, she thought dully, I came to see my son, my only son who lives a continent away in a house with green lawns and dogwood blooming outside the windows, who has two sons, his images. I came to visit and I broke down on the road like an old car.

She could smell the sickly sweet stench of her own skin. Her whole body had an aura of decay.

The smell reminds me of something. Something years ago. I was young, but my skin still carried this smell.

I have only to live until the morning. It is time.

Time had so many different patterns. After her father died, when they were very poor with only his small pension to support them, Willie May went off to work at the Convent of the Holy Angels. Thirteen, tall and strong, and afraid. For three years she lived in a maze of echoing halls that smelled of floor wax and furniture polish and a laundry that smelled of steam and bleach and starch for the stiff white coifs and wimples the nuns wore. Three years of small hard beds in tiny rooms. Of weariness and sick exhaustion. Of prayers and echoing Gregorian chant. And a great emptiness. Occasionally in the garden as she swept the covered walkways, she could hear children shouting as they walked to school. She envied them and their living fathers whose hard-earned money sent them laughing along the sidewalks.

Eventually her mother remarried, a police sergeant named Joseph Reilly, a widower nearly sixty. "Hello, Willie May," he said, when she came back from the convent. "I married your mother." "Okay," she said. He smiled then, and it was settled.

He liked to cook, and despite his name he cooked Italian style. Her mother was beginning to grow fat on spaghetti and sausage and peppers, all glistening with olive oil.

He was a quiet man who spent every evening at home listening to the radio, sitting in his special chair (one he had brought with him to her mother's house) with his feet propped on a stool. He was a kind man and treated her like his own child. Each birthday he bought her a pair of white gloves to wear to church, and every Christmas he gave her a box of Evening in Paris cosmetics, blue bottles held in shining white satin.

There was no talk of her returning to school, the time for that had passed. On her sixteenth birthday she went to work at Woolworth's, at the big store on Decatur Street. She sold potted plants and stood all day behind the counter near the front window, and when she wasn't busy she watched the street outside. The cars and the big delivery vans and the green streetcars rocking unsteadily past on their small clacking iron wheels. Women in print dresses and hats, breathless and harried from the excitement of shopping. Office messengers with brown envelopes and packages and long cardboard tubes. Girls in navy blue school uniforms, arm in arm, and boys gathered at the corner by the traffic light. Bookies and numbers runners whose territory this was; she grew to recognize them and smile, and they lifted their hats to her in passing.

As she watched she felt her quietness and her loneliness slipping away. She felt herself become a part of things, no longer a child looking in, but an adult and part of the busyness and bustle that was life. Her hands, broadened and thickened by the convent work, their nails clipped very short and square across, grew soft and slender, and she filed her nails into careful ovals. She buffed them too, until they had a high shine; she might have worn nail polish of a color to match her lipstick (they sold those sets at the cosmetic counter at the back of the store), but the management did not allow that.

She had money of her own now, and the delicious expectation of each week's pay. (Dutifully she gave half to her mother, the rest was hers.) Sometimes she would stand for long minutes, half-smiling, half-dozing, smoothing the bills between her manicured fingers, pressing the coins against her palms until they left their imprint on her skin.

Every evening on the streetcar home, she stared through the dirty finger-smeared window, lulled by the steady rocking, and dreamed half-visions of the future. She had never done that before. She had met only one day at a time, fearful. Now she was the future, a series of busy days. Beyond grimy windows the littered crowded streets were mysteriously inviting. She lived now in a state of great excitement, with a fluttering in her stomach, a feeling of endless energy, a sense that flowers were beautiful and rain was lovely, that colors were brighter than they had ever been before, that something wonderful was about to happen. She had no experience of it, but she thought this must mean that she was happy.

One day John Denham walked past Woolworth's big front window. They stared and blinked and then laughed at the sight of each other grown up. They had been children together; he'd lived two blocks away. In those half-remembered days before her father's death, they had played and adventured together. "When you get off work," he said, "I'll be waiting for you." He rode home with her on the streetcar, but he wouldn't come near her house. "Your mama wouldn't like me."

"Why not?"

"She won't like any boy hanging around you. I'll see you after work tomorrow."

He did, every evening. They talked the whole way home, nervously, rapidly summarizing the years. He told her that years ago his family had moved across town to share a house with his aunt. "Way out," he said. "Nothing but swamps behind us. We used to go crawfishing a lot." Once, he told her, he'd gone back to their old neighborhood and people said she'd gone off to the convent.

"I thought you were going to be a nun," he said.

"Not me." She held up her soft manicured hands, admiring them against the scratched varnish of the car seats. "Mama went to work but she couldn't make enough to keep me and the house both, and then Father Lauderman heard that the convent needed somebody, and that somebody turned out to be me."

"They teach you anything?"

"Sure. Cooking—would you believe they've got thirty-seven nuns there. And embroidery and crochet. And a lot of prayers."

"Okay," he said, "say me a prayer."

"I get plenty enough prayers in church on Sunday," she said. "Anyway, the next stop is mine."

He got off with her and they stood talking until a car came going the other way. He swung on, she walked home.

And so she saw him six days a week. She learned that he still lived at home with his parents and his orphaned cousins and his grandmother. That he'd finished Jesuit High School and right away was lucky enough to get a job with the post office, delivering mail. "I like it," he said. "I couldn't ever stand being inside at a desk all day long."

"I like my job too," she said.

"What do you do on Sundays?"

"Go to mass. Do my laundry and my ironing and be sure my clothes are ready for the week. And I help my mother with her garden, and in the evenings there's always the radio programs."

"You don't work much in the garden, not with hands like that."

"I didn't know you noticed my hands."

"Sure I notice. I notice everything about you."

She felt pleased and shy.

"But your Sundays don't sound like any fun to me."

"I like it just the way it is," she said. But in truth she didn't like it as much as she had.

"Where do you go to church? St. Rita's?"

"Mama and I go to the eleven o'clock every Sunday, rain or shine. She wouldn't miss it."

"What would you say if I told you I'd be there? That'd surprise you, wouldn't it? Well, I used to go to that church when I was a kid living just down the street from you, and I might just take myself back there again. Oh, I wouldn't talk to you, just spy on you. I know they get a big crowd for mass, so you see if you find me. And I bet you can't."

On Monday he said triumphantly, "You had a blue skirt and a white blouse and a tie like a man's, and you had to sit in the middle of a pew because you got there late, and you dropped your purse because you were so busy looking for me."

"I don't think that is a funny game," she said.

"I'm tired of it too." He popped a match against his thumbnail and lit a cigarette. "Let's not go to church next Sunday. Let's go out to the lake and walk along the seawall and have a look at all the big boats. I'll meet you at the streetcar stop at the end of Prentiss Street."

She did not meet him. She felt tired and out of sorts that Sunday, but she worked very hard in the garden, spraying the tomato plants with tobacco water to control aphids, staking and tying the beans.

"You are such a big help," her mother said. "You've got such a lot of energy."

The following day John Denham said, "You sure did miss a good time yesterday."

"I told you I was busy."

"Sure you were," he said. "I'll believe anything."

Day after day he waited for her. "Who's your boyfriend?" the other girls at Woolworth's asked. "He's not a boyfriend, he's just somebody used to live in my neighborhood."

The September rains began and he carried a big gray post office umbrella. The interior of the streetcars smelled of wet mud and musty sawdust, but the windows were washed clean by the pounding rain.

"You can't work in that precious garden now," he said.

"Not much any more," she said.

"So let's go out this Sunday."

"I am busy on Sundays," she said. "I have very important things to do."

"What's more important than me?"

She hesitated, not wanting to tell him, not really, but telling him anyway. "I crochet."

"All day? You're crazy."

"No." This time she didn't try to explain how pleasant Sundays were—with the street quiet and empty except for a few wandering dogs. Even kids' games sounded muted on Sundays, without so much screaming. She'd sit on the front porch with her mother, while Joseph read the newspaper and then, finished, slept soundly in his special rocking chair. Sometimes they were so silent and still that mourning doves perched on the railing and watched them. In chilly weather they sat in the parlor. Joseph dozed in the chair that he had brought in from the porch, the bright red patterned cushions almost hidden by his bulk. Her mother read aloud from the *State Times* or the *Diocesan Chronicle*, news of weddings and births and deaths. She herself sat surrounded by baskets of yarn, all colors, pale sea green her favorite. Her crochet hook flashed faster and faster, in and out, catching, dragging, snaring. The soft wool nets slipped away from her hands, completed.

"Okay," John said, "so what do you crochet that takes all day, every Sunday."

"They're called fascinators," she said. "You saw me wearing one the other day."

"That head scarf thing?"

"Not a scarf," she said. "They're pretty and they're warm. I always used to wear mine to church, I made them in two or three different colors to match the altar vestments."

"What?"

"It seemed respectful," she said. "Well, ladies began stopping me, wanting to know where I got them, because the department stores don't have anything nearly so nice. I made some for them, and I found I could do it very fast. So I put a notice in the *Chronicle*. Now I take orders, any color if you bring me the wool and any stitch if you show me what it is. I've got lots of orders for Christmas. People don't mind what they spend at Christmas."

"Money," he laughed, "is that all you ever think about? You got a job and you still want more."

"I've been poor," she said slowly, trying to explain, "and the convent took me in and the nuns taught me needlework, all kinds of needlework. It was like they were making me a present of it. And I can use it now."

"You are plain crazy," he said.

Still, every day after work he waited at the streetcar stop. It was December now, with cold winter rain. The early azaleas showed their buds and the sasanquas opened their flat pink and white flowers.

"Something likes this weather," she said to him, pointing to the gardens as they passed.

"Not me," he said. "Look," he said, "make one of those fascinators for me and I'll give it to my mother for Christmas. She'll be expecting something."

"Okay," she said.

"They look kind of pretty on you, so maybe they'll do something for her too."

She felt herself flushing, as pleased as if it had been a proper compliment.

After Christmas the rain stopped. In the parks camellias bloomed and all the big purple azaleas.

"Come to the park with me this Sunday," he said. "We'll look at those flowers you're so crazy about and then we'll go to the aquarium and watch them feed the seals."

"I work on Sunday," she said primly.

"You're not still making those stupid scarfs," he said. "Christmas is over."

"I'm making baby dresses."

"Don't tell me the nuns taught you that."

"They taught me to smock," she said. "People want real smocking on their baby clothes and I add little embroidered rosebuds too."

"And people buy that?"

"All I can make," she said.

"Okay," he said. "I'm going to walk by your house this Sunday and I am going to see."

"You're checking up on me," she said, and was flattered by the thought. "If you walk past I am going to pretend I don't know you."

"What makes you think I'm going to talk to you?" he said. "I just want to look."

He did. He walked by slowly, looking at the houses on both sides. She did not lift her head from her work, not even when he walked back again.

"I hope you are satisfied," she said.

"You are crazy, I knew it."

"No."

"You don't ever think of me, I bet. You won't even miss me when I'm gone."

She stared at him. "Where are you going?"

"Got your attention that time, didn't I? You heard about this little thing called the draft, and yours truly is 1A. They're going to haul me off any day now."

"I forgot."

"Well, old Uncle Sam ain't going to let me forget. Hey, look, next stop is yours. You better ring the bell."

They stood talking longer than usual that day, leaning against the rough trunk of one of the young oak trees at the corner.

"I bet you won't even miss me when I'm out there getting shot at."

"There ain't any war," she said, "not unless you know something I don't."

"They're drafting an army," he said. "You don't make an army if you don't plan to use it."

The last azaleas faded, purple wisteria ran wild along the fences, lost its flowers and put out its leaves; high up on the old buildings the Rose of Montana vine began to show its small pink flowers. Then one day he wasn't waiting at the streetcar stop, and she rode home alone. He wasn't there the next day, or the next. The weather turned stormy, fishing boats scurried back into port. It rained so heavily that the streets flooded and she waded home in waist-deep water. By morning the water was down; children were fishing for crawfish in the ditches, all of them playing hooky from school.

Finally he was back, thin and tired-looking. "I got my induction notice," he said, "four or five other guys too. We all took annual leave and got drunk. Then we took the train to Chicago just for the ride."

She wasn't too sure exactly where Chicago was, though she did remember learning about it in geography class. So he had just gone off like that, to a spot on the map. . . .

"We decided we didn't much like Chicago so we came back. Here's your streetcar, didn't you notice?"

Again he disappeared without a word.

"What happened to your boyfriend?" Norma, who sold cosmetics, asked.

"The army," she said. "And he's not my boyfriend."

Norma lifted her eyebrows. "Too bad."

Evenings Willie May rode home alone, feeling strange and a little hurt that he had not said good-bye. He shouldn't have just disappeared, she thought.

Joseph retired from the police force, complaining of pains in his chest. The doctor told him to stop drinking beer and lose weight; her mother fussed over him, fixing special meals which Joseph wouldn't eat. She hid his beer. He started spending afternoons at the Paradise Bar, two blocks away. He liked their draft, he said, a lot better than bottles.

Willie May herself had so many orders for children's dresses that her mother had to help with the cutting and some of the simple sewing and the ironing and the folding in tissue paper. And she still worked at Woolworth's. In the summer heat, the air in the store turned musty and sweaty and heavy. The tall fans barely pushed it along the aisles. The floorwalkers complained all day long about dust on the counters, and the clerks polished and rearranged them constantly. Aphids appeared like white frosting on all the potted coleus. Two stock boys took them to the back loading platform and dabbed at the bugs with rubbing alcohol.

In August Willie May got her first order for a christening dress, a peau de soie robe over a long lawn shift. She worked on it for a month, carefully dusting her hands with talcum powder so that her sweating fingers left no mark on the white material.

One Sunday as she and her mother sat on the porch and Joseph dozed in the hammock he had slung between two mulberry trees in the yard, John Denham sauntered up the walk and stood with one foot on the steps, grinning. His hair was so short that he seemed quite bald and he was in uniform. "I got leave," he said. "You want to take a ride out to the lake and get an ice cream?"

"I've got to finish the dress," she said.

Her mother took the material from her hands and carried it carefully inside.

He laughed. "Your ma says yes."

"I suppose so," she said. She was very confused and she did not like the feeling at all. "You surprised me," she said. "I don't like being surprised."

"Look, don't blame me," he said; "the army owns me now."

Her mother said from inside the screen door, "It will take her just a few minutes to freshen up. Would you like some iced tea, what did you say your name was?"

So they caught the streetcar to the lake and ate ice cream cones and walked along the seawall and looked at the muddy water and sat on benches under small pine trees and listened to a band play marches and waltzes and opera overtures. Children skated on the concrete walks and chalked the outlines of hopscotch games. The young women were there in their summer dresses, full skirted and starched crisp against the summer heat. The young men were in uniform.

"What's the matter with you," he said. "You're scowling."

She answered truthfully, "I felt afraid, all of a sudden."

He grinned and put his arm around her. "Baby, you got nothing to be afraid of when I'm with you."

"Oh," she said. And didn't tell him she knew he was wrong about that.

They settled finally on a shady bench near a fountain. They could hear the water trickling and bubbling in the wide basin.

"Look," he said. "You ever think about yourself? Like what you're going to do next? And why you want to do it?"

"No," she said.

"Well, you should. Now, you're a good-looking gal. A real pretty face and a nice figure even if you are too thin. But then, you can be pretty disagreeable and grumpy and you can set that mouth of yours tight like a nun."

She stared at him, anger beginning in a flush.

"But I still think we ought to get married."

She stopped, realized her mouth was open, and shut it with a click of teeth.

"It kind of makes sense. We get married, and you stay at your mother's house, and I come back when they give me leave. You keep working and if I get killed you get the insurance. I'm sure as hell worth more dead than alive."

Two children were running across the open field, their dresses bright multicolored spots on the green. Water dribbled from the bronze urn held high by a fat bronze boy on the edge of the fountain.

It isn't real, she thought.

"We go meet my family tonight. I already met yours. Tomorrow I see the priest and it'll all be arranged when I pick you up after work tomorrow. What do you say to that?"

"All right," she said. "Fine with me."

The banns were announced at three masses the next Sunday, and they were married that evening. It was just about the only free time the priest had, there were so many weddings on such short notice.

He came back twice on leave before war started and he was sent to England. Willie May left Woolworth's for a job at the shipyards. It was hard and dirty work—but she saved her money carefully and watched the total grow slowly month after month. In the second April of the war, her mother died in her sleep. Then Joseph remembered his children in Texas and grew lonesome for them and his grandchildren, and went to spend his last days with them. He did not write, so she never knew exactly how many last days he had.

There were few letters from John, but she did not worry. He was a headquarters clerk and they never got shot at, he told her. "I'm still handling the mail, only now I'm getting paid a lot less for doing it." He was a corporal, then a sergeant. "If you don't hear from me," he said, "you know I'm all right."

In a way she was glad he didn't write, nor expect her to write very often. She was just too tired. She worked the graveyard shift at the shipyards—the pay was better—and she never quite got used to sleeping in the daytime with children shouting just outside the window. Once she had her picture in the shipyards' paper: a group of four women, waving to a newly completed PT boat. She clipped that out and sent it to John. She did not sew or knit or crochet any more; her hands were too stiff and heavy. Occasionally, holding a pencil awkwardly, she would sketch a child's dress. She always felt better then, when she could dream about the clothes she would make one day for other people's children, lovely things she herself had never had.

When the war was over, she got a long letter from John, the only one ever. He'd been drinking, he said, and he'd been thinking. . . . There'd been some talk about them having to go into occupation forces, but the captain said that was just stupid, maybe the unit would go, but any guy with nearly five years' service could get out if he wanted to. . . . And he wanted to. "So one of these days you'll see me come walking up to the yard and maybe I'll have one of those big FOR SALE signs on my shoulder and we'll go for a paddle in the canal. Like we used to. You remember?"

She did. It was the best game of the long rainy summers of that faraway childhood.

First the oldest and the boldest and the strongest children gathered the large wood and metal signs one particular realtor installed at his buildings. C ME FOR SALE C. BELL the signs said in red and black letters. The children stole them from walls and lawns and hid them away until heavy rains filled all the drainage ditches and canals. Then each large sign became a raft for two children, their paddles the curved fronds of the tall palm trees.

Willie May smelled the freshness of rain-cleared air and the nutty odor of her own sweat. She was aware also of the presence of another child. (Had that been John? She didn't know.) She saw her arms (long and thin and spotted with mosquito bites) and she saw the brush-burns on her knees (large dark scabs always bleeding). She was shivering with pride and excitement: the smell of drainage water, the smell of sweet decay, was the smell of freedom.

She was never afraid, though they all knew it was dangerous. Childhood sheathed her, protected her.

The children slid down the grass-spotted mud banks of open drainage ditches to launch their rafts on the slow-moving water. Buoyed by its wood frame, the sheet of tin floated a fraction of an inch above the surface. Each stroke of the paddle sent a thin sheet of water across it.

Because the city was built on perfectly flat land, it was drained after every heavy rain by huge pumps concealed in brick buildings. (Keep out of the canals, all the mothers screamed, you'll drown, they'll pick you out of the screens at the pumping station with the drowned dogs and the drunks, and the runaways from the state hospital. . . . None of the children paid attention, though they once did see a body floating. The police were already there, grappling for it.)

The grassy ditches led into wider concrete-lined canals where rusting iron pipes high over their heads dripped small streams of water. Here the surface was slack and oily, showing only the faintest pull of the distant pumps.

Soon they passed under High Street Bridge. A man named Duke, who worked in the gas station on that corner, had made himself guardian of that stretch of canal and watched it all day long. He'd rescued so many children from the water that newspapers often did stories about him. Willie May had seen pictures of him, beaming, dripping wet, holding a child in his arms. Sometimes he was too late; the children were drowned. He snagged their bodies with a long hooked pole and dragged them out. Then the newspaper picture showed him holding a small wrapped bundle.

Willie May remembered him clearly, shouting, leaning over the side of the bridge, one arm reaching down to catch them, a thick hairy arm with a hand so huge it filled the sky.

The children crouched down, swinging their palm frond paddles like bats against him. Sometimes they felt the air from his grasping arm against the backs of their necks. (If he caught you, he took your raft and sent you home.) "You'll kill yourself, you damn fool kids," he shouted. They shouted back at him in their high reedy voices, "No, no, no."

Farther down the canal there was a dark-haired woman who sat in her backyard under a medlar tree. She waved to them, silently.

Even farther along there was an old man, a very old man, who always wore a grayish bathrobe and held a glass of red liquid in his hand. He called to them, using the same words every time: "You pass on my canal, and you never stop to talk to me. Come talk to me and I will give you some cream soda." And he held up the red-filled glass and rattled the ice against its sides.

Though he was much too old and frail to chase them, they were afraid, and never looked directly at him as they passed. He might have the evil eye.

Now, listening carefully, they heard the sucking, gurgling sound of fast-moving water. They were nearing the point where their canal emptied into a still larger one, where the water was very swift and the pumps less than a mile away through a great brick-lined underground culvert.

Already ripples surged across the tin surface of their raft. They dug in their paddles, turned the raft into the side. They landed with a thump and a splash. Quickly, they scrambled up the slope and stood on the concrete parapet to watch.

The empty raft, freed of their weight, floated off. It slipped into the main canal, its prow bobbing, nodding to itself, as trickles of water splashed across its tin deck. The raft shifted from side to side, anxiously, nervously, then began spinning in circles, traveling faster and faster. Until it vanished into the darkness of the brick tunnel.

Willie May and the other child watched it disappear, their adventure half over, only the trip home left. Stretching and whistling, arms out, they pranced like acrobats along the narrow concrete edge. Tiring of that, they wandered through strange yards, teasing dogs, stealing medlars or pomegranates or figs, according to the season. At Calhoun Street, at the traffic light, they hitched rides on the backs of trucks, hunched down carefully out of the drivers' sight. If they were very lucky, they might catch an iceman's truck and find a handful of ice flakes under the dark canvas.

Among those children had been John Denham, her husband. He remembered, even if she didn't. But then she always had trouble remembering John. When he walked into her living room that November day in 1945, still in uniform, duffel bag on his shoulder, she blinked with surprise. He'd never seemed quite real to her.

He went back to work in the post office. She was pregnant three months later with a boy, their only child, named Michael.

While she waited for his birth, while her body grew thick and full and her work-stiffened hands became soft and pliable again, she began setting up her own business: children's dresses. She got out the designs that she had drawn so awkwardly during the war years, and she selected the best, carefully, lovingly. Her designs were always ornate, the colors always unusual—her clothes would be easy to recognize. A year later she sold the first of her special christening dresses, one with a cape of seed pearls to be used later in a wedding veil. For that, because she did it herself alone, there was a waiting period of five months.

"Those women are crazy enough to order that far in advance?" John said. "My God, Willie May, they've got to call you as soon as they find out they're pregnant."

"Yes," she said smugly, "they do."

"But our kid didn't have a fancy dress when he got baptized."

"I didn't have the time," she said with a smile.

She hired three women, then five, and that was all.

John said, "If you advertised, you could sell a hell of a lot more. You could have a real factory, not just five people, you could be growing."

She shook her head. "I don't want to advertise, I want the mothers and the grandmothers to hear about me. I want them to see my dresses and then want to buy them. Sure, I could hire more people right now, but I want the customers to wait. They will. The Mary Lynne Shop gave me an order yesterday, even when I told them it would be four months before delivery."

"Crazy," John said.

"No," she said, "they know my clothes are hard to get and expensive."

"And they like that?"

"Yes," she said, "that's exactly what they want."

Their son, Michael, was healthy and strong, polite in his catechism class and good in school. The three of them lived quietly, well-organized and orderly. Every Sunday after ten o'clock mass they went to John's family for midday dinner. Sunday afternoons they went for drives in their new Plymouth, stopping in the park to watch the child play. They went to a downtown movie on Saturday night and Bingo on Thursday. John went out with the boys on Friday night. Sometimes he did not come back to the house at all, but went directly to work on Saturday morning. He kept his post office uniform neatly folded in the trunk of his car.

Eventually those Friday evenings became whole weekends. Willie May scarcely noticed. She still took their son downtown on Saturday evenings to the big movie house with its curving stairs and crystal chandelier and velvet curtains. And she went to John's family for Sunday dinner, saying only, "John won't be here." His parents never asked about him.

She decided on a name for her company. Until then her dress labels carried only three gold fleurs-de-lis (she'd seen them on the banner of St. Louis King of France). Now she added *Beatrix Designs*, named for the author of Michael's favorite book, *Peter Rabbit*.

Somewhere in those years, once, John asked, "You want to take a vacation? I got all this annual leave coming to me. I got to use it or lose it."

"I don't know of any place I want to go," she said slowly.

"A couple of the boys are talking about driving over to Morrisport for some fishing. We can rent a camp there. And I might just go."

"Fine," she said.

Quicker than she thought possible, Michael was finishing high school, and John took fishing vacations several times a year. It took her a couple of days to notice that he had not returned from one of them. Only then did she discover that his clothes were gone.

Feeling oddly embarrassed, as if she were peeping into an uncurtained window, she asked his family about him. He had retired, they said; he had twenty years' service.

She supposed he still lived in town, but it did not occur to her to look for him. The boy she had played with, sailing the drainage ditches after a heavy rain, the young man who had appeared at the counter in Woolworth's, the soldier who had walked into her house—they were all different, detached, set apart by time. They were none of them connected to the balding, middle-aged husband and father.

These things, they were all of them beyond her reach. Forces changing her life, and beyond her control. Impersonal, like wind and rain. Unquestioned.

Why should she be thinking of John now . . . She had not taken a

Seconal last night and so she'd been up very early, long before day showed the other side of the drawn hospital blinds.

"Good morning, Mrs. Denham. Your son's already called to tell us that he's on his way."

"I will be glad to leave."

She let her eyes wander lazily around the room, across the pictures—soft landscapes and seascapes—the two large chairs, the flowers.

A better room to die in, she thought, than ever I was born in. But I don't die here today. Today I go home.

Whispering rubber voices of wheelchairs across polished corridor floors. Into cars. Into other corridors and other cars. Endless whispering.

Long before she boarded the plane, she was so tired she could scarcely hold her head upright.

It will be too much for me, she thought, I should not have tried. It will be too much for me. I shall die on the way. But no, I didn't drown on the raft all those years ago. I balanced and paddled and reached the end and got home safely.

Propped against the vibrating plane wall she dozed, woke to pain. Michael was there. "Here, Mother." White pills and a fuzziness that did not change the pain, only pushed it farther away. As if it were happening to somebody else. In another place, another time.

Michael said, "Mother, this is Dallas. We'll be here for a little while. Would you like a change of scene? Would you like to see the new airport?"

Look at something I will never see again? No. I have seen enough. I carry enough images inside my head to need no more. My world grows smaller, the edges peel back, an orange shedding its skin.

But who would think an hour could be so long . . . Time doesn't rush toward its end. It groans and creaks and creeps along. Like the beat and the wheeze of the heart, its clock. Each tick like a slow hammer stroke, a gong sounding to mark something or other. Whatever.

She opened her eyes and saw people in the plane as skeletons, she saw right through their flesh, saw their bones, saw their blood running through its appointed channels.

She thought: Were I ever so small, a microbe, a molecule, I would ride my raft along those red courses, I would follow those warm canals, exploring.

She floated on the warm canals, she saw the flaws in the bone, inspected them carefully: the chips and the old breaks and the dusty grit of arthritis. She noted them all, and also the swirls and the eddies and the cumbersome debris all along the warm red courses,.

Long before the plane left Dallas, she herself left the ground, flying. The air was soft, silvery birds flew so close to her that their feathers tickled her cheeks. She brushed them away.

Michael said, "Mother?"

But he was not with her, he was far away, held in the plane, and his voice was faint.

She was flying, alone, complete. She saw rushing toward her, rushing past her, everything. Leaves uncurled, people rose from their beds. Cats crouched, claws tearing fur across backs. Copulation: a jumble of arms and legs. She saw hospitals and bodies lying open and bloody until they were sewed back together missing some part or other. She saw rain falling and snow falling and flowers opening their buds like ticking clocks. She saw people brushing their teeth and people weeping in corners. She saw police dozing in squad cars. She saw bitches strain in birth and puppies born like chains of pearls. She saw suns rise and stars dance in their paths across the seasons. She saw ants and oceans and curving endless space. She saw her house, the one she had lived in all her life. She saw a leaf fallen in the gutter. And swamp water bubbling with its own gases, shivering with the swarms of life beneath.

Secure in her power and boastful of her strength, she raced the plane home. And won.

She was waiting at the airport when Michael pushed her wheelchair through the gates. She sniffed at the thin figure sagging sideways, dribble of saliva draining from the mouth, eyes half open but unseeing.

Filled with distaste, she joined them for one more, the last, passage in this trip. Another trailing hiss of rubber wheels across shiny machine-polished floors, another car, another ride.

She grew impatient with their progress and tried to lift herself from the car to float on the layers and levels of the wind. This time she could not. Her power drained, she was trapped inside the tin shell, inside her shattered body.

Michael was there and Michael would let her out. Michael would open the door as soon as they reached home. Until then the endless pale concrete highways, looping rises and the turnoffs, dark night and day all one and the same. Sun and shade. Highways like ribbons, streams of concrete.

They stopped finally and Michael opened the doors and lifted her out.

She was too tired now to rise and soar and find the wind. She would need help. In the sky there seemed to be something . . . a kite. She could ride a kite.

"Is that a kite, Michael? Over there in the sky?"

"No, Mother," he said, "there isn't anything there."

There were other people, but she did not bother noticing them. She stayed hidden behind her eyelids, thinking about all the roads she had traveled that day, the twists and turns that had brought her home. And this was her house, she knew it by its smell. She was home. She smiled to herself, ignoring the distant voices. Was that Michael calling? Well, she would not answer.

She discovered that she was floating, lightly, delicately, on water flickering and iridescent with oil film. Was somebody with her? John? But John was dead years ago. She was alone. Her body was small and light and when she dabbled her fingers in the water, her hand was a sunburned child's hand. The day was sunny and there was a very slight breeze. In the sky there were fluffy white clouds that people called bishops, they were so fat and smug and self-important looking. The water flowed swiftly, carrying her past familiar trees: fig and medlar branches drooping with out-of-season fruit. The bridge now, the High Street Bridge. There was no one on it today, no hand stretched down to bring children home safe from danger. The water made little cooing, coaxing sounds. . . . past the spot where the old man sat, the old man who offered them cream soda to stop and talk to him. No one tempted her today. The raft was moving very fast now, streams of water like banners on each side.

Here was the end of the familiar journey, here was where they always paddled to the side and scrambled away home. But now she had no paddle. And the current was swifter than she ever remembered. No stopping. The raft moved lightly, steadily, floating like a leaf, turning gently, seeming to know its way.

She had never been here, where the water was wide and the sun sparkled on tiny surface waves. She had never dared come this far before and she was astonished at how easy it was, how smooth and how silent.

The raft began to spin in circles, the sun and the clouds flickered across the sky. On both sides was the cream color of hospital walls, and there was nothing to see on them, only rising emptiness.

Then, as she knew she must, she saw the tunnel ahead. Just as she had seen it from the banks of childhood. She looked at it wonderingly, unsurprised. It waited. The raft sailed directly into it, into the dark.

Toni Cade Bambara

A Tender Man

The girl was sitting in the booth, one leg wrapped around the other cartoon-like. Knee socks drooping, panties peeping from her handbag, ears straining from her head for the soft crepe footfalls, straining less Aisha silent and sudden catch her unawares with the dirty news.

She hadn't caught Cliff's attention. His eyes were simply at rest in that direction. And nothing better to do, he had designed a drama of her. His eyes resting on that booth, on that swivel chair, waiting for Aisha to return and fill it. When the chatty woman in the raincoat had been sitting where the nervous girl sat now, Aisha had flashed him a five-minute sign. That was fifteen minutes ago.

He hadn't known he'd mind the waiting. But he'd been feeling preoccupied of late, off-center, anxious even. Thought he could shrug it off, whatever it was. But sitting on the narrow folding chair waiting, nothing to arrest his attention and focus him, he felt crowded by something too heavy to shrug off. He decided he was simply nervous about the impending student takeover.

He flipped through a tattered *Ebony*, pausing at pictures of children, mothers and children, couples and children, grandparents and children. But no father and child. It was a conspiracy, he chuckled to himself, to keep fathers—he searched for a word—outside. He flipped through the eligible bachelors of the year, halting for a long time at the photo of Carl Davis, his ole army mate who'd nearly deserted in the spring of '61. He was now with RCA making $20,000 a year. Cliff wondered doing what.

The girl was picking her face, now close to panic. In a moment she would bolt for the door. He could imagine heads lifting, swiveling, perfect strangers providing each other with hairy explanations. He could hear the women tsk-tsking, certain that their daughters would never. Aisha came through the swinging doors and he relaxed, not realizing till that moment how far he had slipped into the girl's drama. Aisha shot three fingers in his direction and he nodded. The girl was curled up tight now, Cliff felt her tension, staring at the glass slide Aisha slid onto the table. She leaned over the manila folder Aisha opened, hand screening the side of her face as though to block the people out. She was crying. The sobbing audible, though muffled now that the screening hand was doubled up in her mouth. Cliff was uncomfortable amongst so many women and this young one crying. Cliff got up to look for the water fountain.

Up and down the corridors folks walked distractedly, clutching slips of colored papers. A few looked terror-struck, like models for the covers of the books he often found his students buried in. Glancing at the slips of green or white, checking them against the signs on the doors, each had a particular style with the entrance, he noted. Knocking timidly, shivering, Judgment Day. Turning knobs stealthily and looking about, second-story types. Brisk entrances with caps yanked low, yawl deal with me, shit. Cliff moved in and out among the paper-slip clutchers, doorway handlers, teen-agers pulling younger brothers and sisters along, older folk pausing to read the posters. The walls were lined with posters urging VD tests, Pap smears, examinations painless and confidential. In less strident Technicolor, others argued the joys of planned parenthood.

Cliff approached the information desk, for the sister on the switchboard seemed to be wearing two wigs at once and he had to see that. The guard leaned way back before considering his question about the water fountain, stepped away from a woman leaning over the desk inquiring after a clinic, gave wide berth to all the folk who entered and headed in that direction, then pointed out the water fountain, backed up against the desk in a dramatic recoil. Cliff smiled at first and considered fucking with the dude, touching him, maybe drooling a bit on his uniform. But he moved off, feeling unclean.

At the water fountain a young father hoisted his daughter too far into the spout. Cliff held the button down and the brother smiled relief, a two-handed grip centering now the little girl, who gurgled and horsed around in the water, then held a jaw full even after she was put down on the floor again.

"This place is a bitch, ain't it?" The brother nodding vigorous agreement to his own remark.

"My wife's visiting her folks and I'm about to lose my mind with these kids." He smiled proudly, though, jutting his chin in the direction of the rest of his family. Two husky boys around eight and ten were doing base slides in the upper corridor.

"Man, if I had the clap, I sure as hell wouldn't come here for no treatments." His frown made Cliff look around. In that moment the lights seem to dim, the paint job age, the posters slump. A young girl played hopscotch in the litter, her mother pushing her along impatiently.

Yeh, a bitch, Cliff had meant to say, but all that came out was a wheezy mumble.

"My ole lady says to me 'go to the clinic and pick up my pills.' Even calls me long distance to remind me she's running out. 'Don't forget to get the pills, B.J.' So I come to get the damn pills, right?" He ran his hand through his bush, gripping a fistful and tossing his head back and forth. "Man oh man," he groaned, shaking his head by the hair. The gesture had started out as a simple self-caress, had moved swiftly into an I-don't-believe-this-shit nod, and before Cliff knew it, the brother'd become some precinct victim, his head bam-bam against the walls. "Man oh man, this crazy-ass place! Can't even get a word in for the 'What's your clinic number?' 'Where's your card?' 'Have you seen the cashier?' 'Have you got insurance?' 'Are you on the welfare?' 'Do you have a yellow slip?' 'Where's your card?' 'Who's ya mama?' Phwweeoo! I'm goin straight to the drugstore and get me a crate of rubbers right on. I ain't putting my woman through this shit."

"Daddy." The little girl was yanking on his pants leg for attention. When she got it, she made a big X in the air.

"Oh, right. I forgot. Sorry, baby." He turned to Cliff and shrugged in mock sheepishness. "Gotta watch ya mouth round these kids these days, they get on ya. Stay on my case bout the smoking, can't even bring a poke chop in the house, gotta sneak a can of beer and step

out on the fire escape to smoke the dope. Man, these kids sompthin!"
He was starting that vigorous nodding again, watching his sons approach. Cliff couldn't keep his eyes off the brother's bobbing head. It
reminded him of Granddaddy Mobley so long ago, playing horsy,
whinnying down the hallway of Miss Hazel's boardinghouse, that head
going a mile a minute and his sister Alma riding high, whipping her
horse around the head and shoulders and laughing so hard Miss Hazel
threatened to put them out.

"Yeh," he was sighing, nudging Cliff lest he miss the chance to dig
on the two young dudes coming, punching invisible catcher's mitts,
diddyboppin like their daddy must've done it years before. "Later for
them pills, anyway. It's back to good ole reliable Trojans."

"Pills dangerous," Cliff said.

"Man, just living is a danger. And every day. Every day, man."

"We going to the poolroom now?" the older boy was asking,
nodding first to Cliff.

"I want some Chinese food." The younger seemed to be addressing
this to Cliff, shifting his gaze to his father long after he'd finished
speaking.

"Hold it, youngbloods. Hold on a damn minute. I gotta catch me
some sleep and get to work in a coupla hours. Yawl bout to wear my ass
out."

"Daddy."

"Oh damn, I'm sorry. Sorry." The brother made two huge X's in
the air and dropped his head shamefaced till his daughter laughed.

"Man, you got kids?"

"Yeah" was all Cliff said, not sure what else he could offer. It had
been pleasant up to then, the brother easy to be easy with. But now he
seemed to be waiting for Cliff to share what Cliff wasn't sure he had to
share. He bent to take a drink. "Daughter," he offered, trying to
calculate her age. He'd always used the Bay of Pigs invasion as a guide.

"They sompthin, ain't they?" the brother broke in, his children
dragging him off to the door. "Take it slow, my man."

Cliff nodded and bent for another drink. Bay of Pigs was the
spring of '61. His daughter had been born that summer. He bit his lip.
Hell, how many fathers could just tick off the ages of their children,
right off the bat? Not many. But then if the brother had put the

question to him, as Aisha had the day before—What sort of person is your daughter?—Cliff would not have known how to answer. He let the water bubble up against closed lips for a while, not sure what that fact said about the man he was, or at least had thought he was, hoped he was, had planned to be for so long, was convinced when still a boy he could be once he got out of that house of worrisome women.

Aisha had come quietly up behind him and linked arms. "Hey, mister," she cooed, "how bout taking a po' colored gal to dinner." She pulled him away from the water fountain. "I'm starving."

Starving. Cliff looked at her quickly, but she did not react. Starving. He stared at her, but she was checking the buttons on her blouse, then stepping back for him to catch the door. She moved out swiftly and down the stairs ahead of him, not so much eager to get away, for she'd said how much she liked her job at the clinic. But eager to be done with it for the day and be with him. She waited at the foot of the stairs and linked arms again.

Cliff smiled. He dug her. Had known her less than a week, but felt he knew her. A chick who dealt straight up. No funny changes to go through. He liked the way she made it clear that she dug him.

"Whatcha grinnin about?" she asked, adjusting her pace to his. She was a brisk walker—he had remarked on it the day before—Northern urban brisk. I bet you like to lead too when you dance, he had teased her.

"Thinking about the first time I called you," he said.

"Oh? Oh." She nodded and was done, as though in that split second she had retrieved the tape from storage, played it, analyzed his version of what went down, and knew exactly what he had grinned about and that was that. He had kidded her about that habit too. "You mean the way I push for clarity, honesty?"

That was what he had meant, but he didn't like the cocky way she said it with the phony question mark on the end. She was a chick who'd been told she was too hard, too sure, too swift, and had made adjustments here and there, softening the edges. He wasn't sure that was honest of her, though he'd never liked women with hard edges.

"No," he half-lied. "Your sensitivity. I like the way you said, after turning me down for a drink, 'Hey, Brother—' "

"I called you Cliff. I'm not interested in being your sister."

He hugged her arm. "Okay, 'Hey, Cliff,' you said, 'I ain't rejecting you, but I don't drink, plus I got to get up at the crack of dawn tomorrow to prepare for a workshop. How about dinner instead?' "

"And that tickles you?"

"It refreshes me," he said, laughing, feeling good. It wasn't so easy being a dude, always putting yourself out there to be rejected. He'd never much cared for aggressive women; on the other hand, he appreciated those who met him halfway. He slowed her down some more. "Hey, city girl," he drawled. "This here a country boy you walkin wid, ain't used to shoes yet. The restaurant'll be there. Don't close till late."

"I'm starving, fool. Come on and feed me. You can take off them shoes. I'll carry em."

He hugged her arm again and picked up his pace. It was silly, he told himself, these endless control games he liked to play with assertive types. He was feeling too good. But then he wasn't. Starving. She had raised that question: Can you swear no child of yours is starving to death? Not confronting him or even asking him, softening the edges, but addressing the workshop, reading off a list of questions that might get the discussion started. The brother next to him had slapped his knees with his cap and muttered, "Here we go again with some women lib shit." But a sister across the aisle had been more vocal, jumping up to say, "Run it down to the brothers. Let's just put them other questions on hold and stay with this one a while," she demanded. "Yeah, can you swear?" Her hot eyes sweeping the room. "Can you deal with that, you men in here? Can you deal with that one?"

The discussion got sidetracked, it'd seemed to Cliff at the time. Everybody talking at once, all up in each other's face. Paternity, birth control, genocide, responsibility, fathering, mothering, children, child support, warrants, the courts, prison. One brother had maintained with much heat that half the bloods behind the walls were put there by some vengeful bitch. Warriors for the revolution wasting away in the joint for nonsupport or some other domestic bullshit. "Well, that should point something out!" a sister in the rear had yelled, trying to be heard over a bunch of brothers who stood up to say big-mouth sisters like herself were responsible for Black misery.

Starving. Cliff had spaced on much of the discussion, thinking about his daughter Rhea. Going over in his mind what he might have said had he been there to hear Donna murmur, "Hey, Cliff, I think I missed my period." But he had been in the army. And later when the pregnancy was a certainty, he was in Norfolk, Virginia, on his way overseas, he thought. And all the way out of port he lay in his bunk, Donna's letter under his head, crinkly in the pillowcase, gassing with Carl Davis about that ever-breathtaking announcement that could wreck a perfectly fine relationship—Hey, baby, I think I'm pregnant.

He had not quite kept track of the workshop debate the night before, for he was thinking about parenthood, thinking too of his own parents, his mother ever on the move to someplace else his father'd been rumored to be but never was, dragging him and his little sister Alma all over the South till the relatives in Charlotte said whoa, sister, park em here. And he had grown up in a household of women only, women always. Crowded, fussed over, intruded upon, continually compared to and warned not to turn out like the dirty dog who'd abandoned Aunt Mavis or that no-good nigger who'd done Cousin Dorcas dirty or some other low-down bastard that didn't mean no woman no good.

"You're unusually preoccupied, Cliff," Aisha was saying gently, as if reluctant to intrude, but hesitant about leaving him alone to wrassle with the pain he was sure was readable in his face. "Not that I know you well enough to know what's usual." He followed her gaze toward the park. "You feel like walking a while? Talking? Or maybe just being quiet?"

"Thought you were starving?" He heard an edge to his voice, but she didn't seem to notice.

"I am. I am." She waited at the curb, ready to cross over to the park or straight ahead to the Indian restaurant. Cliff disengaged his arm and fished out a cigarette, letting the light change. Had he been alone, he would have crossed over to the park. He had put off taking inventory for too long, his life was in a drift, unmonitored. Just that morning shaving, trying to fix in his mind what role he'd been called on to play in the impending student takeover, he'd scanned the calendar over the sink. The student demands would hit the campus paper on the anniversary of the Bay of Pigs.

He'd made certain promises that day, that spring day in '61 when the boat shipped out for Vietnam they'd thought, but headed directly for the Caribbean. He'd made certain promises about what his life would be like in five years, ten years, ever after if he lived. Had made certain promises to himself, to the unborn child, to God, he couldn't remember to whom, as the ship of Puerto Ricans, Chicanos and Bloods were cold-bloodedly transported without their knowing from Norfolk to Cuba to kill for all the wrong reasons. Then the knowledge of where they were and what they were expected to do, reminded of the penalty for disobeying orders, he'd made promises through clenched teeth, not that he was any clearer about the Cuban Revolution than he was about the Vietnamese struggle, but he knew enough about Afro-Cuban music to make some connections and conclude that the secret mission was low-down. Knew too that if they died, no one at home'd be told the truth. Missing in action overseas. Taken by the Vietcong. Killed in Nam in the service of God and country.

"Worries?" Aisha asked, "or just reminiscing?"

He put his arm around her shoulders and hugged her close. His life was not at all the way he'd promised. "I was just thinking," he said slowly, crossing them toward the restaurant, "about the first time I came North as a kid." He wasn't sure that was a lie. The early days came crowding in on him every time he thought of his daughter and the future. And his daughter filled his mind on every mention of starving.

He hadn't even known as a boy that he was or for what, till that Sunday his aunts had hustled him and Alma to the train depot. But Granddaddy Mobley didn't even get off the train when it slowed. Just leaned down and hauled them up by the wrists, first Alma, then him.

"Hop aboard, son," he'd said, bouncing the cigar to the back of his jaw. "This what you call a rescue job."

Son. He had been sugar dumpling, sweetie pie, honey darling for so long, as though the horror of Southern living in general, the bitterness of being in particular some poor fatherless child could be sweetened with a sugar tit, and if large enough could fill him up, fill those drafty places somewhere inside. So long hugged and honey-bunched, he didn't know he was starving or for what till "son" was offered him and the grip on his wrist became a handshake man to man.

Dumfounded, the women were trotting along after the still-moving train, Cousin Dorcas calling his name, Aunt Evelyn calling Granddaddy Mobley a bunch of names.

"Train, iz you crazy?!" Aunt Mavis had demanded when she

realized that was all the train intended to do, slow up for hopping off or kidnapping. "Have you lost your mind?" Cliff could never figure to whom this last remark was said. But he remembered he laughed like hell.

Granddaddy Mobley chuckled too, watching Cousin Dorcas through the gritty windows, trotting along the landing, shaking her fist, dodging the puffs of steam and the chunks of gravel thrown up by the wheels, the ribbons of her hat flying in and out of her shouting mouth.

Leaning out of an open window over his sister's head, Cliff could make out the women on the landing getting smaller, staring pop-eyed and pop-mouthed too. And when he glanced down, li'l Alma was looking straight up into his face the way she did from the bunk beds when the sun came up, the look asking was everything okay and could the day begin. He grinned back out the window, and grinned too at his sister cause yeah, everything would be all right. He couldn't blame the women, though, for carrying on like that, having taken all morning to get the chicken fried and the rugs swept and the sheets boiled and dough beat up. Then come to find old Mobley, highstepping, fun-loving, outrageous, drinking, rambler, gambler and everything else necessary to thoroughly scandalize the family name, upset the household with his annual visits, giving them something to talk about as the lamps glowed at night till next visiting time, ole Mobley wasn't even thinking about a visit at all this time. Wasn't even stopping long enough to say hello to his daughter, not that she was there. Just came to snatch the darling little girl and the once perfect little gentleman now grown rusty and hardheaded just like his daddy for the world.

"We going North with you?" Alma had asked, not believing she could go anywhere without her flouncy dresses, her ribbons, and their mother's silver hairbrush from the world's fair.

"That's right."

"We going to live with you?" young Cliff had pressed, eager to get things straight. "To live with you till we grown or just for summer or what?"

Instead of answering, the old man whipped out a wad of large, white handkerchiefs and began to unfold them with very large gestures. The children settled in their seats waiting for the magic show to commence. But the old man just spread them out on the seats, three for sitting on and one for his hat. Cliff and Alma exchanged a look, lost for words. And in that moment, the old man leaned forward, snatched Alma's little yellow-haired doll and pitched it out the window.

"And you'd better not cry," he said.

"No, ma'am."

Cliff laughed and the old man frowned. "Unless you in training to take care of white folks' babies when you grown."

"No, ma'am."

Cliff had smiled smugly, certain that Alma had no idea what this rescue man was saying. He did. And he looked forward to growing up with a man like this. Alma slid her small hand into his and Cliff squeezed it. And not once did she look back after her doll, or he at the town.

"I met your wife in the bus terminal—"

"Ex-wife," Cliff said, jolted out of his reverie.

Aisha poured the tea. "Ex-wife. Met her last Monday and—"

"You told me."

"I didn't tell you the whole thing."

Cliff looked up from his plate of meat patties. He wasn't sure he wanted to hear about it. Every time he had tried to think of his daughter, he discovered he couldn't detach her from the woman he'd married. Thinking about Donna made him mad. Thinking about his daughter Rhea just made him breathless. Rising, he jingled change in his pocket and stalled for time at the jukebox. That was the first thing Aisha had said to him when they were introduced just four days ago on campus. "Hemphill? I think I know your wife, Donna Hemphill. Ran into her at the bus terminal less than an hour ago."

After his own class of the day and a quick meeting with the Black student union, he'd sought her out in the faculty dining room, convinced that his chairman would at least give her the semi-deluxe treatment, particularly considering his taste for black meat (or so the rumor went, though he rarely did more toward orienting new faculty members than pointing out their cubicle, shoving a faculty handbook at them, and warning them about the "Mau Mau," his not-so-affectionate name for the Black student union). She had pursued the topic the minute Cliff had seated himself next to her, remarking quietly that his wife had seemed on the verge of collapse. He welcomed the mention of Donna only for the opportunity it offered to point out that one, she was very much an ex, two he was single, three he found her, Aisha, attractive. Beyond that, he could care less about Donna or her mental state. Aisha had remarked then—too sarcastically for his taste—that this very ex-wife with the mental state was the woman who was raising his daughter. He had eaten the dry roast beef sullenly, grateful for the appearance of his colleague Robinson, who swung the conversation toward the students and the massive coronaries they were causing in administrative circles.

Some Indian movie music blared out at Cliff's back as he picked out one of the umpteen rhythms to stroll back to the table doing, slapping out the beat on his thigh.

"I didn't say this before"—Aisha was reaching for the drumming hand—"cause you cut me short last Tuesday. I'm sorry I didn't press it then on campus, cause it's harder now . . . that I know you . . . and all."

"Then forget it."

She slid her hand back to her side of the table and busied herself with the meat patties. He drummed on the table with both hands, trying to read her mood. He felt he owed her some explanation, wanted even to talk this thing out, his feelings about his daughter. Then resented Aisha for that. He drummed away. The last thing he would have wanted for this evening, the first time they'd been together with no other appointments to cut into their time, the last thing he wanted, feeling already a little off-center, crowded, was a return to that part of his history that seemed so other, over with, some dim drama starring a Cliff long since discarded. Cliff the soldier, Cliff the young father, Cliff the sociology instructor—there was clarity if not continuity. But Cliff the husband . . . blank.

He had pronounced the marriage null and void in the spring of '61. On the troop ship speeding to who knew where, or at least none of the dudes in that battalion knew yet, but to die most probably. He'd read the letter over and over, and was convinced Donna was lying about being pregnant and so far advanced. He was due home for good soon, and this was her way to have him postpone thinking of a split. He and Carl Davis had gassed the whole time out of port about what they were going to do with their lives if they still had them in five months' time. Then some of the soldiers were saying the fleet was in the Caribbean. And all hell broke loose, the men mistakenly assuming—assuming, then readying up for shore leave in Trinidad. The CO told them different, though not much. First there was a sheaf of papers that had to be signed, or court-martial, papers saying they never would divulge to press, to family, to friends, even to each other, anything at all regarding the secret mission they were about to embark upon. Then they got their duties. Most work detail the same—painting over the ship's numbers, masking all U.S. identification, readying up the equipment for the gunners, checking their packs and getting new issues of ammunition.

"We're headed for Cuba," Carl Davis had said.

"That's crazy. The action's in Vietnam."

"Mate, I'm telling you, we're off to Cuba. T. J. was upside and got the word. The first invasionary battalions are Cuban exiles. They'll hook up with the forces there on the island to overthrow Fidel Castro."

"You got to be kidding."

Carl had sneered at Cliff's naïveté. "Mate, they got air coverage that'd made the Luftwaffe look silly. We rendezvous with a carrier and a whole fleet of marines moving in from Nicaragua. I'm telling you, this is it."

T. J. had skidded down the stair rail and whispered. "They got Kennedy on a direct line. Kennedy! Jim, this operation is being directed from the top."

"Holy shit." Cliff had collapsed on his bunk, back pack and all, the letter crumpling under his ear. A child was being born soon, the letter said. He was going to be a father. And if he died, what would happen to his child? His marriage had been in shreds before he'd left, a mere patchwork job on the last leave, and she'd been talking of going back home. His child. Her parents. That world. Those people.

"I never knew Donna well," Aisha was saying. "We worked at Family Services and I used to see her around, jazz concerts, the clubs. I pretty much wrote her off as a type. One of those gray girls who liked to follow behind Black musicians, hang out and act funky."

Cliff looked at Aisha quickly. Was she the type to go for blood? He'd had enough of the white girl–brother thing. Had been sick of it all, of hearing, of reading about it, of arguing, of defending himself, even back then on the tail end of the Bohemian era, much less in the Black and Proud times since.

"Use to run into her a lot when I lived downtown. The baby didn't surprise me—hell, half of Chelsea traffic was white girls pushing mulatto babies in strollers. We used to chat. You two seemed to be always on the verge of breakup, and she was forever going down in flames. I got the impression the baby was something of . . . a hostage?" She seemed to wait for his response. He blanked his face out. "A hostage," she continued, seeming to relish the word, "as per usual."

The waiter slid a dish of chutney at Cliff's elbow, then leaned in to replace the teapot with a larger, steamier one. Cliff leaned back as the plates and bowls were taken from the tray in some definite, mysterious order and placed just so on the table. Cliff rearranged the plate of roti and the cabbage. The waiter looked at him and placed them in their original spots. Cliff sneaked a look at Aisha and they shared a stone-faced grin.

"Cliff?" She seemed to call to him, the him behind his poker face. He leaned forward. Whatever she had to say, it'd be over with soon and they could get on with the Friday evening he had in mind.

"I asked Donna on Tuesday to give up the child. To give your daughter to me. I'm prepared to raise—"

Cliff stared, not sure he heard that right.

"Look. She's standing in the bus terminal having a crying jag, listing fifty-leven different brands of humiliations and bump-offs from the Black community. She's been trying to enroll your daughter in an independent Black school, at a Yoruba cultural center, at the Bedford-Stuyvesant—"

"Bedford-Stuyvesant?"

"Yeah, your wife lives in Brooklyn."

"Ex-wife."

Aisha spread her napkin and asked very pointedly, "You were not aware that your daughter's been living in Brooklyn for two years?" Cliff tried to remember the last address he had sent money to, recalled he had always given it to Alma. But then Alma had moved to the coast last spring . . .

"Hey, look, Cliff, I've noticed the way you keep leaning on this 'ex' business. I'm sure you're sick to death of people jumping on you, especially sisters, about the white-woman thing. Quite frankly I don't give a shit who you married or who you are . . . not now . . . I only thought I did," she said, spacing her words out in a deliberate challenge. "What does interest me is the kid. I'll tell you just what I told her, I'm prepared to take the girl—"

"Hold it. Hold it." Cliff shoved his plate away and tried to sort out what he was hearing. If only he could have a tape of this, he was thinking, to play at his leisure, not have to respond or be read. "Back up, you're moving too fast for me. I'm just a country boy." He smiled, not surprised that she did smile back. She looked tired.

"Okay. She's been trying to move your daughter into cultural activities and whatnot. Very concerned about the kid's racial identity. For years she's always been asking me to suggest places to take her and how to handle things and so forth. So I'm standing in the bus terminal while this white woman falls apart on me, asking to be forgiven her incompetence, her racism, her hysteria. And I'm pissed. So I ask her—"

"Where's the nigger daddy who should be taking the weight."

Aisha studied her fork and resumed eating. Cliff clenched his jaws. She was eating now as though she'd been concentrating on that chicken curry for hours, had not even spoken, did not even know he was there. Was that the point of it all, to trigger that outburst? And it had been an outburst, his face was still burning. Was she out for blood? It was a drag. Cliff reached for the chutney and sensed her tense up. She looked coiled on her side of the table, mouth full of poisonous fangs. She was a type, he decided, a type he didn't like. She had seemed a groovy woman, but she was just another bitch. She had looked good to him less than half an hour ago, bouncing around in the white space shoes. Had looked good in that slippery white uniform wrinkling at her hips. And all he thought he wanted to do was take her to his place and tell her so, show her. He thought he still might like to take her home to make love to her—no, to fuck her. The atmosphere kept changing, the tone, the whole quality of his feelings for her kept shifting. She kept him off balance. Yeh, he'd like to fuck her, but not cause she looked good. Cliff tore off a piece of roti, then decided he didn't want it. Looked at her and decided he was being absurd. What had she said she was pissed about? Donna, an unhinged white woman raising a Black child. Why had he been so defensive?

"This was a bad time to meet," he heard himself saying. "I wish he had met at some other time when—"

"Look, sugar," she spat out with a malice that didn't match the words, "no matter when or where or how we met, the father question would've come up. And I'd have had to judge what kind of man you are behind your whole sense of what it means to bring a child into the world. I'm funny that way, mister."

"What I was thinking was," he pressed on, shoving aside the anger brewing, clamping down hard on the urge to bust her in the jaw, not sure the urge to hold her close wasn't just as strong, "in a year or so you might have met me with my daughter. I've been considering for a long time fighting for custody of Rhea."

"How long?"

"Off and on for years. But here lately, last few weeks . . ." It occurred to him that that was exactly what he'd been trying to pull together in his mind, a plan. That was what had been crowding him.

"Donna said she'd talk to you about it, Cliff, then get back to me. It was a serious proposal I was making."

"She hasn't called me. Matter of fact, we haven't talked in years."

"Uh-hunh." She delivered this with the jauntiness of a gum-cracking sister from Lenox Avenue. Cliff read on her face total disbelief of all he'd said, as though he couldn't have been really considering it and not talk with the child's mother. He was pissed off. How did it get to be her business, any of it?

"Anyway, Brother," she said, shifting into still another tone, "I'm prepared to take the child. I've got this job at the clinic, it'll hold me till summer when the teaching thing comes through. My aunt runs a school up on Edgecombe. She's not the most progressive sister in the world, but the curriculum's strong academically. And there're several couples on my block who get together and take the kids around. I'm good with children. Raised my nephews and my sisters. I'd do right by the little girl, Cliff. What do you want to ask me?"

Her voice had faded away to a whisper. She sipped her tea now, and for a minute he thought she was about to cry. He wasn't sure for what, but felt he was being unjustly blamed for something. She hadn't believed him. That made him feel unsure about himself. He watched her, drifting in and out among the fragments of sensations, questions that wouldn't stay formed long enough for him to get a hold of. He studied her until his food got cold.

She wasn't going to sleep with him, that was clear. He knew from past experiences that the moment had passed, that moment when women resolved the tension by deciding yes they would, then relaxed one way, or no they wouldn't, and eased into another rhythm. Often at the critical point, especially with younger women, he'd step into their timing and with one remark or a caress of the neck could turn the moment in his favor. He hadn't even considered it with Aisha. There had seemed time enough to move leisurely, no rush. They'd had dinner that first night, then he'd had a Black faculty meeting. He'd picked her up last night to get to the workshop, and after they'd had coffee with Acoli and Essa and talked way into the night about the students' demands. He hadn't even considered that this evening, which just a half-hour ago seemed stretched out so casual and unrushed, would turn out as anything but right.

Hell, they weren't children. They had established right from the jump that this would be a relationship, a relationship of meaning. And he'd looked forward to it, had even thought of calling Alma long distance and working Aisha somehow into the conversation. He knew it would please his sister, for he knew well how it pained her whenever he launched into his dissertation on Black women, the bitterness for those Black women who had raised him surfacing always, and for the others so much like them—though Alma argued it wasn't so—who'd stepped into his life with such explosions, leaving ashes in their wake. And Alma argued that wasn't so either, just his own blindness contracted from poisons he should have pumped out somehow long ago cause they weren't reasonably come by either. He was sick of his dissertation, the arguing, the venom, even thinking about it.

"You can imagine, Cliff . . . well, the irony of it all, meeting you right after seeing Donna after all these years of running into her, hearing about you . . . Look, it's very complicated—my feelings about . . . the whole thing."

"How so?" He poured the last of the hot tea into her cup and waited. She seemed to study the cup for a long time as though considering whether to reject it, wait for it to cool, drink it, or maybe fling it in his face. He couldn't imagine why that last seemed such a possibility.

His sister Alma would have argued that he simply expected the worst always and usually got it, provoked it.

"On the one hand, I'm very attracted to you, Cliff. You care about the students. I mean . . . well, you have a reputation on campus for being—" She was blushing and that surprised the hell out of him. He decided he didn't know women at all. They were too weird, all of them. "Well, for being one of the good guys. Plus you so sharp, ya know, and a great sense of humor. Not to mention you fine." She was looking suddenly girlish. He wanted to laugh, but he didn't want to interrupt her. He was liking this. "And I dig being with you. You're comfortable, even when you're drifting off, you're comfortable to be with." He bowed in his seat. They were smiling again.

"On the other hand"—she cocked her head to signal she hoped to get through this part with the same chumminess—"well . . ." She drank the tea now, two fingers pressed on each side of the Oriental cup, her face moving into the steam, lips pursing to blow. If they ever got around to the pillow talk, he'd ask her about her gesture and whether or not it had been designed to get him. He found all this blowing and sipping very arousing, for no reason he could think of.

"On the other hand," she said again, "while you seem to be a principled person . . . I mean, clearly you're not a bastard or a coward . . . not handling the shit on campus like you been doing . . . but—" She put the cup down.

"Hey look. It's like this, Cliff. I don't understand brothers who marry white girls, I really don't. And I really don't see how you can just walk away from the kid, let your child just . . . Well, damn, what is your daughter, a souvenir?" It was clear to Cliff that his reaction was undisguised and that she was having no trouble reading his face. "Perhaps"—she was looking hopeful now, his cue to rise to the occasion—"perhaps you really have been trying to figure out how to do it, how to get custody?"

"I considered it long before we even broke up. When I first heard that the child was an actual fact, was about to be born, I was in the army. As a matter of fact, I was up to my neck in the Bay of Pigs shit." He had never discussed it before, was amazed he could do it now, could relate it all in five or six quick sentences, when times earlier he hadn't even been able to pull it together coherently in a whole night, staring at the ceiling, wondering how many brothers had been rerouted to the

Philippines to put down the resistance to Marcos and the corporate bosses, how many to Ethiopia to vamp on the Eritrean Front, and how many would wind up in southern Africa all too soon, thinking they were going who knew where. How many more caught in the trick bag of colored on colored death if all who knew remained silent on the score, chumps afraid of change?

Cliff had always maintained he despised people who saw and heard but would not move on what they knew. His colleagues who could wax lyric analyzing the hidden agenda of SEEK and other OEO circuses engineered to fail, but did nothing about it. Bloods in his department grooming the students for caretaker positions, all the while screaming on the system, the oppression, hawking revolution, but carefully cultivating caretakers to negotiate a separate peace for a separate piece of the corrupt pie, claiming the next generation would surely do it. And even Cousin Dorcas and Aunt Mavis years before, going through a pan of biscuits and a pot of coffee laying out with crystal clarity the madness of his mother's life, chronically on hold till she could just get to that one more place to find the man never where folks said he'd be. But never once wrassling the woman, their sister, their kin, to the floor, demanding she at least put the children on her agenda, if not herself. And Cliff himself, heroic in spots, impotent in others, he had postponed for too long an inventory of his self, his life.

"The Cuban people were ready. They kicked our ass. That first landing troop ran smack into an alligator farm in Playa Girón and got wiped out. The second got wasted fore they even got off the beach. And all the while our ship was getting hit. Cannonballs sailing right between the smoke stacks of the ship. And Kennedy on the line saying, 'Pull back,' realizing them balls were a warning, a reminder of what could happen in the world if the U.S. persisted."

Aisha poured him a glass of ginger beer and waited for him to continue. Cliff felt opened up like he hadn't been in years.

"The idea that I might be killed, that my wife Donna would move back to her parents, my child growing up in an all-white environment . . . I use to run the my-wife-is-an-individual-white-person number . . . I dunno . . . it all scared the shit out of me," he was saying, not able to find the bridge, the connection, the transition from those thoughts, those promises made in Cuban waters and what in fact he lived out later and called his life.

"When we broke up, I turned my back, I guess," he said, finding his place again, but not the bridge. "I use to see my daughter a lot when my sister Alma lived in the city. And if I could just figure out how to manage it all, have time for my work and—"

"Your work?" she said, clutching the tablecloth. "Your work?" she sneered. "You one of those dudes who thinks his 'real' work is always outside of—separate from—oh, shit."

He felt her withdraw. He would make an effort to draw her out again, even if she came out blazing in a hot tirade about "women's work" and "men's work" and "what a load of horseshit." He would do it for himself. Later for the them that might have been.

"We were discussing all this recently in class—'The Black Family in the Twentieth Century,' my new course."

"Yeah, I know," she said.

"You know?"

"My niece is in your class. She tapes your lectures. Big fan of yours, my niece."

"Oh." Cliff couldn't remember now just what he had wanted to say, had lost the thread. Aisha had motioned the waiter over and was scanning the dessert list. He shook his head. Dessert was not what he wanted at this point.

He had handed back the students' research papers on their own families when the vet who sat in the back got up to say how odd it was that their generation, meaning the sophomores or juniors, despite the persistent tradition in their own families of folks raising children not their own, odd that this younger generation felt exempt. How many here, someone in the front of the room had asked then, can see themselves adopting children or taking in a kid from the streets, or from a strung-out neighbor, as their own? Cliff had expected a split down the middle, the brothers opting for pure lineage, the sisters charging ego and making a case for "the children" rather than "my child." But it didn't go down that way. The discussion never got off the ground. And after class, the vet had criticized Cliff for short-circuiting the discussion. Cliff hadn't seen his point then. But now, watching Aisha coax the recipe for some dessert or other from the waiter, he could admit that he had probably spaced.

Naturally he'd been thinking of his daughter Rhea, wondering how many others in the class had children and whether it would be fruitful to ask that first. The problem was, he could never think of Rhea without also thinking of Donna. Even after he refused to visit the child on his wife's turf, preferring the serenity of Alma's home for the visits, Rhea was still daughter to the woman who'd been his wife. And he was outside.

He'd been so proud when as a baby she had learned to say "Daddy" first. That had knocked him out. His sister had offered some psycholinguistic-somethinorother explanation, completely unsolicited and halfway unheard, about a baby's physical capacity to produce *d* sounds long before *m* sounds. Cliff paid Alma no mind.

But as the baby grew more independent, more exploratory of the world beyond her skin, he realized why she could say "Daddy" so much sooner. Cause Mommy was not separate, Mommy was part of the baby's world, attached to her own ego. He was distinctly different. Outside. It was some time before Mommy was seen as other. And still later that Rhea could step back from herself and manage "Rhea," then "me." Meanwhile he was outside. Way before that even he was outside—pregnancy, labor, delivery, breastfeeding. Women and babies, mothers and children, mother and child. Him outside. If only she had looked more like him, though in fact she resembled Alma more than Donna. But still there was distance. He knew no terms for negotiating a relationship with her that did not also include her mother. How had Donna managed that? Hostage, Aisha had said.

He chuckled to himself and stared at Aisha. He started up a nutty film in his head. All over the country, sisters crouching behind bushes with croaker sacks ready to pounce and spirit away little mulatto babies. Mulatto babies were dearer, prizer. Or sisters shouting from the podiums, the rooftops, the bedrooms, telling warriors dirty diapers was revolutionary work. Sisters coiled in red leather booths mesmerizing fathers into a package deal. He clamped down hard on fantasies leaching poisons into his brain. Package deal—me and the kid.

"Were you proposing to me by any chance?" he asked just for the hell of it.

"Say what?" She first looked bewildered, then angry, then amazed. She burst out laughing, catching him off-guard when she asked in icy tones, "Is that basically your attitude? Big joke?"

He shrugged in innocence and decided to leave it alone. She was bristly. Let her eat her pastry and drink her mint tea, he instructed himself. Put her in a cab and send her home. He wanted time to himself, time to take a good look at the yellow chair Alma had bequeathed to him when she moved to the coast. Its unfolding capacity never failed to amaze him. It would make a better bed than the Disney pen he'd spied in a children's store that morning. He was feeling good again.

He leaned forward and Aisha slid a forkful of crumbly pastry into his mouth. She was looking good to him once more. He grinned. She jerked her chin as if to ask what was he about to say. He wasn't about to say anything. But he was thinking that no, they hadn't met at the wrong time. It'd been the right time for him. The wrong time for them maybe. But what the hell.

"What did you want to be when you grew up?" she asked. He leaned in for another forkful of pastry. "Just don't be like your daddy" rang in his ears. "A tender man," he said and watched her lashes flutter lower.

The question he would put to himself when he got home and stretched out in that yellow chair was what had he promised his daughter in the spring of '61. He smiled at Aisha and leaned up out of his chair to kiss her on the forehead. She blushed. He was sure he could come true for the Cliff he'd been.

Madame Bai and the Taking of Stone Mountain

1

Headachy from the double feature, she tells Tram and Mustafa that she'll take a rain check on dinner. The rest of the household, after all, expect her back by ten o'clock for an English conversation lesson.

"A coffee?" Mustafa suggests. He answers himself with a groan. The only decent cup of coffee to be had in Atlanta is at the house. "Home, then," he shrugs and saunters across the street for a paper.

She views it all as a bit of footage. That is what seeing her neighborhood, the city constantly on the news has done to her perception. Figures moving out of the Rialto into the wind. Man and woman wait on curb. Third figure crossing street. Mustafa's coat, elegantly draped around his shoulders, falls in soft, straight folds, his sleeves swinging like regal robes. From the back he could be her father. All he needs, she's thinking, is a horn case and his beret set a bit more ace deuce.

"Rain check?" Tram gazes at the wintry sky perplexed, wrinkles scarring his broad-boned cheeks. She mumbles an explanation of the figure of speech, standing at the curb hipshot as her mother would. But she does not tap her foot. She can't chance it with the wind beating at her back and her still wobbly from that particular loss. It's a new way to be in the world, she's discovering—unmothered.

"Rain check." Tram nods, dipping his chin down to his arms crossed against his chest, and shoves up his quilted sleeves. He stands against the wind an untippable figure, a pyramid. She shifts her weight to match his stance.

Two young bloods, in defiance of the curfew, shoot out of Luckie Street and race between cars bouncing over the parking lot braker. She takes this in as though through a viewer, widening the lens to incorporate a blind man tapping along the pavement toward them. There is, she decides as Mustafa rejoins them, too lively a curiosity behind the dark glasses. She watches warily as the blind man stops behind the boys inspecting the *kung fu* posters outside the Rialto, his chin stuck out as if to sniff the wind, as if to catch the aromas from the restaurant farther on, as if to smell out his prey. To her list of suspects—Klan, cops, fiend in clerical cloth, little old ladies with poisoned cookies, monsters in Boy Scout gear, young kids in distress used to lure older ones to their death—she now adds blind people.

Mustafa reads the headlines. She does not correct his pronunciation. She's watching the blind man who has hooked his cane in the crook of his arm and is following the boys down Forsyth.

"Oh God," she mutters, bracing herself against her companions and ready to call out a warning. But the boys scoot down a side street toward Central City Park and the blind man continues straight ahead toward Marietta Street. She exhales.

"Yes?" Mustafa is studying her, his eyebrows arched so hard in query, his narrow forehead all but disappears under his beret.

"What?" Tram, hunched and shivery, growls.

She flops her hands around by way of explanation. Her companions exchange a look. Their landlady/friend/English instructor bears watching, the look says. Tram lifts an elbow for her to catch on. Mustafa tucks the paper away and sweeps his coat open. But he doesn't pull his sweater cuffs down. She hesitates. His wrists are deformed. They move up Forsyth, heads ducked, bodies huddled. She's grateful, wedged between the two, for the warmth and support. And grateful too that Mustafa has not offered his latest theory on the missing and murdered children of Atlanta. He doesn't usually talk freely in the streets, reserving his passionate tirades against global fascism for the late-night talk fests in the kitchens, having learned a hard lesson.

They hung him from the barracks ceiling by the wrists. The Israelis whose parents had had them baptized in '36 then sent to the convent school in Mustafa's district to save them from the Nazis. The same convent school Coptic Christians of the district sent their children to save them from the backwardness of Jordanian society. The same district whose faithful evicted the French nuns to save Islam from the infidels. Mustafa, a brash young student, had been relating the take-over of the old convent school by the Israelis, who'd converted it into an army barracks "to save the city from terrorists." Too much irony in too loud a recitation, Mustafa was hustled in for interrogation.

"Whatcha got up your sleeve, Chinaman?"
selfsame line delivered in badly dubbed stereophonic sound, followed by a whistling knife spun from a tobacco-brown silk sleeve that pinned the speaker's shoulder blade to a beam in the rice shop. Courtesy of Hong Kong Eternal Flame Films, Limited.

"I'm talking to you."

Four white punks in gray, hooded sweatsuits have slipped up alongside and cut them off. They carry what looks like a three-foot grappling hook, something you'd drag the river with. She freezes.

"Whatsa matter?" the leader leers, jiggling the pole. "No speaky de English?" The Confederate flag snaps down at the sharpened end.

Mustafa slides his arm away and quickly rolls his paper into a bat. She fingers the pick comb in one pocket, her key ring in the other. Tram is in a crouch, staring hard at the belt buckle insignia of the big-bellied punk. In the East it would be the reassuring Shorinji *kempo* figure, but in the West the interlocking z's have been corrupted into the swastika. They're jabbing the pole straight at Tram's midsection, the flag snapping like a whip, like teeth.

"Chinky Chinaman no speaky de English." The leader nudges Big Belly with his hobnailed wristband, grinning to his cohorts. "Speak gook then," he prods Tram, no grin.

She does not see the lunge or the spin, only Tram's fists, pulled out of sleeves, striking as he lands. Two of the punks slam hard against the donut shop window. The others stumble between the two newspaper boxes near the curb. Mustafa gets off a few good whacks before his weapon buckles. The clang of the pole against cement propels her. She's leaning hard on the skinniest punk flung against the donut shop window, her pick in his gut, her keys grating across the bridge of his nose. Brothers in the shop have left the counter to rush to the window.

"The cruel and lively Thai boxer legs," Mustafa is announcing to the crowd at the glass, bouncing Big Belly off the *Wall Street Journal* box. She hears glass shatter and half expects to see the donut shop window break away in slow motion, falling. She brings her knee up into the groin as she rams both elbows down hard between collarbones.

Tram's final kick-spin ends with one foot catching the leader on the side of the head, the other foot shoving Big Belly into the street. She and Mustafa rush the two who are scrambling backward over a spatter of glass into the gutter. Brakes screech, tires squeal as the hooded ones race across toward a construction site where the Loews Grand used to be. They leap hurdles of haystacks and sandbags and disappear.

"Well, all right." A brother in seaman's cap and sweater, his body moving in sportscaster replay, retrieves Mustafa's coat and slaps it on. "Welcome to Margaret Mitchell Square," he laughs and hands her her keys.

"That was some set-to," an elderly gent with jelly on his front tooth says, hand raised high to give five but not sure who to give it to. She extends her hand. The brothers size her up—twentyish, redbone, whatcha doin' with these foreign jokers, whatcha story? She knows that look. The gent gives a stingy five as though she, skin-privileged, doesn't need it. And then the two rush back into the warmth of the shop, leaving her with a bad feeling.

Mustafa is brushing off his coat and adjusting the beret. Tram is standing back hard on his heels, the wind plastering his sweater against his chest so that eight separate segments of abdominal muscles lift like bas-relief. He looks like sculpture, she's thinking, the raised scar on his rib cage a length of packing twine, his quilted jacket a packing mat—statuary ready for shipping.

"Let's go home," Tram says squinting when his examination of the construction site shadows fails to produce a sneak attack of rock and rubble.

Once again they hook arms and, huddled, move to the bus stop, saluted by raised coffee mugs and soup spoons.

She hopes the bus will be overheated. Though her companions shelter her from the wind, she is chilled through, brittle, on the brink of cracking. They talk in French, Mustafa recounting each blow in the battle, being droll, inviting her to join in, Tram complaining that breaking bones is not why he studies the arts, not why he's come to Atlanta to await the arrival of the celebrated Madame Bai.

"With these two fingers," he explains, shoving two blunt-nailed fingers near her nose, "I can go home and help heal the wounds of war."

"The first to create the phrase 'What is up the sleeve, Chinaman?' did not meet this *kung fu* fighter," Mustafa chuckles. She ghosts a smile, clamping her jaws tight.

"I'm Vietnamese," Tram says flatly, ignoring the compliment and wagging his two fingers against Mustafa's lapels. "They go in so quick to snatch out disease, no scar tissue forms," he says, snipping off a button.

"Fine hands," Mustafa says, eyebrows arched.

Tram drops the button in Mustafa's palm and shoves his arms up his sleeves once more. "Not Chinese," he adds with a warning grunt. She closes her eyes for a moment, hoping Mustafa will not offer the usual taunts that provoke Tram into a diatribe against Bruce Lee and all things Chinese and launch the rest of the household into endless debate over whether Mao makes it a Gang of Five. Tram leans over to peer for the bus. Mustafa attempts to fit a cigarette into an ivory holder. His hands are shaking, she notices, ruining what might have been an elegant portrait: Jordanian poet, ivory tusk smoldering, coat collar blown against chin. Tobacco shreds down his coat. She looks away and thinks of the figures in Madame Tussaud's, of her mother waxy and spent.

"There will be news on the television," Mustafa says, tossing the broken butt away. "Another child found murdered."

Tram catches her from behind under the armpits before she knows she is falling. Mustafa leads her to the curb waving an oversized hanky. She dumps lunch into the gutter.

2

Madame Bai arrives on a dismal day the week of inauguration. There are two *kung fu* movies playing at the Rialto. There are always two *kung fu* movies playing at the Rialto. The bill is not in honor of the warrior-healer woman revered in *shaolins* and *ashrams* around the globe, honored by masters of the arts, quoted in the reliable texts. The Tai Chi Association silk-screens a batch of T-shirts. But the *yin-yang* figure is not bordered by the trigrams that signal the flag of Korea. Madame's presence in the city is not the occasion for the artwork. Not a line of copy is devoted to Madame's arrival in Atlanta, magnet city for every amateur sleuth, bounty hunter, right-wing provocateur, left-wing adventurer, do-gooder, soothsayer, porno-film maker, scoop journalist, crack shot, crackpot, or cool-out leader not born from the fires of struggle.

The Reagans moving in, Carter moving out, and the hostages coming home from Iran hog the news. The best of medical and psychological help is mobilized for the hostages. Less than little is available for Vietnam vets suffering from shell shock, stress, and Agent Orange genetic tampering. Gifts of things, of cash, of promising jobs await the returnees. But a minister on TV tells people not to send a dime to the parents of Atlanta: "They were getting along without our help before their children got killed. They can get along without our help now." Speeches are made about the hostages, about Carter, about the new President Reagan. Phrases like "not racially motivated" and "no connection between the children's murders and violence in other places" are fed to Atlantans. "The parents are not above suspicion," the FBI poison pen leaks. And as solidarity groups move to mount a movement, "The parents did it," say the authorities.

Yellow ribbons flap from flagpoles, trees, door knockers, wrists in the northeast section of the city. In the southwest green ribbons and black armbands are worn solemnly. The red, white, and blue is waved in *The Thunderbolt* and *Soldier of Fortune*, as articles urge good patriots to beat back the colored hordes rising to take over God's country.

Tram runs a vacuum over the dining room floor, lifting the skirt of the tablecloth pointedly to rout the household from its round-table discussion over the latest National States Rights Party rag. It features faces of African Americans superimposed on apes' bodies. Mustafa, wearing an elaborate headdress of pillowcases and carrying a hammer, goes to tack a sign of welcome on the door for Madame Bai. Panos, at the top of his lungs, sings anti-junta songs and restrings his *oud*. Jean-Paul at the ironing board composes aloud angry op-eds on the refugee situation. Maaza, the Ethiopian film maker, and Madas, the Chilean novelist, fold sheets and discuss a collaborative project built around the visiting Madame with English narration to be supplied by their land-lady/English instructor/friend.

She's in the kitchen inching out saffron into the rice and grumbling. The couple from Bahia are mincing peppers and listening.

"Democratic action can be taken too far," she complains. A collective vote was made to postpone lessons—and with it, her salary—until Madame is settled in her studio school. Tram yells over complaints, singing, and hammering to review once more the self-defense system Madame Bai had designed especially for women, a sleight-of-hand technique in which one masters critically quick placement on critical organs while maintaining an ingratiating mien and nonaggressive stance. So quick a placement, it bypasses the notice of the aggressor. So deft a placement, the violent mind is discouraged.

"In days to follow," Mustafa on cue calls from the doorway, "the rogue is coughing blood and urinating red."

"But he continues to think he's tough and won," croons Panos.

"Yeh, yeh," says Maaza, bored.

"All one needs," she mumbles to the Bahians, "is seven years of anatomy and fifteen degrees in one or more arts."

They assemble in the living room to wait like schoolchildren, the house aromatic with rosemary, curry, *ouzo*, and stinking with *nuoc nam* that couldn't be voted down. She is prepared for a light-filled eminence to grace them like song, for an amazon to perform strike-rock-fist on the door, for Madame to pole-vault like dragon fire through the window, or to materialize *ninja*-style in the shadows of the fireplace. Madame Bai arrives like an ordinary person, steps in behind Tram on soft cloth shoes. Bows, sits, eats, fusses with her hair, pinning her grayed topknot with two golden carved fibulae from her grandmother's chest as she explains. With Tram as translator, Madame jokes, converses, and proves herself to be the sagelike wonder he'd promised all along. And by 9 P.M. Madame has stolen away all of her students. A collective decision is made to redistribute the usual thirty dollars a week for room, board, and English lessons into fifteen dollars for her and fifteen dollars for Madame.

"There's such a thing as taking democratic action too far," she complains for months at Madame's studio. They begin with a roster of thirty—adepts from the Oracle of Maat, instructor from the *tai chi* group near Lonox Plaza, two medicine men and a clan mother from Seminole County in Florida, herbalists from Logos, *shiatsu* therapists and rolfers from the massage school, Fruit of the Nation from the Bankhead mosque, two ex-bodyguards from Mayor Jackson's elite corps, and her erstwhile students of English grammar and conversation. By Easter she is experiencing a body-mind-spirit connection she'd imagined possible only for disciples in the nether mountain ranges of Nepal. Attendance drops off steadily as the weather turns warm, her boarder/students returning to the fold and restoring the good health of her budget. Most of her nights are spent plowing through *Gray's Anatomy* and sticking pins in the red dots of her pressure point chart. Her days are spent working with defense teams, bat squads, and root watchers. She's made a marshal of the citizen search team for her calm and logical way in the woods.

By late May, when the media converges on Wayne Williams' drive across the Chattahoochee Bridge, complaints are rife at the studio. No mats, no *ka-li* charts to study. No striking bags or apparatus for stretching the legs. No *shurikens*, iron fans, *nunchaku* sticks for practice. Not even an emblem to patch on a sweater, transfer to a shirt, solder on a key ring. Wholesale defection begins in June when headlines around the country announce the fiend has been nabbed. One man charged with two counts of murder, the case hanging literally by a thread, a bit of carpet fiber that changes color as the days advance but no journalist seems to notice. One man, two counts, leaving twenty-six "official" deaths still on the books and an additional thirty-eight or more not being discussed. Eight hundred police are withdrawn from the neighborhoods. One hundred state patrolmen returned to the highways. Roadblocks vanish. Helicopters disappear. Neighborhood security groups disperse. Search teams disband. Safety posters come down. Bumper stickers tatter. Amnesia drifts into the city like fog. "Let the Community Heal Itself," say the sermons. She grunts and continues training. The Medfly in California, a tsetse epidemic in Atlanta, she masters butterfly metamorphosis and requires only five hours of sleep at night.

Madame smiles and wishes the departing students well on their journey. Madame smiles and intensifies training for those that remain. At the studio, at the house, throughout the neighborhood, she is learning to be still as her mother used to counsel, to silence the relentless chatter inside in favor of the small-voiced guide she is experiencing as a warm hand steering at the base of her spine. The cadres of the neighborhood call her the Alarm Clock. She keeps the block security tight and keeps watch over the children.

3

They are sitting in a sauna with a name she cannot even pronounce. Nerves frayed, mind seared, muscles screaming for release, she sits beyond endurance till she is the sauna, focused. Madame dismounts from the only cushion in the room and glides to the center of the circle and sits. She looks at Madame's back and traces the carver's journey along the golden fibulae to the points. She senses a summoning, as though her mother had set a space heater down before her, then dragged it slowly away by its cord for her to follow. Madame sending out her power, she concludes, rising to walk round into the light. She sits back on her heels before Madame, palms on her thighs, poised, ready. Madame's face turns from skin to old parchment, an ancient text she's being invited to read.

"One question, daughter." Madame says it in English after a long while. She waits, as if all her life this question has been forming. Not a favor to tax her friendship, nor a task to test commitment, but a question coming together, taking shape, her shape. Daughter. It drives deep within to jimmy open a door long closed, padlocked, boarded over. She leans against the boards, feels the grain of the wood as it swings wide to a brilliant and breezy place she's not visited since the days when she was held dear and cherished simply because she was she and not a pot to mend or dress to hem or chair leg to join.

She smiles at Madame by way of signaling, Let the test begin. Then panic gathers behind the door to shove it to. She gathers the weight of her years into a doorstop. Test. She's heard of disciples who roam the earth unkempt and crazed by a *koan* a master has posed for solution: Where does the dark go when the light is switched on? Why does the arrow never reach the mark despite the illusion of the bowman? The door pushes against her back. She heaves against it, listing. The warm hand at the power base rights her. The door swings wide again.

"Stone Mountain," Madame says finally.

Stone Mountain. A rock to prop a door with. A rock dropped into the pool of the mind. For a moment, she's in a muddle. Rocks rear up out of the ocean. She scrambles across the rock ledge braille-reading the fossils embedded deep within. Stone Mountain. It tumbles down into the waters. She surfaces, crawling across the wet rubble in a quarry. Stone. From ledge to peak to cliff she follows the goat trail, shreds of fleece caught on briars and shrubs. She gathers it all within the pouch of her shirt. Mountain. Could it be a Red Army libretto in the repertoire of the Peking Opera? Someone near beats out a tattoo on a knuckle drum. Her mother used to pummel her, knuckles against both temples, when she was too impatient to be still and receptive.

She exhales and lets it flow to her. Stone Mountain. Of course. A mere thirty-minute ride out by U.S. 78. Stone monster carved tribute to the confederacy Mountain. Tourist-trap entrapment of visiting schoolchildren lured under the spell of the enslavers of Africans, killers of Amerinds. Lewdly exposed mammoth granite rock of ages the good ole boys hide in from history. Eight hundred and sixty-five feet high, the guide books say. Five hundred and eighty-three acres. The sacred grove of grand dragons, wizards, greater and lesser demons who crank out crank notes in the name of Robert E. Lee, Jefferson Davis, and Stonewall Jackson riding across the monument on horseback. She smirks.

Madame lifts her brows. Everything above Madame's eyes slides up and back, taking her hair line out of view as though someone is standing behind, tugging at mask and wig, about to reveal the woman as a person she has known always, who has been there all along, just beyond peripheral vision, guiding her through the various rites of passage.

"What is it for, Stone Mountain?" Madame asks with her face in place.

For? To rally the raunchy, Madame, to celebrate the. She clutches the ropes as the scaffolding swings against the side of the mountain scraping her knuckles. For this you summon me? You could have called the Chamber of Commerce, asked any schoolboy at the Peachtree Academy, checked the nearest public li. Balanced, she leans against the cool, damp rock and traces the sculptor's line across hind parts, boot stirrups, folds in the uniforms. For? Any almanac, encyclopedia, atlas could have told you what. Wind and rain have eroded the line of the nose here, a ripple of hair there. An ice pocket just below Stonewall's hand, holding the reins loosely, proves just deep enough to drive the chisel point in. Eighth Wonder of the World, some say, Madame, and. The hammering enlarges a hairline fissure running from the brim of one hat to the forelegs of the first horse. Five sticks of dynamite shoved in just so can bring the whole thing tumbling down. They say, Madame, that staunch materialists who favor symbols over reality can be thoroughly demoralized if. A people's army should focus on.

"Teacher." The word blows through her chest cavity, a breeze amplified in that resonating chamber. The words to be spoken already reverberating around the room, releasing the circle from the sauna. She hears the slap of flesh against wood, a signal, an army awaiting direction.

"Stone Mountain is for taking, Madame."

Alice Walker

The Welcome Table

for sister Clara Ward

I'm going to sit at the Welcome table
Shout my troubles over
Walk and talk with Jesus
Tell God how you treat me
One of these days!
   —Spiritual

The old woman stood with eyes uplifted in her Sunday-go-to-meeting clothes: high shoes polished about the tops and toes, a long rusty dress adorned with an old corsage, long withered, and the remnants of an elegant silk scarf as headrag stained with grease from the many oily pigtails underneath. Perhaps she had know suffering. There was a dazed and sleepy look in her aged blue-brown eyes. But for those who searched hastily for "reasons" in that old tight face, shut now like an ancient door, there was nothing to be read. and so they gazed nakedly upon their own fear transferred; a fear of the black and the old, a terror of the unknown as well as of the deeply known. Some of those who saw her there on the church steps spoke words about her that were hardly fit to be heard, others held their pious peace; and some felt vague stirrings of pity, small and persistent and hazy, as if she were an old collie turned out to die.

She was angular and lean and the color of poor gray Georgia earth, beaten by king cotton and the extreme weather. Her elbows were wrinkled and thick, the skin ashen but durable, like the bark of old pines. On her face centuries were folded into the circles around one eye, while around the other, etched and mapped as if for print, ages more threatened again to live. Some of them there at the church saw the age, the dotage, the missing buttons down the front of her mildewed black dress. Others saw cooks, chauffeurs, maids, mistresses, children denied or smothered in the deferential way she held her cheek to the side, toward the ground. Many of them saw jungle orgies in an evil place, while others were reminded of riotous anarchists looting and raping in the streets. Those who knew the hesitant creeping up on them of the law, saw the beginning of the end of the sanctuary of Christian worship, saw the desecration of Holy Church, and saw an invasion of privacy, which they struggled to believe they still kept.

Still she had come down the road toward the big white church alone. Just herself, an old forgetful woman, nearly blind with age. Just her and her eyes raised dully to the glittering cross that crowned the sheer silver steeple. She had walked along the road in a stagger from her house a half mile away: Perspiration, cold and clammy, stood on her brow and along the creases by her thin wasted nose. She stopped to calm herself on the wide front steps, not looking about her as they might have expected her to do, but simply standing quite still, except for a slight quivering of her throat and tremors that shook her cotton-stockinged legs.

The reverend of the church stopped her pleasantly as she stepped into the vestibule. Did he say, as they thought he did, kindly, "Auntie, you know this is not your church?" As if one could choose the wrong one. But no one remembers, for they never spoke of it afterward, and she brushed past him anyway, as if she had been brushing past him all her life, except this time she was in a hurry. Inside the church she sat on the very first bench from the back, gazing with concentration at the stained-glass window over her head. It was cold, even inside the church, and she was shivering. Everybody could see. They stared at her as they came in and sat down near the front. It was cold, very cold to them, too; outside the church it was below freezing and not much above inside. But the sight of her, sitting there somehow passionately ignoring them, brought them up short, burning.

The young usher, never having turned anyone out of his church before, but not even considering this job as *that* (after all, she had no right to be there, certainly), went up to her and whispered that she should leave. Did he call her "Grandma," as later he seemed to recall he had? But for those who actually hear such traditional pleasantries and to whom they actually mean something, "Grandma" was not one, for she did not pay him any attention, just muttered, "Go 'way," in a weak sharp *bothered* voice, waving his frozen blond hair and eyes from near her face.

It was the ladies who finally did what to them had to be done. Daring their burly indecisive husbands to throw the old colored woman out they made their point. God, mother, country, earth, church. It involved all that, and well they knew it. Leather bagged and shoed, with good calfskin gloves to keep out the cold, they looked with contempt at the bloodless gray arthritic hands of the old woman, clenched loosely, restlessly in her lap. Could their husbands expect them to sit up in church with *that?* No, no, the husbands were quick to answer and even quicker to do their duty.

Under the old woman's arms they placed their hard fists (which afterward smelled of decay and musk—the fermenting scent of onionskins and rotting greens). Under the old woman's arms they raised their fists, flexed their muscular shoulders, and out she flew through the door, back under the cold blue sky. This done, the wives folded their healthy arms across their trim middles and felt at once justified and scornful. But none of them said so, for none of them ever spoke of the incident again. Inside the church it was warmer. They sang, they prayed. The protection and promise of God's impartial love grew more not less desirable as the sermon gathered fury and lashed itself out above their penitent heads.

The old woman stood at the top of the steps looking about in bewilderment. She had been singing in her head. They had interrupted her. Promptly she began to sing again, though this time a sad song. Suddenly, however, she looked down the long gray highway and saw something interesting and delightful coming. She started to grin, toothlessly, with short giggles of joy, jumping about and slapping her hands on her knees. And soon it became apparent why she was so happy. For coming down the highway at a firm though leisurely pace was Jesus. He was wearing an immaculate white, long dress trimmed in gold around the neck and hem, and a red, a bright red, cape. Over his left arm he carried a brilliant blue blanket. He was wearing sandals and a beard and he had long brown hair parted on the right side. His eyes, brown, had wrinkles around them as if he smiled or looked at the sun a lot. She would have known him, recognized him, anywhere. There was a sad but joyful look to his face, like a candle was glowing behind it, and he walked with sure even steps in her direction, as if he were walking on the sea. Except that he was not carrying in his arms a baby sheep, he looked exactly like the picture of him that she had hanging over her bed at home. She had taken it out of a white lady's Bible while she was working for her. She had looked at that picture for more years than she could remember, but never once had she really expected to see him. She squinted her eyes to be sure he wasn't carrying a little sheep in one arm, but he was not. Ecstatically she began to wave her arms for fear he would miss seeing her, for he walked looking straight ahead on the shoulder of the highway, and from time to time looking upward at the sky.

All he said when he got up close to her was "Follow me," and she bounded down to his side with all the bob and speed of one so old. For every one of his long determined steps she made two quick ones. They walked along in deep silence for a long time. Finally she started telling him about how many years she had cooked for them, cleaned for them, nursed them. He looked at her kindly but in silence. She told him indignantly about how they had grabbed her when she was singing in her head and not looking, and how they had tossed her out of his church. A old heifer like me, she said, straightening up next to Jesus, breathing hard. But he smiled down at her and she felt better instantly and time just seemed to fly by. When they passed her house, forlorn and sagging, weatherbeaten and patched, by the side of the road, she did not even notice it, she was so happy to be out walking along the highway with Jesus.

She broke the silence once more to tell Jesus how glad she was that he had come, how she had often looked at his picture hanging on her wall (she hoped he didn't know she had stolen it) over her bed, and how she had never expected to see him down here in person. Jesus gave her one of his beautiful smiles and they walked on. She did not know where they were going; someplace wonderful, she suspected. The ground was like clouds under their feet, and she felt she could walk forever without becoming the least bit tired. She even began to sing out loud some of the old spirituals she loved, but she didn't want to annoy Jesus, who looked so thoughtful, so she quieted down. They walked on, looking straight over the treetops into the sky, and the smiles that played over her dry wind-cracked face were like first clean ripples across a stagnant pond. On they walked without stopping.

The people in church never knew what happened to the old woman; they never mentioned her to one another or to anybody else. Most of them heard sometime later that an old colored woman fell dead along the highway. Silly as it seemed, it appeared she had walked herself to death. Many of the black families along the road said they had seen the old lady high-stepping down the highway; sometimes jabbering in a low insistent voice, sometimes singing, sometimes merely gesturing excitedly with her hands. Other times silent and smiling, looking at the sky. She had been alone, they said. Some of them wondered aloud where the old woman had been going so stoutly that it had worn her heart out. They guessed maybe she had relatives across the river, some miles away, but none of them really knew.

A Sudden Trip
Home in the Spring

For the Wellesley Class

1

Sarah walked slowly off the tennis court, fingering the back of her head, feeling the sturdy dark hair that grew there. She was popular. As she walked along the path toward Talfinger Hall her friends fell into place around her. They formed a warm jostling group of six. Sarah, because she was taller than the rest, saw the messenger first.

"Miss Davis," he said, standing still until the group came abreast of him, "I've got a telegram for ye." Brian was Irish and always quite respectful. He stood with his cap in his hand until Sarah took the telegram. Then he gave a nod that included all the young ladies before he turned away. He was young and good-looking, though annoyingly servile, and Sarah's friends twittered.

"Well, open it!" someone cried, for Sarah stood staring at the yellow envelope, turning it over and over in her hand.

"Look at her," said one of the girls, "isn't she beautiful! Such eyes, and hair, and *skin!*"

Sarah's tall, caplike hair framed a face of soft brown angles, high cheekbones and large dark eyes. Her eyes enchanted her friends because they always seemed to know more, and to find more of life amusing, or sad, than Sarah cared to tell.

Her friends often teased Sarah about her beauty; they loved dragging her out of her room so that their boyfriends, naive and worldly
young men from Princeton and Yale, could see her. They never guessed
she found this distasteful. She was gentle with her friends, and her
outrage at their tactlessness did not show. She was most often inclined
to pity them, though embarrassment sometimes drove her to fraudulent
expressions. Now she smiled and raised eyes and arms to heaven. She
acknowledged their unearned curiosity as a mother endures the prying
impatience of a child. Her friends beamed love and envy upon her as
she tore open the telegram.

"He's dead," she said.

Her friends reached out for the telegram, their eyes on Sarah.

"It's her father," one of them said softly. "He died yesterday. Oh,
Sarah," the girl whimpered, "I'm so sorry!"

"Me too." "So am I." "Is there anything we can do?"

But Sarah had walked away, head high and neck stiff.

"So graceful!" one of her friends said.

"Like a proud gazelle" said another. Then they all trooped to their
dormitories to change for supper.

Talfinger Hall was a pleasant dorm. The common room just off the
entrance had been made into a small modern art gallery with some very
good original paintings, lithographs and collages. Pieces were constantly being stolen. Some of the girls could not resist an honest-to-God
Chagall, signed (in the plate) by his own hand, though they could have
afforded to purchase one from the gallery in town. Sarah Davis's room
was next door to the gallery, but her walls were covered with inexpen-
sive Gaugin reproductions, a Rubens ("The Head of a Negro"), a
Modigliani and a Picasso. There was a full wall of her own drawings, all
of black women. She found black men impossible to draw or to paint;
she could not bear to trace defeat onto blank pages. Her women figures
were matronly, massive of arm, with a weary victory showing in their
eyes. Surrounded by Sarah's drawings was a red SNCC poster of a man
holding a small girl whose face nestled in his shoulder. Sarah often felt
she was the little girl whose face no one could see.

To leave Talfinger even for a few days filled Sarah with fear.
Talfinger was her home now; it suited her better than any home she'd
ever known. Perhaps she loved it because in winter there was a fragrant
fireplace and snow outside her window. When hadn't she dreamed of

fireplaces that really warmed, snow that almost pleasantly froze? Georgia seemed far away as she packed; she did not want to leave New York, where, her grandfather had liked to say, "the devil hung out and caught young gals by the front of their dresses." He had always believed the South the best place to live on earth (never mind that certain people invariably marred the landscape), and swore he expected to die no more than a few miles from where he had been born. There was tenacity even in the gray frame house he lived in, and in scrawny animals on his farm who regularly reproduced. He was the first person Sarah wanted to see when she got home.

There was a knock on the door of the adjoining bathroom, and Sarah's suite mate entered, a loud Bach concerto just finishing behind her. At first she stuck just her head into the room, but seeing Sarah fully dressed she trudged in and plopped down on the bed. She was a heavy blonde girl with large milk-white legs. Her eyes were small and her neck usually gray with grime.

"My, don't you look gorgeous," she said.

"Ah, Pam," said Sarah, waving her hand in disgust. In Georgia she knew that even to Pam she would be just another ordinarily attractive *colored* girl. In Georgia there were a million girls better looking. Pam wouldn't know that, of course; she'd never been to Georgia; she'd never even seen a black person to speak to, that is, before she met Sarah. One of her first poetic observations about Sarah was that she was "a poppy in a field of winter roses." She had found it weird that Sarah did not own more than one coat.

"Say listen, Sarah," said Pam, "I heard about your father. I'm sorry. I really am."

"Thanks," said Sarah.

"Is there anything we can do? I thought, well, maybe you'd want my father to get somebody to fly you down. He'd go himself but he's taking Mother to Madeira this week. You wouldn't have to worry about trains and things."

Pamela's father was one of the richest men in the world, though no one ever mentioned it. Pam only alluded to it at times of crisis, when a friend might benefit from the use of a private plane, train, or ship; or, if someone wanted to study the characteristics of a totally secluded village, island or mountain, she might offer one of theirs. Sarah could not comprehend such wealth, and was always annoyed because Pam didn't look more like a billionaire's daughter. A billionaire's daughter, Sarah thought, should really be less horsey and brush her teeth more often.

"Gonna tell me what you're brooding about?" asked Pam.

Sarah stood in front of the radiator, her fingers resting on the window seat. Down below girls were coming up the hill from supper.

"I'm thinking," she said, "of the child's duty to his parents after they are dead."

"Is that all?"

"Do you know," asked Sarah, "about Richard Wright and his father?"

Pamela frowned. Sarah looked down at her.

"Oh, I forgot," she said with a sigh, "they don't teach Wright here. The poshest school in the U.S., and the girls come out ignorant." She looked at her watch, saw she had twenty minutes before her train. "Really," she said almost inaudibly, "why Tears Eliot, Ezratic Pound, and even Sara Teacake, and no Wright?" She and Pamela thought e.e. cummings very clever with his perceptive spelling of great literary names.

"Is he a poet then?" asked Pam. She adored poetry, all poetry. Half of America's poetry she had, of course, not read, for the simple reason that she had never heard of it.

"No," said Sarah, "he wasn't a poet." She felt weary. "He was a man who wrote, a man who had trouble with his father." She began to walk about the room, and came to stand below the picture of the old man and the little girl.

"When he was a child," she continued, "his father ran off with another woman, and one day when Richard and his mother went to ask him for money to buy food he laughingly rejected them. Richard, being very young, thought his father Godlike. Big, omnipotent, unpredictable, undependable and cruel. Entirely in control of his universe. Just like a god. But, many years later, after Wright had become a famous writer, he went down to Mississippi to visit his father. He found instead of God, just an old watery-eyed field hand, bent from plowing, his teeth gone, smelling of manure. Richard realized that the most daring thing his 'God' had done was run off with that other woman."

"So?" asked Pam. "What 'duty' did he feel he owed the old man?"

"So," said Sarah, "that's what Wright wondered as he peered into that old shifty-eyed Mississippi Negro face. What was the duty of the son of a destroyed man? The son of a man whose vision had stopped at the edge of fields that weren't even his. Who was Wright without his father? Was he Wright the great writer? Wright the Communist? Wright the French farmer? Wright whose white wife could never accompany him to Mississippi? Was he, in fact, still his father's son? Or was he freed by his father's desertion to be nobody's son, to be his own father? Could he disavow his father and live? And if so, live as what? As whom? And for what purpose?"

"Well," said Pam, swinging her hair over her shoulders and squinting her small eyes, "if his father rejected him I don't see why Wright even bothered to go see him again. From what you've said, Wright earned the freedom to be whoever he wanted to be. To a strong man a father is not essential."

"Maybe not," said Sarah, "but Wright's father was one faulty door in a house of many ancient rooms. Was that one faulty door to shut him off forever from the rest of the house? That was the question. And though he answered this question eloquently in his work, where it really counted, one can only wonder if he was able to answer it satisfactorily—or at all—in his life."

"You're thinking of his father more as a symbol of something, aren't you?" asked Pam.

"I suppose," said Sarah, taking a last look around her room. "I see him as a door that refused to open, a hand that was always closed. A fist."

Pamela walked with her to one of the college limousines, and in a few minutes she was at the station. The train to the city was just arriving.

"Have a nice trip," said the middle-aged driver courteously, as she took her suitcase from him. But for about the thousandth time since she'd seen him, he winked at her.

Once away from her friends she did not miss them. The school was all they had in common. How could they ever know her if they were not allowed to know Wright, she wondered. She was interesting, "beautiful," only because they had no idea what made her, charming only because they had no idea from where she came. And where they came from, though she glimpsed it—in themselves and in F. Scott Fitzgerald—she was never to enter. She hadn't the inclination or the proper ticket.

2

Her father's body was in Sarah's old room. The bed had been taken down to make room for the flowers and chairs and casket. Sarah looked for a long time into the face, as if to find some answer to her questions written there. It was the same face, a dark Shakespearean head framed by gray, woolly hair and split almost in half by a short, gray mustache. It was a completely silent face, a shut face. But her father's face also looked fat, stuffed, and ready to burst. He wore a navy-blue suit, white shirt and black tie. Sarah bent and loosened the tie. Tears started behind her shoulder blades but did not reach her eyes.

"There's a rat here under the casket," she called to her brother, who apparently did not hear her, for he did not come in. She was alone with her father, as she had rarely been when he was alive. When he was alive she had avoided him.

"Where's that girl at?" her father would ask. "Done closed herself up in her room again," he would answer himself.

For Sarah's mother had died in her sleep one night. Just gone to bed tired and never got up. And Sarah had blamed her father.

Stare the rat down, though Sarah, surely that will help. *Perhaps it doesn't matter whether I misunderstood or never understood.*

"We moved so much looking for crops, a place to *live*," her father had moaned, accompanied by Sarah's stony silence. "The moving killed her. And now we have a real house, with *four* rooms, and a mailbox on the *porch*, and it's too late. She gone. *She* ain't here to see it." On very bad days her father would not eat at all. At night he did not sleep.

Whatever had made her think she knew what love was or was not?

Here she was, Sarah Davis, immersed in Camusian philosophy, versed in many languages, a poppy, of all things, among winter roses. But before she became a poppy she was a native Georgian sunflower, but still had not spoken the language they both knew. Not to him.

Stare the rat down, she thought, and did. The rascal dropped his bold eyes and slunk away. Sarah felt she had, at least, accomplished something.

Why did she have to see the picture of her mother, the one on the mantel among all the religious doodads, come to life? Her mother had stood stout against the years, clean gray braids shining across the top of her head, her eyes snapping, protective. Talking to her father.

"He called you out your name, we'll leave this place today. Not tomorrow. That be too late. Today!" Her mother was magnificent in her quick decisions.

"But what about your garden, the children, the change of schools?" Her father would be holding, most likely, the wide brim of his hat in nervously twisting fingers.

"He called you out your name, we go!"

And go they would. Who knew exactly where, before they moved? Another soundless place, walls falling down, roofing gone; another face to please without leaving too much of her father's pride at his feet. But to Sarah then, no matter with what alacrity her father moved, foot-dragging alone was visible.

The moving killed her, her father had said, *but the moving was also love.*

Did it matter now that often he had threatened their lives with the rage of his despair? That once he had spanked the crying baby violently, who later died of something else altogether . . . and that the next day they moved?

"No," said Sarah aloud, "I don't think it does."

"Huh?" It was her brother, tall, wiry, black, deceptively calm. As a child he'd had an irrepressible temper. As a grown man he was tensely smooth, like a river that any day will overflow its bed.

He had chosen a dull gray casket. Sarah wished for red. Was it Dylan Thomas who had said something grand about the dead offering "deep, dark defiance"? It didn't matter; there were more ways to offer defiance than with a red casket.

"I was just thinking," said Sarah, "that with us Mama and Daddy were saying NO with capital letters."

"I don't follow you," said her brother. He had always been the activist in the family. He simply directed his calm rage against any obstacle that might exist, and awaited the consequences with the same serenity he awaited his sister's answer. Not for him the philosophical confusions and poetic observations that hung his sister up.

"That's because you're a radical preacher," said Sarah, smiling up at him. "You deliver your messages in person with your own body." It excited her that her brother had at last imbued their childhood Sunday sermons with the reality of fighting for change. And saddened her that no matter how she looked at it this seemed more important than Medieval Art, Course 201.

3

"Yes, Grandma," Sarah replied. "Cresselton is for girls only, and *no*, Grandma, I am not pregnant."

Her grandmother stood clutching the broad wooden handle of her black bag, which she held, with elbows bent, in front of her stomach. Her eyes glinted through round wire-framed glasses. She spat into the grass outside the privy. She had insisted that Sarah accompany her to the toilet while the body was being taken into the church. She had leaned heavily on Sarah's arm, her own arm thin and the flesh like crepe.

"I guess they teach you how to really handle the world," she said. "And who knows, the Lord is everywhere. I would like a whole lot to see a Great-Grand. You don't specially have to be married, you know. That's why I felt free to ask." She reached into her bag and took out a Three Sixes bottle, which she proceeded to drink from, taking deep swift swallows with her head thrown back.

"There are very few black boys near Cresselton," Sarah explained, watching the corn liquor leave the bottle in spurts and bubbles. "Besides, I'm really caught up now in my painting and sculpting. . . ." Should she mention how much she admired Giacometti's work? No, she decided. Even if her grandmother had heard of him, and Sarah was positive she had not, she would surely think his statues much too thin. This made Sarah smile and remember how difficult it had been to convince her grandmother that even if Cresselton had not given her a scholarship she would have managed to go there anyway. Why? Because she wanted somebody to teach her to paint and to sculpt, and Cresselton had the best teachers. Her grandmother's notion of a successful granddaughter was a married one, pregnant the first year.

"Well," said her grandmother, placing the bottle with dignity back into her purse and gazing pleadingly into Sarah's face, "I sure would 'preshate a Great-Grand." Seeing her granddaughter's smile, she heaved a great sigh, and, walking rather haughtily over the stones and grass, made her way to the church steps.

As they walked down the aisle, Sarah's eyes rested on the back of her grandfather's head. He was sitting on the front middle bench in front of the casket, his hair extravagantly long and white and softly kinked. When she sat down beside him, her grandmother sitting next to him on the other side, he turned toward her and gently took her hand in his. Sarah briefly leaned her cheek against his shoulder and felt like a child again.

4

They had come twenty miles from town, on a dirt road, and the hot spring sun had drawn a steady rich scent from the honeysuckle vines along the way. The church was a bare, weather-beaten ghost of a building with hollow windows and a sagging door. Arsonists had once burned it to the ground, lighting the dry wood of the walls with the flames from the crosses they carried. The tall spreading red oak tree under which Sarah had played as a child still dominated the church-yard, stretching its branches widely from the roof of the church to the other side of the road.

After a short and eminently dignified service, during which Sarah and her grandfather alone did not cry, her father's casket was slid into the waiting hearse and taken the short distance to the cemetery, an overgrown wilderness whose stark white stones appeared to be the small ruins of an ancient civilization. There Sarah watched her grand-father from the corner of her eye. He did not seem to bend under the grief of burying a son. His back was straight, his eyes dry and clear. He was simply and solemnly heroic; a man who kept with pride his family's trust and his own grief. *It is strange,* Sarah thought, *that I never thought to paint him like this, simply as he stands; without anonymous meaningless people hovering beyond his profile; his face turned proud and brownly against the light.* The defeat that had frightened her in the faces of black men was the defeat of black forever defined by white. But that defeat was nowhere on her grandfather's face. He stood like a rock, outwardly calm, the comfort and support of the Davis family. The family alone defined him, and he was not about to let them down.

"One day I will paint you, Grandpa," she said, as they turned to go. "Just as you stand her now, with just"—she moved closer and touched his face with her hand—"just the right stubborn tenseness of your cheek. Just that look of Yes and No in your eyes."

"You wouldn't want to paint an old man like me," he said, looking deep into her eyes from wherever his mind had been. "If you want to make me, make me up in stone."

The completed grave was plump and red. The wreaths of flowers were arranged all on one side so that from the road there appeared to be only a large mass of flowers. But already the wind was tugging at the rose petals and the rain was making dabs of faded color all over the green foam frames. In a week the displaced honeysuckle vines, the wild roses, the grapevines, the grass, would be back. Nothing would seem to have changed.

5

"What do you mean, come *home?*" Her brother seemed genuinely amused. "We're all proud of you. How many black girls are at that school? Just *you?* Well, just one more besides you, and she's from the North. That's really something!"

"I'm glad you're pleased," said Sarah.

"Pleased! Why, it's what Mama would have wanted, a good education for little Sarah; and what Dad would have wanted too, if he could have wanted anything after Mama died. You were always smart. When you were two and I was five you showed me how to eat ice cream without getting it all over me. First, you said, nip off the bottom of the cone with your teeth, and suck the ice cream down. I never knew *how* you were supposed to eat the stuff once it began to melt."

"I don't know," she said, "sometimes you can want something a whole lot, only to find out later that it wasn't what you *needed* at all."

Sarah shook her head, a frown coming between her eyes. "I sometimes spend *weeks,*" she said, "trying to sketch or paint a face that is unlike every other face around me, except, vaguely, for one. Can I help but wonder if I'm in the right place?"

Her brother smiled. "You mean to tell me you spend *weeks* trying to draw one face, and you still wonder whether you're in the right place? You must be kidding!" He chucked her under the chin and laughed out loud. "You learn how to draw the face," he said, "then you learn how to paint me and how to make Grandpa up in stone. Then you can come home or go live in Paris, France. It'll be the same thing."

It was the unpreacherlike gaiety of his affection that made her cry. She leaned peacefully into her brother's arms. She wondered if Richard Wright had had a brother.

"You are my door to all the rooms," she said. "Don't ever close."

And he said, "I won't," as if he understood what she meant.

6

"When will we see you again, young woman?" he asked later, as he drove her to the bus stop.

"I'll sneak up one day and surprise you," she said.

At the bus stop, in front of a tiny service station, Sarah hugged her brother with all her strength. The white station attendant stopped his work to leer at them, his eyes bold and careless.

"Did you ever think," said Sarah, "that we are a very old people in a very young place?"

She watched her brother from a window of the bus; her eyes did not leave his face until the little station was out of sight and the big Greyhound lurched on its way toward Atlanta. She would fly from there to New York.

7

She took the train to campus.

"My," said one of her friends, "you look wonderful! Home sure must agree with you!"

"Sarah was home?" Someone who didn't know asked. "Oh, *great*, how was it?"

"Well, how was it?" went an echo in Sarah's head. The noise of the echo almost made her dizzy.

"How was it?" she asked aloud, searching for, and regaining, her balance.

"How was it?" She watched her reflection in a pair of smiling hazel eyes.

"It was fine," she said slowly, returning the smile, thinking of her grandfather. "Just fine."

The girl's smile deepened. Sarah watched her swinging along toward the back tennis courts, hair blowing in the wind.

Stare the rat down, thought Sarah; *and whether it disappears or not, I am a woman in the world. I have buried my father, and shall soon know how to make my grandpa up in stone.*

Molly Best Tinsley

Mother Tongue

More than time had passed since summer, the evening my father
sat my mother down opposite him in the kitchenette and promised her
things would get better. In a restrained voice he read out loud his orders
for Sweden, a choice assignment to the Naval Attaché in the American
Embassy. He reminded her that he had dreamt of such a chance.
Stockholm was a beautiful city, he said. "Clean. Picturesque." He
watched for the effect of his words on my mother's downcast face. She
twirled a fingernail in the sweat on her glass of iced tea. There was no
sound except the window fan in the living room vainly sucking at the
muggy Norfolk heat. "We'd all be together," he said finally, knowing
that was no clincher. "For a year."

As though drifting in and out of sleep, she had registered objections. There was mention of me—"Cynthia's happy here. She's got her
feet on the ground in junior high." I supposed that was true. I had
heard her ask often enough, what did my father know about us children
anyway that she didn't have to tell him?

"Over there," he had countered, "she goes to a fancy private school
and the Embassy picks up the tab." And I supposed from his tone that
was something to be desired. My welfare was as rhetorical an issue to
me as it was to them. On my seventh school in as many grades, I'd
learned not to care where I was. My mother was partly right, I did tend
to confuse the stability of indifference with being happy.

She had finally conceded as she always did, with a stiff correction
of her posture, as if she knew some other, more important private

victory had been sealed. And now here we were, aliens camped in a village outside Stockholm, in a house of shabby yellow stucco, facing an early winter. I say *camped* because our household goods had been shipped by accident to England. My father and mother, Charles and I each had a cot and one worn blanket, courtesy of our landlord. Georgie, the baby, slept in the biggest suitcase on his own bunched clothes. Our father fixed the hinges so that no matter how much Georgie wiggled in his sleep the lid couldn't drop and smother him.

As foreseen, I was enrolled in *L'Ecole Française Internationale*, a four-story facade of reddish stone in the middle of the city, in a special class for children of diplomats. It must have been clear to the Sisters from the start that my knowledge of French was limited to what I had learned in Norfolk from a Miss Lafave during a brief exposure to ballet. But they were unfathomable women, the Sisters, in their dark skirts and heavy black stockings, their faces drawn like long grey masks. No matter how poignantly I tried to dramatize my ignorance, I could not move them to either compassion or anger. They simply expected me, from my first day and every night thereafter, to memorize whole pages in their language on the subject of *Mesopotamie*, *l'Esquimaux*, or *la famille Lebrun*. My failure also to memorize the correct pronunciation was simply a matter of fact, to be brought to the attention of the rest of the class almost daily and met with a terrible silence. Time after time, I tried with humble eyes and posture to plead my good faith before old Madame Sibouet, who simply stared up at me over her spectacles and nibbled the inside of her lips while the room slowly filled with sounds of derision.

I soon learned not to mention these humiliations at home, for the certainty of living together for a full year was making my parents edgy and temperamental. Actually, none of us was used to it. I loved my father desperately. Very tall and thin, he had a narrow, bronze moustache at a time when such adornments were daring. He could be deployed on the other side of the world but he would see to it that bouquets of flowers were delivered to my mother and me on our birthdays: *Always, Frank*, promised the neatly printed card. *Always, Father*. Home on brief leaves, he was a limitless source of practical wisdom—how to bluff a large dog; how to extinguish different kinds of fires. During his weeks on shore, I used to stand behind his chair while he watched "The Cisco Kid" or "Dragnet" and scratch his head. Later when he was back on cruise I tried to remember the smell of his scalp.

But his steady presence now was like living a story you know will not end well. It meant always performing and waiting to hear the one thing you did wrong. "It's only a little thing," he'd say, "but those little things pile up." What about the mistakes piling up, burying me at school? He could never accept my mother's need to keep to herself. "Relax," he instructed her. "If you would just relax," and I could feel her silence get brittle and unsafe. I had to work to protect it, fussing at Charles and Georgie lest their mischief and blind demands become the last straw, cause it to buckle, casting us all down into something worse than silence, the bitter currents of blame.

Yet no matter how careful we children were, out mother could always stare suddenly off over our heads and wonder, "How in God's name did I ever fall for this one?" We could be about to take our places on the floor, at the corners of a sheet spread with Saturday's lunch— hardbreads and *lingon* jelly, sweet butter and cheeses, her favorite strong-smelling Port-Salut among them. The sunlight could be streaming through the wide window and warming the bare wood around us. Georgie could manage not to kick over his jar of milk. And still she asked, "What in God's name am I doing here?" and drained the taste from everything.

Our father sat cross-legged, a knife in one hand, a wedge of Gouda in the other. "Caesar's armies marched on bread and cheese," he would announce, passing slabs around on the blade.

"The more I think about it," she went on, still with a distant, speculative look, "the more I think things were fine in Norfolk."

"You mean, without me," Father said.

I broke the corner off a piece of hardbread, tossed it in the air, and caught in on my tongue.

"I mean, where it wasn't impossible to cook a decent meal for the children. Where we had a table to eat at. Where they had beds to sleep in."

I threw another piece of bread over my head, arched and fell backwards trying to capture it in my mouth.

"Where I had a place to sit."

"If you took an interest in something besides those frigging books,"

Father said. She was staying up late every night, propped in a corner of the living room, rereading, by the light of its tarnished fixture overhead, the historical novels she had hand-carried onto the ship.

"I had plenty of interests in Norfolk," she said, wrenching me upright by one arm. We had lived there a long time for us—two years in the same grey-shingled house. She had established rosebushes against its sunny south side, and in back, she'd unrolled a wire fence around a playhouse left by a much earlier tenant and filled it with six Rhode Island Red hens. Every day she poked around in their odorous feathery litter for the bright surprise of an egg, free of cost. But she could never get them to settle down enough to lay.

Charles was throwing crumbs of hardbread all over the sheet.

She smacked his arm and then turned to me. "Is this how you set an example?"

On weekend afternoons, my father went off on long walks, along the residential lanes of the village and down to the horseshoe of shops on the shore of Lake Malaren. He invited me to go with him. He said we should meet our Swedish neighbors, but our Swedish neighbors did not believe in gratuitous meetings and preferred to watch us from behind delicately parted curtains. For the return route we bought a bag of macaroons or, my father's favorite, a few pieces of marzipan. Now and then we passed a knot of girls my age. "*Hej*," they cried in unison, their knees flexing in the quick curtseys my father's age demanded. "*Hej*," he called back, to my embarrassment, his mouth full of sweet, scooping up air with his hand. "Come here a sec. *Komm.*" He held out our open bag as bait. But they giggled and shied off. "The Swedes are a cold people," he told me.

One Saturday as we approached our house, each bracing in silence to reenter, a girl was standing on one of the stone posts that flanked the steps up into the yard. The sun low and at her back, she loomed above us, then spread her arms and jumped, scooting to where we stood in the road. "Welcome to Sweden," she said, as though we had just arrived. She was too intent on pronouncing the *w*'s correctly to smile.

"*Tack*," my father said, the word for *Thank you*. He could barely control his delight. "*Tack so mycket.*" Without taking his eyes off her, he ordered me, "Quick, go get the book," as though she were about to run away.

She was smaller than I, though her face made her two or three years older. It was thin and cheekless, with a wide thin mouth and teeth a discomfiting grey. The upper lip dipped very long at the center, like a flap over the lower, and gave her a wry expression, the expression of someone not about to escape, someone appraising the situation with an eye to moving in. What I wanted to do was disappear inside with my mother; but I dawdled back with my father's book.

He riffled through it and put a question together syllable by syllable.

The girl's face pinched and wrinkled with the effort to understand. "May I have a look?" she asked. Then her face slackened. "Oh, it is Pia Brandberg. My-name-is-Pia."

"*Tack*," he said emphatically. "*Tack so mycket.*" He eked out another sentence from the book with "Cynthia" at the end.

"Cynthia," said Pia. The *th* drew her tongue out and back over her upper lip.

I glanced at her and made my mouth smile. I didn't like the way her straight hair separated to show the rims of her ears.

"So much for the language barrier," my father boasted to me sidelong.

"In the future," Pia said, "you must ask like so: *Vad heter du?* What-are-you-called. It is the Swedish idiom." She guessed I had no idea what an idiom was. "I shall teach you," she said. Her small eyes glittered with purpose.

On a good day at school, no one paid any attention to me. Bad days left me in such despair I hardly knew who I was. What had happened to the opportunities my father had touted, to make friends from other lands? There was the Egyptian, Ada, a single black braid down her back as thick as my wrist, with an aloof beauty beyond her years; there was Tulla from Finland, whose round face and rough red cheeks seemed to promise friendliness; and Geeta from India, dark and thin, with a gooey red spot between her eyes. They had in common a language I could not seem to learn.

And then there was Wendy, the daughter of the American ambassador, who according to school legend, had mastered French overnight, who found my struggle to remember which consonants not to pronounce entertaining. Mornings in the cloakroom before we donned the school smock, she showed off her frilled blouses and furry sweaters, each monogrammed with her initials. She wore a gold pin etched with *Wendy* and tortoiseshell barrettes shaped like *W's*. For larger political reasons which I could never have grasped, the Sisters allowed her free and capricious play in the class. She was the one who shot my attempts at recitation with snickering rounds, until I gave in myself to spasms of anxious laughter. Sometimes these spilled into incontinence—*accidents*, my mother called them with Georgie—and all I could do was to pray the knee-length smock would hide their traces. At home in secret I washed them out.

Perhaps it was Wendy's ridicule at school that fueled the contempt I felt for Pia Brandberg. Afternoons and Saturdays, I dreaded the scratching at our door, and when I dragged it open, the elfin, unsmiling face announcing, "It is Pia."

Did she think I couldn't see that?

"The persistent Pia," my father called her affectionately. It was fine for him—to try out a few Swedish idioms and then pawn her off on me.

"What shall we do now?" she always asked, as if we had just accomplished something mutually satisfying, as if we faced an array of choices.

Nothing, I wanted to shout. *Just leave me alone.* She never showed up with anyone else; she'd never been among the girls Father and I passed on our walks, girls who now and then strolled by our house, chatting in steamy bursts, darting sidelong looks around the yard, stirring my hopes. Their faces brightened by the cold, they seemed to exude gregarious well being. Might they be trying to make contact? Would they speak English? Wasn't the inevitable presence of Pia, spidery thin, homely Pia, scaring them away?

"I can't come out now," I might say diplomatically.

"Quite fine," said Pia. "I shall wait." Then while I watched from the kitchen window, she scrambled up onto one of the stone pillars on which she'd first appeared to us and, arms spread to perfect her balance, leaped back and forth between the two like an angel guarding the gates.

She worked on teaching me a game that involved juggling balls off the wall of our garage—she was an expert juggler and could keep four going, interspersed with handclaps, knee slaps, and full turns. Half-hearted, I fumbled around with two balls, and even though she allowed me extra misses per turn, she did most of the juggling while I watched.

As darkness crept into the afternoons, she invented a form of hide-and-seek that didn't permit you actually to hide your entire body, but rather position it in such a way that in the deepening twilight it could be mistaken for something else—a shrub, a mound of rock. It was another game that guaranteed her advantage, for she could melt into the dusk with me standing practically beside her. I finally let my brother Charles play with us, so I wouldn't always be *it*. Often as I held myself still and breathless, arms angled from my body, perhaps, like the branches of the hemlock beside me, I could hear the cries of other players, other games, carrying on the cold air from other yards, and I wondered at life's unfairness, that it offered me nothing more than one weird friend, my own kid brother, and the challenge of trying to pass for a tree.

By November, it was dark at three o'clock and still there came the scratching on the door and the announcement, "It is Pia."

"What shall we do now?" I sighed.

"A bloose," she said one afternoon. "We shall sew for you a bloose."

"A bloose?"

"I shall teach you. With a collar, like so. And a pocket, perhaps. Do you wish for pockets?"

"A blouse," I said. It had never occurred to me to wish for pockets or blouses, much less to imagine the creation of either to be within my power. In fact, I didn't care about clothes. My mother discouraged it; she was in charge of figuring out what I needed, and more important, what we could afford. I had never expected this to include furry sweaters or monograms. Now when packages of coarsely woven long underwear showed up on my dresser, through no wishes of mine, I assumed I was going to need them, and grotesque or not they would have to be worn.

"Quite right, a blouse," Pia said. "Shall you come, have a try?"

Her proposition was mildly disquieting—*wish for something*, it said, and what's more, that something might be gotten for nothing. I could hear my mother's reproach. Trying to act as though my following her was a duty to friendship, no more, no less. I entered Pia's house for the first time. It was down a block toward the village center, a large cottage whose faded blue paint hung from the wooden siding in shreds. Inside, a single lamp gilded the layer of dust on a grand piano in the living room. Cobwebs filled in the legs of a carved wooden horse on the hearth in the kitchen and threaded the blue and white plates on a shelf above. A pure white cat rubbed my ankles. Pia's mother bustled aimlessly in a dark dress and baggy apron. Her hair was pulled back in a bun to display the same pointed face as Pia.'s She seemed terribly grateful to see me with her daughter and insisted on serving us hot chocolate, with a dollop of whipped cream. The way my mother's set expression was an unfocussed scowl, Pia's mother's was a smile, twitched into place several times a minute, turned almost to a simper by protruding eyeteeth.

But Pia was fresh with her mother. I didn't need to know Swedish to understand, *None of your business*, or *See what I care*. It made me very uneasy to hear her rudeness and ingratitude echo unpunished, and I felt obliged to counter them by meeting Fru Brandberg's bleached blue eyes as often as I could and returning her smiles, twitch for twitch. When she left the kitchen for a moment, Pia dragged me away from the table, into the hall and up a narrow staircase. "That was a revolting perform-ance," she hissed over her shoulder. I didn't understand. To which of us three was she referring? To what?

The next thing I knew I was flung into the elaborate, demanding world of Pia's room under the eaves. It seemed to contain everything, packed in with compulsive efficiency. There were no empty spaces. The sloping ceiling and walls were covered with maps, over which were tacked photos, postcards, labels, envelopes, signs. Feathers and dried flowers and pieces of colored glass dangled from threads at the one window. Rugs overlapped on the floor; dolls and stuffed animals lay heaped on the bed. Dresser and desktop held stacks of assorted boxes and books. A bookcase on one wall had been converted by upright dividers into an elegant mansion for the smaller dolls. Pia had made all the furniture herself, from more boxes, papier mâché, scraps of wood and fabric and yarn. There were wire chandeliers, crocheted rugs, framed pictures, bowls of fruit, tiny down pillows and quilts on each bed.

"So this is your room," I said emptily, when it seemed I had to say something. The last thing I wanted was for her to think I was compar-ing it to the one I had been assigned at home, a servant's cubicle on the first floor off the kitchen, while the rest of the family slept upstairs.

Pia went right to the kneehole of her desk and pulled out a basket and from it a pile of neatly folded remnants of cloth. "These are for you to choose," she said.

It was too much. "I should go home," I said.

"For the *blouse*," she said.

"I don't really need a blouse," I said. "Why don't we make *you* a blouse?" She always wore the same dull sweaters, the same rumpled grey ski pants.

"Do you wish flowers or no flowers?" She stared at me blankly. I let out a sigh. "Flowers."

"Like so?" She pulled a doll from the crowd on the bed, tidied it up, then held it in front of me. It was wearing a blouse of flowered print, with tiny buttons, a collar trimmed with lace, and pockets.

"Did you make this one?" I asked.

"I make everything," she said.

She lifted my arms away from my sides and began measuring me with her tape. Her quick, light touch caused me to flinch, but that she ignored. Soon she was unfolding the cloth on the floor and cutting through it with long, crunching shears. Then she sat down at the old machine on her desk and began rhythmically pressing the pedal with her foot while she tugged at the cloth above, her pursed face rapidly aging with concentration. I continued to stand there until I realized there was nothing else for me to do. With tentative relief, I sat and slowly let myself loll back on the bed among the dolls. I had had my fill at school of being taught the impossible. It also seemed to me that the less I had to do with the blouse, the greater its chances would be of becoming one, and my chances of deserving it. So she worked by the light of a green-shaded lamp, and I watched from the shadows, and sometimes her foot pumped slowly and other times it broke into a convulsive race, faster than the eye could see.

After a very short time, she stood up and pointed to the floor in front of her. I rose and let her spread out my arms again. She draped me with flowered fabric, smoothed it across the back, pulled it down in front, and straightened the shoulders. It was a shapeless tunic at this stage.

"It's nice," I said politely, actually pleased to find its appeal no stronger. She slipped it off and showed me the side seam, the special way she had double-sewn it to enclose the rough edges. "That's nice too," I said, and I was feeling more relaxed, enough to kneel beside the bookcase and study the decoration of each compartment. Pia invited me to touch things, as I wished, but I kept my hands folded in my lap.

After another stint of pedaling she stopped, reached over, grabbed a handful of my sweater and said, Take it off." I obeyed her the way my mother taught me to obey the doctor. Then Pia helped me slip the blouse on over my undershirt.

There was no mirror in that room, but from what I could see of my arms and front, I thought I must look very stylish. Two puffy sleeves had attached themselves to the tunic, sleeves that gathered in a ruffle at each cuff. I studied Pia's face for a confirmation, but could learn nothing from the way she fussed at the fabric, lapping it closed in the front, a fan of silver pins pressed between her lips. It was a little tight somewhere—across the back, or at the armholes—but this was a constraint I could live with. When she reached into her pants pocket and disclosed a handful of red plastic buttons shaped like hearts, another sigh escaped me. I saw myself in the cloakroom at school, and Wendy silent with envy. Pia's stern expression never changed.

She snapped her fingers twice. "Give it me," she mumbled through pressed lips.

I peeled the blouse off and handed it to her. She sat down at the machine. Oddly contented, I lay back on the bed and drew a crocheted afghan around my bare shoulders. "Did you make this too?" I asked her, hugging it around myself. I felt oddly, blandly sociable.

"I make everything," she reminded me.

Again her foot rose and fell on the pedal, her deft hands guided the fabric under the pulsing needle, the machine chattered hypnotically. On the train home that afternoon, I had been working to memorize another passage from *Une Jolie Maison à la Campagne*, home of the family Lebrun, and for some reason it returned now to my mind in perfectly pronounced cadences—the roof touched in all seasons by the sun, the balcony adorned by the red pompons of a climbing rose, Madame Lebrun happily knitting on the *rez-de-chausée*, while beside her a canary sang in its cage.

There came a pause in the rhythm of the machine. "Pia," I said, "do you know how hard it is to speak French? I don't think I'm ever going to learn."

"I suppose not," she replied without looking up.

"You don't?" I hadn't expected her to agree with me.

"It is not your mother tongue."

"I don't care what it is," I said. "It's a dumb tongue."

"Because you are at home in English." She began pumping at the pedal.

I thought about this for a while, found her certainty reassuring. "But you learned to speak English," I reminded her above the noise of the machine.

Her foot stopped. "But I am not at home," she said. "I try for many years, but I am not at home." She began pedaling again and fiddling with my blouse, and as I watched, I seemed to feel every tug and stroke of her hands on the cloth, as though it were part of my body, threaded with my nerves. She pinned and basted and clipped the collar, and my neck bristled at the touch. It was a sensation too unfamiliar to understand, but I wished it might never stop. Until Pia announced that it was time for me to go, I watched those hands avidly, but it was still not enough. As I walked back to our house in the dark, I thought that it would be just like Pia to come calling for me tomorrow with her mind set on doing something else.

I never did see my blouse again. I asked after it once or twice, knowing that it must exist somewhere, lacking only its heart-shaped buttons—I could have sewn them on myself. "That isn't necessary," Pia told me. "I must fix it," she said vaguely. I didn't really pursue the matter; in fact, giving up the blouse was easy. After months of adjustments and resignations, losses in translation, what was one more?

The next day after school, I went straight from the train station in the village to Pia's and knocked on the door. No one answered. The window upstairs glowed dully. I was about to knock again when Pia's voice spoke up from the shadows, "I do not wish to be in that house." There was a woodstack at the far end of the porch and she was perched, chin to knees, upon it. She wore nothing over her usual sweater and pants. "It is quite intolerable," she said.

"You'll catch cold," I said.

"It's nothing." She slid down and stamped her feet.

"We could go to my house." I hoped she could see as clearly as I did what an empty prospect that was.

She shivered. "It is always nothing." She shouldered open the door. In the kitchen Fru Brandberg glanced up from where she stood clutching the sink. Her eyes and nose were swollen and red. I made myself look away, kept moving behind Pia, until the dim intricate warmth of her room surrounded me. I threw down my books, dropped my jacket, sank onto the foot of the bed with the relief of someone arriving, after long absence, home.

Something was bothering Pia. She paced the channel between bed and bookcase, stopped at the window, pulled on her long upper lip.

"What shall we do?" I asked.

She began to draw in the steam on the glass—a square inside a circle, a circle inside that square, and so on, until things all ran together. As if this had given her an idea, she asked, "Do you wish to play with the dolls?" She was teasing me, I thought, for she reached over and picked from the pile behind me the one wearing the miniature of my blouse.

"Sure," I said, and accepted the others she tossed in my lap—a mother with cottony hair and an apron, a father in felt trousers, then like an afterthought, the male twin of the girl in the blouse. I carried them to the bookcase, knelt, and began amenably to arrange them in the living room. Meanwhile, I assumed, Pia would begin working on my blouse. The mother doll, having acquired a tiny book from a basket, was bent into a striped satin chair to read. The father, who didn't bend, lay on the matching sofa, leaving the boy to play some boy's game on the floor along the back wall. I was deciding what room, what activity to assign the girl when Pia began pounding on the bookcase with her fist and shouting in Swedish.

It was a strange creature she clutched around the middle and shoved headfirst into my comfortable scene—a bald baby doll painted black, swaddled in black cloth, and under its chubby rubber arm, the one prop Pia had not made, a miniature lead gun.

From its little mouth hole where the toy nipple went were coming those loud incomprehensible commands.

"Pia," I said.

She snatched the girl from my hands and threw her into the living room, toppling the spool lamp and the mother in her chair. She snarled again in Swedish, then turned to me and said calmly, "Put up their hands."

I began to understand. I reached into the room for the father, half the size of the black baby, and adjusted his arms. I was working on the mother when Pia's Swedish became soft and sibilant She jerked her head in my direction, then made the same sounds, by which I understand they were my lines—rather, the mother's lines—so I tried to reproduce them. Then flatly, out of the side of her mouth, Pia translated: "Please, I have done nothing. Please, don't shoot me right through the heart."

As the scene went on, the intruder forced mother, father, daughter to take off the meticulous clothes Pia had made for them and assume embarrassing positions on the round doily rug in the middle of the room. And I continued to repeat the lines Pia fed me in Swedish, mimicking every melodramatic inflection, curious to hear the English translations that came afterwards in quick neutral asides. "Would you like to see a trick?" the girl asked. "I will do anything you wish, but please don't kill me." The father began to rage at the mother for not locking the door, until the black baby threatened to cut his fingers off. The mother tried at first to be polite, offering the baby food, and was pitched again onto the floor. "What have I done," she cried, her legs thrust straight into the air. "Oh what have I done?"

Before long I wasn't pretending the emotion; it rose up to meet the Swedish Pia pronounced for me as though I knew just what it meant. The more I understood the showdown in the bookcase, the more I forgot everything else. There came a point, and I could not say when, when the script became bilingual, though the parts in original English still came to me by surprise, like translations from another tongue. The girl muttered nasty insults behind the baby's back. The father threatened the baby impressively with the full power of the U.S. Embassy, but was butted aside. From where he landed facedown beside the couch, he demanded that his own life be taken to spare the rest. My eyes filled at the nobility of his intention. But the mother had other ideas. She sidled up to the baby and whispered in my voice, "Why don't you just take the girl instead? We don't need her. Take her and leave the rest of us alone."

It was a terrible thing to hear. For a few seconds I was stunned silent, waiting, I think, for some objection from the father, but he was not moved to speak. Then more to escape what I felt than to give it expression, I started to whimper. I was still holding the mother doll, and I pressed her to my chest like a hurt child. "Oh Pia," I cried, "no mother would ever say that." I rocked back and forth in distress. "No mother could."

My tears seemed to elate her. Her eyes grew bright and her chin jutted sharp as a trowel. She picked up the father doll and threw the girl down in his place, then poked at her with his foot, exploding with a string of Swedish. Breathing as if she had just come running from far away, she blurted the translation: "It doesn't matter what happens to this one. I shall never think of her as mine."

She looked at me expectantly. I studied the mother doll in my hand as though its shape and construction would tell me what to say. There was nothing left. When I glanced up, Pia was still looking at me. I felt slightly dizzy, seemed to be staring out of a deep cave. I returned to whimpering.

All this time the boy doll sat neglected against the back wall. Now I heard fumbling amid the furniture and looked up to see the black baby point the gun at the boy's head, and fire it throatily. The boy fell sideways and expired without a word.

Walking home in the dark, I felt sick to my stomach. What had happened? I thought of Pia's own words, "a revolting performance." I had spoken forbidden words, thoughts, I had cried, sunk to some unspeakable depth. Hoping to avert discovery and punishment, I made a promise to the starless sky never to visit Pia's room again.

For three days I kept it, assuming all the while persistent Pia would come to call for me and manage cleverly to break me down. When she never did, the promise faded into the shadowy irrelevance of other guilty reflexes, like smiles for Fru Brandberg. By the end of the week, I was trudging to Pia's house, trying to look less like a sinner defying hell than a martyr approaching the stake. Her front door opened before I could knock, and there she stood like fate, that sharp, needy face, the pallid skin, urgent eyes. She raced up the stairs by twos, I went after with attempted dignity. She greeted me on her threshold with the dolls. Hating her, and myself, I accepted them from her trembling hands.

Where was the flowered blouse, with the lace trim and heart-shaped buttons? It seldom entered my mind, caught up as I was in the black baby's hypotheses of sensual violence. At school, when Madame Sibouet was her most impassive or Wendy her most supercilious, I imagined the most satisfying reprisals in which they were stripped of their power and pretense, along with their clothes. Then one day in real life, I scored a victory over Wendy, who hung over my desk and whispered, "You don't even know what *pee* is," grinning to expose the gap between her upper front teeth.

My breath caught: I thought she had somehow discovered the dreadful secret of my accidents.

She shifted her weight from one patent-leather shoe to the other, shook her curls, and tapped on my desk. "Knock, knock. Who's there. Stupid. Cynthia doesn't even know about *pee*."

"Pia's a name," I gasped. "I have a friend called Pia."

Wendy doubled over with a fake laugh. "She says it's a *name*." Geeta chuckled and rolled her bulging eyes.

Maybe I saw *Pia* spelled in my mind, maybe it was just that I had to say something, anything, to deny the old truth, that I deserved their contempt many times over. A desperate answer came to me, something I'd forgotten I knew from seventh grade in Norfolk. "You mean *pi*." I tried to sound contemptuous myself. "Pea is a green vegetable. Pi is equal to three point one four."

Wendy's cute features went blank, and I realized, in disbelief, that my answer was the right one. "You should learn to pronounce English better," I said hoarsely before she flounced off.

After school in Pia's room meanwhile, we worked to embellish our basic scene. We set matchstick fires in a glass ashtray and, threatening the family with the same fate, threw their smaller furnishings into the flames. There was open warfare now among family members, as each offered to strike a different bargain with the baby. In the end, Pia always took over and brought off the recurring finale when the baby announced to the boy doll, "Now you're going to get it," and he did.

It must have been my father, the sailor, who once told me that the farthest stars have burned themselves out by the time their beams prick out night sky. It may be the same with shared secrets—no matter how dazzling, how outrageous their shine, it is phantom light, its source exhausted once shown. As the weeks passed, the scenes Pia and I staged began to lose energy. There was a limit to the delinquent novelties our minds could come up with. As the passion subsided, the black baby seemed silly. We began watching, hearing ourselves, and each other. That first revulsion I had felt toward Pia and what we were doing returned unchecked.

I think Pia was having a similar reaction to me. Her lines grew stilted, began presenting themselves in carefully composed but listless English. One afternoon when I arrived at her house after school, Fru Brandberg opened the door and gave me to understand that Pia had gone to the Milk Central on an errand, and I felt relieved. The next two days I went straight home and, as if for penance, memorized more attentively than ever before a long passage about winter *chez la famille Lebrun*—how the snow covered the earth and wove a light lace on the branches of the trees, how the boy named Maurice made balls of it, and his sister Jeanne slid happily on the ice, while the blackbirds, which were called crows, flew about the house seeking something to eat, but found nothing.

My partnership with Pia might have ended then, I think, with the dwindling of novelty and need. French was no longer impossible, Wendy no longer invincible, and our household goods arrived, no worse for their detour to Liverpool. But then one night, just as we were sitting down to dinner at our long-lost-chrome-legged kitchen table, my mother happened to mention what she'd learned from the woman who lived behind us: two years before we arrived in Sweden, Pia's brother had killed himself—put a gun to his head, pulled the trigger, very messy. It was information passed from woman to woman by pantomime and sheer resolve, for neither spoke the other's language. Apparently Pia's mother had dreamt of a career as a concert pianist for her gifted son, while Pia's father, who sold vacuum cleaners, wanted his boy to become an engineer. The boy didn't want to become an engineer. Or a concert pianist. He wanted to go to America and play jazz. His mother cried, his father laughed. So. My mother pointed at her temple. "Please pass the meat loaf," she said.

My stomach was churning. Spread in front of me were our familiar Melmac plates, the matching aluminum glasses, the hen saltshaker, the rooster pepper mill. Georgie was where he belonged, in the old wooden high chair, scrubbed almost paintless. The rooms beyond had filled up with more familiar things, unpacked, arranged in order. As though he were the expert, my father said the place had begun to look like home. How could this, what my mother said, be true?

"Apparently Mr. Brandberg went north after it happened. He chops down trees. His wife gets a little money every month."

There was a tinted sepia portrait of Pia's brother sitting on a square of yellow lace on the Brandberg's grand piano. I remembered the close-set eyes, their brown stare mocked by too-pink lips and cheeks. Pia had said he didn't live with them any more. Her mother had nodded, twitching smiles. There had been no sign of a father anywhere.

"We should all of us try to be nice to Pia," my mother said.

I could feel myself flush under her gaze. Why was she looking at me? I didn't shoot Pia's brother. How could she dare pretend to look sad over this death of someone she didn't know? "Two hands," I reminded Georgie, who was raising his cup of milk.

"Cynthia," my mother said, as though she had an inkling of the games Pia had taught me.

"I *am* nice to her," I said. The fact was Pia was too imperious and preoccupied to notice whether you were nice to her or not. But what did my mother know? This wasn't one of her books. This wasn't picturesque.

"Does she ever mention?" my mother asked.

"Angie," my father said.

"I'm only curious," she said.

"I don't think it's any of your business," I said haughtily. I would defend my friend Pia, the juggler, the hider, the maker, from her easy words.

"Cynthia," my father said.

"You would think that poor child would have mentioned it." My mother's tone implied I was withholding information. "The poor child has lost more than a brother, after all."

In my mind I saw Pia in her kitchen, picking at her dinner, separated from her inconsolable mother by two empty chairs. I looked across at Georgie, who had gone red-faced and Buddha-like the way he did when he was doing his business; then over at Charles, chewing potatoes and beets with his mouth open. The fact was I *had* known for some time the story my mother had just reported with such self-importance. Maybe not the gaudy details, but the same dark, furious core. Tomorrow afternoon, I would call for Pia, we would turn our backs on these tables, these intolerable houses, we would walk the dark road out of the village arm and arm.

"Still waters run deep," my mother said. If that was supposed to be some wise reference to Pia, who talked and moved incessantly, she couldn't have been more impertinent.

"Dow," said Charles, pretending to shoot himself in the head with his finger. "Dow, dow, dow."

She turned on him ferociously. "Don't ever let me see you," she said, slapping his hand out of the air. Charles tucked his fist in his armpit and laughed.

Zoe

She liked to be the first to speak. It wasn't that she wanted to be nice, or put them at ease; it was her way of warning them not to be, of setting the tone she liked best: bemused, even ironic, but formal. She didn't want any of them thinking she was someone to cultivate. Whenever those voices, low and strained, interrupted her life downstairs, whether they came late at night from the front hall or mornings from the kitchen, she slipped into the one-piece camouflage suit she used as a bathrobe, wrapped the belt twice around her slim waist, and ascended to meet her mother's latest. She liked to catch him with breakfast in his mouth, or romance on his mind, and then before he could compose himself, announce, "I am Zoe, her daughter," offering a little bow and a graceful hand, limp as a spray of japonica.

It usually left him stammering, fumbling—this blend of childlike respect and self-possession. If he'd already begun to imagine her mother recharging his life with pleasure and purpose, Zoe's winsome presence made such visions more intense, then tipped them into unsettling. Though he'd never gone in for kids before, he might find himself thinking at first how agreeable it would be to have a delicate creature like her around, slender, long-legged, with pale freckles across her nose. These days she has her auburn hair bobbed at the ears so it curls up shorter in back above a softly fringed nape. But if he thought for a moment how much the child must know, her poise could seem ominous—all the things *he* didn't know, was hungry to find out, but might not want to hear.

"So what's it like, living with her?" one of them asked Zoe once, as if he expected soon to be sharing the experience, to be given exclusive credit for recognizing that her mother was an extraordinary woman. He reminded Zoe of a large rabbit—a confusion of timidity and helpless lust.

"There's never a dull moment," Zoe answered, sweet but nonchalant. "I meet a lot of interesting men." That was stretching things. Most were rabbits.

Often they felt called upon to tell Zoe, "Your mom's a great lady." Did they think Zoe was responsible for raising her mother and not the other way around? Or that she had a choice of mothers? Or that she couldn't guess what they meant, that her mother was something else in bed, that they'd never done it to a Sibelius symphony before?

Since the age of five when her parents split up, Zoe Cameron and her mother, Phyllis Rush, have lived beyond the D.C. Beltway in The Colonies of Virginia, clusters of townhouses subtly tucked into one hundred acres of rolling woods, whose inhabitants readily paid a little more to get aesthetic design and proximity to nature. Set against the ridge of a hill, with cathedral ceilings and an expanse of glass to the south, Zoe's mother's unit welcomes light, draws it in to challenge her work—heavy terra cotta, here and there a dull giant bronze—set off by white walls. Each piece has been given a woman's name, yet they are only parts of women, global buttocks and thighs, pairs of breasts larger than the heads mounted upon them—Leda, Electra, Helen, truncated. They are one reason Zoe stopped bringing home friends, who tended to stare about in stunned silence or whisper words like *gross* and *perverted*. Zoe has learned contempt for kids her own age, who cannot understand true art. Yet she hates her mother's women: fat, naked blobs. The bald definition of nipple or vulva makes her sick. There are more of them on exhibit in the local gallery her mother manages in The Commons. The public tends not to buy them, but Phyllis does enter them in shows and they have won awards, including a purchase prize at the Corcoran. After that, a man from the *Washington Post* came out to photograph Phyllis at home in her skylit studio. Zoe declined to be in any of his shots. He took her mother to dinner in Great Falls. When Zoe came up the next morning to leave for school, he was in the kitchen alone making raisin toast. He offered her a slice, trying to act as if he owned the place, but she drank her sixteen ounces of water as if he weren't there. It was easier than ever to resist that sweet yeasty aroma, tainted as it was by his male pride.

As far as Lucas is concerned, Zoe would give anything to go back and start over again with the moment she arrived home in the early afternoon to find his body sticking out from under the sink. Thinking her mother had finally called someone to fix the dishwasher, Zoe set her wide-brimmed hat down on the table and looked on absently as the body twisted and grunted with its efforts. Her hunger had been stubborn that day, conjuring extravagant food fantasies that almost sabotaged a test in pre-calculus. But she had conquered temptation, and now what she wanted was plenty of water and maybe a carrot to get through until dinner.

"Let me out of here," came a roar, all of a sudden, followed by bumping sounds and *great god*'s, and the upper part of the man extricated itself from the cabinet. His knuckles were smudged with black, his once-starched shirt was sharply wrinkled, and he rubbed the top of his head ruefully, but when he saw Zoe, his expression flexed in a smile. "Well, look at you," he said. "Don't you look out of this world!" And not expecting such a remark from a repairman, Zoe, who was known to become transfixed by her own image whenever she found it reflected, who that day was wearing one of her favorite suits—broadly padded shoulders over a short slim skirt, a blue that turned her eyes blue—could not bring herself to disagree, nor think of anything to say back. She did try her ironic geisha bow, but in the same instant noticed the roaches hurrying over the sill of the sink cabinet and out across the kitchen floor in a dark stream.

Before she knew it she had emitted a soft scream, more out of embarrassment than fear. She had certainly seen roaches in the kitchen before, those nights when she gave in to temptation and felt her way up the stairs in the dark. Thinking it was almost like sleepwalking, she was almost not responsible for what she was about to do: forage for food, cookies, bagels, leftover pasta, cinnamon raisin toast drenched in butter. When she turned on the light, there they always were collected on some vertical surface in clusters of imperceptible activity, and she caught her breath in disgust, but went on to get what she had come for. "They must have a nest under there," the man said, a little out of breath. He was somehow hopping and stooping at the same time, slapping at the creatures with one of his moccasins. "How about giving me a hand here?"

Zoe looked down helplessly at her clothes, her inch-high patent heels.

"How about insecticide, a spray or something?"

"If we have any, it's in there." She pointed to the cabinet from which they kept coming. The floor around him was awash with brown spots. Some had been hit and were finished moving. "Close the door," Zoe cried. When she realized the sense of her suggestion, she repeated it more calmly.

He smacked the door shut, and the stream was cut off. "Good thinking," he said.

She pursed her lips to hide her pleasure. Producing a fly swatter from the closet in the front hall, she commenced ceremoniously to slap at the remaining roaches from the comfortable distance its handle allowed. "Mother," she called.

"She went to the store," the man said, rubbing his bare foot along his pants leg, then replacing his shoe. "I thought I'd keep myself busy until she got back."

That was when Zoe realized he wasn't a plumber and that she had been inexplicably foolish. Her mother, who scorned home maintenance, who refused to spend any time on fixing things when she could be making something new—why would her mother suddenly hire a plumber? "I am Zoe, her daughter," she said, with a final stroke of the swatter, but it was too late.

"I assumed as much," the man said. "From the side you're a dead ringer." He introduced himself: Lucas Washburn. He had light, almost frizzy hair and eyebrows, no cheekbones to speak of, and his nose must have been broken once and never set straight. His skin was fissured from past acne, and his eyes were a flat, changeless gray. He was not handsome, Zoe decided, but there was something about him. His hair was cropped short, his skin evenly tanned, his khaki pants creased. Clean—in spite of his disarray, he seemed oddly, utterly clean.

"I assumed you were the plumber." Zoe pulled the broom out from beside the refrigerator and began with dignity to sweep roach hulls into a pile.

"I can see why. I hear you're down to one bathtub."

Zoe stiffened at the forced intimacy, the hint of sympathy. She normally did not interfere in her mother's affairs, patiently allowing what Phyllis would call nature to take its course. But this man, with his long cheekless face, who had poked around under their sink, discovered their roaches—he was not at all her mother's type, and the sooner he was history, the better. "And it happens to be my bathtub downstairs, which gets pretty inconvenient if you think about it. One of her quote friends pulled the soap holder off the wall in *her* tub and half the tiles came with it, and the guest tub has a leak that drips into the front hall. Actually, the whole house is a total wreck." She finished, and made herself laugh, but in the silence that was his reply, she heard her words echo like a blurted confession, false notes, as if something were playing in the background in a different key. Blasé wasn't working.

"If I had my tools," Lucas said, "we could get this sink to drain, and I could take a look at those tubs. Next time I'll bring my tools."

That is a lot to assume, next time, Zoe thought, and to her surprise, that was what she said.

Lucas nodded solemnly, then turned his back on her and began washing his hands. Should she explain that her mother had very liberal views, that if men and women were allowed to live naturally, without the inhibitions imposed by society, they would choose to spend their nights in each other's beds all the time, different other's beds as the impulse moved them, mornings parting, more often than not, forever? And that was all right with her, Zoe, for it was much worse when a man of her mother's showed up a second time, all twitchey and trembly, and suggested doing something that included her, and her mother, seduced by some transient vision of family, agreed.

"I appreciate the warning," Lucas said, drying his long hands finger by finger. Then he added, "Maybe I've got something in common with those guys in there"—he jerked his head toward the roach settlement—"I'm pretty hard to get rid of."

That night her mother and Lucas fixed strip steaks, steamed artichokes, wild rice. As she often did, Phyllis set up small folding tables on the balcony off the living room in view of the sunset, but Lucas moved the hibachi to the backyard below to comply with the county fire code. ("What fire code?" Phyllis asked. She had never heard of any fire code.) Zoe went downstairs to change into a faded denim jumpsuit, espadrilles. She rolled a fuchsia bandana into a headband and tied her curls down, Indian-style. She freshened the strip of pale blue shadow on her lower lids, all the while aware that Lucas was right beyond the glass door, the drapes that don't quite meet, calling arguments up to her mother in favor of well-done. Phyllis stuck to rare. Her face blank and impersonal, Zoe made a last appraisal in the full-length mirror. She pushed a fist into her sucked-in abdomen. *I hate my stomach,* she thought. You couldn't trust mirrors; they could be designed to make people look thinner. All the ones in stores were deceptive that way.

Lucas sawed off huge blocks of meat and swallowed them almost whole. Her mother plucked her artichoke, petal by petal, dragged each one through her lips slowly, her subtly silvered eyelids drooping with the pleasure. She had a strong jaw, and a wide mouth, with large teeth—but she knew how to recontour her face with light and shade, to make her eyes seem bigger, mysterious. Yes, Zoe had her nose, rising fine and straight from the brow, nostrils flared back, so that if you happened to have a cold or be cold, their moisture was open to view. Zoe had learned to carry her head tilted slightly forward, to make it hard for anyone to see into her nose.

To Lucas' credit he seemed not to be noticing Phyllis' sensual performance. He was expressing his suspicion that her clogged dishwasher and drain stemmed from a failure to scrape dirty dishes thoroughly; a small chicken bone in the trap, for example, was all it took to start an obstruction.

Phyllis threw her head back and laughed. "You sound like my mother," she said.

Lucas wasn't fazed. "You're talking to someone who's trained to eliminate human error." Lucas flew for Pan Am; Phyllis had picked him out of the happy-hour crowd in the lounge at Dulles Airport after dropping off a friend.

Phyllis stroked his closest arm. "That's Mother all over again."

"Another word for it is *accident.*"

"It's only a dishwasher," Phyllis said, sullenly, and the fatalist in Zoe settled back with the vaguest sense of loss to watch this man ruin things with her mother long before he could get the bathtubs fixed.

In a steady, almost uninflected voice, he was talking improvements. He could see a brick patio in their backyard, and redwood planters and a hexagonal redwood picnic table. Zoe saw clumsy strategy, tinged with pathos. He frankly admitted he was tired of living on the tenth floor of a condo in Hunting Towers. Between his job and the apartments he unpacked in, he never had his feet on the ground. "It's about time I got my feet on the ground," he said. Phyllis suggested he sprinkle dirt in his socks.

She was being strangely tolerant; maybe he had touched off an attack of what she called her *passion for reality*, when practical dailiness, what everyone else did, became the exotic object of curiosity and desire. Lucas was neither suave nor witty. If you sanded his face, he might be handsome. Zoe guessed he had what her mother would call a good body, though she, Zoe, had trouble looking at a male body long enough to form a complete picture of one. She tended to focus on them piece by piece, and they stayed like that in her mind, a jumble of parts. Her mother often said it was an insult to women the way men let themselves go after a certain age, after they had good incomes. Phyllis herself kept her weight down by smoking and thought women should band together and hold men to the same physical standards everyone held women to.

"Why me?" Phyllis asked Lucas, and seemed genuinely to wonder. "For how many years you've been tied to no place particular and been perfectly happy? Why pick on my place? Maybe I like it this way."

"Look at that," Lucas said, pointing above them at a strip of white streaks and blotches on the cedar stain. "Look at the mess those birds have made of your siding. Starlings. They must have a roost in the eaves. I'd have to take care of that before I'd put in a patio right under their flight lines!"

Phyllis pulled forward a lock of her thick dark hair. "I don't begrudge them that. It's nature." She gave a quick yank, then let the breeze lift an offending gray strand from her fingers.

"Like roaches under the sink."

Zoe held her breath as her mother lit a cigarette. Was he joking or criticizing? Either way he had no right; either way her mother would finally put him in his place. Then why was she stretching, smiling languidly at his rudeness? "Everyone has them," she said, blowing a plume of smoke. "They're a fact of life."

"You don't have to give in totally," Lucas persisted.

"It isn't in me to go around poisoning things."

Her mother's reasonableness was a puzzle to Zoe. *Why him?* she kept asking herself, until the answer came to her, all at once: it made her a little queasy. It was obviously something to do with sex that gave Lucas this power, this license. Wasn't her mother always declaring that everything came down to that? It must be something sexual he did to her mother or for her, which she, Zoe, for all her determined precocity, had not yet figured out. Then she felt very empty—empty as though she had failed an exam, empty because she didn't want to think of Lucas that way. In the back of her mind, she had been hoping he was different, and she didn't even know she was hoping until he turned out to be the same—just another male, who in the irresistible flux of life must soon disappear. Well, she could care less.

That night Zoe ate. Once dead silence told her Lucas and her mother had settled down, she stole upstairs in the dark, removed from the freezer a half gallon of vanilla ice cream and went back down to her room. She sat on the bed, and gazing at the photos of lithe models she had cut from her magazines, began to spoon ice cream into her mouth. Each mouthful hit her empty stomach like a cold stone. It made her feel a little crazy; she couldn't think straight anymore. She swung between defiance—when she agreed with herself that this was incomparable pleasure, no matter how high the price, this cool, bland sweetness, this private solitude—defiance, and despair. "Eat up," she heard her mother encouraging, as she had all evening, though never showing concern when Zoe didn't. "She eats like the proverbial bird," her mother told Lucas. And then Lucas had said, "Do you know how much a bird eats? One of those starlings, for example? They eat something like four times their body weight in one day."

Ah Lucas, the way he looked at Zoe then, as if he knew that sometimes she forgot she must be thinner. She forgot the terrible burden of stomach and hateful thighs, which kept you from ever being wonderful, and she ate, and having forgotten, she ate more, to forget she forgot. One hand around the damp, softening box of ice cream, in the other the spoon, hands like bird claws, eating like a bird. Her stomach danced madly as it filled with birds. Her whole body felt in motion. She strutted across her own mind, plump-chested, preening; she opened her wings and took off, soared and swooped above the balcony where Lucas, the flier, watched captivated. And then the ice cream was gone, and all that motion froze, like someone caught in the act. She looked down at her denim thighs spreading against the bed; she could barely get both hands around one. Her stomach was monstrous, almost pregnant. She was losing her shape. She would turn into one of those crude female blobs of her mother's. The thought alone was all it took to convulse her, as, eyes closed above the toilet, she imagined all the birds escaping from the cage of her ribs.

Afterwards she would not allow herself to sleep. Awake burned more calories, burned flesh from bones. She held one hand to the hollow of her throat and felt her heart beating fast and hot as a bird's.

This afternoon Zoe found her mother nestled in the wine velvet cushions of the sofa, her legs drawn up under a long Indian cotton skirt, smoking with one hand, sipping maté tea with the other. From the dull puffiness of her mother's eyes, Zoe could tell she had been crying. *It is all right to cry,* Phyllis has always said. *It is a natural response of the body. Holding it back is harmful.* Zoe hates it when her mother cries, hates to see the pain, the rivulets of mascara, the surrender.

"The bus was a little late today," Zoe says, hitching the knees of her linen pants and perching on the chair opposite.

Her mother pulled herself upright, bare soles on the floor, began carefully to shift the position of everything around her—the huge pillows, ashtray, teapot, the extra cup, which she filled and handed to Zoe. "You're not happy," she told her daughter.

"I'm not?" Zoe asked, with a careful laugh.

"Oh, Zoe, you don't have to pretend. But why, when two people love each other, can't at least one of them be happy? You'd think they could pool their resources and work on one of them. Tell me something you want, Zoe, okay?"

"Kids my age just aren't very happy." Her mother was in one of her moods. "We grow out of it. It's no big deal."

"But what would make you happy? We could manage it."

"You must have had a bad day," Zoe said.

Phyllis took a long pull on her cigarette. "For six hours I have tried to work." She didn't exhale but let the smoke seep out as she talked. "I felt like any minute my hands were going to do something no one has ever done before, but they never did. Nothing. I might as well have been kneading bread. At least I'd have something to show for my time."

"Let's go to the mall," Zoe suggested. She and her mother have always had a good time shopping for Zoe's clothes. When Zoe was small, her mother said, it was like having a doll. Now Zoe has her own ideas, and Phyllis, rather than objecting, seems able to guess almost infallibly what they are—sophisticated angular lines, in pastels or white and black, plenty of defining black; Phyllis combs the racks, and brings a steady supply of possibilities into the fitting room for Zoe to try. Phyllis has always shopped for herself alone and piecemeal, at craft fairs, antique markets, Episcopal church rummage sales in Leesburg, Fairfax. She's owned her favorite jacket for over twenty years—brown leather with a sunrise appliquéd in faded patches and strips on the back.

"I'm going back to pots," Phyllis said dramatically. "Tomorrow I'm hooking up the wheel."

"Let's go to the mall." Zoe bounced twice in the chair to demonstrate eagerness. "I need summer things. That would make me happy."

Her mother paused, searched Zoe's face. "Lucas gets in at five," she said finally. "I think he'll be coming right over."

"Lucas?" Why the flare of panic? Zoe had not seen him since the afternoon of the roaches, assumed that, like one of her mother's moods, he had passed.

"That's what he said last week before he left. He had back-to-back European runs. He said he'd be carrying his tools in the trunk of his car." Her mother's voice quavered, as if she were afraid of something, too.

"What did *you* say?"

Her mother went into a prolonged shrug. "I said all right."

"Well, you must like him then," Zoe said dismissively, deciding it was all right with her, at least one of them would be happy.

"I don't know. I don't understand him. I don't know what he's after." She laughed nervously.

"Mother," Zoe said, stressing each syllable. This was no time for either one of them to act innocent.

"Do you know what he said to me? He said, 'Why do you women assume that's all you've got to offer?'" Phyllis shook her hair violently. "We shouldn't be talking like this."

"We always talk like this."

"I know, but . . ."

"Don't be weird, okay? You've got to tell me what's going on." That has been, after all, Zoe's main fare—knowing. "I can handle things."

"I was asking him to spend the night."

"So?" Zoe had handled that countless times. Then all at once question and answer came together in her mind. "He didn't spend the night?" A rush of feeling, worse than any amount of fear, washed away her strength. She fell back into the chair, crushing her linen blazer.

"He said, number one, it wasn't safe anymore and I should know better, and number two, that it didn't matter because he'd promised himself the next time he met a woman he liked he would wait to sleep with her for six months." Her mother spoke haltingly, as though his reasoning mortified her.

"He said he liked you anyway?"

"He said he'd been through enough relationships that began with great sex. He can't afford another."

Zoe pulled herself up straight again. "Did you tell him what you think, about tapping into the flow of nature, and creating the sensuous present?"

"I can't remember," her mother said faintly, then all at once roared angrily through her teeth. "Forget him," she said, bounding up, jabbing each foot into a thong. "Let's go. He's too damned controlled. Forget him."

"I don't mind staying here and waiting to see if he shows up." Zoe's voice was playing tricks on her, first whispering and then suddenly wanting to shout. "It would be nice to have the plumbing work."

Lucas arrived around seven, looking as if he'd never thought for a moment that he wouldn't. He was wearing fresh khakis and a white knit shirt, with the last of four neck buttons open. He had stopped somewhere to rent a giant ladder, which he had tied onto the ski rack of his perfectly restored Karman Ghia. If there was awkwardness in the rather formal greetings he received from mother and daughter in the front hall, he didn't seem to notice; he was more interested in introducing the two of them to his plumber's pliers, assorted wrenches, a drain snake, a staple gun, and a roll of six-inch-wide screening. He was ready to work.

"You must be hungry," Phyllis said. "I've got pastrami, Swiss cheese. A wonderful melon. Aren't you too tired for this? I mean, what time is it for you? It must be after midnight. You ought to sleep. I can make up the couch," she added quickly.

He wasn't ready to sleep. He'd spent all that time in the air dreaming of feet-on-the-ground work, making mental lists of things to do. He had promised to return the ladder the next morning, and the sun was already dropping into the trees in back. "First things first," he said, unlashing the ladder from his car. He took one end, Phyllis and Zoe the other, and he led them back into the house, down the front hall, miraculously through the living room, without bumping a life-sized bronze of staunchly planted legs and hips—the Arch of Triumph, he had dubbed it last week. Out on the balcony, he pressed his end over the rail and took over theirs.

He dug the ladder firmly into the grass below, then produced a shoelace from his pocket and tied one end around the staple gun, the other around a belt loop. He slipped the roll of screen up his arm, swung a leg onto the ladder, and descended. When he reached the ground, he stamped his feet a few times as if to get used to it. "Come on down," he called back to them. Zoe had never been on a ladder before—the whole thing made her think of burning buildings, great escapes—she scrambled over the edge, linen pants, Capezios and all, and breathing deep against the slight sway, carefully eased herself from rung to rung. She was afraid of losing it if she looked down, so turned her eyes on her mother's face, where she found the blank patient expression of someone lying low.

"I think I'll use the stairs," her mother said, and disappeared. By the time she slid open the glass door, Lucas had extended the ladder twice to the impossible height of three stories. "It's simply physics," he had told Zoe, waving away her offer to steady the bottom. "It can't go anywhere." He had one foot on the first rung.

"Wait a minute, wait a minute," Phyllis said.

Lucas froze, eyes front, hands in midair.

"What are you going to do?"

"I am going to staple this stuff over the vents in the soffit, to keep the birds from getting up under your eaves and building nests and shitting on your siding." It took great control for him to speak that slowly, clearly.

"And you have to do it right now? I mean, it must be two in the morning."

Lucas looked at his watch and then back at Phyllis, stared at her as if he were having trouble translating her language. He didn't want to sleep, he didn't want to stop and wait for sleep to overtake him, he wanted to push himself until he dropped—at least that was what Zoe recognized.

Phyllis clenched her jaw, swallowed visibly. "I don't know whether I'm being pushed around or cared for."

"Give it a while," Lucas said, "and you ought to be able to tell the difference." Unblinking, he watched her, as she appeared to consider this. Then her shoulders fell forward.

"I'll be inside," she said.

Lucas was on the ladder, his feet over Zoe's head, when she realized that she must love him. She wasn't sure why—maybe because he didn't belong to her mother, maybe because there was something so definite about him, but it wasn't a boyfriend sort of love. He didn't have to return it; in fact she would rather he didn't. He just had to stay there, in her life, and let her watch him while he fixed things, and she would privately love him. The ladder flexed in toward the house.

"You sure this will hold you?" she called up to him. "What if the three pieces come apart?"

"I checked everything out," he called from the higher rungs. "But thanks for your concern."

She pursed her mouth. He was pressing the strip of screen against the eaves with the fingertips of one hand. With the other he tried to bring the staple gun into range, but he couldn't get it there: the shoelace was too short. He cursed and then tugged again, but only managed to hike his pants up on the right side where he'd tied it. The ladder shuddered, and Zoe clutched it for all she was worth.

Then resolutely, Lucas climbed up a rung, and then another, until his head and shoulders ran out of ladder, the tips of which had come to rest just below the gutters. He wrapped his legs around the top rungs, twisted his right hip toward the house, and blindly felt the screen into place, firing the staple gun along its edges, clunk, clunk. He wavered precariously at each recoil. She gaped up at him in wonder, and not just his body at the odd foreshortening angle, but his whole heroic being seemed clear to her, shining. She was still afraid he would fall, but just as sure that there was a way to fall, a way to land so you didn't get hurt, and Lucas would know what it was.

In a few minutes he was down, and without pausing to comment or change the arrangement with the inadequate shoelace, had moved the ladder and mounted it again. He did this three times, four. And Zoe remained dutifully at its foot, face upturned, holding him in place with her eyes.

At first she thought her ears had begun to ring from craning her neck so long. She covered and uncovered them—the noise was outside, she had never heard it start, and now it had grown in volume to something shrill and unpleasant. Beyond the cluster of townhouses to the south, a long cloud of black birds hung in the pale violet sky. They were their own fixed path, funneling in from the invisible distance, spreading to rest in the saved trees at the base of the back slope. The shrieking came from the trees; when you looked closely among the leaves, it was as if each branch was thick with black fruit. Zoe had never seen anything like it.

When Lucas came down to move the ladder for the last time, she said, "They don't like what we're doing." It did seem their shrieking was directed at the two of them. "Maybe they think you've caught one of their friends up there behind the screen," Zoe said, to be amusing, but Lucas said it was just what starlings did, gather for the night in communal roosts. They had probably been there every night since early spring, carrying on, making a mess. She had just never noticed it.

"I guess I'd rather sleep up under our eaves where I could get comfortable than have to balance all night on a tree branch," said Zoe.

"Starlings are the roaches of the bird world," Lucas called down meaningfully as he climbed one last time. A few minutes later he was finished, sliding the ladder back to carrying size with loud clanks.

"Could you see whether they've built any nests yet up there?" Zoe asked.

"Didn't look," Lucas said.

"Probably they haven't yet." She gazed skeptically at the streaks and blotches on the siding.

"Hard to say. It is that time of year. You know," Lucas went on, "being a pilot, there's no love lost between myself and birds. I could tell you a story or two about the accidents they've caused, hitting propellers, getting sucked into jet engines, gumming up the works. A couple months ago out of Kennedy a bunch of gulls sailed right up into one of my engines two minutes after takeoff."

"That's weird. What happened to them?"

"The point isn't what happened to them. The way a jet turbine works, it's got these finely balanced blades. A bird carcass gets in there and the engine chokes up." Zoe made a little gagging sound of revulsion. "Look," Lucas said, "that engine was ruined. I had to fly out over the Atlantic and dump 100,000 pounds of fuel before that jumbo was light enough to land minus an engine. That's good money down the drain, not to mention the danger. When you look at it that way, it's them or us."

Zoe could tell that she was being tested. She wasn't supposed to waste sympathy on the gulls, act squeamish at their fate. That was all right. She could see that a jumbo jet was more important than a handful of birds. Lucas was realistic. How much he knew about certain things—clear, definite knowledge. She searched her mind for something comparably definite to say, something to suggest she was in agreement with him on the issue of birds. But all that came to mind in that driving clamor of bird screams was a jumble of her mother's pronouncements, bitter and nebulous as a mouthful of smoke.

Lucas has showered in Zoe's tub and crashed on the sofa, which Phyllis fixed up for him. There was nothing for mother and daughter to do then but retire early to their own rooms upstairs and downstairs, leaving him the middle. Was it because Lucas was watching that Zoe hugged her mother before they parted, something she never did willingly, unless for a camera? And why her mother's body seemed so sadly appealing to her arms—her mother's odd scorched smell, so suddenly sweet—Zoe didn't know.

Zoe won't be able to eat tonight because she doesn't dare try to sneak by Lucas. That is all right. She would much rather know he is stationed there at the center of the house, a guardian of order. Stomach clenched around its treasured pain, she lies awake thinking about this man—his determination on the ladder, when he thanked her for her concern. She goes over and over these moments in her mind, savoring them. She imagines that she has emptied herself in order to be filled more purely and perfectly by his image. When she closes her eyes, he is all she sees, poised at the foot of the ladder, then at different stages of his ascent. *Give it a while*, he keeps telling her, and she knows that he does what he does because he cares.

He has climbed far above her now, and the ladder keeps lengthening. He is climbing far beyond the roof of the house, so far she can hardly see him. Her stomach begins to ache with worry. Then the dreadful noise begins—she knows even while it is dim and distant, it is dreadful. She tries to call a warning to Lucas, but he is too high to hear, and soon the noise is deafening, and the sky darkens with enemy starlings. Lucas is engulfed by a black cloud of them; Zoe screams as loud as she can, but nothing can be heard over that noise. Then as she looks up, something comes sliding down the ladder, something shapeless, shrunken lands at her feet. She wakes up in terror, the noise still in her ears.

She must calm herself. She is awake now. She is safe inside. There are no birds, they are all asleep in the trees, balancing somehow on their branches without falling.

But that noise still shrieks in her ears, and she must make sure. She turns on the light and stumbles to the window, pulls the drape aside, tries to peer beyond the glass, through the reflection of her own room, her own body, all arms and legs, wrapped in a large men's T-shirt. She is awake now, yet it seems the noise has filled her room, and she drags open the glass door to let it out. The night air flows in, chills her into alertness. The noise inside dissipates, met as it is by another sound from above, beyond the screen, softer, but as shrill and relentless, the sort of sound, like crickets, or running water, you could confuse with silence unless you had been warned it was there.

Ntozake Shange

From *Sassafrass, Cypress & Indigo*

"Indigo, I don't want to hear another word about it, do you understand me. I'm not setting the table with my Sunday china for fifteen dolls who got their period today!"

"But, Mama, I promised everybody we'd have a party because we were growing up and could be more like women. That's what Sister Mary Louise said. She said that we should feast and celebrate with our very best dresses and our very favorite foods."

"Sister Mary Louise needs to get herself married 'fore she's lost what little of her mind she's got left. I don't want you going round that simple woman's house. You take my good velvet from 'tween those dolls' legs. Go to the store and buy yourself some Kotex. Then you come back here and pack those creatures up. Put them in the attic. Bring yourself back here and I'm going to tell you the truth of what you should be worrying about now you sucha grown woman."

"Mama, I can't do that. I can't put them away. I'll have nobody to talk to. Nobody at all."

"Indigo, you're too big for this nonsense. Do like I say, now."

"Mama. What if I stopped carrying Miranda in the street with me, and left my other friends upstairs all the time, could I leave 'em out then, could I? Please Mama, I know they're dollies. I really do.

Sassafrass and Cypress kept all the things they made when they were little, didn't they?"

"That's a lie. Don't you have all their dolls? I can't believe a girl as big as you, wearing a training bra and stockings to school, can't think of nothing but make-believe. But if you promise me that you going to leave them in your room and stop asking me to sing to 'em, feed 'em, and talk with 'em, you can leave them out. Now go on to the store."

Indigo left her lesson book on the kitchen table, went to her mother tearing collards by the sink, and gave her a big hug. Her mother's apron always smelled like cinnamon and garlic no matter how many times it was washed. It smelled of times like this when her mother felt a surge in her bosom like her nipples were exploding with milk again, leaving her damp and sweet, but now it was Indigo's tears that softened her spirit.

"Indigo, you're my littlest baby, but you make it hard for me sometimes, you know that."

"Mama, I can make it easier today 'cause I awready know what it is you were gonna tell me when I came back from the store."

"You do, do you?"

"Yeah, you were going to tell me that since I became a woman, boys were gonna come round more often, 'cause they could follow the trail of stars that fall from between my legs after dark."

"What?"

"The stars that fall from 'tween my legs can only be seen by boys who are pure of mind and strong of body."

"Indigo, listen to me very seriously. This is Charleston, South Carolina. Stars don't fall from little colored girls' legs. Little boys don't come chasing after you for nothing good. White men roam these parts with evil in their blood, and every single thought they have about a colored woman is dangerous. You have gotta stop living this make-believe. Please, do that for your mother."

"Every time I tell you something, you tell me about white folks. 'White folks say you can't go here—white folks say you can't do this— you can't do that.' I didn't make up white folks, what they got to do with me? I ain't white. My dolls ain't white. I don't go round bothering white folks!"

"That's right, they come round bothering us, that's what I'm trying to tell you . . ."

"Well if they bothering you so much, you do something about 'em."

"Is that some sass coming' out your mouth?"

"No, M'am. It's just I don't understand why any ol' white person from outta nowhere would want to hurt us. That's all."

Indigo moved to her mother, with a seriousness about her that left the kitchen emptied of all its fullness and aroma.

"I love you so much, Mama. & you are a grown colored woman. Some white man could just come hurt you, any time he wants, too? Oh I could just kill 'em, if they hurt you, Mama. I would. I would just kill anybody who hurt you."

Holding her child as tight as she could, as close into herself as she could, the mother whispered as softly as she could, as lovingly as she could: "Well, then we'll both be careful & look after each. Won't we?"

Indigo sort of nodded her head, but all she remembered was that even her mother was scared of white folks, and that she still wrote out the word Kotex on a piece of torn paper wrapped up in a dollar bill to give to Mr. Lucas round to the pharmacy. This, though Indigo insisted Mr. Lucas must know what it is, 'cause he ordered it for his store so all the other colored women could have it when they needed it. After all, even her mother said, this bleeding comes without fail to every good girl once a month. Sometimes her mother made no sense at all, Indigo thought with great consternation. On the other hand, as a gesture of goodwill & in hopes that her littlest girl would heed her warnings, the mother allowed Indigo one more public jaunt with Miranda, who was, according to Indigo, fraught with grief that their outings were to be curtailed.

Weeping willows curled up from the earth, reaching over Indigo & Miranda on this their last walk in a long friendship, a simple, laughing friendship. Miranda thought the weeping willows were trying to hug them, to pull them up to the skies where whether you were real or not didn't matter. Indigo, in her most grown-up voice, said, "No, they want us to feel real special on this day, that's all." Miranda wasn't convinced, and neither was Indigo, who managed to take the longest walk to the drugstore that her family had ever known.

After following the willows' trellises till there were no more, Indigo reverently passed by Mrs. Yancey's, back round to Sister Mary Louise's, down to the wharf where she & Miranda waved to her father who was living in the sea with mermaids, & then 'cross to the railroad tracks looking for Uncle John. Indigo liked colored folks who worked with things that took 'em some place: colored folks on ships, trains, trolley, & horses. Yoki was a horse. Uncle John did go places, and after that night with Mrs. Yancey in the street, Indigo figured him mighty powerful.

In between two lone railroad cars was Uncle John's wagon. Sequestered from ill-wishers & the wind, there he was chatting away with the air, the cars, or Yoki. Sometimes men of Color disappear into the beauty of the light, especially toward day's end. It's like clouds take on color & get down on the ground & talk to you, or the stars jump in some black man's body & shine all over you. Uncle John was looking like that to Indigo's mind, just brushing away, leaving Yoki's coat glimmering like dusk.

"Good evening, Uncle John."

"Humph." Mr. Henderson turned round knowing full well who'd come calling, but not wanting to let on. "Oh. If it ain't my girl Indigo. & who's that ya got witcha?"

"This is Miranda. We're going to Mr. Lucas' to pick up something." Indigo was quite careful not to say what she was going to the drugstore for, 'cause her mother had said not to say anything to anybody.

"Indigo, Mr. Lucas' place way off from heah, don't ya think?"

"Well, Uncle John, that's some of it, but not all of it."

Laying down his brush, pulling a stool from the other side of a fire where he was cooking either a chicken or a pigeon, Uncle John motioned for Indigo to take a seat.

"Some of it, but t'aint all of it, ya say? Well, I would be guessin' the rest of it be a matter for discussion."

"Yes, Uncle John. I want you to tell me something. I'm asking you 'cause you been doin' what suits your own mind since I was born."

"No, long fo' that, chile."

"Well, anyway, I want to keep on talkin' with all my dolls. You know they my very best friends." Indigo was talking so fast now, Uncle John started walking in a circle around her so as to understand better. "& Mama wants to put 'em way 'cause now I am a woman & who will I talk to? I can't seem to get on with the chirren in the school I go ta. I don't like real folks near as much." Indigo had jumped off the stool with

Miranda in her arms, much like a woman daring someone to touch her child. Uncle John stood still for a minute, looking at the shadows of the rail cars on Yoki's back.

"Indigo, times catch up on everybody. Me & Yoki heah been catched up by trains & grocery stores. Now you bein' catched up by ya growin' up. That's what ya mama's tryin' to say to ya. Ya gotta try to be mo' in this world. I know, it don't suit me either."

Miranda was crying, nestled in Indigo's elbow. Uncle John mumbled to himself, & climbed in his wagon. Indigo stayed put. Folks said that sometimes, when Uncle John had said all he had to say, he got in his wagon & that was that. Other times folks said Uncle John would get in his wagon & come back out with something to keep your life moving along sweeter. So Indigo didn't move a muscle. Miranda prayed some good would come of all this. They still hadn't gone to Mr. Lucas'. Indigo could hear Uncle John humming to himself, fumbling in that wagon. He was looking for something for her so she could keep talkin' & not have to be with them real folks & all their evil complicated ways of doing. The last of the day's sun settled on Indigo's back, warmed the taut worry out of her limbs, & sat her back down on the stool, jabbering away to Miranda.

"See, you thought that I was gonna just go on & do what Mama said & never play witya no more or go explore & make believe. See, see, ya didn't have no faith. What's that Sister Mary Louise is all the time sayin'?"

"Oh ye of lil faith . . ." Miranda rejoined.

Uncle John didn't come out of his wagon first. A fiddle did. Uncle John was holding it, of course, but he poked the fiddle out, then one leg, his backside, and the other leg, his precious greying head, and the last arm with a bow in his grasp. Indigo & Miranda were suspicious.

"What we need a violin for?" Miranda sniggled.

"Hush, Miranda, Uncle John knows what he's doin'. Just wait a minute, will ya?"

Uncle John sure nuf had intentions to give this fiddle to Indigo. His face was beaming, arms wide open, with the fiddle & bow tracing the horizons, moving toward Indigo who was smiling with no reason why.

"Indigo, this heah is yo' new talkin' friend."

"A fiddle, Uncle John?" Indigo tried to hide her disappointment, but Miranda hit her in her stomach. "Uh, that's not what I need, Uncle John." She sat back on the stool like she'd lost her backbone. Uncle John was a bit taken back, but not swayed.

"Listen now, girl. I'ma tell ya some matters of the reality of the unreal. In times blacker than these," Uncle John waved the violin & the bow toward the deepening night, "when them slaves was ourselves & we couldn't talk free, or walk free, who ya think be doin' our talkin' for us?"

"White folks, of course," snapped Indigo.

Uncle John's face drew up on his bones like a small furious fire. His back shot up from his legs like a mahogany log.

"Whatchu say gal?? I caint believe ya tol' me some white folks was doin' our talkin'. Now, if ya want me to help ya, don't say nary another word to me till I'm tellin' ya I'm finished. Now, listen. Them whites what owned slaves took everythin' was ourselves & didn't even keep it fo' they own selves. Just threw it on away, ya heah. Took them drums what they could, but they couldn't take our feet. Took them languages what we speak. Took off wit our spirits & left us wit they Son. But the fiddle was the talkin' one. The fiddle be callin' our gods what left us/be givin' back some devilment & hope in our bodies worn down & lonely over these fields & kitchens. Why white folks so dumb, they was thinkin' that if we didn't have nothin' of our own, they could come controllin', meddlin', whippin' our sense on outta us. But the Colored smart, ya see. The Colored got some wits to em, you & me, we ain't the onliest ones be talkin' wit the unreal. What ya think music is, whatchu think the blues be, & them get happy church musics is about, but talkin' wit the unreal what's mo' real than most folks ever gonna know."

With that Uncle John placed the fiddle in the middle of his left arm & began to make some conversations with Miranda & Indigo. Yes, conversations. Talkin' to em. Movin' to an understandin' of other worlds. Puttin' the rhythm in a good sit down & visit. Bringin' the light out a good cry. Chasing the night back round yonder. Uncle John pulled that bow, he bounced that bow, let the bow flirt with those strings till both Miranda & Indigo were most talkin' in tongues. Like the slaves who were ourselves had so much to say, they all went on at once in the voices of the children: this child, Indigo.

When Indigo first tried to hold the fiddle under her neck like the children in the orchestra at school, Uncle John just chuckled, looked away. When she had it placed nearer her armpit & closer to her heart, with the bow tucked indelicately in her palm, he said, "Now talk to us, girl." Indigo hesitated, pulled the bow toward the A string, took a breath, & stopped. "I don't know how to play a violin, Uncle John."

"Yeah, ya do. Tell Miranda somethin' on that fiddle. 'Cause after today, ya won't be able to reach out to her like ya do now. Ya gonna haveta call her out, wit that fiddle."

Indigo looked at Miranda lying on the stool & then back at Uncle John whose eyes were all over her face, the fiddle, the bow. & in a moment like a fever, Indigo carried that bow cross those fiddle strings till Miranda knew how much her friend loved her, till the slaves who were ourselves made a chorus round the fire, till Indigo was satisfied she wasn't silenced. She had many tongues, many spirits who loved her, real & unreal.

The South in her.

It was already so late Mr. Lucas had started to lock up his shop. Only the lights in the very back were still on. Indigo held onto her violin with its musty case religiously, & she beat on the door of the pharmacy like somebody possessed. "Please open up, Mr. Lucas. It's a emergency," she shouted. Mr. Lucas, portly & honey brown, peered out the door thru the lettering: Lucas' Pharmacy, Oldest Negro Drugstore in Charleston, S.C. Between the "S" & the "C" there was Indigo's face, churning & shouting. Mr. Lucas opened up remarking, "An emergency is somebody dyin' or a woman who needs some Kotex." Indigo was stunned. "Hi, Mr. Lucas, how'd you know that?"

"Oh, I been in this business a long time, Indigo. Tell your mother she almost missed me this time."

"Oh, it's not for Mama, it's for me." All of a sudden Indigo blushed & shrank. She'd gone & done what her mother had asked her please not to do. Mr. Lucas took a step toward Indigo, like he was looking for the woman in her. He'd seen younger girls than Indigo who were busy having babies. He'd even seen girls more comely in a grown-woman manner than she who didn't bleed at all. But here was this girl with this child body & woman in her all at once. It was difficult for Mr. Lucas to just go & get the Kotex. He wanted to keep looking at this girl, this woman. He wanted to know what she felt like.

Indigo heard somebody talking to her. She saw Mr. Lucas coming toward her & somebody talking to her. Telling her to get the Kotex &

get home quick. Get the Kotex & get home quick. Indigo ran to the back of the store, grabbed the blue box, stuffed it under her arm with Miranda & whipped thru the aisles with Mr. Lucas behind her, lumbering, quiet. The fiddle was knocking all kinds of personal hygiene products off shelves: toothpaste, deodorant, shaving cream. Indigo almost dropped it, but she held tighter, moved faster, heard somebody telling her to get home quick. She got to the doors, started to look back & didn't. She just opened the door as best she could without letting go of anything & ran out.

Mr. Lucas stood in the back of his pharmacy, looking at his S.C. Certification, his diploma from Atlanta University. He knew he might be in some trouble. Didn't know what had got hold to him. Every once in a while, he saw a woman with something he wanted. Something she shouldn't have. He didn't know what it was, an irreverence, an insolence, like the bitch thought she owned the moon.

"Yeah, that's right." Mr. Lucas relaxed. "The whole town knows that child's crazed. If she says a thing, won't a soul put no store in it."

The South in her.

Ridin' the
Moon in Texas

Houston Rodeo & Livestock Show ain't never seen the same since we come riding in from Arcola. All colored and correct. Long-sleeved shirts, cowboy hats, chaps, spurs, covered wagons, and a place all our own in Memorial Park. Ain't never seen that many niggahs in Memorial Park no way, least not at 4:30 in the morning. Perking coffee over open fires and warming each other with bourbon and one rodeo yarn after another. Ain't nothing white folks can do bout it, even Sam Houston enlisted this black fella could talk five Indian languages—five and English, of course. Even Sam Houston had enough sense to ask this niggah to go talk some sense to them Cherokees, so's they wouldn't fight gainst Texas independence. Well, we independent now and riding proud right down Hwy. 59 to Texas Avenue. Don't understand why that woman didn't buy those boys some hats. She knows cain't no man be in a trailride or a rodeo without a hat. Shame, too. They came all the way from Abilene to sit by the wayside with them other folks. Just looking. And I'll say one thing. That flock of niggahs on them gorgeous horses and them wagons, now that was something to look at! Must be why ain't none of us forget it. The trailride and all. And the rodeos. The black ones, of course, white folks don't quite have the hang of it. I mean, how you sposed to look, your image, on your horse, It takes a colored point of view.

"Twanda, whatcha gone do tonight? Louisiana Red is up for everything from bronc-busting to steel-dogging!"

"Oh go on gal, you know I cain't do nothing but barrel racing. Sides, I've got some business out yonder."

"Whatchu mean, you got some business out yonder? You ain't plannin' on messin' with me or them hard-head cowboys come to laugh at us tonight. You know this is our night, the All-Women's Rodeo, Navasota, Texas, honey. We the stars this evening, girl, even if you do gotta itch in your twat—them races come first—you got some business out yonder—huh!—you better check Dallas—you really gonna let that Jamaican chick use your horse for calf-roping?"

"Her horse is sick. She's an allright broad. You know she was champion two years in a row."

"But not with your horse."

"You know you can be one petty bitch when you wanna."

"I spose that's why you gonna investigate your business out yonder?"

"Listen, honey, I'ma see about Dallas. He misses me if I'm gone more than a hour and before a race he just gets beside himself and I gotta sweet talk him and snuggle up to him, specially fore I put that bridle thru his mouth—he don't like that thing at all—I sure do like them Oak Ridge Boys. Listen, can't ya hear it?"

"Hell, no. Why don't cha just ride bare back."

"I might—"

"Sure."

"No, I might saunter thru the night bare back on Dallas; naked as a jay bird."

"Oh yeah, where?"

"Out yonder, I told ya."

"Girl, you know you don't make no sense sometimes. Did you pay up for the bronc-busting and barrel racing?"

"Course I did. Cost me seventy dollars. That's why I gotta get Dallas feeling high and sweet. We gotta win alla that money back and then some."

"You signed up for the breakaway?"

"Hell, no. That ain't no rodeo. That's some real bullshit. Can you rope a runaway calf?"

"Some folks cain't."

"Well, that ain't shit to me. Rope the damn thing and tie it in eight seconds. That I can understand. Breakaways just some other way for the 'pro-mo-tors' to make some more dough."

"So what? There's money in it."

"And a lotta fools, too."

"Go on now. See bout Dallas. I'ma get me a beer and some barbecue. Thank God, they finally playing Charlie Pride. I just love how that man can sing. Love me some Charlie Pride."

The night was fresh, more like morning should be. The grass and brush beyond the rodeo arena were moist and seductive, begging to be touched or lain on. The moon sat up in the sky like a hussy in red with her legs wide open. So what if all the women riders from Muskogee to Lubbock, Marshall to Lafayette, showed for the All-Women's Rodeo? Just last year, Susie Louise won bronc-busting and she was four months pregnant. Her momma won calf-roping and her daughter ran away with the steel-dogging. Shit. What a night that was. Take a look at those men come to look at us. I can't believe Lee Andrew had the nerve to tell me he came out here cuz he likes to see the expression on my face: see me change from pretty to ugly. Talk about nerve. I'ma bring me one of my pretty cowboys right on back here. It's so quiet. Most like there wasn't no rodeo going on. Maybe I'll ride Dallas by that rhiney boy with those dogging arms, the one in the black and red satin shirt with white fringe and red suede chaps dangling silver coins. He's the one whispered "I'm a black man who wants to ride off on a filly." Yeah, mister. I got something for your ass. God, I wonder how James is doing? I forgot to call the hospital once the ambulance carried him off. That bull stamped all over his ass and he ain't but so big. Big as a minute actually. Not much bigger than a minute. Jesus. That gore was more than I could handle. And that fool Joe-Man had the gall to say I didn't have no heart cuz I was paying up for calf-roping instead of seeing to James. Shit. James finished his event. How was I gonna calf-rope and see to James. Humph. that's awright, Dallas. We're just warming up, that's all. Getting a feel for the wind and the ground round here. Come on, I'ma kick it up! See if we can get neath these tree limbs and over that stream without hurtin' ourselves. Watchu say, baby? That's a boy. Do like momma say and she'll give you a bright shiny apple. That's a boy. Let's get it. Go for it. There ain't nothing out here but prairie and me and you and the wind. So that makes it the moon, the wind and a little satisfaction. Those folks crazy now, they playing Otis Redding. Come on, now. Show momma whatcha can do. She needs some satisfaction too. Right, baby? Do it for momma.

"Breakaway:
"Nancy Bourdan—Houston—Score 57.
"Sally Johnson—Midnight, Mississippi—Score 55.
"Molly Hanks—Conroe, Texas—Score 52."

"No, man, just give me a beer from that cooler in your truck. I ain't out here to compete tonight. How can I do that? This is All-Women's Rodeo—ain't it? Well, ain't it?"

"Yeah, that why I'm out here, cain't really tell if a woman's a woman til you see how she could ride a horse."

"You right bout that, bro!"

"Gimme that beer and a joint."

"I'ma get some more barbecue but I'ma say one thing. Just one thing. The ladies is the horses. If you get my meaning. But the way my lady friend ride is fantastic. All that tension and excitement from the Diamond L all the way out here to Navasota to Madisonville. Now they got some great rodeo in Madisonville, but you know I got three daughters and I'ma black man and I'd rather have my girls here than anywhere else."

"Oh, man, go and get the barbecue."

"Whatever you say, Bubba. Watch the horses all right. These gals ain't got no more scruples than that white bitch, whatcha call it, Belle Starr?"

"Yeah, man. I got it covered. Just get the beer, man, and let me know if you see that sassy gal what races barrels."

"There's Bo-Peep with those damned armadillos in a pond of draft beer. When these guys gonna learn armadillos get drunk. They chasing beer. They ain't racing. That's all right, Dallas. We'll just ignore that. Okay, baby."

"Hey, Twanda."

"Huh?"

"Ain't that what they call you, Twanda?"

"Some do, some don't. What it to you?"

"That's a nice-looking animal you got there."
"I know that. You got a nice-looking face too."
"It's just a cowboy's face."
"I know that. Come on, Dallas."
"Hey, don't ride off like that."
"Whatcha think I'm on a horse for, to stay still somewhere? Let's go, Dallas."

"All right, everybody clear the arena—it's time for the Cotton-eyed Joe."

"Well, cain't you dance, gal?"
"Whatchu mean? Of course I can!"
"Twan, let's me and you gone and do the Cotton-eyed Joe."
"Shit yeah. If you can keep up with me."
"Watch me, baby. Careful how you do that horse and you'll see what all I could do. What all I could do for you, baby."
"Sure, hot stuff."

"Calf-Roping:
"Agnes Moralez—San Antonio, Texas—Score 7.6.
"Sally Johnson—Midnight, Mississippi—Score 8.1.
"Louisiana Red—Lafayette, Louisiana—Score 7.2"

I cain't exactly explain how it happened, but out there somewhere how the prairie snapped up the last bits of night. Bubba and Twanda raced free as sepia roses on their horses' bare back. Holding the manes and each other the way you'd have to when you're dealing with a steer and you come out grinning and then be screaming. They fell out near a smooth mossy cloud neath a cypress tree. "Guantanamera" blasting from the arena.
Guantanamera, Gaujiro, Guantanamera.

Twanda was murmuring, "I'm in the rodeo cuz my momma was and my first night out I won ninety dollars just for running round barrels. You cain't beat that, for running round barrels." Bubba somehow quieted her. He was unsettled by her drive. She had to win. She was one with her horse. She had no sense of anything sides speed and her animal, but that was when she was racing. She said. She liked he was a champion. She said, "Look a heah, I'm a champion too," when she wrapped that huge silver buckle round her slight waist. The hairs from her thighs creeping like ferns from her navel. Women and horses. Black women and horses. An all-women's rodeo. What next? Bubba slapped his thigh and reached for that joint and Bud.

Twanda pulled him to her and let him play with a piece of grass she slipped tween his lips. Then she lay back on his shoulder. Let the sky celebrate her victory: Twanda Rochelle Johnson—Barrel-racing—17.5—First Place—$532.

She smiled, contented; remembered that business she'd had out yonder. Out on the prairie where black folks have always felt at home. She pulled the straw outta Bubba's mouth. He didn't know what was happening til she sang a cowgirl's song / sweet & tough / soft and rough:

let me be a chorus of a thousand / tongues

and your lips dance on a new moon / while

Daddy Cool imagines synchopated

niggahfied erotica on Griggs Road

We'll have skimmed the cream off the milky way / made a permanent ellipse by the yet uncharted tail of Halley's Comet / these tongues and lips make a time step of Bojangles in fast forward / merely slow motion in a sultry dusk / so natural / is the tone of your chest under the gaze of the wild stallions by the waterfalls, enveloped by scarlet blossoms like a woman's heart / your sweat seeps into my mouth / we sleep / deep / deep / like in Texas."

"Hey, ain't that the Judds—ain't that something."

"We gone sleep / deep / deep like in Texas."

Opal Moore

A Pilgrim Notebook

Part I: The Odyssey

The man. he
sped bold across the landscape
broke barriers of time   space
He was   simultaneous
He was yesterday   today   tomorrow . . .
    —*The Pilgrim Diary* (1)

Country music is good company if you're alone, if it's a quarter to dawn, if it's all you can get in the middle of Missouri, middle of nowhere. The words of an old song ran through Ben's head, *luv the one ya with . . . ya got-ta . . .* Ben leaned into fifth gear *luv the one ya with* as he watched the changing sky, as he only half watched the winding road, as he squealed into a sudden curve, as the sky bloomed pink.

He wanted Jazz. A little Miles. Trumpet mellow into morning. Or saxophone—the moaning sax . . . oh yes. How-ever, in the absence of Jazz, he had been known to settle for The Chi-Lites, The Delphonics. The Moments talkin about: I found Luv on a 2-way street . . . Wanted Jazz. Motown would do. But if you're alone on the road at a quarter to morning in the absence of Jazz and with no possi*bil*ity of soul, country music can grow on you. Ben tapped a finger to the rhythm. The sky was a bruised pink.

He sped out of another curve, foot heavy on the accelerator. The little sports car's tail end wagged.

"Like a frisky woman itchin' to get loose," the rental guy had said, "she's just a little dangerous if you don't keep her in a firm hand," They had both laughed.

Her name was *Arroyo II*. Just on the market. She was cute but no BMW. She was flashy. She was candy-red outside with a creme interior. Ben had smiled as he slipped into the creme.

Luv on a 2-way street . . . Ben stretched out, in his mind, in *Arroyo II*, his She-machine. Inside, he was borderless, infinite. Anything was possible in this car, in this picture postcard landscape complete with pretty cows on endless fields and quaintly crumbling haybarns. And the space—wide fresh-air country sky—was a welcome relief from the elbow-to-elbow anonymity, crush and secrecy of the city. He raced boldly across his picture of a landscape. He was complete. He felt like yesterday, today *and* tomorrow. *you are ev'rything, and ev'rything is you, ooh ooh ooh* . . . Ben smiled a smile like horizon. The chilly half-circle of sun dangled before him like a gold coin slipped in a pocket.

Ben twisted the rearview to an odd angle to check the knot of his tie. Perfect, as expected. Everything was perfect (except for the music, of course). But even that was ok. Today he could love what he didn't love: a backwoods view, a country tune. Even Saundra's bad mouth, the way she always managed to say what he didn't need to hear when he least needed to hear it. Like this morning, could have been a stellar beginning. Like a saxophone solo: her warm sighs, her tapering backside sliding across new linen, his lyrics. But no. She has to roll over and put her mouth on this trip—in that voice, like satin ripping:

"You drivin 400 miles to witness a football pat on the ass? You could watch that on TV all day *and* save gas." Saundra could be depended upon *not* to understand. Sometimes the girl was ok. She was certainly the make and model he preferred in women: recent year, low wind resistance, . . . but then her mouth would open and reveal such *serious* flaws in workmanship. What he was doing today was not play. It was business—it was, it was like an odyssey.

Ben touched his tie, readjusted his rearview to watch his progress, watch the road lay down behind him in submission. Everything was "go"—smooth road newly laid leading from here to . . . well, to wherever he chose to go. Who could say what the future held? Except for Saundra, who knew?

Green signs, white and blue signs leaped up to tally his progress, point the way, take him past all the wrong exits to the right ones. Ben just had this *feeling* that this ceremony for his friend Billy was a signpost of the 90's, that the day would mark the decade clear as any of these man-made signs posted along the roadside.

Ben flipped the station dial (a little country goes a long way). He listened to news reports—hog futures and weather, Bushwhacking and the oil war, evangelists begging, car salesmen pitching. He twisted the dial, barely listening, hearing only the rumble of his thoughts:

"As of today," he'd announced to Saundra, "Billy Mills, I mean, William Randolph Mills, is no longer just a man. He's a landmark. A signpost in the pageant of history."

"He's unemployed," said Saundra. "What kind of signpost is that?"

"This is history in the making," said Ben.

"Um," she'd said and watched him prepare.

Ben had decided his closet was too drab. He'd bought everything from the skin out, brand new. At Fields, he'd gone through suits, ties, shoes, everything. He'd inquired about a manicure, shampoo and haircut at a salon. And finally, he'd decided to rent the car. His old 1970 Chrysler was steady—a classic really—but it just wouldn't do for the occasion. It just did not make *quite* the right . . . statement. He needed a chariot—the *Arroyo II*. Throughout his preparations, Saundra's eyes had worn an expression of bored ridicule.

"It's not like it's the *real* Hall of Fame," she said. "It's just some small town, small college homecoming-halftime filler stuff."

Women. They simply did not understand men—a man's style is to play the game all the way through to the end. Even if the stakes seem small. Even if it looks like you can't win. Even if it takes a lifetime to tally the score. Even if nobody but you ever knows the game has been played. The college's Hall of Fame might seem like nothing, but no black player had ever been named. Billy had played like a champion on an unknown team, and had gotten nothing for it. Couldn't she *see* that no victory was insignificant? This was one more capitulation, a psychological Berlin Wall falling, quietly, with no fanfare, but it had been a long time falling and so it was still victory. Still sweet. A small victory for 1959 was better than none. Fifty-nine had been a bruiser. Nobody talked about '59. Everybody talked about THE SIXTIES. But they couldn't have had a 60's without 1959. In 1959, he and Billy and a few other brothers had been imported to this small nowhere town for purposes of football and not a damn thing else. Townies'd never seen black folks before—not in the flesh. He remembered the pale stares of wide-eyed girls, hard and vulnerable—and dangerous, to a handful of black men mailordered to the middle of nowhere. In 1959 he and Billy had made a vanguard—a front line. *They* had stood pissing into the headwind; *they* had faced the backsplash. *They* had survived. And sometimes a ceremony 31 years late was all you got. He'd explained all this to Saundra, with her mouth turned down, looking at him out of the tops of her eyes.

To Saundra, born in the year of The King's death, 1959 was pre-history—biblical at best. Even the people who'd been there were trying to forget. Billy himself had said of the nomination, "Man, it's nothing. It's no big deal." Ben had had to explain to him the importance of it—that the record of his excellence, of his perseverence, his *games*manship, his courage when the chips were down—*that*, not football, was his contribution. It was a life lesson that he, Ben, personally would *never* abandon. Billy had shook his head. 'Man,' he said, 'you always *been* deep.'

Ben smiled to himself.

> he sped bold
> across the landscape
> a warrior
> black and determined
> veteran of Time
> fearless
> on his way to be overcome.
>
> —*The Pilgrim Diary* (27)

Ben flicked at a speck of lint on his trouser leg. Tested the razor crease in the subtle tweed. Caressed the perfectly tied silk blend burgundy tie. He leaned over to glimpse himself in the mirror. He was the same now as then. No. He was better. Definitely better. He'd kept his football weight. His hair. Most often, he could go without his glasses, even though women told him his glasses made him look more distinguished. He was among the top salesmen in his region. And, he was wiser. His motto: put the past in the past. He told every young black executive he met, past is passed. Today is today.

Ben rearranged himself in his cockpit. He was streamlined for forward motion. Today was the blossoming of a seed planted long ago and forgotten. *Well, but I mean, is this little Hall of Fame lollipop parade likely to turn into some sort of job? Cause, I mean, it's a job the man needs—not another ball game plaque. Is it any money in it?* Saundra. Famous last words. Ben twisted the radio dial as if her voice were a stray telecast. He cracked the window an inch. The cold blade of morning air was a relief. Brisk country morning air can clear a man's head of debris. The road curved sharp and sudden.

It was not easy living with a woman who did not understand reality. Billy was not just some guy out of a job. He was a symbol. Ben put the accelerator to the floor, cocked his jaw. The little car's tail end lashed decidedly.

Except for Saundra, who knew? Someday Billy's story might be told. A transcendent tale, a modern *Iliad* and *Odyssey*. New heroes and magical conquests. Like the ancient tales of the griots, the entire history of a man and his kind read from the inward eye. Too bad how the great epics were now interred in books, how the stories no longer resided in the hearts of men. Ben straightened his tie. Twisted the radio dial. Nothing but static and country music. *What if you drive all the way down to that god-forsaken place and nobody else shows up? I mean, if the man is out of work, he can't really afford to waste the time. Can't afford to waste the gas!* Like the static in the radio, Saundra's voice could not be fine-tuned out of his head.

> a pilgrim soul
> in a foreign landscape.
> it is an epic tale
> of the overcome.
>
> —*The Pilgrim Diary* (495)

Doggedly, Ben tried every frequency along the radio dial. A man could only stand so much of this backwoods banjo shit. He settled for news finally. A woman newscaster, her voice smooth and practiced, fought through the static:

"Early last evening a county woman was forced into the back seat of her own car where she was repeatedly assaulted."

"Jesus!" said Ben, his eyes scanning the crisp clean panorama of country. What a horrible thing. A violation really. Out here. Didn't fit. He winced a little as he imagined a helpless woman stumbling across the hard cold ground. . . . "The woman's assailant was unknown to her," the newsvoice said. Ben's finger hovered at the dial.

"The assailant was described (don't let him be black) as a black man . . . (What else?) . . . 5'11", 160 pounds, wearing dirty jeans and a dirty green shirt. He was last seen walking along the highway."

The "assailant" was also a fool.

"The woman managed to drive her own car to a nearby farmhouse where she received assistance. Police were summoned . . ." The news-cast wavered and fluttered. Ben leaned into a curve. The broadcast ceased abruptly in a rage of static. The newslady voice succumbed with a struggle.

Ben breathed out slowly. "Damn," he said.

The sky ahead seemed to be darkening. The sun, so promising earlier, seemed to fade as it climbed higher into the sky.

They're after you man

Ben checked his watch. Longines. Second anniversary—third wife. Shifting out of a curve, he put a heavy foot on the accelerator. She probably picked him up. A hitchhiker. When would these white girls learn anything? Not that he didn't feel bad for the girl. . . . *they're after you man, after you for sure.*

He shut the window—the invigorating country air had become numbing. The landscape slid by grey and threatening. Ben loosened his tie a bit, checked the rearview mirror frequently. He wondered if he could make it to the auditorium by noon.

> glancing over one shoulder, he ran.
> hands palms forward
> like a blind man's hands
> touching the future first
> before he stumbles in.
> feet in a furrow, plowed out, he
> ran. agonizing forward like a dream,
> aching slow awkward in the ditch
> green Arrow shirt
> plastered in cold sweat.
>
> —*The Pilgrim Diary* (999)

Rough farmland stretched infinite on either side of a strip of highway. Somewhere out there was The Assailant, identified Black. In the silence of no radio, Ben entertained the thought of him, The Assailant, on foot. The report had to be wrong. Couldn't have been a Black man. On no. Black man would've put her ass out, made *her* walk to the nearby farmhouse (where she received assistance . . .) while he put a few strategic miles between him and the jailhouse. The car, being identifiable, presented its own problems of course. But he could have eventually ditched the car and hopped a bus or train. Park a car in a mall parking lot and it's not likely to be found for a month. Of course that would add a charge of grand theft auto to the assault, but what did it matter if you did not intend to get caught? Then again, there were probably no reputable malls in Hicksville. Still there were fields. Miles and miles of unsupervised space. Was it possible for a man to walk a country unnoticed?

A large dark bird flapped into view interrupting the smooth yellow centerline of Ben's thoughts. The bird stood still, seemed to watch him approach in his speeding rent-a-sports-car. The bird watched with only a casual interest. Or was it arrogance? Ben put the nose of the racing car right down the dividing line—CHICKEN! he yelled. The bird flapped leisurely to the shoulder, cocked one wing and stared. Ben watched the bird diminish to a black speck in the quick distance of the rearview mirror, but oddly, he felt himself shrinking in the bird's cold black eye.

Ben's eyes lingered on the makeshift lean-tos and rotting sheds that sprinkled the passing fields. He noted how the harvested cornstalks were shaved to cruel spikes making his toes curl involuntarily inside their soft Italian leather casings. He discovered a new tightness in the pit of his stomach. It reminded him of the day before yesterday. The ink could not have been dry on her contract before the new "boss" had come in announcing, like it didn't make a difference, that "they" should not expect any bonus this year.

"The profit margin just doesn't warrant it," she'd said.

she

Not that he had anything against women. But who would have believed that one would be put over his division? Ben tapped a steady rhythm on the steering wheel.

She didn't dress like an executive. Briefcase full of nothing but Kleenex, probably. Full of lip gloss, electric haircurler, fingernail polish to dot the runs in her pantyhose probably. Who would have thought . . .? Ben shook his head. Thumped the steering wheel sharply. The little car swerved dangerously into the opposite lane. It didn't matter. He had her in a firm hand. And he was alone in this middle of nowhere—no Jazz, no soul, no sound. It was the same sound he'd felt in that room full of salesmen when she looked dead at Ben and said, "You men had better get off your laurels, they're spreading." She'd looked dead in *his* face when she said no bonuses as if he were responsible somehow. And everyone's eyes had followed hers, looking at him. It was then that he had heard his aloneness. It was as if they expected him to provide an explanation, or apologize. The down profit margin wasn't *his* fault. He was the best in his division. His numbers were at the top, up there with the best in the region. Maybe she didn't know that? Her eyes had singled him out. It was not paranoia. He had not imagined that the very next day his best account—he'd spit blood to build that account—had been taken from him—handed over like an ice cream come to their "boy," the division runt. She *had* known. "We need *team* players," she'd said to Ben. "Sometimes you've got to *pass* the ball to win the game."

Ben swallowed. The insides of his mouth stuck like gummy paper. Team players! He was a man, alone—The Assailant, scaling a wall one narrow foothold at a time. He could hear "them" holding their breath, waiting for a misstep. What damn laurels?

she

Didn't even dress like an executive.

Road signs flashed past overhead but Ben did not need signs. He had seen his future murdered in their eyes, in the eyes of the men who would like to see him eat filthy humble pie.

she's after you hotshot

He didn't need signs. He'd seen the writing on the wall. He was no fool. He'd smiled in her face, invited her to lunch and put in for a transfer all in the same day.

Team play. That was the line they bought your soul with. The line they used on Billy. Billy Mills could've dusted them all. He'd been *star* material. He could've broken every record in the book that year. But he went for that "team player" bullshit. Could've been NFL, but he'd nodded and grinned while they nailed him to the bench, "team player" plastered across his chest. The hell with the team. Ben would play "the game," but by a winner's rules. He was no Billy Mills. Billy was a good guy, but he hadn't used his head. He'd gambled his future against a cheap trophy and a few grins. Life was no sport. A smart man knew when to concede defeat. Cut and run. What is honor when your pockets are picked clean?

The sun pulled clear of the treeline just to disappear behind a cloud. Ben glanced in his rearview. The black bird was, of course, long gone. Its cold indifferent stare remained.

No FM, no tape deck, no sounds. That was the trouble with these rental deals. You paid through the nose for a set of fancy bare bones— AM, four wheels and a gas tank. The Chrysler was old, but at least it had insides. It had character. It had a tape deck. Why had he left it behind? He couldn't remember. Ben felt stripped as he raced breakneck through a bass-ackwards state full of black tar, one long yellow line, and dead cornfields everywhere. . . .

Ben bitched. Flipped the radio on for another try but nothing had changed and so he turned it off again. Silence. Barren fields. Blunt, cruel. Infinite visibility. No alleyways to duck down, no supermarkets to dodge through and out the back way, no holes to disappear into. He thought of the first and last time he'd driven through the South, Mississippi that is. Dense foliage buttressing broad stretches of bald land. The Beautiful, laced with a horrible feeling of dread. The passing trees, close and deep. They had seemed to threaten him with their green, secretive silence. And the dust—the dust really was red. It had occurred to him then that one step, one misstep, would be enough to cast him backwards into a history he did not care to relive. *the past is passed.* The past is never past. The past was like one of those big redwoods. You cut off the top and leave what you can't get at. Even safe inside his car, safe inside his era, he'd felt as if he were running—only steps ahead of some ancestor African—disoriented, afraid, rough feet clouded in red dust, running in circles. . . . He'd sworn that he would never return to Mississippi. But in the end, it didn't matter. The world was Mississippi. Ben thought of the bird and felt unlucky.

> hauling ass
> pedal to the metal
> plan in his pocket
> for to overcome.
> he will round the bend
> see too late
> too late
> the flaw in the picture
> pit in the peach
> see the man run
> crash into fate.

—*The Pilgrim Diary* (9,999,999)

The sporty little car was surrounded by implacable fields of harvested crop squeezing in on the black two-lane stitch. The fancy red toy shot forward escaping out of the pinch. Every blind curve tugged at Ben's stomach, every billboard was concealment, every car stalled on the side of the road, an ambush.

The sky was darkening at the edges, something gathering ahead. Maybe rain. Ben tugged at his tie, fatigued. A man with a fundamental resemblance to himself was being sought in America. In the country. In the neighborhood. There was something mercurial about the air, heavy and falling to the bottom, weighing at the bottom of this bland rural picture, like a tickertape disaster bulletin rolling silently at the foot of a TV screen. *The Assailant was described as . . .*

It was instinct that eased Ben's foot from the accelerator slowing the sleek car to well below the limit. He swallowed the bitter juice that kept squeezing into his mouth. Billboards hung against the grey sky. STUCKY'S, next exit. Bright markers popped red and white and green against the pallid sky: JOHN'S PIT STOP 2 mi. Bright-faced, pink-faced people, too happy to eat, smiled all the way to their back teeth because of MARY ANNE'S HOME COOKED FOOD, 4 mi. The road was exhausting.

He ought to stop for a breather. A quick bite, some bad coffee, a little grim-faced sullen-faced waitressing, smudgy fingerprints on the john door might cheer him up. MARY ANNE'S—that was the ticket. A short detour. A quick bite.

MARY ANNE'S. Fly-specked, dust-dark window glass. Shantytown eatery. A hand-lettered sign propped in the window declared the establishment OPEN FOR BUSINESS. But it was not OPEN. Why not? It just wasn't.

OPEN. The word seemed to hang there like a smirk because, on the back side of every OPEN there is always the hidden CLOSED. Ben knew that it did not really matter which side of the sign was showing, only what was hidden made any difference.

The wind was a high whine. Dead leaves clung to their tree limbs as if winter had not already claimed them, rattling, vibrating like fingers on open hands. Thousands of hands. He looked at the door of Mary Anne's, locked and bolted, looking like it had never been open, never would open; looked at the OPEN sign so misleading. He wanted to take the door full throttle, *make* it OPEN, feel it opening, feel the scream of glass breaking. The reined power of the car's idling engine surged up through Ben's legs like an electrical current, quick, like zero to sixty in six; perilous, like a fast car leaping, fishtailing on loose rock, out of control, snatching a slender reflector pole, bending dragging it to the ground before skidding to a shuddering stop. *Arroyo II*, and Ben, hung on the downside of a ditch.

Ben flung himself out of the car and crawled, scrambled up the embankment, his thin shoes snagging and turning in the hard, pitted ground. Water came, cold, into his eyes as he stood, toes at the line where asphalt crumbled into country dust, stood looking back in the direction from which he had come, expecting nothing, anything. After a moment, he knelt, rubbed the chalk from his shoes, wondering how far he could run in them.

he
be hauling ass
awkward in them ditches
singin "in a *coooold* sweat"
by John Brown
or H. Rap
or James of the same name.

I seent 'im yesterday
say he be 'round today,
'less he don't get here
til tomorrow. . .

—*The Pilgrim Diary* (Prologue)

A Happy Story

"What's this story about?" Everett leans over my shoulder. He really wants to ask "when will dinner be ready?" But he will not have it spread about that he is a traditionalist.

"It's about a woman," I say as he inspects the contents of pots with an air of disapproval. I continue. "Intelligent. Attractive. Educated. A career is possible if she plays her cards right." Everett has thrown open the refrigerator door, is standing, feet apart, fists on hips, as if silently demanding that certain foods present themselves for his until-dinner-gets-ready snacking. I continue. "But one morning she wakes up to realize that despite her efforts, she is living the same life her mother led. She feels desperate at this idea—"

Everett is desperately opening up foil wrappers. Finds one cold pork chop.

"—and in that moment, she begins to plan her own suicide."

"Why?" mumbles Everett around a mouthful of pork chop. "I thought she was so intelligent."

"Maybe she's intelligent enough—" I say to his back as he returns to his armchair enclave, "—intelligent enough to wonder if surviving is worth the trouble."

Everett rattles his newspaper. The TV drones. I sweep up crumbs from the table and deposit the abandoned pork chop foil wrapper in the trash can. Slowly I recover my thoughts, make a few scribbles on my yellow pad.

"Why don't you ever write a *happy* story?" Everett says, moments later, newspaper crumpling in his lap. I pretend I don't hear him, wish that I hadn't.

"Angel? Didja hear me? Why can't you write a *happy* story for a change?" I don't even look up.

"You know one?" I say. "Tell me a happy story and I'll use it," I say. When I do look up, his eyes are waiting. We look at each other. I smile, feeling some triumph. "Tell me," I say, "and I'll write it."

Everett is a determined optimist; I call it self-delusion. I am a realist; he calls it "bad disposition." I say that he pretties up life with pretense. He says that I don't consider the cloud's silver lining. I say you're liable to be struck by lightning standing in a thunderstorm looking for a silver lining. He says I live for bad news. "Tell me a happy story," I persist. "I can't wait to write it."

His tongue is working inside of one cheek; maybe he's thinking . . . or maybe he's just after a sliver of pork chop caught between his teeth. He seems to regard me with infinite patience and pity. But now, his unflagging optimism comes to rescue his face from furrows of doubt. I see firm determination light his eyes. He will, now as ever, rescue me from myself. I am caught off guard by my own laughter; it comes snorting unladylike from my nose.

"Come on," I say, "Lay this fairy tale on me."

It has to be a fairy tale. All stories with nice happy endings are— either that, or gothic romance. But I prefer fairy tales. At least they don't pretend to be in any way real—just morality tales cloaked in an entertainment. Snow White bites the poison apple but does not die— she lives happily ever after (and the bad queen dies a horrible death). An ancient wish for moral justice, but certainly no reflection of life, where victims don't sleep but die, and bad queens suffer fame and millions made on the Vegas circuit.

The problem with fairy tales is that they end just where true stories begin. What if the story of Snow White continued beyond the grand wedding, and her prince carried her to a land called Newark, to a tenement castle subdivided for multiple family dwelling? And what if his princely income waned, and his ardor, as her body sagged with childbearing, and the mirror chanted a different tune, and Prince Charming—whipping up his trusty steed—stumbled across a younger damsel in distress upon the urban glade? And the matronly Snow White became the poison-toting neglected wife. . . .

It would not take much to convince me that happiness *is* the darker side of life: suburban housewife pushing husband and kiddies off to work and day care just to crawl back into illicit daydreaming; the unrequited lover tasting the most profound ecstasy at the lip of the poison cup. . . . I try to return to my *own* thoughts, abandon this tired academic problem of art vs. life. But Everett has been pondering.

"You could write a story about my mother," he says.

"Your mother's story is not happy," I say.

"My mother is a saint," he says.

"Saints do not happy stories make. Saints are tragic," I point out. "In order to even qualify for sainthood, one must suffer inordinately and die pathetically for the purpose of inspiring pity, guilt, and other behavior inhibiting emotions. Not a prescription for a truly happy story."

"But it's their triumph over suffering," he says, "That's the happy part."

"The happy part is that it was *their* suffering and not *yours*." I think this, but I don't say it. Everett can't stand being *al*ways wrong. So I nod at his last protest even if I don't agree. Because nobody overcomes hardships: we merely survive them, like car wrecks, to haul the scars around with us until we die. But I nod as if the saintly mother story is a possibility to consider. Heartened by this, Everett continues:

". . . And mama has spent her whole life trying to help other people. As hard as her life has been, she could always find something to give. Isn't that happy?" Everett pauses. Studies my face which I make sure is giving away nothing. He waits for my acquiescence on his last point; I can't give it. So I tell him flat out, "That's the saddest story there is. Along with being the oldest." Everett's face tightens. The words sound harsh. Maybe the truth will go better with a musical accompaniment. So I toss aside my writing, flip through albums for something mellow—something sad.

I wouldn't object to writing his mother's story if, in her old age, she had put hard times behind her and was now enjoying some ease and peace of mind. But Everett's mother is living in the same two-story walkup of her childhood—the same, but different, because it's older, more decrepit. The beams are termite riddled, the front porch is a hazard, and her new neighbors are young acid heads who don't know the difference between sleep and death. It is not triumph but the height of tragedy—the final kick: sacrifice rewarded with pain. Maybe it is irreverent to say that her story is the oldest story on record, but it is: a mother sacrificing body and mind for children who will eventually spurn her (or idealize her) but never recognize what was traded for their lives. It is old. It is sad. . . . It is true. It is not happy. And now I hope that Everett can realize the magnitude of the thing he has so frivolously proposed. It's easy to *say* "write a happy story," but when you get down to the brass tacks of it, the task is formidable.

Of course I could manufacture happy tales unending if I made them out of wish instead of life: flawlessly beautiful men and women living lives full of satisfaction; modern episodes of Ozzie and Harriet; heroic tales of John Wayne justice, Right prevailing over Wrong; evil creatures disarmed with a fortuitous bucket of water—

The stove hisses vehemently.

"Your pot is boiled over," says Everett cocking one eye to the stove, then to me. I cross the kitchen, deliberately sly, watching the foaming white water smear down the sides of the saucepan, sizzle into the hot recesses of the stove where it will congeal into an impossible to remove glue.

"What about Alice?" says Everett.

I think about my friend Alice, now a very big costume jewelry magnate on the East coast. She *is* a success story.

"Is Alice happy?"

"She made more money last year than most people ever see— outside a Monopoly game," Everett says.

I swab the stove top with a soppy dishcloth. "Is she happy, you think?" Everett doesn't answer. I stir pots.

"What's *this* story about?"

"Alice's happy story fragment. It's not finished."

"How much've you got?"

"I've got:

"At seven, Alice was a pretty girl. Everyone always said so. Especially her uncle, her mother's step-brother, who had Sunday dinner with them every week without fail.

"But they were poor, so Alice's mother had no chicken for Sunday pots, but depended on her step-brother to bring fish that he caught at the lake. He always brought an extra fish for Alice who hated fish but was always made to thank her uncle for her extra portion with a kiss.

" 'You see Alice, a pretty girl will always get more,' he whispered to her every Sunday without fail, and endlessly, like the smell of fish that she came to associate, not with a meal, but with her uncle. With his breath, his shirt, his fingers that squeezed her quick and rough whenever she had to kiss him.

"Men told Alice she was pretty. Alice's mother said, 'You must think you're cute, or somethin',' and slapped her when she was angry. But Alice loved her mother. She knew the slaps were not from lack of love, but because her mother hated fish also. So Alice gathered pretty trash, lost buttons, bright chips of glass, and strung them for her mother who wore them on 'chicken days'—Christmases and Easters— to make Alice smile."

"That's happy?" Everett asks incredulous.

"Well . . .," I say, "She never went hungry."

"The uncle is a lech."

"She overcomes that hardship," I say. But Everett has heard enough.

"Alice never had any uncles like that," he says.

"How do you know?"

"And she was never poor."

"This is fiction, not biography," I say. "Besides, a story should be universal. Every girl has an uncle, or *some*body, like that."

"Did you?"

"This is fiction, not autobiography," I say.

Everett takes a deep exaggerated breath. "Alice's family was well-off, she went to college, majored in Business Administration. She married, had two sons, and in her spare time, she blasted her way into the costume jewelry market and made a killing." The world according to Everett.

I amend. "Alice was a neglected child who hung around college campuses, married a rich man's son, had two sons right quick, divorced the rich man's son, sued for humongous alimony, bought herself a nanny, and a costume jewelry business," and reality reigns once again.

"You don't have to put it like that. You could emphasize the success part," says Everett.

I sweep gleaming vegetables from the chopping board into the skillet. The hot butter gives a long sigh. "So," I say. "A happy story is a story with the sad parts snipped away. And writing is an aberrant form of—cosmetology?"

I don't agree with this dishonesty, but I have to admire Everett's clear vision, a man for whom happiness is attainable through good sound planning—or a good pearl eraser. Later, as I clear and wash up from dinner, I wonder if he isn't right about Alice. With one son in jail, the other a part-time hairdresser and her series of interesting but impermanent men, she was surely, I had thought, in pure agony. I scrub pots. Ironic that Everett would be the one to suggest that a woman's happiness could exist despite the failure of children and men.

Everett seems to have lost interest in this quest for the happy story, but I am tortured by it. The problem is the thing itself—happiness. What is it? The attainment of what I *think* I want, or just the absence of grief? Who has it? How did they get hold of it? Hang onto it? Or is it just mind control—looking for the bright side while constantly living in the dark? Is it the predictable routine of Everett's mother's last years, whose whole life was spent in flux? Is her happiness the mere absence of the awful unexpected, the knowledge that there are no new disasters? That her own death is no longer frightening—that it is a not altogether unpleasant prospect? The idea that every eventuality can be met? The reason that she can refuse to be rescued from the dilapidation of life, finally insist upon having some things her own way and not worry about the consequences? There might be a certain satisfaction in this.

Still, how sad if happiness boiled down to a kind of good-natured fatalism. I wanted my happiness to be more perfect, even if that made it impossible to obtain. Even if it had to remain the property of childhood ignorance, or of memory.

"Are you trying to say you've never been happy?" says Everett.

"I would never say that."

"What was the happiest time of your life?"

"Happiest?" I repeat, balancing a stack of plates to a high shelf. "It's so hard to speak in degrees. . . ."

"Give me one time," he says. "When?"

"When?" I repeat.

When. Everett's voice is like the crossed arms of my old piano
teacher. Mrs. Poindexter. One hand always gripping a ruler. "Give me
the time," she would say, smacking the ruler against her narrow backside for the tempo. And I played, struggling to meet the demand.
Everett waits. I rifle through my life, days, and years, in search of a
single convincing moment. I think it must be something wholly selfish
and completely satisfying—

Like the time two nickels bought me two whole Big Time candy
bars to eat all by myself and *not* share. It had taken me all day to shake
little sisters and supervision. The city air had smelled sweet to me as I
ran, full tilt, without stopping, to the basement store. The agony,
sweet, of impossible choices: candy necklaces or candy mint juleps or
"wine" candy sours. But I had already known I wanted the Big Times
that were hurt-yourself good and never enough when you had to split
one two ways, or three, or four. But I had two nickels and a little bit of
time. . . . Except I remember the candy didn't taste as good as I had
expected. Maybe they were stale. Or maybe it was because I ate them
so fast, afraid of being discovered, afraid of the sudden cry of: "dibs
dibs!" our unrefusable demand to share. Or worse, some unexpected
adult demanding to know "—and where'd you get the money for that?"
Because a nickel for candy was unusual, and two was rare if not
completely unheard of. And the nickels were "borrowed" from my
grandmother's mantel. No, this was not a happy memory. The selfish
moment is always spoiled by guilt.

A happy moment would, evidently, have to be some occasion of
selfless generosity or sacrifice. When I was oh, maybe ten years old, my
sisters and I had saved a wool sock full of money. A collection of nickels,
quarters and even some dollar bills. We counted it constantly, thoroughly excited at our thrift. We discussed what to do with the money,
but could think of no purchase exciting or satisfying enough to justify
spending all of that money, close to thirteen dollars. It must have been
Palm Sunday, or some other special occasion. It could not have been an
ordinary Sunday when we carried our treasure in its black wool "bank"
to Sunday school, and we decided to give a whole dollar in offering.
Our Sunday School master must have smelled our excitement, or our
money, because she kept on begging and prodding, saying: "Oh, our
class has never won the distinction of best offering. A little bit more,
and we might earn a special blessing." (One more dollar). And: "Oh!

wouldn't it be something if the children of the Sunday School out-
shined the adults in their offering to God?" (*Two* more dollars). And: "I
just checked and we're still five dollars lower than the Elders' collection
plate." In defeat, we emptied the entire remains of our sock savings into
the plate. . . . And, in a moment, a great cry rose up in the church.
Three daughters had given thirteen dollars to the collection plate.
Wasn't that a wonderment! Wasn't that the spirit of God at work! But
there was jealousy in the House of God because a rally cry went up.
The adults reached into their deep pockets and came forth with dollar
after dollar. Even so, we almost earned our special blessing, which was
little enough reward I thought, when my own father came forward with
five dollars in his hand. The adults grinned. I wept. No. Selfless
generosity was, and always had been, for the birds. How could I have
forgotten that even joyful giving *must* offer *some* small reward.

The last possibility: happiness must be some simple uncompli-
cated moment when your purposes—no matter how unambitious—go
unthwarted.

Like I had my own house once. And once, I had a certain recognition for particular kinds of Saturday afternoons, early dusk, mild
uneventful days. Yes, summer Saturdays, early dusk, just as the worst
of the midday heat has dissipated, and every window is thrown open to
the deepening air, the beginning breeze; rooms stretch out infinite in
growing shadows. I am part of the shadows, sweaty, rank. But every
surface is scrubbed, rubbed to gleaming. Leisurely, slow, I lean in to
every doorway and everything is perfect order: perfumed linen, gleaming glass, dark scent of wax and incense burning into dusk. And jazz
saxophone mellow on the box—Standing sour and damp, old clothes
sticking to me, scalp pricking sweat, lifting my shirtfront to the breath
of a breeze, knowing I am the only imperfection within this small
perfection made by me. And I, for the moment, am my own creation.
It is not the weekly grind of housework that satisfies, but purposes
being met without interference. Completion. The signature on the
painting. The flourish at the end of the performance.

"Climbing into the wonderful world of Calgon is bliss," I say to
Everett. "I have been happy."

"Taking a bath is happiness for you?" he says, voice cracking. His
look is scorching. I guess I have missed a beat somewhere. I suppose I
ought to include *him* in it somehow.

I return to myself in an incredibly hot bath, so hot I am floating up like the mist, so perfect my thoughts burst open like the bubbles I nudge with my toe. I can dissolve into the sweat of mirrors that multiply me, disappear into the yellow brilliance of saxophone straining toward the treble—a single superb note the horn blower discovers at the top of the riff. He blows, bending at the knees until his chest caves—holding it . . . holding on. . . . It is the uncertainty of the moment that inspires absorption: knowing the sweetness of the bath can't last, knowing how hot dissipates to tepid, knowing that the record will end. That the silence will be broken . . . by a faint sound—the deadbolt sliding back under the key. Joy is the prior regret for the sweet ending of an irretrievable moment. I tell Everett that his returning home from an absence and I'm brand new in the bathtub is an intensely exquisite experience.

Everett considers this—tongue busy. But I'm dissatisfied. What is this feeling I'm looking for, so fleet, like a bubble I burst with my toe? Why should it be that I can recall injuries and slights to no end, have at my disposal infinite evidence of the world's injustice, malice, and casual cruelty. And disappointments: like discovering that there *is* no magic— no benevolent and timely fairy godmother to rescue us from the daily cinders and rubble; that the bread crumbs strewn to show us the way are *al*ways food for birds, or the hustling industrious ants, leaving us all standing, faces tipped, staring up into a knit of blankness. Where are the matching memories of joy so powerful, so engulfing, enough to muffle the continuous pummeling of life?

This is a happy story with a dole of sadness, like the surplus bread handed out to the poor. Like the rich man whose joy in his richness is tainted with a worry that the poor might get too much. . . .

My neighborhood church is a dispensary to the poor. I volunteer to hand out surplus food to the needy. Sometimes cheese, sometimes bread. The Reverend Lester hands out religion. "Jesus fed the multitude with five loaves and two fish," he preaches a popular sermon.

"You givin' out fish too, Rev'rend?" a young woman asks.

"They given out fish," someone passes it on.

"*Some* folks got fish," another says, dissatisfied. "They ran out."

The people stand in lines. I think of fish dinners, back yard fish fries, slapping mosquitoes on summer nights, pungent hot sauces, cold beer and lemonade. Mountains of catfish, perch, fried golden crisp, the hot steam trapped inside the skin. How it would take all day to get ready with errands and cleaning the fish, and sweeping stray children from underfoot. The air full of expectation and no one too impatient.

A woman stands in front of me, her hands held forth for her portion. Her expression is sour. She looks at the smooth blocks of cheese thinking of fish. She takes the cheese, hands the large weight of it to her small child standing beside her. The child wobbles with the burden.

"There never was any fish," I say to her.

"Sure," she says.

"It was just a rumor," I say, but she stalks off. She wants to know who is in charge. My eyes are met by the direct stare of the woman standing behind her. She is elderly; her skin in smooth like rubbed, cured wood. After a moment, she smiles.

"The good Lord didn't need fish nor bread to do what he done. Don't never call *that* no rumor," she tells me, mocking-stern. "God bless," she says, receiving the cheese into her arms carefully. "I gives some of this to my nephew," she says. "He don't qualify. He earn $10.00 over the limit." Her smile is full of yellow gold, a bright chip drawing the vague light of the dim room to a single brilliant mite. She leaves me with my own smile.

"The happiest day of my life was the day we were married," Everett confesses to me, then waits. Then he says, "What about you?"

"I'm still working on it," I say.

"You weren't happy on our wedding day?" he says.

"Well," I say, "I didn't want to take *your* happiest day."

"But it *was* the happiest? So far? Right?"

Everett no longer asks me about my stories. Now I *make* him listen.

"This is a story about happiness," I say. "It's not finished." Everett says nothing. "This is what I have so far," I say.

"Alice always loved weddings. So, as a young girl, she resolved to have several. Each one would be more beautiful than the last, each husband more beautiful than his predecessor. Therefore, the spareness of her first wedding and the sparsity of beauty in the face and form of her first husband did not disturb her excessively. When the aged preacher misread a few of the vows, it was not devastating to Alice who, later, had to console her new husband's anger regarding the matter.

"'You didn't plan to keep all those promises anyway,' she chided him, laughing, teasing. The accusation shocked him at first, as he did not expect her to know this, and he protested the fidelity of his heart. But, a day later, when Alice found her husband's eyes wandering behind an unfamiliar woman, he smiled, licked his lips and resolved to be more careful.

"His name was Cheever. Cheever did not have good looks but knew 'how to make him some money.' He said this often and Alice, who was always agreeable, agreed.

"But Alice did not despise Cheever for his lack of handsomeness. She felt genuinely grateful to him—he's been her escape route from home, from her uncle's fish smell. She was satisfied with her marriage and learned how to keep house out of magazines, cooked out of books, and drew designs with colored pencils which she pinned all over her walls until they lived inside a montage of faint scribbly color. She even pinned the light designs to the bedboard above their heads. And sunny mornings when she woke to Cheever thrusting love at her from behind, matter-of-factly like a drowsy bear rubbing an itch against a slender bark, she had only to lift her eyes to study the outlines of dreams, outside the sudden odor of private lust.

"One day, when Cheever had gone, Alice crawled back into the spoiled sheets that held her daydreams. And behind her lids grew a tree supple and bending beneath the jewels that budded on the tips of its branches. She plucked one red fruit and made it disappear inside the warm dark of her palm."

"She's living in a dream world," says Everett. "Her husband is selfish and inconsiderate. *And* ugly. Where does the happy part come in?"

"It's coming," I say.

I am still writing the story of the woman—intelligent, ambitious, attractive, educated. Did I say intelligent? Because she is no longer planning suicide, realizing it was a waste of her time since death is already scripted and requires no additional preparation. Realizing that her mother's life contained some moments of joy because she was a woman who worked towards the completion of tasks small and large and always spoke of her life without excluding any of its parts.

Mary Hood

A Man
Among Men

1

His old man lay in Grady Miller's best steel casket with the same determined-to-die look on his face that he had worn throughout his final two months of decline, from the night Olene had run red-eyed back through the Labor Day rain with his uneaten supper on its wilting picnic plate to report, "He's gone in that camper and put on his nightshirt and gone to bed. For keeps." She had shaken the rain from her jacket and scarf, using one of the green-checked napkins to dry her face. "He's talking funny. I don't like the way he's talking. Made me lay out his dark suit where he could see it and told me, 'No shoes, no use burying good leather, just see my socks are clean,' all because of a dog. A dog!"

"Daddy thought the world of Smokey Dawn," Thomas pointed out.

He and the old man had spent their entire holiday looking for the hound, as far south as Buck's Creek, all around the public hunting lands, calling, calling from the windows of the truck. She had never stayed out so long. She had never trashed in her life. From time to time the old man raised his arm and hissed, "Listen," his bladey hand like an ax. Once it was the waul of a blue-tailed rooster, strutting in a dried cornfield; it almost sounded like the dog. The cock stepped toward them, icy eye taking it all in. "Shoot!" The old man fell back against the seat, disappointed. They drove on.

There was a strange feel to the weather; the sky was so overcast the morning glories in the corn were still open wide. "Weatherbreeder," the old man said, staring at the clouds, but he wasn't looking for rain. In a few miles he spotted them—three buzzards—freckles on the flannel belly of the afternoon. The old man tensed up and leaned forward, still hoping, and peered down the dirt lane to where she lay in the gold-enrod. Before Thomas got the truck full-stopped, his daddy was scrabbling out. He thrashed his hat all around to keep the birds aloft. He still had that sense he was rescuing her. His tough old shoes barely cleared the dust as he hastened toward the corpse, stumbling over pebbles and lurching on, stiff-footed.

Thomas lagged back, letting him handle it. He lit his cheroot on the third match; there was an east wind, mean and cold, shaking the young pines. Handfuls of sparrows sifted themselves out of the blow, deeper and deeper into the thickets.

His daddy was shivering.

Thomas shed his jacket and offered it to the old man, who wasn't dressed for the knifing wind. He took it, knelt, and wrapped the dog in it. "I reckon it was her heart," he said, beating his parchment fist against his chest. "No bigger than a fiddle when I got me my first redbone pup, Billy Boy it was." He looked away as Thomas lifted the dog and carried her back to the truck. The old man walked alone, counting up his losses: "After Billy it was Babe . . . and Ginger Tom out of Babe and French Lou—she had the straightest legs of them all— and Red Pearl and Rabbit Joe, one-eyed but it never cost him a coon, heart like a tiger . . . did I say Racing Joe? And Joe's Honey and Honey's Nan . . ." He flinched when Thomas slammed the tailgate: a solemn closing, the end of an era. They headed home. "And Jolly, and Honey's Nan, I mention her yet? And Prince Ego and Skiff. And Smokey," he said, "Smokey Dawn." He stared toward the darkening west, his eyes cold and gray as a dead-man's nickels. "Well, that's about it." They rode in silence then.

By the time Thomas parked, at home, the old man's interest had waned to a single, final point. "Dig it deep" was how he put it. "I don't want a plow turning her up some day." He headed for his mobile home and went in and closed the door.

When Olene saw the windbreaker over the dog's body, she said, "I'm not washing that in my machine."

"Dean's not home yet?"

"I'm not worried." She laughed. "When you're seventeen you run on nerve and Dr. Pepper, not Daylight Saving. You'll have to bury her yourself."

It was already raining—the first huge cold drops—when he went to get the mattock.

Olene had never had much patience with the old man's sulks. "Do something," she said, after supper, just as the phone rang. She went scraping the old man's untouched food into the garbage. "Turned his head to the wall, not one bite would he taste, and me on my feet chopping and cooking since noon." All the time Thomas was on the phone she kept reciting her welling grievances at his back. She broke off when he reached for his uniform jacket on its hook.

"Now what?

He zipped the jacket to his chin, then unzipped it halfway; he dug out his truck keys and clipped his beeper to his belt. "A car hit a deer on the quarry road."

"Couldn't someone else?"

He unlocked the cabinet and took down his service revolver. "I had last weekend off, remember?"

"We didn't do anything."

He loaded the gun and clicked it shut. "I'll just step on across and check on Daddy before I go." Lightning showed the walk to be running like a brook. "And it's not a camper," he said as he plunged out into the deluge.

He splashed across the flagstones to the mobile home. The windows were open; it was cave-damp and dark inside. The wet curtains dragged at his hands as he cranked the jalousies shut. He turned on the lights and ran the thermostat up. At the bedroom door he hesitated. "It's Thomas," he announced softly.

"Come on."

Thomas took the old man's hand and clasped it; it was cold. His daddy puzzled him out a feature at a time from his pillows. He shook his head; they were strangers. "I recollect you now," he bluffed. "We were running Blue Jolly and Nan . . ." He trailed off, uncertain. "That old coon—tail shot off four years back—no fight left in her, no fight. So fat she dropped into the dogs and just let 'em rip. No play in the pack for that. Funny . . ." He yawned for breath. "Funny . . ." He opened his eyes and stared all the way through Thomas, clear out the other side into the young century when someone, someone . . .

"*Who?*" he asked irascibly. He focused again, present tense. "My memory's shot to chow," he confessed. He glanced indifferently around the room, recognizing nothing but his suit on the chair. "I'm checking out of here," he announced abruptly, flailing himself upright, then falling back, exhausted. "You help me, mister?"

Thomas nodded.

"You notify my son, Little Earl—Earl Teague, Jr.—on the Star Route . . ." He gestured with his thumb, south.

Thomas watched the pulse wriggle in the old man's temple. Was he just sulking, like Olene said? Or was it another of the little strokes that left him more and more a stranger?

"Daddy?" Thomas said, sharp, calling the cloudy eyes back into focus.

Frowning, he examined Thomas' face and resumed, "Highly thought of . . . in the book . . . look him up . . . Earl Teague, Jr. He'll come take care of me."

"But what about Thomas?" Thomas asked, for the record.

The old man seemed to have dozed off.

"Daddy?"

He blinked awake. "Who is it?"

"Thomas."

"Not him," he said, irritated. He had never suffered fools gladly. "He's dead." He looked at Thomas and yawned.

You son of a bitch, Thomas thought. He wanted to shake the old man, wake him, make claims. But what was the use of that now? Or ever? When Little Earl was killed by the train, hadn't his daddy stared at Thomas standing by the closed coffin and asked, "Why couldn't it have been you?"

That was when Thomas knew.

2

His old man lay in Grady Miller's front parlor between the adjustable lamps casting their discreet 40-watt pink-of-health upon him head and foot. He was dressed in his Sunday best. Olene had tucked a rose into his lapel. She came up to Thomas standing there and ran her arm through his. "Isn't he sweet?" she said, giving the little bouquet of buds and baby's breath a pat, smoothing the streamers across the old man's chest. GRANDDADDY was spelled out in press-on gold letters on the satin ribbon. She had ordered that, in Dean's name. The boy hadn't seen the old man since the last week of the hospital stay, when life-support was all that tethered him to the world. He hadn't seen him dying, and he hadn't seen him dead. Thomas' simmering resentment of that finally boiled over on Saturday night when Dean came in late for supper, said he wasn't hungry, and announced that the clutch had torn out of his Chevy again.

"Ten days!" Thomas said. "This time it lasted ten days!"

"Three weeks," Olene corrected. She looked it up in the check-book. "He can drive mine."

"He won't need it; he's coming with us," Thomas said.

"I can fix it myself in three hours if I get the parts."

"Not tonight." Thomas finished his coffee, standing. He set the cup in the sink.

"I'm not going down there."

"Your granddaddy—"

"Is dead and I'm not. I'm sure as hell not," Dean said. He laughed. He drank what was left of the quart of milk right from the carton. When Thomas backhanded him, it knocked his sunglasses and the empty milk carton across the kitchen. One of the lenses rolled over by the trash.

"No!" Olene stepped between.

"I'd beat his ass till it turned green if I thought it would do any good," Thomas said, over her head. Still he couldn't see into the boy's eyes. How long had it been since they *saw* each other? He turned away, shrugged off Olene's restraining hand. In the silence, which prolonged, the boy wiped the milk mustache off with his fist.

When Olene saw the look on his face, she said, "He's just trying to raise you."

"All he raises is objections," Dean said.

Thomas headed up the stairs, two at a time, to shave and dress for the wake. "Don't wait up," Dean bragged as he left. He took Olene's car.

It was the first time he had stayed out all night that they didn't know where to find him.

On Sunday morning (the old man's funeral would be that afternoon) the beeper summoned Thomas on a dead-body call. He left
Olene and the men's Bible class on honor guard at Miller's and headed
across town to Doc Daniels' pharmacy. Doc was the one who had
spotted the body in the weeds, followed the footprints from his broken-
in back door out through the frost and down the gullied fill-dirt specked
with soda cans and gum wrappers. Doc had called, "Hey! HEY!", a
wake-up call in case it was sleep and not death he had been stalking, but
when he got close enough to be fairly sure he hurried back to the phone
to spread the news. The EMS driver got there first and made a tentative
diagnosis—overdose—but now they were waiting on the coroner and
Thomas to arrive.

When Thomas got there, Doc led the way again, down the clay
bank, his white bucks getting pinker with every dusty step. Thomas
was in a hurry; Doc caught at his sleeve to stay apace. He was panting
to keep up. Together they leaped the last gully. All the way Doc was
telling, telling, fixing his magnified gaze on Thomas' profile.

"Look at him," Doc accused, as they came to the corpse.

A boy, curling a bit toward the fetal pose, lay on his left side. For a
moment Thomas thought he knew him—a trick of the mind after a
sleepless night—dirty sneakers, faded jeans, blue windbreaker, watch
cap. He swayed, rubbed his eyes, then knelt for a closer look, resting his
hand on the boy's stiff, angled knees.

Behind him Doc was saying, "This makes the sixth time I've been
robbed. I've got payments to make like anyone else—"

Thomas searched the boy's pockets for ID. He flipped through the
haggard wallet. Doc leaned forward, squinting. "So who gets the bad
news?" he wondered.

Thomas stood up. "I'll tell them," he said, and started up the bank
to his truck. He took the time to smoke one of his little cigars. He
answered no questions. The crowd moved back to let his truck pass. He
drove fast though there was no hurry.

He crossed the tracks at midtown and turned right onto a forgotten
road hardly more than an alley paralleling the rails. He headed south
till the paving turned to gravel; it peppered the underside of his truck as
he negotiated the lane's washboard heaves and hollows. He rolled his
window up against the dust rather than slow down.

The road dead-ended in a grove of blighted elms beyond a bare yard, clean-swept with a broom in that country way of deterring snakes. Mazes of rabbit fence held back the frost-nipped remains of faded petunias. On the staggering mailbox, in decrescendo, red paint not a season old announced ELSiE BLaND beneath the former tenant's name, shoeblacked out. A dingy cat leaped up onto the truck hood, settled on the cab roof, and held aloof from Thomas' hand. From the grayed house came the sound of fast sad blues, decades old, scratchy— an ancient, sturdy record salvaged from attic or rummage sale. Before Thomas crossed the porch the music sped up to 78 rpm; people were laughing. They didn't hear him.

He knocked again. Louder.

A laughing woman materialized behind the rusty rump-sprung screen door, wiping her eyes with her fingers and shaking the tears away. "Sounds like mice in them cartoons," she explained. She leaned into the dark to call, "Jude? Jude! You shut that down now, *shut* it." To Thomas she said, "It's Sunday, I know, but I didn't reckon it'd hurt anything for him to listen. We been to church this morning, early." She guessed he was a preacher.

Because they did not know each other, because he had come in his pickup truck instead of the cruiser, because she did not notice the blue light on the dashboard behind the windshield reflecting October, because he was dressed for his daddy's funeral and wasn't in uniform, he could see she had no idea at all who or what he was. He held up his badge and said, "It's the Law, ma'am. I'm Tom Teague. Are you Mrs. Bland?" And because he had come on official business and there was more than courtesy conveyed in his manners—some additional intimation of apology for bad news, perhaps the worst news—the solemnity communicated itself through the rusty screen and into her heart instantly and flamed up into remorse, as though the fires of regret and grief had long been laid and awaited but the glint of Thomas' badge to kindle them.

"My boy Ben! Killed oversea in the service!" she screamed, voicing her oldest premonition, her dreams that woke her, brought her to her knees in the nightwatch. She had a map of the world with Lebanon marked on it in ballpoint, circled and circled, to help her focus her prayers.

"No," Thomas said. He tried the door. It was latched. "Mrs. Bland . . ." he appealed. Something in his tone arrested her wild attention.

The needle scratched loudly across the old record and resumed playing again, at proper speed, the fast sad blues. She settled her eyes on Thomas'.

Quieter, she said, "Then it's about Ray." She unhooked the screen and admitted trouble into her scrub-worn rooms. Every windowsill had its beard of green plants in foil-covered pots. Above the mantel with its clutter of photographs hung a lithograph of radiant Christ.

"Jude, honey," his mama suggested, "about time for your train."

Jude came in from the kitchen, a man who would be a boy all his life.

"We got to discuss," she told him. "You go on out." No introductions.

Passing by, the boy stuck out his hand to Thomas. "Please to," he said. The old ladies that Elsie cleaned for praised his manners and his willingness to climb ladders; they let him unclog their gutters for cookies and dimes.

The train at the town limits sounded its whistle. The boy hurried out to admire the pink Albert City Farmers grain cars rolling past on tracks not a city block away.

"Just a little something went wrong when he was borned, a good boy, no trouble, not like Ray." Elsie breathed faster. She aimed her sharp nose at Thomas and angrily asked, "What about him? Tell me what he done."

"I'm afraid it's bad news, Mrs. Bland."

She thought it over. "Bound to be." She pushed herself up out of the chair and fetched one of the photographs from the mantel. She handed it to Thomas. Its cheap metal frame was cold and sharp as a knife. There was the face of the boy Doc had found in the weeds. Thomas cleared his throat. He handed the picture back; for a moment they both held it, then he let it go.

"He's dead," he told her. There was nothing to tell but the truth, and it only took two words. Thomas thought that was how he would want to hear it, if he ever had to. Elsie heard it, Thomas thought, without surprise. She seemed stupefied, though, and it was a minute before she repeated, "Dead." She sat staring at the photograph in her lap.

"He's the one like his pappy," she specified. She just sat there. Silent.

"You'll want to ask me some questions," Thomas suggested.

Elsie looked out the window at Jude. "He purely loves them trains. Don't miss a one. Always try to locate near the tracks for him."

Georgia, Clinchfield, and West Point stock rolled past, slowing, and the British Columbia car with its magnolia logo stopped directly in view as the L&N engines switched back and forth uptown, shunting a feed car aside.

"He's the good one," Elsie said. Canny, she studied Thomas' face, reading there her familiar, bitter lesson. "Ray done bad?" she guessed. She set the photograph back in its place on the mantel. "You don't love them for it, but you love them. There's good in between the bad times." She smoothed a wrinkle in the mantel runner, chased the fold ahead of her fingers to the fringed end, then chased it again.

The train, readying itself for the run north through the deep cuts and poplar hills, revved its engines until the whole house rumbled, making itself felt in every bone.

"The Lloyd Jesus knows I love all my boys!" she cried, her face lifted to the calendar Christ as she wept. When she was calmer she wiped her face on her apron and took her seat again, her tear-shining hands inert on the arms of her chair, her swollen feet in their strutted oxfords braced heel by heel for the truth. "All right," she consented. She sniffed deeply, inhaling the last of her tears. "You tell me what it is. What'll be in them newspapers. Tell me in so many words. I don't want to read about it." Her voice was worn down with speaking up for herself and her sons, husky from making itself heard over mill racket, muffled by sorrows. "I hate to read about it," she explained, then cleared her throat with a sigh and waited.

That was when Thomas, though it wasn't his intention, admitted, "It could have been my own son. I thought it was."

3

His old man lay in Grady Miller's lifetime-guaranteed burial vault, and the mourners—those windblown few who waited for the closing and the anchoring of their wreaths in the raw clay—drifted like dark leaves against the whited wall of Soul's Harbor Church. Olene's sinuses were acting up; she couldn't wear a hat over that hairdo and she had left her scarf in her other coat. She withdrew to the sanctuary of the darkened church itself. Miller's assistants were already folding the chairs, rolling up the fake grass, loading the pulleys and frame and plush seat covers into their van. The pastor gave Thomas a little tap with his Bible as he went by, saying, "We'll keep in touch," and headed briskly for his car. His wife was already buckled in, ready.

There came that general, genteel exodus, with no backward glances, as life went on. The road and margins cleared of traffic and then it was so quiet; there was only the flutter of the canopy's scalloped canvas as the wind rocked it on its moorings. The grave-diggers' words were blown far afield, toward the kneeling cattle, fawn-colored jerseys, on the distant hill. They looked legless; they reminded Thomas of that deer on the quarry road Labor Day night, her front legs sheared in the accident, yet somehow she was still alive.

He had knelt beside her. Her doe eye, widely dilated, stared vacantly up at the sky, her nostrils flaring with each quick breath. She was dying, and it was taking too long.

"Where the hell is the Ranger?"

The inevitable crowd had begun to gather. G. W Laney, first responder, stamped and snorted like a dray beast. He was a volunteer, whose wife had given him an emergency light for his birthday. Its intermittent red sweep refreshed his sunburn and turned the rain to blood. His scanner spat static. Thomas had a headache. He and G. W. laid a tarp over the deer.

"Back 'em up," Thomas told him, and G. W. herded the bystanders deeper into the dark. "Appreciate y'all coming, folks, but how about clearing on off for home now?" They mostly went. Thomas couldn't see how the deer was still alive. He checked her again, ran his hand down her neck.

"I'm not waiting," he decided.

At the gunshot, the door of the ditched car ratcheted open and a young man climbed uphill out into the downpour. Thomas stared. They hadn't told him it was Dean! The boy had a bloody handkerchief tied around his left palm. They stood in the rainy circle of flashlight and Thomas asked, first off, "Whose car have you wrecked this time?"

"Ginnie let me drive. You know Ginnie—Doc Daniels' daughter."

The kind you find dead in a ditch some day, Thomas thought, watching her get out now, her jacket held over her head to keep the rain off her bright hair. Her T-shirt advertised Squeeze Me, I'm Fresh. She sided with Dean, facing Thomas down, two against one.

"It's totaled," Thomas said, surveying the wrecked sedan.

"I'm insured," Ginnie said. "but still I bet Daddy'll shit a brick." She laughed. Dean started to laugh, then didn't. Then did. Ginnie flicked a few tiny cubes of safety glass off his shoulder.

"You been drinking?" Thomas asked, officially. And unofficially.

"Naw, uh, just beer. Just one." Dean shut his eyes, stood on tiptoe, and began touching first one index finger, then the other, to his nose. "See?"

"You need a doctor?" Thomas kept his voice casual as he eyed that blood-blackened bandage.

"It's just a cut." Dean was exhilarated by the adrenalin. "Damn deer bust right out on me! Like a bomb. Clean through the windshield." He avoided looking at that mound under the rain-glittering tarp.

"How fast were you going?" Thomas shone the flashlight along the pavement. "Where'd you brake?"

"You saying it's my fault?" The boy's raw fist in its bandage tightened.

"I'm saying what I'd say to anyone."

Dean crossed his arms over his chest when he heard that and bent a hot, hurt look on his father—part anger, part disappointment—as though he had been handed a stone instead of bread.

Thomas knew that look well enough. "Sue me," he told the boy. The wrecker was backing up to Ginnie's car and the Ranger had arrived, with a notebook to fill with facts. He began asking Dean and Ginnie the hard questions. When he finished and had no charges to file, Thomas offered, "Y'all need a lift?"

Ginnie said, that quick, "We're going with G. W.," and G. W. grinned, because he hadn't asked them and because Ginnie was like that, fixing things to suit her. (She had a way of daring him that sent Dean diving off the rocky cliff over the reservoir at least once a summer, risking his neck for one moment of her laughter, and before the peony of spray had settled around him, before he had surfaced, she was bored, thinking up something else. Thomas had warned them off those rocks, but Ginnie was worth the risk, worth the slow climb back up the cliff to her lacquered toes.) She swung herself up into G. W.'s front seat and Dean got in the back.

"Keep it between the ditches," Thomas had called as they rolled off, white water fluming up from beneath the wide tires of the Jeep.

"How much longer?" Thomas wondered. He had objected to the machine, backfilling, so the men were shoveling by hand.

One of the mourners, with an estimating glance over toward the undertaker's canopy, said "*Now*, I think. They're about done." The grave was covered and the wreaths were being laid. The ribbons rattled in the wind.

Thomas led the way, alone. Friends who had stayed set out in a broken rank behind him, by twos and threes, across the intervening graves, picking their way around the minimal obstacles of granite and marble, not talking. The throaty mufflers of Dean's orange Chevy caught their attention from the moment he rounded the curve by Foster's store. He burned a week's worth of rubber off its tires and stopped in a scour of gravel at the foot of the hill. Thomas turned to watch. They all did.

Dean had a bucket of bronze mums. He came on fast, loping across the field, hurdling the cemetery wall, catching up. They made way for him, but still he hung back, only stepping up to set the flowers at the headstone, between his grandparents' graves. Then he rested on Little Earl's footstone, catching his breath. He had nothing to say when they greeted him. Sullen, he raised the hood of his jogging suit and tied it snug, but they could still see his black eye. He stood suddenly and stamped his foot. "Cramp," he explained, doing some exercises to stretch the kink from his calf. "Gotta work it out." He jogged off east across the field, over unclaimed ground, then down toward the gravel pit, and around again.

As they watched him go, one of the men said, "Give him time, Tom, he's just a kid." That was what Olene was always saying. But wasn't that what everyone had said about Little Earl? Wild as sunspots and dead at twenty-four after losing a race with a locomotive, and not a day in that whole wasted life had he ever thought of anyone but himself.

The others paid their last respects to the old man, calling him a man among men, shaking Thomas's hand, and heading on down the hill to their cars. The diggers, behind the church, loaded their backhoe onto its trailer, threw in their handtools, and drove off.

When they had gone, Dean trotted back. "I wasn't going to come," he said. He pulled up his left sock, then stood not quite facing his daddy. They were alone now.

"You just about missed it," Thomas agreed. Why had he bothered to come? Thomas couldn't look at him, at that bruised eye. Had he hit him *that* hard? Where the hell had he been all night?

"Your mother was worried sick," Thomas said. He fumbled with his matches. Dean didn't say anything, as usual, just looked around. "She's in the church," Thomas told him. The boy shrugged.

"You're the ones who let the air out of the cruiser's tires, aren't you? You and Ginnie." He'd figured that out in fifteen seconds. Did they think he was a fool?

"Sue me," Dean said. Thomas blinked when he heard himself quoted. The boy stepped up to the curb of the plot and balanced on his toes, taller than his daddy, then stepped back down. "I was pissed," he said.

Before Thomas could decide if that was an apology, the door of the church skreeked open, then slammed. Olene stood on the steps, her eyes shaded by her upheld hands as she stared their way. She waved and shouted something, but the wind scattered her words. She gave up, but stayed out, as though she wanted to keep an eye on them. She sat on the top step in what was left of the sun, hugging her cold knees.

"And leave Ginnie out of it," Dean added.

"I figured it was you." Thomas unpocketed his fists to stoop and right a spray of carnations the wind had tipped over. The shoulders of his suit were white from leaning against the chalky shingles of the church. The scent of dying flowers choked him. Just that mere whiff made him remember all the other times, but he didn't want to re-member. A phoebe settled hard, rocking a little on the rusty gate, feebly singing. Thomas concentrated on the bird.

When he caught Dean looking at him, he nodded toward the boy's car and said, "You fixed the clutch." He was getting hoarse.

"Yeah." Dean almost smiled.

The wind was strong enough to lean on, like it would never die. Dean glanced at his watch and sighed. He held out his hand, signaling *five minutes more* to Olene, waiting.

Thomas crossed his arms. "Don't let me keep you."

One by one Dean popped the knuckles of both hands, taking his time. Thomas hated that. "You going to stay out here all night?" Dean asked.

"Look who's talking."

"At least I was warm," Dean said.

Thomas checked the sky. "This time it didn't rain. It always rains." He watched the blue pickup truck bump across Langford's far pasture, and the cows begin walking toward the hay in back. One of the calves bawled and ran to catch up with its mother.

Olene came across the cemetery, making careful steps in her high heels, holding her coat shut. "Thomas?" she called. She lurched, stopped, and removed her shoes, then came on, faster, over the grass. "I'd rather have pneumonia than broken bones," she said. She looked from Thomas to Dean and back again. Thomas took her shoes and put them in the pockets of his suitcoat. She reached up to touch Dean's bruised eye, but he pulled away.

Olene knelt to gather up the remains of the everlasting and lilies she had planted. "Look what they did," she said. The careless mower in his zeal had laid them low. The diggers had chipped the granite corner monogram and snubbed the rose, the only volunteer. Thomas toed a stray clod from his daddy's footstone, which was already in place, part of the package deal when they buried his mother.

"All they've got to do is cut the date of death," Olene said, bending to tap the cold stone. "Its been a while, but they can match Mama Teague's numbers exactly." Olene dusted her hands and hugged her coat tighter to her. "I'm freezing to death," she said. "I'll be next."

"We'll go," Thomas said. Olene ran on and got into Thomas' truck and shut the door, but Dean stayed. Thomas was shivering. He made a giveaway gesture at the ground: farewell. "Maybe Mama can do something with him," he said. "I sure as hell never could."

The phoebe on the iron gate flew out and back, out and back, preying and preening. The wind had finally let up, and for a moment there was no other motion in the world but the lone bird, weakly singing. Then Dean stepped across Little Earl's grave and brushed the chalk dust off Thomas' shoulders, brushed and brushed.

That was when Thomas began to cry.

Manly Conclusions

His wife, Valjean, admitted that Carpenter Petty had a tree-topping temper, but he was slow to lose it; that was in his favor. Still, he had a long memory, and that way of saving things up, until by process of accumulation he had enough evidence to convict. "I don't get mad, I get even," his bumper sticker vaunted. Fair warning. When he was angry he burned like frost, not flame.

Now Valjean stood on the trodden path in the year's first growth of grass, her tablecloth in her arms, and acknowledged an undercurrent in her husband, spoke of it to the greening forsythia with its yellow flowers rain-fallen beneath it, confided it to God and nature. Let God and nature judge. A crow passed between her and the sun, dragging its slow shadow. She glanced up. On Carpenter's behalf she said, "He's always been intense. It wasn't just the war. If you're born a certain way, where's the mending?"

She shook the tablecloth free of the crumbs of breakfast and pinned it to the line. Carpenter liked her biscuits—praised them to all their acquaintances—as well as her old-fashioned willingness to rise before good day and bake for him. Sometimes he woke early too; then he would join her in the kitchen. They would visit as she worked the shortening into the flour, left-handed (as was her mother, whose recipe it was), and pinch off the rounds, laying them as gently in the blackened pan as though she was laying a baby down for its nap. The dough was very quick, very tender. It took a light hand. Valjean knew the value of a light hand.

This morning Carpenter had slept late, beyond his time, and catching up he ate in a rush, his hair damp from the shower, his shirt unbuttoned. He raised neither his eyes nor his voice to praise or complain.

"You'll be better at telling Dennis than I would," he said, finally, leaving it to her.

She had known for a long time that there was more to loving a man than marrying him, and more to marriage than love. When they were newly wed, there had been that sudden quarrel, quick and furious as a summer squall, between Carpenter and a neighbor over the property line. A vivid memory and a lesson—the two men silhouetted against the setting sun, defending the territory and honor of rental property. Valjean stood by his side, silent, sensing even then that to speak out, to beg, or order, to quake would be to shame him. Nor would it avail. Better to shout "Stay!" to Niagara. Prayer and prevention was the course she decided on, learning how to laugh things off, to make jokes and diversions. If a car cut ahead of them in the parking lot and took the space he had been headed for, before Carpenter could get his window down to berate women drivers, Valjean would say, "I can see why she's in a hurry, just look at her!" as the offender trotted determinedly up the sidewalk and into a beauty salon.

She was subtle enough most times, but maybe he caught on after a while. At any rate, his emotional weather began to moderate. Folks said he had changed, and not for the worse. They gave proper credit to his wife, but the war had a hand in it too. When he got back, most of what he thought and felt had gone underground, and it was his quietness and shrewd good nature that you noticed now. Valjean kept on praying and preventing.

But there are some things you can't prevent, and he had left it to Valjean to break the news to Dennis. Dennis so much like Carpenter that the two of them turned heads in town, father and son, spirit and image. People seemed proud of them from afar as though their striking resemblance reflected credit on all mankind, affirming faith in the continuity of generations. He was like his mama, too, the best of both of them, and try as she might she couldn't find the words to tell him that his dog was dead, to send him off to school with a broken heart. The school bus came early, and in the last-minute flurry of gathering books and lunch money, his poster on medieval armor and his wind-breaker, she chose to let the news wait.

She had the whole day then, after he was gone, to find the best words. Musing, she sat on the top step and began cleaning Carpenter's boots—not that he had left them for her to do; he had just left them. She scrubbed and gouged and sluiced away the sticky mud, dipping her rag in a rain puddle. After a moment's deliberation she rinsed the cloth in Lady's water dish. Lady would not mind now; she was beyond thirst. It was burying her that had got Carpenter's boots so muddy.

"Dead," Valjean murmured. For a moment she was overcome, disoriented as one is the instant after cataclysm, while there is yet room for disbelief, before the eyes admit the evidence into the heart. The rag dripped muddy water dark as blood onto the grass.

They had found Lady halfway between the toolshed and the back porch, as near home as she had been able to drag herself. The fine old collie lay dying in their torchlight, bewildered, astonished, trusting them to heal her, to cancel whatever evil this was that had befallen.

Carpenter knelt to investigate. "She's been shot." The meaning of the words and their reverberations brought Valjean to her knees. No way to laugh this off.

"It would have been an accident," she reasoned.

Carpenter gave the road a despairing glance. "If it could have stayed the way it was when we first bought out here . . . you don't keep a dog like this on a chain!"

It had been wonderful those early years, before the developers came with their transits and plat-books and plans for summer cottages in the uplands. The deer had lingered a year or so longer, then had fled across the lake with the moon on their backs. The fields of wild blueberries were fenced off now; what the roadscrapers missed, wildfire got. Lawn crept from acre to acre like a plague. What trees were spared sprouted POSTED and KEEP and TRESPASSERS WILL BE signs. Gone were the tangles of briar and drifted meadow beauty, seedbox and primrose. The ferns retreated yearly deeper into the ravines.

"Goddamn weekenders," Carpenter said. They had lodged official complaint the day three bikers roared through the back lot, scattering the hens, tearing down five lines of wash, and leaving a gap through the grape arbor. The Law came out and made bootless inquiry, stirring things up a little more. The next morning Valjean found their garbage cans overturned. Toilet tissue wrapped every tree in the orchard, a dead rat floated in the well, and their mailbox was battered to earth—that sort of mischief. Wild kids. "Let the Law handle it," Valjean suggested, white-lipped.

"They can do their job and I'll do mine," Carpenter told her. So that time Valjean prayed that the Law would be fast and Carpenter slow, and that was how it went. A deputy came out the next day with a carload of joyriders he had run to earth. "Now I think the worst thing that could happen," the deputy drawled, "is to call their folks, whattya say?" So it had been resolved that way, with reparations paid, and handshakes. That had been several years back; things had settled down some now. Of late there were only the litter and loudness associated with careless vacationers. No lingering hard feelings. In the market, when Valjean met a neighbor's wife, they found pleasant things to speak about; the awkwardness was past. In time they might be friends.

"An accident," Valjean had asserted, her voice odd to her own ears. As though she were surfacing from a deep dive. Around them night was closing in. She shivered. It took her entire will to keep from glancing over her shoulder into the tanglewood through which Lady had plunged, wounded, to reach home.

"Bleeding like this she must have laid a plain track." Carpenter paced the yard, probing at spots with the dimming light of the lantern. He tapped it against his thigh to encourage the weak batteries.

"She's been gone all afternoon," Valjean said. "She could have come miles."

"Not hurt this bad," Carpenter said.

"What are you saying? No. No!" She forced confidence into her voice. "No one around here would do something like this." Fear for him stung her hands and feet like frost. She stood for peace. She stood too suddenly; dizzy, she put out her hand to steady herself. He could feel her trembling.

"It could have been an accident, yeah, like you say." He spoke quietly for her sake. He had learned to do that.

"You see?" she said, her heart lifting a little.

"Yeah." Kneeling again, he shook his head over the dog's labored breathing. "Too bad, old girl; they've done for you."

When the amber light failed from Lady's eyes, Valjean said,

breathless, "She was probably trespassing," thinking of all those signs, neon-vivid, warning. He always teased her that she could make excuses for the devil.

"Dogs can't read," he pointed out. "She lived all her life here, eleven, twelve years . . . and she knew this place by heart, every rabbit run, toad hole, and squirrel knot. She was better at weather than the almanac, and there was never a thing she feared except losing us. She kept watch on Dennis like he was her own pup."

"I know . . ." She struggled to choke back the grief. It stuck like a pine cone in her throat. But she wouldn't let it be *her* tears that watered the ground and made the seed of vengeance sprout. For all their sakes she kept her nerve . . .

"And whoever shot her," Carpenter was saying, "can't tell the difference in broad day between ragweed and rainbow. Goddam weekenders!"

They wrapped the dog in Dennis' cradle quilt and set about making a grave. Twilight seeped away into night. The shovel struck fire from the rocks as Carpenter dug. Dennis was at Scout meeting; they wanted to be done before he got home. "There's nothing deader than a dead dog," Carpenter reasoned. "The boy doesn't need to remember her that way."

In their haste, in their weariness, Carpenter shed his boots on the back stoop and left the shovel leaning against the wall. The wind rose in the night and blew the shovel handle along the shingles with a dry-bones rattle. Waking, alarmed, Valjean put out her hand: Carpenter was there.

Now Valjean resumed work on the boots, concentrating on the task at hand. She cleaned carefully, as though diligence would perfect not only the leather but Carpenter also, cleaning away the mire, anything that might make him lose his balance. From habit, she set the shoes atop the well-house to dry, out of reach of the dog. Then she realized Lady was gone. All her held-back tears came now; she mourned as for a child.

She told Dennis that afternoon. He walked all around the grave, disbelieving. No tears, too old for that; silent, like his father. He gathered straw to lay on the raw earth to keep it from washing. Finally he buried his head in Valjean's shoulder and groaned, "Why?" Hearing that, Valjean thanked God, for hadn't Carpenter asked *Who?* and not *Why?*—as though he had some plan, eye for eye, and needed only to discover upon whom to visit it? Dennis must not learn those ways, Valjean prayed; let my son be in some ways like me . . .

At supper Carpenter waited till she brought dessert before he asked, "Did you tell him?"

Dennis laid down his fork to speak for himself. "I know."

Carpenter beheld his son. "She was shot twice. Once point-blank. Once as she tried to get away."

Valjean's cup wrecked against her saucer. He hadn't told her that! He had held that back, steeping the bitter truth from it all day to serve to the boy. There was no possible antidote. It sank in, like slow poison.

"It's going to be all right," she murmured automatically, her peace of mind spinning away like a chip in a strong current. Her eyes sightlessly explored the sampler on the opposite wall whose motto she had worked during the long winter when she sat at her mother's deathbed: Perfect Love Casts Out Fear.

"You mean Lady knew them? Trusted them? Then they shot her?" Dennis spoke eagerly, proud of his ability to draw manly conclusions. Valjean watched as the boy realized what he was saying. "It's someone we know," Dennis whispered, the color rising from his throat to his face, his hands slowly closing into tender fists. "What—What are we going to do about it?" He pushed back his chair, ready.

"No," Valjean said, drawing a firm line, then smudging it a little with a laugh and a headshake. "Not you." She gathered their plates and carried them into the kitchen. She could hear Carpenter telling Dennis, "Someone saw Gannett's boys on the logging road yesterday afternoon. I'll step on down that way and see what they know."

"But Carpenter—" She returned with sudsy hands to prevent.

He pulled Valjean to him, muting all outcry with his brandied breath. He pleased himself with a kiss, taking his time, winking a galvanized-gray eye at Dennis. "I'm just going to talk to them. About time they knew me better."

She looked so miserable standing there that he caught her to him again, boyish, lean; the years had rolled off of him, leaving him un-creased, and no scars that showed. He had always been lucky, folks said. Wild lucky.

"Listen here now," he warned. "Trust me?"

What answer would serve but yes? She spoke it after a moment, for his sake, with all her heart, like a charm to cast out fear. "Of course."

Dennis, wheeling his bike out to head down to Mrs. Cobb's for his music lesson, knelt to make some minor adjustment on the chain.

"I won't be long," Carpenter said. "Take care of yourselves."

"You too," Dennis called, and pedaled off.

Carpenter crouched and pulled on his stiff, cleaned boots, then hefted one foot gaily into a shaft of sunset, admiring the shine. "Good work, ma'am." He tipped an imaginary hat and strode off into the shadows of the tall pines.

A whippoorwill startled awake and shouted once, then sleepily subsided. Overhead the little brown bats tottered and strove through the first starlight, their high twittering falling like tiny blown kisses onto the wind-scoured woods. It was very peaceful there in the deep heart of the April evening, and it had to be a vagrant, unworthy, warning impulse that sent Valjean prowling to the cabinet in the den where they kept their tax records, warranties, brandy, and side arms. Trembling, she reached again and again, but couldn't find the pistol. Carpenter's pistol wasn't there.

Not there.

For a moment she would not believe it, just rested her head against the cool shelf; then she turned and ran, leaving lights on and doors open behind her, tables and rugs askew in her wake. She ran sock-footed toward trouble as straight as she could, praying *Carpenter! Carpenter!* with every step. And then, like answered prayer, he was there, sudden as something conjured up from the dark. He caught her by the shoulders and shook her into sense.

"What's happened? Babe? What is it?"

But she could not answer for laughing and crying both at once, to see him there safe, to meet him halfway. When she caught her breath she said, "I was afraid something awful—I thought—I didn't know if I'd ever—"

"I told you I was just going to talk with them," he chided, amused. She gave a skip to get in step beside him. He caught her hand up and pointed her own finger at her. "I thought you said you trusted me."

"But I didn't know you were taking the gun with you . . ."

Angry, he drew away. She felt the night chill raise the hair on the back of her neck.

"I didn't take the damn gun! What makes you say things like that? You think I'm some kind of nut?"

"But it's gone," she protested: "I looked."

And then a new specter rose between them, unspeakable, contagious. For a moment they neither moved nor spoke, then Carpenter started for home, fast, outdistancing her in a few strides. Over his shoulder he called back, edgy, unconvinced. "You missed it, that's all. It's there." He would make sure.

She ran but could not quite catch up. "Dennis has it," she accused Carpenter's back.

"Nah," he shouted. "Don't borrow trouble. It's home."

When he loped across the lawn and up the kitchen steps three at a time he was a full minute ahead of her. And when she got there Carpenter was standing in the doorway of the den empty-handed, with the rapt, calculating, baffled expression of a baby left holding a suddenly limp string when the balloon has burst and vanished. The phone was ringing, ringing.

"Answer it," he said into the dark, avoiding her eyes.

Finding the Chain

Ben wrapped a feed sack around the flat rock and hooked it onto the chains. There wasn't more than ten feet of sound hemp or baling wire on the whole farm and he'd used that to tie the dog out of trouble. Not that Shin would've run off; she wanted to run *in*, and she'd already fought a skunk and lost and come rushing back so fast nobody had the wit to grab her and drag her out before she ruined—"It's clean gone, you can just cut it up for stinking rags for all I care now," Cliffie raged—Grandma Gable's Storm at Sea quilt, which was still on the floor from where they had huddled to sleep the night before, cold, damp, and hungry.

By flashlight Ben had found the one can of tomato juice in the trunk of the car and had poured it over the dog, rubbing it into her coat, but there was no way, till he got the chimney swept of bats and birds' nests, to safely heat water to rinse her. She sat at rope's end, still reeking, grizzled pink with tomato and whining with embarrassment. She never had been restrained in her life—it had been honor system all the way, and mutual trust—and now this.

They had arrived late, well past dark, and the first thing Ben had tried to do for them, when they had finally got into the log cabin, was make a fire. It hadn't seemed worth it to pay a deposit to have an electric meter installed for just a weekend, so they came prepared to camp, to cook over the fireplace, and draw water up from the well. Ben laid a good enough fire to get things going and cheerful, only before he could turn his back the house had filled with smoke, all of it coming into the rooms, none of it going up the chimney. They had doused the fire with water and waved damp towels to get the air clear, deciding not to mess with the chimney till daylight.

First thing Ben did in the morning was run Mary J and Drew out to look around, to find something long enough to use to clean the flue. There were snow chains, eaten up with fertilizer, and trace chains, not long enough in themselves, but linked to the swing chains, they were about right. Ben reached up and unhooked the swing, hardly stretching. He left the swing on the porch, flat, and scaled the old ladder to the roof, telling himself, "Easy, easy." The mossy shingles were rain-slick. "No time to be airborne," he said.

He was whistling a little as he dropped the bundled rock down the chimney's crooked throat. Before he could even draw up, on the first sweep, here came Cliffie boiling out of the house like a hornet from a lit nest, yelling *whoa* and cussing like a Christian.

"Are you out of your mind?" she screamed. The echo bounced off the barn. Mary J prissed over to stand by her momma under the umbrella. All Ben could see was spattered shoes and neon anklets from that angle. Everything looked different. He almost laughed, till Cliffie shoved the umbrella back and he saw her face.

"Did soot get all over the house?" he wondered. It might have been an apology, but after all, it wasn't his fault. He had told the boy to run in and help his momma cover the hearth and seal it off with newspapers and duct tape. He'd even tossed the boy his car keys, so he could get the tape from the toolbox in the trunk. Ben reckoned Drew had just skipped off, and not accidentally either. Cliffie said the boy had some adjusting to do, that was all, and she never came down hard on his "pranks." Ben eased over onto his other hip and stretched his bum leg. Bad weather reminded every bone of where it had broken and healed.

"I told him to tell you," Ben said. "Where is he?"

"Don't start on him," Cliffie said. She'd been saying it for over two years, ever since Ben and Cliffie's first date, when Ben had offered Drew his hand and the boy pocketed his fists and turned away, sour as sorrel.

"I'm through *starting* on him," Ben said. Loud enough for the boy to hear, if he were skulking in the barn loft or on the back porch or stretched across the back seat of the car, reading his comics. He knew the boy wouldn't be sorry, early or late, for messing up. He didn't look for Drew to poke his hard head up over the edge of the roof and say, "Sir?"

"I've got news for that little pecker," Ben boomed. "The paperwork's come through. I'm his old man now."

Cliffie looked hurt. "I wanted to tell him!" She leaned on the ladder and stared up, but she wouldn't climb, wouldn't meet Ben halfway. She cocked her head like she heard nothing but bad news from an angel. Tears of rain ran down her face. Ben wasn't fooled. He knew it was rain. She'd laugh it off, or fight it out, or sue, Cliffie would, but never cry. "Not my Cliffie," he said.

She had been about to pull the ladder away and strand him up there, but when he spoke as cheerfully as that, and him wet enough to wring rainwater from his shirttail, she moderated. She and Mary J headed back to the house without another word. "You just cover the fireplace and save me a round trip," he called after them. If Cliffie heard it, she didn't say so. He posted himself by the chimney, listening. He could hear Cliffie comforting the baby, and warning Mary J not to run the batteries down on the transistor . . . Because of the crook in the chimney he couldn't see the light or if the fireplace had been covered, if they were ready. He called down to them—Cliffie had to hear it!— "Now?" and tried to sound like he was enjoying himself. "Say when," he hollered again.

Nothing

"If you can stand it, so can I," he decided, and having given her time enough, and warning—"It be on your head"—he let the bundle fall, giving the chains a good twist and scour, hoping, maybe, for the worst below. That's what it had come to after only twenty-four hours away from the Jim Walter home-on-stilts he had built for her in South End, with a view of the docks and marsh.

When Ben stamped back across the porch and into the house with an armload of wet kindling, he reminded her, "I'm no goddamn pioneer."

Cliffie had been so sick after the baby came she made Ben promise if anything happened—"Now, honey, please, just listen to me"—he'd take her back to her homeplace, have the funeral there, and bury her in the mountains with her family. "Mama's got the prettiest stone, marble, and white as the winter moon. It says WILDROSE WOMAN / GOD LOVED / SORROWS ENDED . . ."

Ben didn't want to hear that kind of talk. He said, "You're going to get well and when you do, we'll all drive up there and see how the other half lives." He promised.

"You mean it?"

Of course he did. But when she got well, he acted as though she had taken advantage of him. It was two years before they finally got away and headed due north. By then, the last of the Gables had died out and Cliffie had been fretting all summer about what was happening to "the things" left in the abandoned cabin. She couldn't locate a cousin willing to go see, or find a tenant steady enough to keep the farm going. Taxes kept coming due, and Cliffie was settling it in her heart that she would have to sell. This would be the last trip. She would bring back with her all that she could not bear to part with, and make her peace about the rest. She wanted them to love the place as she did. She wanted them to know everything, all the little stories. She wanted everything to be perfect, and she was so excited the night before they left that she kept getting up to write down something else on her lists. Ben would turn over in bed, his back to the sudden light, and grumble for her to settle down.

"You could sleep through a war," she told him.

"Not the one I went to," he said.

She had them out of bed and spooning cold cereal toward their zombie faces by five o'clock the next morning. Even then, she was telling them how great things were going to be.

Ben warned her again as they left the last traffic light in Glynn County behind them, "It won't be like you remember it," as though he expected her to reconsider, admit it was a mistake, and tell him to turn around in the churchyard at Sterling and head back to the coast.

"I'm prepared," is what she said.

Ben had never been north of Lyons, where the sallow clay hills begin, except for a class trip to Macon when he was a kid—to see the circus—and his time in the army. He couldn't imagine what there was about red mud for Cliffie to love and miss. He liked the rich flat black sandy land, the rise and fall of the tides, the evergreen oaks . . .

He had to press the accelerator harder all the time now; every mile was uphill. Already his right knee felt stiff. The engine made a dry tapping sound, noisy as diesel, and he prayed the valves and lifters would behave themselves. He had packed extra quarts of oil and a can opener in his toolbox, but he wasn't like Cliffie, he couldn't plan ahead the way she did, for emergency and bad luck. He called it "borrowing trouble," but she'd had a lifetime to get good at it, no changing her ways now. The trunk of the car overflowed with things she had crammed in because they "just might need this up home." Besides the lunch she'd made for them, for the road, she had packed groceries, candles, matches, a hatchet, pillows, blankets, coal oil, and lanterns.

One suitcase contained the clothes they'd need if the weather stayed mild and another was stuffed with sweaters and warm hats and gloves in case it turned cold. "It can get mean in the mountains at Thanksgiving," Cliffie said.

She looked over the seat back to check on Mary J and Drew. They had set out perky enough, full of questions, jokes, quarrels, and fighting for place, but now had subsided into sleep, catching up on the dreams they'd lost in the early start. The dog, Shin, rode between them atop a pile of bedclothes that wouldn't fit in the trunk. She was a medium-sized dog, not young but alert, her hindquarters on the package tray, her front legs stretched out, her chin down, her ears up. She widened her grin into a sour yawn, but her eyes never left off for a moment searching the center line that came at them out of the dark.

"Dog is my copilot," Ben said, glancing in the rearview. Cliffie disapproved of dogs and blasphemy.

"We should've left her with Palma and them. They had room."

"They had room for Mary J and Drew too," Ben pointed out. He didn't want to leave the children behind, but he loved his dog. "She was my family, the same way Mary J and Drew were yours." He'd been wanting to say that for some time, waiting to see if she'd figure it out without having to be told.

The lights from the dashboard lit every hurt and hollow in her face with an eerie green. "We're all Stevensons now," he added, for once saying exactly the right thing whether she admitted it or not. "Little pitchers," she said, putting her long fingers over his mouth to hush him, adding, "Keep your eyes on the road." She sounded pleased.

It was false dawn. They were driving away from sunup. By the time it was true day, they had covered a hundred miles, had almost left the cypress lands behind. Jondi stirred and woke; Cliffie unharnessed him from his carseat and stood him on her lap to see out. "Look, baby boy, now we're getting somewhere."

When they stopped for a fill-up, Cliffie wrote down the mileage and the time and amount. She kept books on everything like that, had clipped coupons in case they had a chance to see some museums in Atlanta. "This isn't just another joy ride," she told them. When the kids wanted Cokes at the service station, she wouldn't let Ben shell out change for them. "We have our own cooler," she reminded them, "pretty soon we'll be stopping for lunch." All along the way she pointed out things she thought they might not notice, and explained history and geography, and what the fall line was and why so many pines grew and how to preserve the indigo snake from extinction. She was always teaching, whether she was in her classroom or not. She had even brought along a library book on the historical markers, so they wouldn't lose time stopping to read them.

"There's not an hour in the world for every little thing," Cliffie said, "but it's good to know what you're missing."

Mary J and Drew argued and begged to take turns reading the book, but they got carsick—"I told you so," Cliffie said—and had to walk it off on the roadside between endless cotton fields. Another good reason to travel U.S. 341, not the Interstate. Plenty of stopping room. "If you want to race, go to Daytona," Cliffie said. "All you smell on a four-lane is exhaust fumes . . . I'd know this was cotton with my eyes shut." She breathed in, in a testing way. "Everything done by machine now," she said. "No more chopping. No more laying by. No more protracted meetings, muddy baptizings, no more one pair of new shoes in November having to last all year." They gathered along the fence—Shin, too—looking. Ben and the kids stretched across to pick a boll or two. "The rains have about ruined it," Cliffie said, as they drove away. Jondi, who had never seen any kind of the real thing, just cotton batting and angel hair and aerosol flakes, kept pointing out the window at the dotted fields and calling, "Snow!"

"I never picked cotton," Ben said.

"I'd rather pick rags," Cliffie said, so bitterly he let up on the gas for a moment. She'd had it hard, so hard he wondered again why she'd want to go back and remind herself of what she'd left behind.

Cliffie had been so sure of the roads, the turns, the old landmarks, but in the rain her memory failed. It had never been but the dimmest daylight all day, and they had driven in rain from Macon on. Cliffie sat right up at the windshield, rubbing it with her hand, trying to see past the headlights. "This isn't where," she realized, looking scared. "Am I losing my mind?" Ben didn't complain; he backed them around in a wide place and they tried again. Finally they stopped at a dark store and Cliffie beat and beat at the door till an old woman dragged open a window in the house and yelled, "They're out of business. What?" Cliffie stepped around a pile of coal, to stand in a puddle and talk. As she came splashing back to the car, she was smiling. "We're just not there yet. Two more miles to Wildrose."

When they drove around the curve and the whitewashed church came into view, Cliffie said, "Of course," meaning *Here we are*, but Ben didn't understand, so he kept on driving, almost past, till Cliffie cried, "STOP!" He slammed on the brakes and they slid around in the mud. "I didn't say have a wreck," Cliffie said. "I didn't say break my nose." She had brought fresh-cut flowers from a florist. "Not artificial, not weeds. When will I ever have the chance again?" she explained, justifying those six red roses kept on ice in the cooler every mile of the way. The buds looked almost black now in the rain. That's how near nightfall it was.

Mary J got to steer the car when it slid off the road and stuck in the mud. Everybody but the dog and baby got out to push. Mary J liked the way her fingers curved around the wheel, and she was glad she still had polish on some of the nails and hadn't gnawed it all off. She had on so many coats of paint she could peel it off in one piece that tasted like banana oil. Kid stuff . . . She felt grown-up, driving, and she knew what she wanted for Christmas: a birthstone ring. "Aquamarine," she said, loving the sound of it, forgetting Jondi was listening. She wanted white gold, like her momma's. She could turn the stone under to her palm, and just let the gold show, like a wedding band. When she got married—didn't know yet *who*, but probably a fisherman, like Ben— she was going to live in a little house right on the marsh, and have a baby sweeter than Jondi, a little girl baby, and drive around in a boat the color of the sky. And if she didn't want to wash the supper dishes, she wouldn't. Her momma couldn't make her. And she wouldn't have to fold clothes or study books any more either. It might be another year or two, she didn't know just when she'd be a woman and could put her feet up and look at magazines and pin her curtains back with paper roses and have flowers everywhere, in a tire ring under the trees, and at the windows. "Window boxes, definitely," she said, sounding enough like her momma to make Jondi sit up and reach.

"Momma," she announced when everybody got back in the car and she slid over to let Ben drive again, "I'm not going to marry till I'm tall enough to see into the soup pot on the back eye. If a boy caint wait that long, he probably doesn't love me anyway. Right?"

Her momma felt her forehead. "I think this child has a fever," she decided. Jondi already had his ears filled with sweet oil and cotton, and coughed. "You next?" she asked. Mary J crawled over the seat back and lay in her corner and imagined what it would be like to be a nurse, like Aunt Palma. She would bring comfort and cheer to all her patients. She would wear a cape the color of midnight and walk quietly down the halls and carry a silver pen in her pocket to write important things on the chart . . .

As she brought luggage in from the car she imagined these were emergency Red Cross supplies. The next day as she carried Grandma Gable's red and gold candy jar from the hutch to set in the center of the table she imagined it was a bottle of blood. She held it to the light and said, "Plasma," and shivered. That wasn't why she dropped the jar. She didn't know why she dropped it. She couldn't believe she had dropped it. How could something that terrible happen? It didn't shatter, it broke in three shards, as if it had been meant to, and lay there empty as a shell. Her momma came running, picked up the perfect lid, kissed it.

"Not my bowl," she said. She knelt and picked up the pieces and tried fitting them together, like a puzzle. Ben came in and put his hand on Mary J's shoulder and said, "It's stopped raining. Why don't you and Drew take this grocery sack and hunt me some pine cones?" When she went out, he was telling her momma, "You going to have a funeral for it, or what? It ain't going to grow back. It ain't flesh and blood."

"You don't understand," her momma said. "I wouldn't expect you to."

Mary J handed Drew the bag. She went to the barn instead, and pulled the door shut behind her. It was so heavy.

Drew wasn't strong enough to drag the barn door open. He

didn't want to play with Mary J anyway. She was too bossy. He looked around, his first chance to explore the farm in daylight, in good weather. It was Thanksgiving day, after noon. They weren't going to have a turkey this time. There was no stove to cook on. They heated soup over the fire. The smoke smelled nice when wind blew it down the roof of the house and swirled it around in the yard. His momma told him to watch the weathervane. She said, "This is the fairing-off shower," and, sure enough, the arrow backed from east to northwest and the rains finally drizzled to a stop. The cold wind was rolling fog over the gray flanks of the Blue Ridge and Drew's momma said she didn't care what the man on the radio had to allow, *she* smelled snow. Drew couldn't smell anything but smoke and skunk-scent the dog had brought back. The ruined quilt hung on the slack line between the barn and the cherry tree. "Crazy place for a clothesline," his momma had said and Mary J and Ben laughed along. Drew couldn't understand. He never understood anything. They'd tell a joke and laugh and he wouldn't get it. At school they called him "Dumbo" partly because he was slow and partly because of his ears. He pulled his cap down over them. He liked winter best, when he could wear a cap all the time. When he was grown up he was always going to wear his hat, never take it off except when they played the national anthem; he'd take it off them, if the other soldiers did. He was going to be in the army. He'd grow. He'd be tall enough. He'd lead the way. "I'm not afraid," he said. He ran in the tunnel the quilt made hanging over the line; he held his breath. When he came out the other side, he took in a chestful of frosty air. It burned. It was getting colder. When he breathed out, he made steam clouds. He found a stick and broke it to length and pretended it was a cigarette, puffing on it, exhaling. It really looked like smoke. He wished Mary J was spying. She'd snitch and then he'd get her back for once . . .

Jondi had an earache and couldn't play outside. He wasn't even supposed to go on the sleeping porch. "Right back in here this minute or I'm coming after you!" his momma said when he went. He was watching Drew play with the chain. Drew had the chain around his shoulder. He dragged it then wrapped it around him again, at the waist, like a belt. He held it in both hands like a snake. He was going away with it. Jondi couldn't see where. Momma came and picked him up and carried him back into the house and set him by the fire. "Don't get in the fire," she said. "Be an angel," she said. When she had gone he crawled over to the shelves. There were no picture books. There was a basket. There was a jar. He liked the jar. It took both hands to carry it back. He sat on the floor and dumped it out. Buttons rolled everywhere. He laughed and chased them. His momma came back angry. "You put them up, look at this floor, I asked you to be an angel."

He reached into the jar and put a handful back. He gathered up another handful and put them back. It was taking a long time.

"Every last one of them," she said. She went away again.

Jondi thought of something fun. He dropped a button down the knothole in the floorboard. It disappeared. He had a savings bank. This was like that. He kept on putting buttons down the hole. He used both hands. Some of the buttons were metal, some were bone. He didn't have to force any; they all went.

"Gone," he said, reaching into the empty jar.

"What have you done with Grandma's button collection?" Momma shouted when she came back. Jondi cried.

Ben said, "I'll crawl up under there and get 'em for you, no use in hearts busting over something I can fix."

When he came back, he set the buttons on the porch. "Blow the dust off and they'll be fine," he told Cliffie. "Good as new." He went whistling off to the barn. He had an idea for a Christmas present for Cliffie, and he hoped there was a shovel around.

Cliffie felt like the whole trip so far had been one long erosion. They didn't appreciate this old place or the things in it. And why should they? "It's just somewhere else they'll probably forget they've ever been." She picked up the jar of buttons and was turning to go back into the house when she noticed the swing still sitting flat on the porch, its chains gone.

Before she could holler *Where?* Mary J came running out of the barn yelling, "Fire!"

Drew heard her. He was in the field, swinging the chain. Turning in a circle holding the chain. Whirling faster and faster till the chain stood flat out from him and pulled at his arms in their sockets. When he couldn't hold the chain any longer, or whirl any faster, he'd let go and tumble backward and the chain would fly out from him ad then drop in the sedge. He had invented the game on his own, and he liked it. His hands were stiff with cold. He didn't know where he had lost his gloves. He had let the chain pull him around in its circle all afternoon, and when he fell, he'd lie there and look up at the sky.

Clouds were coming fast. Low clouds, soft gray clouds. The sun struck through their gaps, casting golden shafts. Shadows raced. The mountains had vanished. Gusts of wind rattled the last soft downy seeds from the sedge and launched them across the pasture. When Mary J ran out of the barn and yelled, "Fire!" Drew was swinging the chain as hard as he could; he felt that this time he might be lifted from the earth and flung. He let go.

As soon as he scrambled to his feet he ran toward the barn. Shin stood at the end of her taut rope and barked. Momma came running down the steps, her hands over Jondi's ears to keep the wind off. "God help us, God help us," she was saying.

Ben had the shovel. He ran into the barn and Mary J and Momma were calling, "Come back! No! Don't"

Drew ran past them. He ran in after Ben. He didn't know why. Maybe he just wanted to *see*. He didn't think. He just ran. He wasn't afraid. He darted around the door and crashed into Ben, who came laughing out of the barn. "False alarm," he said. "That board looks like it's cherry red," he said. "I'd have thought the same thing. Its rosin's catching the sun . . . You did the right thing." Mary J beamed.

"I remember that board," Momma said. "I remember that board so well."

Everybody went back to the house, everybody but Ben and Drew. Ben said, "You come with me." They went back into the barn to put up the shovel.

"I gave you my keys this morning," he said. "Remember?"

"In the car," Drew said. "I left them on the—the—"

"Well, you go find them, and you open that trunk for me, and you get back here warp speed, you hear me? I got a chore for you."

Drew darted out.

"You owe me," Ben said. "If you're not back here in two minutes I'm coming to feed you to the hogs."

Drew said, "I ain't scared of nothing." Then he ran.

Ben was sitting on a crate when Drew came back. It was pretty dark in there. "You still here? Mister?"

It had been more than two years since Ben and Drew declared war. The boy never called him anything but *Mister.* "Here," Ben said.

"What you want me to do now?"

"Help me load this box in the car."

"Just old mud?"

"It's for your momma's Christmas," Ben told him. Maybe it was a crazy idea. "A surprise," he told Drew. "A little bit of here, for there."

"I hear you."

"I'm asking you to keep it a secret," Ben told him. "Man to man. You give your word and you keep it. You do that for me?"

"I'll do it for *Momma*," Drew specified.

"No, you'll by Jesus do it for me," Ben said, "or you won't do it at all."

The boy's chin came up and his lips narrowed. He didn't promise, Ben thought. Goddamn little peckerhead, he thought. Where's the pay-off? He said, "Tell me something nice your daddy did for your momma. Just one nice thing."

Mary J asked Drew, "What do you mean 'crazy'?"

"He's giving her a box of dirt, the reddest dirt he can find, for Christmas."

Mary J wished she had thought of it. She decided right then to give her momma some rocks; she still had time before dark to find them, wrap them in a gunny sack, hide them, in the car under the seat. She'd find the prettiest stones, to outline the flower beds.

Cliffie said, "All I want is that other chain. They were both right here this morning and they got no business being anywhere else tonight." Drew just stood there, looking at her. "And don't stare at me like a refugee," she said. "I know it isn't all your fault. If Ben hadn't taken the swing down, you couldn't have lost the chain off it." She glanced across the yard at the field beyond. She could smell it so plain: snow. No use in telling them that again, getting their hopes up for nothing. But she wanted that chain, and if it snowed, they'd never find it. It would lie out there all winter, forever maybe, if whoever bought the farm left the field fallow. She could remember the day that porch swing got hung. They called it a "courting swing." She was finally old enough to keep company. She went with her daddy to the feed merchant—it was her sixteenth birthday—and watched as the bright links of chain reeled off the spool. He had bought a better grade than just getting by. "We want it to last," he had said. "A hundred years from now, my grandchirren's grandchirren'll be sitting out here in the breeze saying, 'Thank you, Charley Gable.'" He had died the next year.

Cliffie got up and paced. "I'm just going to look some more," she said. "I feel like a mama cat that's lost one of her kittens."

They could see her in the field, passing back and forth, looking down. She came to the far line and just stood there staring north where the Blue Ridge earned its name in fair weather. It was getting on toward sundown now, and the sky was still full of those tumbled clouds, plum-colored and ragged. Far off, crows laughed, fighting the wind.

Mary J eased off her chair and pulled on her jacket. She put her soup bowl in the dish bucket and skipped out.

"Mary J'll probably find it too," Drew said. "She likes being the hero."

Ben said, "I hope she *does* find it. . . . This has been some day." He folded a piece of bread in half and ate it. Two bites.

"What if she doesn't? What if nobody finds it?"

"Your momma wanted to take the swing home with us."

"We still can. They sell chain."

"Some things in this world there's just one of, even when you get something else just as good. Or better," Ben said. He and Drew studied each other, thinking it through.

"Work to do," Ben said, pushing back from the table. "You going to be here, you watch Jondi. Keep him out of the fire." He zipped his jacket and ducked out the door.

Drew said, "Easy when you tall." Meaning life in general. His daddy had been a featherweight Golden Gloves champ, five foot three. Everybody said Jondi was going to be big, big as Ben. "Look at those hands," they'd say. Drew pulled Jondi's hand away from the lantern and balanced the baby on his hip till he could get dressed for outdoors. He set the screen in front of the fire and slipped out the back way. He didn't want them to see him coming, as if he were tagging after.

Jondi jogged along in Drew's arms, asking *Why? Why? Why?* about everything he saw. Drew hoped Jondi wouldn't start crying when he saw their momma on the far side of the field. Drew just wanted to be by himself. He just wanted to find that chain.

But Jondi cried. He wouldn't toddle along, he wanted to be carried.When Drew set him down, Jondi grabbed to his leg like an anchor, and howled. Across the field their momma was calling instructions to him. Drew picked up Jondi and carried him to her.

Back of the house Shin was whining again. She ran as far as she could and then jerked over, held back by the rope.

Cliffie was saying, "Look!" She had found something. Not the chain. It was a little heap of trash, years old, in a ravine where they had brought the things they no longer wanted in the house or barn. A bedspring. A broken TV. Pickle jars. An old antenna. "Here's where they threw out," she said. "Look at this." She picked up the doorknob she had told them about. The white porcelain one that her great grandmother saved for the housewarming, from the other house, the one that burned. Cliffie had told them all about it. They had expected to see it on the front door instead of the deadbolt that had greeted them. They didn't have a key. They could see the key in the lock on the inside. They stood in the rain, locked out, and Ben went from window to window, trying each one. He managed to get the one in the kitchen open wide enough to slip Jondi through. Cliffie shined the flashlight from the porch toward him, calling him, and he had finally arrived at the front door and pulled the key from the lock inside and pushed it under the door so they could get in. All that because Cliffie didn't want to break a window . . .

The porcelain doorknob was chipped and the shaft wrung off. "I guess they knew what they were doing," Cliffie said. She turned her back, closed her eyes, and tossed it over her shoulder, refusing to look at where it fell. "The best way," she said. "I can't save every little thing."

Drew made sure no one was looking, especially not Mary J. He made it look as if he were just wasting time, prowling around in the weeds. Momma was saying, "Grandma always said a field that grows sedge is too sorry to plow." When they had gone on past, still hunting the chain, Drew stooped down and picked up that old white doorknob. It had rolled down the gully a little farther when his momma threw it.

He didn't even take time to rub it off. He couldn't force it into his pocket, so he hid it in his sleeve. His heart was pounding. He felt so proud, as though he had saved a life. He ran with his arm up, so the knob wouldn't slip out of his jacket sleeve. He slowed down when he got back in the field. He walked along kicking at the tufts of sedge, trying to remember where he had been the last time he swung the chain. He wanted above all to find that chain. If Mary J found it, it would be all right, but if he found it, it would be exactly right. She was searching along the crumbly edge of the brook, so he turned upland, his arm raised, his eyes down. He didn't see Shin chew through the last threads of her rope.

They were never going to find the chain. All they were doing was wandering around in the last light, hoping. Shin ran back and forth over the soggy ground, greeting each of them, forgiving them. They had been walking the terraces away from the house, Mary J here, Drew there, Jondi and Shin everywhere, and now that they had come to the far fence row, scattering its sparrows, there was nothing to do but turn back. They were by chance or grace almost in unison now, apart from each other, absorbed, looking down, but moving, pausing, and keeping pace.

It had begun to snow, the first flakes they'd ever seen; only Cliffie had been in snow before. They'd have stopped to enjoy it, to catch the white cool feathers on their hands and tongues, but Cliffie moaned, "That's gonna do it. Amen. Y'all go on."

Ben said, "I wish I had a big magnet."

"Or a giant rake," Mary J said. They closed ranks against the coming dark, against the soft, random flurries, against the idea of giving up. Not touching, still at arm's length, but now shoulder by shoulder, like a chorus line, they swept across the field. Shin barked them along, and raced ahead and then padded back. Finally she took her sober place beside Ben, on the right flank. Drew, on the far left, stumbled, fell, and pushed himself to his knees. The doorknob had flung out of his sleeve and he was so intent on getting it back, on keeping his secret, that he didn't notice the chain. That was what had gripped him. It lay in a loose curve, muddy, and till he touched it, got it in his hands and lifted it, he couldn't believe it. He had seen it in his mind's eye all afternoon; he didn't believe it. Then he jumped up and hollered, "Ben! Momma!

Over here!" and everyone swerved, everyone came clotting around him, reaching, touching. Holding on.

It was funny how they all held on. Even when they turned and headed for the house, its one window lit golden by the oil lamp, the smoke from the hearth fire beaten down flat from the chimney into the bare yard, the air between them and comfort filled with that confetti of feathers, they still held to the chain. It seemed so right. Ben wanted to say, "Don't nobody let go," but he didn't. Some things just have to happen.

Suggestions for Further Reading
and Classroom Use

The stories collected here represent only a small sampling of recent fiction which deals in important ways with southern life and culture. For further reading or for use in the classroom many of these stories might be paired with other books in order to explore common themes and the necessities of different genres.

To set these stories in the context of work by southern women writers, a number of recent critical books are particularly helpful. These studies attempt to define a tradition—or traditions—of writing by southern women and suggest topics and texts for further reading. Especially useful are: Ann Goodwyn Jones, *Tomorrow is Another Day: The Woman Writer in the South, 1859–1936* (Louisiana State University Press, 1981); Louise Westling, *Sacred Groves and Ravaged Gardens: The Fiction of Eudora Welty, Carson McCullers, and Flannery O'Connor* (University of Georgia Press, 1985); Minrose Gwin, *Black and White Women of the Old South: The Peculiar Sisterhood in American Literature* (University of Tennessee Press, 1985).

An interesting perspective on the issues raised by these stories and by southern literary critics is Alice Walker's *In Search of Our Mothers' Gardens* (Harcourt, Brace, Jovanovich, 1983). Her essay "Beyond the Peacock," which appears in that collection, provides an important emphasis on home, on change, and on the relationship of African-American writers both to southern literature by whites and to cultural change. It would be interesting to pair the stories by Walker, Moore, and Spencer with stories by Flannery O'Connor, particularly "The Artificial Nigger" and "Everything That Rises Must Converge."

A historical dimension to the issues these stories raise can be found in several recent novels. A striking development in recent fiction is the number of books that have sought to work through the history of slavery, to bring a contemporary imagination to bear upon the most distinctive and the most horrible dimension of southern history. The parent text for all these novels is Margaret Walker's *Jubilee* (Houghton

Mifflin, 1966), a book which is still not so well known as it deserves to be. Outstanding recent novels by women that come to grips with the meaning of slavery include Toni Morrison's *Beloved* (Knopf, 1987) and Sherley Ann Williams's *Dessa Rose* (Berkley Publishers, 1987). These books, though they are not written by southerners, can, I believe, significantly reshape our sense of southern literary history and of southern history itself. They present powerful evocations of the spiritual and emotional meanings of slavery and show us how indelible, finally, the institution of slavery is in cultural memory. They provide a useful context in which to read stories like Spencer's "The Business Venture," Walker's "The Welcome Table," or Opal Moore's "A Pilgrim Notebook, Part I."

A number of very fine recent novels by African-American women who are not by birth southern can usefully be read in conjunction with this anthology. Particularly interesting in their treatment of the contemporary South are Paule Marshall, *Praisesong for the Widow* (Putnam, 1983); Gloria Naylor, *Mama Day* (Random House, 1988); Marita Golden, *Long Distance Life* (Doubleday, 1989); and Alice Childress, *A Short Walk* (Coward, McCann and Geoghegan, 1979).

Another context in which these stories might be taught, and an area they suggest for further reading, is context of language. Critics of southern literature often remark on its distinctive sense of language, and critics of southern culture sometimes wonder if the distinctiveness of southern language is being lost in the world of mass communication. The work of sociolinguists and others can tell us about the myths and realities of these trends, even as the writers of the stories collected here attempt to reflect the changing nuances of southern speech. Particularly interesting reading in this area are: Shirley Brice Heath, *Ways With Words: Language, Life and Work in Communities and Classrooms* (Cambridge University Press, 1983) and Crawford Feagin, *Variation and Change in Alabama English: A Sociolinguistic Study of the White Community* (Georgetown University Press, 1979).

Like language, culture is always shifting and changing, and these changes have been particularly marked in the South since the time of the Civil Rights movement. Recent work in southern social and cultural history has yielded several books about twentieth-century southern life which might be interestingly paired with stories in this collection. In particular it might be useful to group Margaret Jarman Hagood, *Mothers of the South: Portraiture of the White Tenant Farm Women* (originally published in 1939; rpt. Norton, 1977); Linda Flowers, *Throwed Away* (University of North Carolina Press, 1990), a study of rural culture in eastern North Carolina; Jacquelyn Dowd Hall, *Like a Family: The Making of a Southern Cotton Mill World* (Norton, 1987); the stories by Shirley Ann Grau, which show the changes in southern culture from a middle-class point of view; and Walker's stories and essays.

Attitudes toward sexuality and culture and writing by or about southern lesbians would be an interesting focus for further reading. It would be useful to compare Shange's, Tinsley's, and Spencer's treatment of relationships among women with the relationships in Shange's *For Colored Girls Who Have Considered Suicide When the Rainbow is Enuf* (Bantam, 1980), with Walker's *The Color Purple* (Harcourt, Brace, Jovanovich, 1982), with Mab Segrest's *My Mama's Dead Squirrel: Lesbian Essays on Southern Culture* (Ithaca: Firebrand Books, 1985), with Segrest's poems, and with Rita Mae Brown's novels.

Suggestions for further reading in contemporary fiction by southern women writers can be found in the bibliography appended to *New Stories by Southern Women*, edited by Mary Ellis Gibson (University of South Carolina Press, 1989).

Notes on Contributors

TONI CADE BAMBARA was born in New York City. She holds a B.A. from Queens College and an M.A. from City College of the City University of New York. She is well known as a civil rights activist and as a professor of English and African-American Studies. Her collections of short fiction include *The Black Woman* (1980), *Gorilla, My Love* (1972), and *The Sea Birds Are Still Alive* (1977). She has also edited two anthologies of black literature and written a novel published by Vintage Books, *The Salt Eaters* (1981). In the *New Yorker* Susan Lardner remarked of her stories that they "are notable for their purposefulness, a more or less explicit inspirational angle, and distinctive motion of prose that swings from colloquial narrative to precarious metaphorical heights and over to street talk, at which Bambara is unbeatable."

SHIRLEY ANN GRAU was born in New Orleans and currently divides her time between Metairie, Louisiana, and Martha's Vineyard. She holds a B.A. from Tulane and has published eight books of fiction. Her story collections include *Nine Women* (1985), *The Black Prince* (1955), and *The Wind Shifting West* (1973). In 1965 she received the Pulitzer Prize for Fiction for *Keepers of the House*. Her other novels include *The House on Coliseum Street* (1961), *The Condor Passes* (1971), and *Evidence of Love* (1977). Since her literary debut at the age of twenty-four, Grau has been acknowledged as a master of the short-story form. "As a short-story writer," Mary Rohrerger commented in *Women Writers of the Contemporary South*, "Grau's talent is immense though not revealed by a simple surface reading; for what is beneath the surfaces and interacting with them is what is characteristic of the short-story genre, and Grau has mastered the genre."

MARY HOOD is a native of coastal Georgia and currently lives and writes in Woodstock in the north Georgia foothills. Her short stories and essays have appeared in *Georgia Review, Harper's, Kenyon Review, Best American Short Stories 1984*, and *North American Review*. She has published two collections of short fiction, *How Far She Went* (1983) and *And Venus Is Blue* (1986), and she has recently completed a novel. She is the recipient of a Pushcart Prize, the 1983 Flannery O'Connor Award for Short Fiction, and the *Southern Review*/Louisiana State University Short Fiction Award. Writing in the *Kenyon Review*, David Baker commented that Hood's "is an unsentimental vision of the New South where front porches yield to shopping malls and Camaros outnumber cotton fields." Hood's South, he continued, "finds its families falling apart, its women stranded yet struggling individually to grow stronger, and its very past—the history and nostalgia so important to Southern tradition—vanishing or vanished."

OPAL MOORE was born in Chicago in 1953. She attended Illinois Wesleyan University and the University of Iowa, earning bachelor's and master's degrees in drawing and printmaking. As an art student, she also studied writing fiction and poetry. She completed the Iowa Writers' Workshop in 1982. Her fiction, poetry, and essays have appeared in *Callaloo; Obsidian II; Poet Lore; The Black American in Books for Children* (2nd ed); *Writers for Children: Critical Studies of the Major Authors Since the 17th Century; Black American Literature Forum;* and elsewhere. She is now living in Richmond, Virginia; she is working on a collection of stories and a critical study of the juvenile fiction writer Mildred D. Taylor. She teaches writing and literature at Radford University in Virginia.

NTOZAKE SHANGE was born in 1948 in Trenton, New Jersey, and now makes her home in Houston, Texas, where she is a member of the faculty at the University of Houston. She received her B.A. from Barnard College and her M.A. from the University of Southern California. Highly regarded as a poet, playwright, fiction writer, and screenwriter, she counts among her most recent works *Ridin' the Moon in Texas: Word Paintings* (responses to art in prose and poetry), 1987; *Three Views of Mr. Fuji* (play), 1987; *Besty Brown: A Novel*, 1985; and *From Okra to Greens: A Different Kinda Love Story; A Play with Music & Dance*, 1985. Commenting on the emotional intensity of her work, Shange told an interviewer that "our society allows people to be absolutely neurotic and totally out of touch with their feelings and everyone else's feelings, and yet be very respectable. This, to me, is a travesty. So I write to get at the part of people's emotional lives that they don't have control over, the part that can and will respond."

ELIZABETH SPENCER was born in 1921 in Carrollton, Mississippi. She received her B.A. from Belhaven College in Jackson and her M.A. from Vanderbilt University. She has published numerous novels and collections of stories, including *Fire in the Morning* (1948); *The Light in the Piazza* (1960); *Ship Island and Other Stories* (1969); *The Snare* (1972); *The Collected Stories* (1981); *Marilee* (1981); *The Salt Line* (1985); and *Jack of Diamonds* (1988). She lived for many years in Montreal, Canada, and has recently moved to North Carolina, where she teaches at the University of North Carolina at Chapel Hill. "Like all writers, I think, I write instinctively," Spencer says of her own creative process. "I write because I feel the urge to write and while I'm doing it, the hell with it, but the total pattern is something that recurs as a question: What am I really doing in a large sense? I think I never questioned this as long as I was writing Southern novels because in writing I was simply part of the Southern tradition."

MOLLY BEST TINSLEY grew up in an Air Force family and so comes from "no place in particular." Of her own sense of place and location she says, "Twenty-five years in various suburbs of Washington, D.C., haven't changed this sense of detachment. In my fiction I am trying to connect with the place underlying town, region, country, which I guess I would call *earth.*" She is on the civilian faculty at the U.S. Naval Academy in Annapolis and has published stories in numerous magazines and quarterlies, including *Shenandoah*, *Greensboro Review*, and *Prairie Schooner.* Her first novel, *My Life with Darwin*, was published by Houghton Mifflin in the spring of 1991.

ALICE WALKER was born in 1944 in Eatonton, Georgia, and currently makes her home in San Francisco. She received her B.A. from Sarah Lawrence College and has published essays and fiction as well as poetry, including *In Search of Our Mothers' Gardens: Womanist Prose* (1983) and *Living By the Word: Selected Writings, 1973–1987* (1989); story collections *In Love and Trouble* (1973) and *You Can't Keep a Good Woman Down* (1981); and the novels *Meridian* (1976), *The Color Purple* (1982), and her most recent work, *The Temple of My Familiar* (1990). She has received an award from the American Academy and Institute of Arts and Letters, the Lillian Smith Award of the Southern Regional Council, and a Guggenheim Fellowship. *The Color Purple* was awarded the 1983 Pulitzer Prize for Fiction and the American Book Award for Fiction. Peter S. Prescott commented on this book in *Newsweek*, calling it "an American novel of permanent importance, that rare sort of book which (in Norman Mailer's felicitous phrase) amounts to 'a diversion in the fields of dread.' "